Yellow Boots

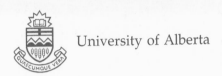

University of Alberta

compliments of

Canadian Institute of
Ukrainian Studies
352 Athabasca Hall
University of Alberta
Edmonton, Alberta
Canada, T6G 2E8

Telephone (403) 492-2972
Fax   (403) 492-4967

YELLOW BOOTS

a novel by
Vera Lysenko

Introduction by
Alexandra Kryvoruchka

NeWest Press

Canadian Institute of Ukrainian Studies Press

First edition 1954. Published by Ryerson Press

Canadian Cataloguing in Publication Data

Lysenko, Vera, 1910-
   Yellow boots
   Previously published: Toronto: Ryerson Press, 1954.
   Co-published by: Canadian Institute of Ukrainian Studies.
   ISBN 0-920897-92-4 (NeWest).-ISBN 0-92-862-73-X
(Canadian Institute of Ukrainian Studies)

   I. Canadian Institute of Ukrainian Studies.
II. Title.
PS8523.Y74X4 1991   C813'.54   C91-091211-4
PR9199.3.L97Y4 1991

CREDITS
COVER DESIGN: Connell Graphics
INTERIOR DESIGN: Bob Young/BOOKENDS DESIGNWORKS
EDITOR FOR THE PRESS: Myrna Kostash
FINANCIAL ASSISTANCE: NeWest Press gratefully acknowledges the
financial assistance of Alberta Culture and Multiculturalism, The
Alberta Foundation for the Arts, The Canada Council, and The
NeWest Institute for Western Canadian Studies.

Printed and Bound in Canada by Kromar Printing.

NeWest Publishers Limited   Canadian Institute of Ukrainian
310, 10359-82 Avenue   Studies Press
Edmonton, Alberta T6E 1Z9   352 Athabasca Hall
                                   University of Alberta
                                   Edmonton, Alberta T6G 2E8

TABLE OF CONTENTS

Author's Foreword

IN THE YEAR 1929, when this story begins, the Ukrainian immigrant settlers who were still pioneering on the Canadian prairie wilderness had not yet lost their power to create a song. Among them there grew up a girl who was moved by the earth and skies to express in song that kinship between man and nature which still exists among peasant people. Living by rites long established, in an isolated community, her ear was tuned to the rhythms of those who broke the land, who built the railroads, and fashioned life for a coming generation. Over the years, her people learned to conform, to yield much of their peasant tradition, since there was so little they could interpose against the robot uniformity of industrialization – only a few symbols of an outmoded life, a carved chest, a folk song, a pair of yellow boots. The old song-makers were dying, the hands that once wove tapestries now tended machines, the treasures of folk lore were forgotten. For all those whose forefathers suffered the anguish which the immigrant must endure when he is called on to surrender his ancestral rites, this story of a girl's search for music is offered as a reminder of their lost inheritance, and to preserve for them something of the old beauty.

Introduction

When the Ryerson Press published *Yellow Boots* in 1954, something new was introduced into Canadian literature. Still the only English-language Canadian novel to treat extensively the experiences of a second-generation Ukrainian-Canadian woman, *Yellow Boots* is also the first piece of Canadian fiction to advance the vision of a multicultural Canadian society with members of diverse ethnic origins participating fully in and making a contribution to the community. Although *Yellow Boots* received good reviews and quiet interest at the time of publication, the full significance of Lysenko's work was not immediately recognized. The views in the novel did not conform to the attitudes and images of the dominant Anglo presence in Canadian literature; as well, most reviewers did not readily appreciate Lysenko's proto-feminist themes. For years *Yellow Boots* was pushed into the margins of the Canadian literary canon and the true concerns and real objectives of Lysenko's work were often missed by the reading public.

Lysenko's purpose in writing *Yellow Boots* was not to give fictional expression to her autobiography. Only recently have the documents and information that provide a better understanding of the life and works of Vera Lysenko been made available.[1] The facts show that, in reality, Vera Lysenko's personal history was in many ways different from that of Lilli Landash, the protagonist of *Yellow Boots*. Although, like Lilli, Lysenko was the daughter of Ukrainian immigrants, Lysenko's parents, Peter and Anna Lesik,[2] did not immigrate to Canada because of a desire to hold land, as was the case with Lilli's father, Anton. Lysenko's parents fled their home in Tarashcha, a town south of Kiev, Ukraine, in 1903, because of religious persecution. The Lesiks were members of a Protestant sect known as the Stundists, and their rejection of the traditional Ukrainian Orthodox and Ukrainian Catholic denominations made them outsiders to the Ukrainian communities in their homeland and in Canada.

When they arrived in the New World, the Lesiks settled in North Winnipeg where, in 1910, Vera Lysenko was born, the fourth child in a family of six children. As she grew to maturity in the multi-ethnic, working-class neighbourhood she witnessed events such as the Winnipeg General Strike and the flu epidemic in 1919, and the suffering of families in the aftermath of World War I. These experiences engendered in her a strong social conscience, a firm sense of class solidarity, and socialist political views. Lysenko's sympathies were with those whom she saw as oppressed by a system that exploited immigrants, women, labourers and farmers. Even at an early age, Lysenko deplored the injustices which were apparent around her and she resolved to use her intellectual resources and literary talent to promote an awareness of the inequities that she abhorred.

In order to achieve her goals, Lysenko read a wide range of materials. She was determined to become a scholar and excelled in all of her academic endeavours. Unlike Lilli Landash, Lysenko had the opportunity to acquire a solid education. At the age of fourteen, she graduated from St. John's Technical High School with the highest honours and awards, and because of her outstanding academic achievements, won a Province of Manitoba Scholarship that enabled her to go through university.

In 1930, Vera Lysenko received her B.A. (Honours) English from the University of Manitoba and earned the distinction of being one of the first Ukrainian Canadian women to complete a university education. On convocation day, Lysenko solemnly proclaimed in her diary, "I now dedicate my learning, my gift and my pen to continue the advancement of ideas and progress in our country." Shortly after making this commitment, Lysenko left Winnipeg with the hope of fulfilling her promise to render service and to establish herself as a writer.

The years that followed were not easy. Even with her education and talent, Lysenko found that career opportunities for a single woman were extremely limited, particularly in the midst of the depression. She first went to Alberta, and, while in Edmonton, studied and practised nursing for a brief period before leaving the health-care field to teach high school until 1936. Then, Lysenko moved to Eastern Canada where she held a succession of jobs as a saleswoman, teacher, factory hand, night-school instructor, domestic servant, research clerk, and journalist. These experiences opened her eyes to the exploitation of women workers who were paid less than their male counterparts, or forced into ghettoized industries such as the garment trade. Lysenko's exposé, "The Girl Behind That Bargain" (published under the name Vera Lesik in *Chatelaine*, October 1936), stripped away the façade of glamour in the fashion industry and revealed that companies amassed huge profits while female employees were paid starvation wages.

Driven by her commitment to social reform, Lysenko continued to write articles on progressive themes using various pseudonyms. *The Clarion*[3] published her work regularly, and she also became a contributor to *Ukrainske Zhyttia* (*Ukrainian Life*), a newspaper published by the pro-Soviet Ukrainian Labour-Farmer Temple Association (ULFTA). In the early 1940s, Lysenko did translations of French novels for the *Magazine Digest*,[4] and her political articles often appeared in that publication under distinctively Ukrainian pen-names. As Vera Lesik she wrote book reviews and essays for the *Globe and Mail* and worked as a reporter for the *Windsor Star* until 1943 when she left to start writing her first book, *Men in*

Sheepskin Coats: A Study in Assimilation.

The research for *Men in Sheepskin Coats* was no small or simple task. Lysenko was pioneering as the first Ukrainian-Canadian author to write, in English, a history of her people in Canada. The project required a great deal of time and financial support, which presented a major problem for a beginning author like Lysenko. After unsuccessfully approaching various Ukrainian organizations for funding, she turned to the Association of United Ukrainian Canadians (the successor to the ULFTA)[5] for assistance. Several leaders in this group responded by offering personal donations in return for editorial control. Her original manuscript was scrutinized by Ivan Navizivsky (John Navis), Peter Krawchuk, and Pylyp Lysets, the latter acting as her main advisor. These patrons were actively involved in the Communist Party of Canada and used their positions as editors to advance their own political views. Lysenko's original manuscript, which was entitled "They Came from Cossack Land,"[6] was more than 600 pages in length, but the published version is 312 pages, including a bibliography. Not only did Lysenko's sponsors change the title and structure of the text, but they also made deletions and alterations to better reflect their own particular notions of how the history should be presented.[7]

Unfortunately, Lysenko was somewhat naive about party politics, and failed to realize that by getting involved with Communist activists she was bound to be identified with their movement. When she set out to write the book, her motives were straightforward. Her intentions were not to advance any particular political views but "to explain the great romance of migration of my people to Canada" and show how "the destiny of the Men in Sheepskin Coats was bound up with the destiny of Canada." Lysenko had hoped "to bring forward a broad picture of Ukrainian-Canadian life over a period of fifty years." At first, it appeared that Lysenko had succeeded when the reviews of *Men in Sheepskin Coats* were published in the

English-language press upon its appearance in 1947. The work received praise from many reviewers who welcomed the book as a significant contribution to the study of Canadian history. Historians such as John Murray Gibbon, author of *Canadian Mosaic*,[8] extended congratulations and compliments, and it seemed that Lysenko's efforts on behalf of Ukrainian Canadians were finally being recognized.

However, trouble erupted when Watson Kirkconnell, an influential Canadian academic with strongly conservative views, accused Lysenko of engaging in left-wing propaganda. A supporter of the anti-Communist Ukrainian Canadian Committee, he sent an unsolicited and sharply worded critique to the book's publishers[9] in which he attacked Lysenko's work and made unsubstantiated allegations about her political affiliations: "An interesting combination of authentic research and Communist propaganda is *Men in Sheepskin Coats* by Vera Lysenko." He went on to declare that "[u]nfortunately this appetizing dish is laced with political arsenic." Nevertheless, Kirkconnell admitted that the bulk of *Men in Sheepskin Coats* was "an excellent and readable account of the settlement of Ukrainians in Canada and their advancement in two generations to positions of affluence and distinction." While later acknowledging that the work was "an admirable summary of the Ukrainian cultural legacy," he took specific exception to some material in the book which, in his view, tainted the entire work. Notwithstanding her sincere intentions in writing a history of Ukrainians in Canada, Lysenko was inadvertently caught in the middle of a political battle.[10] The timing of the release of *Men in Sheepskin Coats* placed her in an especially awkward position, as she had begun work on it in 1943, when the Soviet Union was an ally of the Western Powers, but the actual publication of the book (in 1947) occurred just when the Cold War rhetoric was beginning to intensify. Kirkconnell's critique, an edited version of which was subsequently published in the *University of Toronto*

Quarterly,[11] stung Lysenko to the quick, and in a later, unpublished autobiographical work, she was to protest that:

> It seemed all the more shameful to me, this attack on me, the most vicious ever made on a Canadian writer, with its distortion of irrelevant facts, its aggrandizement of minutiae, its exaggeration of the least important aspects of my theses (Rooted Sorrow 200).[12]

On 9 March 1948, Vera Lysenko swore in an affidavit[13] that she was not and had never been a member of "the Communist Party, the Progressive Labour Party, the Ukrainian Labour-Farmer Temple Association or the Ukrainian Canadian Association."[14] An extensive interview with Lysenko convinced Frank Flemington, one of the editors at the Ryerson Press, that she was not a Communist and had never intended to promote their cause. In a memo to Dr. Lorne Pierce (Senior Editor, The Ryerson Press), Flemington indicated his support for Lysenko and described Kirkconnell as a "fanatic looking for a fight." In a follow-up letter to Kirkconnell, Flemington suggested that legal action was being considered. Kirkconnell subsequently toned down his attack in the published version of his critique, but the damage was done and the allegations regarding Lysenko's political affiliations persist, especially in the Ukrainian community, to this day.

The injury to Lysenko's career and health was tremendous. For several years she suffered terribly, endured public humiliation, and did not publish. Nevertheless, she was determined to keep on writing. As a direct result of the Kirkconnell episode, and because she was committed to rectifying what she regarded as a deplorable situation regarding the representation of immigrants and ethnic characters in Canadian literature, she decided to write fiction:

> Seldom indeed does one encounter a character of, let us say, Slavic origin, in Canadian fiction, except in the role of an illiterate, a clown, a villain or a domestic servant. One exception

can be noted: the Ukrainian Canadian heroine, Anna Prychoda, of Morley Callaghan's novel, They Shall Inherit the Earth. Yet Anna ... possesses no distinctly Ukrainian traits; she might as well have been of French, Irish or Icelandic ancestry; Callaghan made no attempt to limn out the particular characteristics and problems of the second generation to which his heroine presumably belongs. The magnificent drama of migration and assimilation to Canada's Western lands of a polyglot population has not appealed to Canadian writers, mainly for the reason that consciously or unconsciously they still prefer to think of the non-Anglo-Saxon as a comic or uncouth personage, unworthy of elevation to the dignity of literary subject-material (*Men in Sheepskin Coats* 293-4).

Lysenko considered it important that writers of the second and third generation find "the opportunities for fresh and original expression in literary and artistic forms" (*Ibid.* 294) by utilizing their own life experiences, and those of their parents and grandparents. Lysenko felt that such material would yield distinctive qualities in the development of truly Canadian themes. She noted that a major feature which distinguished Canada from countries such as England was the influence of its various ethnic groups upon social and cultural life: " . . . yet Canadian culture as such will not come of age until it embraces in its entirety the manifold life of all the national groups which constitute its entity" (*Ibid.* 294). According to Lysenko, if the Canadian government recognized "all our groups – Icelandic, Swedish, Polish, Czech, etc. – it might stimulate a genuine artistic renaissance" (*Ibid.* 294). She argued that the way to secure national unity was "by giving to each of our component parts a consciousness of individual worth and dignity" (*Ibid.* 295). Invigorated by her patriotic objectives, Lysenko ended a painful hiatus in her writing career and in 1954 published her first novel, *Yellow Boots*.

In telling the story of Lilli Landash, Lysenko drew on the actual life experiences of a young woman whom she had befriended years before she began writing *Yellow Boots*. The real "Lilli" had endured the cruelty of a tyrannical father who, like Anton Landash, was more interested in acquiring land than he was in his daughter's well-being. Still a girl when she decided that she could bear the abuse no longer, the real "Lilli" left the settlement in rural Manitoba and sought a new life in the city of Winnipeg, where she found work and met Lysenko. The two became good friends and Lysenko was greatly moved by "Lilli's" determination not only to survive but to use her talents to succeed in life. The young girl matured into a woman of great beauty. She worked to educate herself and learn all the social graces. In time, "Lilli" advanced from holding jobs as a domestic and factory worker to become a seamstress and then a designer with her own dressmaking shop: soon she was also working as a fashion model, and enjoyed a very successful career.

This true story was the model for the plot in *Yellow Boots*. But, in filling out the design of her novel, Lysenko worked her own vision into the story of Lilli Landash. Lysenko believed that in order to develop a sense of one's identity it is necessary to confront one's ethnic past and then retain that heritage while moving out into the larger community. She agreed strongly with the admonition of the Ukrainian bard, Taras Shevchenko, that Ukrainians should learn about foreign cultures but not forget their own. Through the character, Lilli Landash, Lysenko personifies this ideal. By casting Lilli Landash in the role of a singer or artist, Lysenko uses song as a device by which minorities can be given a voice. Through song, Lilli is able to preserve her own rich cultural background while sharing it with others, and then going on to learn and sing their songs. This then was one way in which diverse ethnic groups could learn to live together with mutual respect.

Just as Lilli Landash uses her vocal talents to communicate the important message that there can be "unity in diversity," Vera Lysenko employs her literary skills, and the English language, to preserve and promote her own Ukrainian heritage while making a contribution to Canadian literature. In the writing of the *Canadian* novel, *Yellow Boots*, Lysenko reflects the tradition of many great *Ukrainian* writers of the past.[15] The result is a work that defies conventional realism. Although *Yellow Boots* has a foundation in actuality, for the most part it exhibits the qualities of a folktale. Vivid accounts of Old-World customs and the resonances of folklore are cross-stitched throughout the telling of the brutal realities of pioneer and immigrant life in Canada. Detailed descriptions of Ukrainian food, myths, song and dance stand out like vibrant strands against the background themes of exile and isolation. Symbolism and imagery are threaded throughout, while knots of historical references to starvation in Ukraine; the first wave of immigrants to Alberta; the depression caused by drought; and the railroad gang's dangerous and lonely lives poke through the pattern of the plot. As Ukrainian poets have always done, Lysenko also pays homage to nature, portraying a prairie landscape that is alive, responsive and a source of inspiration and strength. She draws on her Ukrainian background in order to educate her readers about her people and the experiences shared by all who participate in the building of this country and the shaping of Canadian culture.

Yellow Boots, then, has a place in Canadian literature as a realized work of ethnic fiction. However, *Yellow Boots* is important also in Canadian feminist literature. Always writing a little ahead of the times, Lysenko presents a strong female protagonist, Lilli Landash, who " . . . in the end would prove to be stronger than her father." Under valued as a person because she was born a "puny female," Lilli experiences immediate rejection by her family. Her father who "had set his heart on a son – a tall, handsome fellow who would inherit the farm and further Landash's ambitions of becoming a great landowner," treats her like "a parcel of unsatisfactory goods." She is the "gypsy brat" that even her mother views as an alien to the family, and there is no protest made when Lilli is sent away, at an early age, to work for her aunt. Lilli "belongs to Anton Landash." After her return from her aunt's place, Lilli finds that she has conquered death only to be exploited by her father. He uses her as a workhorse, denies her an education, and literally "cuts her out of the family picture." Despite the abuse, Lilli develops her own means of survival. She seeks solace in nature and the prairie, finds release in singing and, when her father tries to trade her in marriage to a man she finds repulsive, Lilli takes the radical step of fleeing to the city. Undoubtedly, Lilli Landash proves that she is an independent spirit that "cannot be beaten."

Although Lilli owes much to the two male teachers in her life, she feels a particular kinship with Tamara, "an exceptional woman, a woman who in other circumstances might have blossomed into a brilliant and productive personality, but placed in this primitive community, could only dash her head against the wall of prejudice." Tamara's defeat, when a mob of settlers accuses her of being a witch and drives her to a tragic end, "had pointed out the way for Lilli's own rebellion," and in so doing leads Lilli to pursue her own emancipation:[16]

> Up to this evening she had not questioned the old beliefs, but now a great rent appeared in them and she exclaimed to herself, "Lord, what darkness is in their minds!" Brought up in this isolated homestead, Lilli had had no basis for comparing her parents' world with the outside world, from which came only dim echoes, sometimes, in the speech of MacTavish or a visitor. Nevertheless she felt by intuition that another way of life was possible. . . . (*Yellow Boots* 179-80)

Although Lilli throws off the "old beliefs" and seeks a new life in the city governed under Canadian law, she retains the best of the cultural and spiritual strengths of her Ukrainian heritage as she integrates herself into the New-World community.

Of significant note in *Yellow Boots* is the fact that the

retention of Ukrainian culture is carried out by the women. Granny is a folk poet who passes on the stories of days gone by. The festivals are highlighted by food preparation conducted by the females, and the art, embroidery and home healing are all done with feminine hands. "The Marriage Rites" are actually female initiation rites; there are no similar rituals for the male. And the "yellow boots" that are passed from mother to daughter contrast sharply with the "great tan peasant boots" worn by Anton "as MacTavish had seen them tramping across the furrows of the newly-broken earth." Lilli, then, is fulfilling her womanly role when she responds to her brother Peter's charge:

> Take back with you what is best in our past and preserve it for us. . . . The land, that is our job . . . but yours is to cherish the old and give it new meaning. Through these songs, other people in our country can look into the hearts of our people, whom they once despised, and see what beauty is there. You'll speak for all of us. (Ibid. 339)

Ironically, not only is Lilli the woman who outdoes the success of the men in the novel by means of her talent and personal fortitude, but also "she who had fled that environment had built her life upon all the old traditions which had constituted its essence, while those who had remained behind had yielded to modernism."

Thirty-seven years after the first publication of *Yellow Boots*, Canadian readers are more prepared to examine the issues upon which Lysenko touches. The ethnic groups in Canada are pressing for recognition as Canadians who have indeed made an indisputable contribution to the building of this country. Canadian women are struggling to have all of their rights acknowledged, along with recognition of the particular difficulties faced by women who are doubly marginalized, like Lilli Landash. For Canadians today, *Yellow Boots* is indeed a resonant work. With the republication of this book, Vera Lysenko takes her place in Canadian literature and the social consciousness of our time.

Alexandra Kryvoruchka
University of Alberta
Edmonton
February, 1991

I am grateful to Mrs. Olga Vesey, Jars Balan, Peter Krawchuk, Myron Momryk and Elizabeth Hudson for having provided some of the information used in this introduction. I also extend my sincere appreciation to Professor Enoch Padolsky, who provided me with the opportunity to begin my work on Vera Lysenko, and encouraged me constantly during the early stages of my research.

1. See the present author's article "Reintroducing Vera Lysenko – Ukrainian Canadian Author," *Journal of Ukrainian Studies* 27 (Summer 1990): 53-70. Most of the biographical material in this Introduction is drawn from this source.
2. Lysenko felt that the name Lesik was not readily recognized as Ukrainian. The directing force in her life and writing was her pride in her Ukrainian immigrant roots and her determination to be accepted as a Canadian writer without surrendering her ethnic heritage. For these reasons she took the distinctively Ukrainian pen-name Vera Lysenko when she wrote her major works.
3. A paper published in 1939-40 by the Communist Party of Canada (publication was illegal owing to the imposition of the War Measures Act). Formerly known as *The Daily Clarion*, the paper underwent another change of name when it became the *Toronto Clarion* (1940-41).
4. A commercial publication published in Toronto, October 1930-December 1947. In 1948, production of the magazine was moved to the United States.
5. The Communist Party and the ULFTA were outlawed by an Order-in-Council on 4 June 1940 (see Jars Balan, *Salt and Braided Bread*, 54-55). Therefore, in June 1942, the Ukrainian Association to Aid the

Fatherland changed its name to Association of Canadian Ukrainians, and in 1946, the former ULFTA was reconstituted under the name Association of United Ukrainian Canadians (AUUC).

6. The manuscript is privately held. I am grateful to the holder for having made the manuscript available to me in order that I might make a thorough examination and collate Lysenko's original work with the published version of the text.

7. Information regarding the sponsorship, "consultants," and editing which took place was obtained from Peter Krawchuk, personal interviews 6 May 1988 and 7 January 1991. "There is a new kind of glasnost now. Time to tell what took place. She was right. Our approach was distorted." Peter Krawchuk, 7 January 1991. For a detailed description of the unpublished manuscript, as well as the events surrounding the publication of *Men in Sheepskin Coats*, see Chapter 2 of the present author's "Vera Lysenko – Ukrainian Canadian: The Expression of Her Dual Nationality in Her Life and Works" (unpublished M.A. thesis. University of Alberta, 1991).

8. J.M. Gibbon, *Canadian Mosaic: The Making of a Northern Nation* (Toronto: McClelland and Stewart, 1938).

9. Correspondence and memos relating to the Kirkconnell incident are held in the Lorne Pierce Collection, Queen's University Archives.

10. See Thomas M. Prymak, *Maple Leaf and Trident* (Toronto, 1988) for a complete discussion of the issues.

11. See Watson Kirkconnell, "New Canadian Letters," *University of Toronto Quarterly*, 1947, Vol. xvii: 425-29.

12. Held in the Lysenko Papers, Public Archives of Canada. Access is restricted.

13. Deposited in the Lorne Pierce Collection, Queen's University Archives.

14. Lysenko's associates and friends, and members of the organizations in question, confirm that she had no formal political ties. In personal interviews and correspondence with numerous individuals who knew Lysenko professionally and personally, the fact that she was a woman of integrity who had a strong social conscience was consistently emphasized. There appears to be no doubt regarding the truthfulness of the affidavit.

15. Although Lysenko did not learn to read and write in the Ukrainian language until she was an adult, she was well acquainted with works written by Ukrainian authors. A daily custom in the Lesik home was that Lysenko's mother would read Ukrainian literature to the family.

16. See also Gordon Philip Turner, "The Protagonist's Initiatory Experiences in the Canadian *Bildungsroman*: 1908-1971" (unpublished PhD thesis, University of British Columbia 1979), 154-65, for an interesting discussion of *Yellow Boots* as a female *Bildungsroman*.

PART ONE
Rites of Spring

1
THE DEATH RIDERS
❦

THE MOTION of the jigger upon the steel track drummed into the consciousness of the sick girl as she struggled to arrange into some pattern of comprehension the brightness of the skies and the rushing prairie. Where was she going? How did she get here? Who were these men? She heard a voice above her, alien in accent:

"You've been travelling a rough road, young one."

A big, whiskery hand groped about to make sure the blanket was anchored fast about the girl's shoulders. In that livid face, the dark eyes blinked, wary, fearful, as the girl stared back at the Irish countenance of Mike O'Donovan, the section foreman. Only a tremor of the nostril indicated that she had heard his words.

"I wonder if she'll last the journey?"

In the quiet of the spring afternoon, the put-put-put of the track motorcar on which the two men and the girl were travelling across the Manitoba countryside sounded like an outboard motor, and the land appeared like the sea, stretching out in every direction to the curved horizon. The jigger seemed to be floating like a toy on top of an immense plate. Only the rails, which stretched like two silver ribbons to the great northern lakes, gave any sense of direction.

Mike's companion, Ian MacTavish, who had recently arrived from Ontario to teach school in the district, turned his head back from the front seat, where he sat driving the jigger. "She looks more like a wild animal than a child," he said, staring curiously at the girl.

She shut her eyes and she was back once again in the swamp country, hearing the bellowing of cattle, the barking of the dog and the screech of the wind as it tore the leaves from the trees. In the distance she could hear the howling of wolves. Desperately she looked about and could recognize no feature of the landscape in the growing twilight. She was lost! Perspiration oozed down her face in fat drops.

As he observed with consternation the sweat upon the girl's skin, the teacher inquired, "Think she has any chance?"

"Hm?" The old section foreman murmured absently. He had been looking out over the prairie, where the coming of spring had caused a great stirring. Wisps of smoke arose from tree stumps cleared; occasionally they saw the flicker of a scarlet shawl and striped skirt as some woman moved before the whitewashed cottage of a homestead; or a solitary man in sheepskin coat emerged suddenly from the shadow of a poplar bluff. At this hour of late afternoon, the air was suffused with particles of gold, giving a luminous quality to the landscape. Over it all, the song of the meadowlark rang like a constant, recurring chime.

"Think she has any chance?" the teacher repeated.

"Not much, I'm afraid," replied the section hand with regret. "She's a game youngster. It's a pity."

"Whose girl is she? Why is she being moved?"

The old man's eyes returned to the girl in his arms. "She belongs to Anton Landash, about fifteen miles down the line. Quite a ride for a girl close to death. They had her working at her uncle's before she took ill."

'Working? A girl of that age? She can't be more than nine." MacTavish contrasted the feeble child with the man who held her. Like a discus-thrower, the shoulders of the old railroader were muscle-padded from heaving the spike maul on the extra gangs. His face, burned brick red through decades of prairie summers, and his eyes, like two chips of prairie sky,

4

gave him an appearance as elemental as the land over which they were passing.

"More likely eleven,' said the Irishman. 'Small for her age. It's hard to tell about some of these immigrants' children. They don't always keep a record of births. Look at these hands." Mike held up one of the hands which had slipped from beneath the cover, and MacTavish turned his head to see. "More like a labourer's than a girl's." The hands, calloused and with joints abnormally enlarged, were long for a child, with veins bulging out like scars. "The land can't wait for them to grow up. It takes away their childhood. Riding up and down this line, on these homesteads I've seen young girls doing tasks grown men would do among us."

Within the mind of the sick girl, the terror was increasing. The spring floods had obliterated the roads, so that she had lost her bearings while driving the cows home. It was then she had seen it – a light like a hand holding a lantern, coming from the direction of the swamp. What was it the old folks said about swamp fires? "They're the spirits of people who've committed a terrible crime, and if you've sinned, the light will follow you." The light was following her now, almost directly overhead. She stood paralyzed for a moment, then screamed and ran . . .

Meanwhile, the old section-boss was scrutinizing the profile of the man in the front seat. Seen thus, the teacher's face had a fox-like appearance, with its brush of sandy hair, sharp nose and greenish-grey eyes. A rough tweed jacket was draped carelessly over his shoulders. "He's a likely one," thought the railway man. "Tough – he won't balk at wild conditions."

MacTavish felt exhilarated at his novel experience. "You know," he said, indicating the track motorcar. "I've never been on one of these things before." He felt grateful that a chance encounter on the road with the old section-hand had led to this unpremeditated ride.

"It's a good way of getting acquainted with the land and the people," replied Mike from his back seat. "Especially if you've an eye to the country."

"Do you often carry passengers?"

"Sometimes, when it's not possible to reach a place by ordinary means. The train goes through here only twice a week."

He stopped talking in order to wave to two children standing by the track. As soon as they recognized the jigging sound of the track motorcar, they came running from the fields to wave to the men, "Jigger's comin' down the track!" The section-men were a race apart to the children of the Canadian prairies. Detached from the earth, they sped across the land, appearing without notice and vanishing without trace. Where did they come from? Where did they go? Bending in alternate rhythm, they appeared to execute a dance as they pumped the lever up and down to propel the hand-car.

"Wonder what's going on in her mind," said Mike as he passed his hand over the girl's feverish face. "She seems to be having a nightmare."

As the girl ran from the swamp fire, her bare feet splashing against the wet grass, the noise was echoed by the humming in her ears and the thudding of her heart. Feet torn by the stones over which she ran, she tripped and fell headlong into a pool of water. Much later, drenched to the skin and spattered with mud from head to foot, she had finally stumbled into the home of her aunt and had fallen unconscious upon the floor.

Her irregular breath alarmed Mike and he bent over her. "I think the ride is disturbing her," he said. "Rough for a sick one."

The girl in his arms stirred and opened her eyes. "How do you feel, pee wee?"

She was silent. Her eyes were clouded, as though she had not adjusted herself to her surroundings. Mike repeated the question, "How do you feel?"

The girl spoke for the first time. Her voice was low and husky, with a tremolo which might have been caused by weakness. "I all right. I fine."

The teacher commented: "What a fierce, independent little person! She looks at us at though to say that she doesn't expect anything from us."

"Yes," agreed Mike. "That's how her people are – proud, not asking for help though they were thrown on this wilderness and left to shift as best they might." He addressed himself again to the girl: "What's your name, young one?"

She did not answer. "Can't speak English very well," said Mike. "Not likely she's had much schooling. You'll find other kids wild as this one in your classes. The last teacher left because she couldn't stick it out to the end of the term."

"I'm not likely to run away,' said MacTavish, his eyes narrowing with scorn, then, in a sudden change of mood, "You know, I feel close to the earth here." As he crouched upon the jigger, he tried to absorb the vastness about him.

"Well, there's nothing to interrupt your view," said Mike. "Railroaders say this is the flattest roadbed in the world, so you won't feel cramped here. As for your pupils – " he shrugged. "You'll be digging where nobody's dug before."

As the girl's eyes met Mike's, he smiled at her, and she consented to release a tentative smile, as though her smile muscles were unaccustomed to use. "You look like real man," she said in wonder.

"Yes," said Mike. "Here, pinch me." He took her thumb and forefinger and pinched his cheek. "Oi!" he exclaimed as if in pain. A smile flickered on the girl's face. "She doesn't think I'm quite human," said Mike. "No wonder. Perhaps she feels there's something strange about this trip. Strange for me, too. It's the first time I've been riding a jigger with death breathing down my back, and I don't like it." He was developing an affection for the girl. How long, in his wandering life of a railroader, since he had held a child in his arms!

The teacher turned his head back now with a quizzical expression, for he was getting to like the old railroader, and wanted to know more of his history.

His name for one thing sounded a little too apt to be likely, for anyone who looked more like a Mike O'Donovan than the section foreman, MacTavish had never seen. He put the query, therefore:

"Is your name really O'Donovan?"

"Yes, really," chuckled Mike. "Why, don't I look like an O'Donovan?"

"Too much so," replied MacTavish. "It sounds as if you had made it up to suit your face, which certainly looks like the map of Ireland. People don't always have names that fit them so exactly."

"Maybe so," admitted the section-foreman comfortably. "But I think you'll find they ease into them as people ease into a tight-fitting pair of boots."

Another point had been puzzling the teacher: although he was not so naive as to imagine that an Irish section foreman must necessarily talk like a stage Irishman, he was curious to know how such a man had come to his present status in life, and so he asked, "You sound like an educated man. How is that?"

"How is it I'm working on the section-gang?" Mike O'Donovan grinned as though he had heard the question before, many times. "Well," he drawled, "you'll find all sorts on the gangs – scholars, tramps, criminals, saints – I met a chap once who claimed he was the son of an English lord. The roving life gets in your blood. I suppose you'd say, some people are born to be wanderers – It's a way of life."

While speaking, he did not notice the expression on the face of the girl in his arms, and if he had, he might not have understood it, for how could he know that she, too, was a wanderer?

Now the fluty tremolo of the meadowlark sounded again,

from all directions seemingly, so that it was difficult to spot him. "They seem to be all over the prairie," said the teacher, his eyes darting from side to side, trying to locate the bird.

"Meadowlark on fence post," whispered the girl, her eyes indicating the position of the songster.

"Why, so it is!" exclaimed Mike, giving a quick nod in the direction of the yellow-breasted bird. "Imagine her noticing that, in her condition!" He asked, solicitously, "Tired, little one?"

The girl closed her eyes, then opened them again, as a sign of assent.

"We'll have you to your father's soon."

MacTavish was startled by the expression of fear which passed over the girl's face at the mention of her father, and inquired, "What kind of man is her father?"

"Landash? He's a fierce dreamer," replied Mike, trying to recall the many odd stories he had heard about Landash, and to piece them into a composite picture of the man. "A fanatic, some call him, because he has ambitions of becoming a big landowner. He built a log house which is the talk of the district, for it's as big as a barn." Mike looked thoughtfully at the girl, and sensed the tension behind that grave face. "Want to be back at your father's, young one?" He was not surprised when she whispered, "I like you should be fadder."

Tenderness was a new emotion whose existence she knew of by instinct, but had had no personal experience of. She savoured it like a new flavour, disturbing but pleasant. It served as a bulwark against the prospect of meeting again that terrifying figure who was her father, Anton Landash.

How long ago was it since she had seen him – five years? She was six, and even then an independent person, standing against the wall, impassive, while her elders debated her future. "Take that one," said her mother at last to her aunt, a coarse-grained woman far advanced in pregnancy. "She'll help you with the children and cost little to feed as she's small." Her

9

aunt stuck a toothpick into her mouth and laughed: "At least it won't be hard to find room for her." That day, she had left the big log house of her father and had gone to work for her aunt, until a week ago, when she had fallen ill and had shown signs of becoming a corpse. It was then that her aunt had delivered her to the old section-hand, to be returned, like a parcel of unsatisfactory goods, to her family. If only the journey would last forever, so that she would keep on travelling, that she could remain suspended in space, so to speak, neither returning to her aunt's nor to the home of her father!

Unexpectedly now, on the road which ran parallel to the railway, there appeared a fantastic procession, composed of four or five rough green wagons driven by oxen. These wagons were filled with men in sheepskin coats and women in leather boleros, long coloured skirts and white turbans. They were on their way to a silver-domed church on top of a smooth round hillock.

Mike's companion stared at the scene. The people in their shaggy coats looked as if they had only lately sprung from the earth. "Who are these people?" he exclaimed.

The abrupt emergence of this primitive congregation in the midst of bare Manitoba prairie was like a mirage on the desert, and this resemblance was increased when the tarnished gold stubble was lit by the rays of the sun.

Ha, ha, ha! Like a rubber ball, the sound of their merriment bounced wildly over the flat prairie. Ha, ha, ha! A feeble echo, like a nestling's cheep, resounded from Mike's arms. "Laughing, are you, little one?"

The girl implored him with her eyes. "Want to see them, eh?" She blinked her eyes as he lifted her in his arms.

"They're like something out of a history book," marvelled Ian MacTavish. He might have exclaimed, as an Englishman had years before him, on seeing a similar sight in Alberta, "I have seen it – the very beginning of things!"

"Hi! Hi!" the men called as they snapped their whips, the final "ee" of their call being prolonged like the curling of a whip. The sound intrigued the teacher. "Hai, hai!" he called back, but his voice sounded thin in comparison. Mike took up the call and cracked it out with such sharpness that the people in the wagons applauded. "Hai, hai!" they returned the salute. Mike smiled. "When they first came here," he said, "people among whom they settled liked that call so much they named a town in Saskatchewan after it – Hyas."

Then, without warning, the entire congregation burst into song. The tenor, singing almost in a falsetto, initiated the melody, elaborated upon it, prolonged the piercing note until the whole countryside seemed to express the profound sorrow of a persecuted people. The chanting, in polyphonic harmony, swelled in a crescendo as the soaring voices poured forth their melody. The whole prairie had come to life.

"Good Lord!" exclaimed the teacher. He had never heard such spontaneous choral harmony before. "What are they singing? Is it a custom among them, or do they burst into song on any occasion?"

"Do you know," Mike replied, "that's a question I used to put to them myself when I used to hear them sing on the section-gang. They sang often then, ballads, so I thought, of their old country, and when I asked them what they were singing about, they would always reply, "How once we were free."

The two men gazed in silence at the scene, which was like a painting by some primitive artist wielding a huge brush and throwing colour from his palette in a kind of frenzy. Everything was exaggerated – the people, the music, the landscape. An excitement mounted in the hearts of the two men, a feeling that here was a phenomenon of peculiar import, part of the creative processes of life itself. It was difficult to believe that this was the year 1929 in the new world.

Meanwhile, it was extraordinary to see what was

happening to the dying girl. Her features were all alight and there was a glow in her eyes, which were enormous and almond-shaped, with thick lashes fanning out against high cheekbones. The intensity of her feeling communicated itself to the men, even though she was almost inarticulate. "O music lovely, O music lovely!" she gasped, a vein throbbing at her temple.

"Why the pee-wee is trembling," observed Mike. He passed his hand over her face. "She has music in her soul, like her people."

Far down the road, the shrill voice of the tenor, holding the melancholy note with all the strength of his powerful lungs, still yearned with all the nostalgia of a vast and lonely land.

"That's a sickly child to be descended from such robust people," mused his companion, as he recalled the big-bosomed women, full of colour and exuberance, with their glossy hair, their musical voices and free laughter. He could not reconcile the evidences of modern civilization – telephone wires, grain elevators, railways – with the primitive character of the people. Out of what travail had that melancholy song been born? "Where do they come from?" he asked the old section-hand.

Mike searched in his memory for what he could recall of their antecedents and history. "They come from some province of the old Austrian Empire," he began slowly. "Bukovynians, they call themselves. They've been coming into this country for thirty years and more now. I worked with a gang of them in British Columbia, when we were building the Canadian Northern and the Grand Trunk Pacific. They worked like giants – " The railroader paused as he recalled that scene in the Canadian Rockies, with the men of the gang puffing their cigarettes, and laughing in their childlike way.

By this time, the track motorcar had been set in motion, and was chugging down the tracks.

"I wonder what they will become, or their children." MacTavish pulled up his leather glove as he tried to relate the future of these people to his own mission among them.

Mike considered. "They're still pioneering, when pioneering days are over for most of the other settlers. Do you know, when they first came here, I saw them plough the land as people used to in England in the time of Alfred the Great." He paused as he watched, in the distance, the figure of a young farmer ploughing the land. "But I think they'll get ahead; they've already made their mark on the land."

His companion now turned his head back again to look at the sleeping girl, on whose face the marks of death were only too plain. "You know," he said, "I've never seen the country or the people as I've seen them today, and it's all because of this little girl. The whole land's come to life."

"If you want to see clear," Mike pointed out, "see through the eyes of a child." He was obsessed, too, with the thought that near death, everything was intensified.

The girl was not awake when Mike delivered her to her father. The two men saw him from a distance, standing beside the railway crossing, near his wagon, a cigarette glowing red between his fingers. The jigger slowed down, emitting a series of put-put's as it slid to a halt. Mike got off painfully from his cramped position, taking care not to disturb the girl. He walked slowly to the girl's father, carrying the girl in his arms.

"I am Anton Landash," said the man at the crossing.

"We've brought the little girl to you," said Mike and handed the girl over. The two men exchanged glances, Mike appraisingly, Landash arrogant and resentful at having to claim the wretched child.

His tall, lean figure was accented by an extraordinary black cape. Underneath, he had an embroidered sheepskin bolero and a scarlet kerchief was tied under his cleft chin. In the deepening twilight, Landash resembled more the hero of some mid-European operetta than a Canadian farmer, with his swarthy complexion, aquiline nose and glittering eyes.

"Take good care of the child now," Mike admonished,

experiencing a feeling of deprivation. In the last hour he had established an intimate understanding of the child, and now, in all likelihood, he would never see her again. "Perhaps you might send for a doctor," he suggested.

Landash's lips curled as he looked at the dry little husk in his arms. In that still face, breath was not discernible. "Too late for doctor, I think," he said. "Better to send for priest."

Mike, torn with desire to give dignity, somehow, to the girl's death, stood in the twilight, staring at Landash. He discovered that, despite their outward dissimilarity, there was an inner likeness between father and daughter – the intensity of feeling which both brought to the simplest phrase, the rhythm of their speech, the impression both gave of inner resources not easily exhausted.

Anton watched him with hostile eyes. "You have good ride?" he asked, indicating the track motorcar with some amusement.

"A clear night and a clean track," replied Mike, conscious that what he said was almost like a valedictory for the girl.

After exchanging a few uneasy commonplaces with this harsh, uncompromising man, he reluctantly turned back to the jigger, where MacTavish was waiting.

"A harsh man," he sighed as he set the jigger in motion. "I could hardly bring myself to give the girl over to him." He looked down the long steel track which was paling now in the fading light. "It's hard to believe that fierce little light will go out," he said.

2
THE SHROUD MAKERS
❦

THE EXPECTED guest had not yet arrived. All day long, visitors had been coming and going in the house where the young girl lay, awaiting the approach of death, while the square yellow candles by her bedside sputtered, their fat tears oozing painfully down their sides.

The house steamed with the yeasty smell of baking, to provide a funeral feast for mourners who would come from a distance. A large batch of mushroom dumplings was simmering on the stove, supervised by Granny Yefrosynia, who looked rather like an agaric mushroom herself, in her orange blouse, green calico skirt and white turban with chin strap. Granny loved colours and wore them all together; they suited her unique personality, which, also, was full of colours.

The sick girl wakened from her sleep. She saw people moving about, their bare feet smacking like wet rags against the rammed earth floor. It was early evening, and grotesque shadows cast by the coal-oil lamp pantomimed upon the white-washed walls like a procession of dancers clothed in mourning.

A woman, who must be her mother, with the ancient resignation of the peasant stamped on her face, sat near the bed, sewing upon a shroud. Sedate, melancholy, harsh, there was still, in the look of Zenobia Landash's eyes and the brooding curve of her mouth some hint of rich peasant fantasy.

Zenobia laid down her needle for a moment and raised her spatulate fingers to adjust her kerchief, tied gypsy fashion about her smooth brown braids. Her black sateen dress, plainly fashioned, was decorated at the neck with strings of coral beads. She recalled with some compunction how her brother-in-law had arrived hastily on horseback the previous day to impart the news. He had approached the house, hat in hand, as was the custom when announcing an approaching death. "Ai, ai!" Zenobia had shrieked, guessing the import of his visit.

"I have come to ask you to receive her at home, as it is not fit she should die in our house," said her brother-in-law.

"Bring her home, then," said Zenobia. Although without sentiment for her daughter, she had feared the censure of her neighbours, and had on that account hired two mourners to preside at the deathbed of the child. They sat now beside her, one a withered crone with potato-like features, as though she had been lately pulled up from the earth; the other, known as Tamara, a widow of great dignity and tall stature, dressed in a long black robe.

"It is not by chance that we called her the Luckless," remarked Zenobia, "since from birth she had been attended by misfortune."

"Ai, ai!" lamented the crone. She reached for a dish of pumpkin seeds and cracked one expertly between her few remaining teeth.

Granny Yefrosynia remarked, in her hoarse, yet not unpleasant voice: "Death takes his harvest whenever he chooses." She went to the stove, sampled the dumplings with a judicious nod, and gave the pot a brisk stir with the wooden ladle.

The sick girl strove to re-orientate herself. She looked at the woman beside her, and her lips formed the appeal, "Mother!" But she could not utter a sound; the woman was alien to her; there was no tenderness in her. She groped about desolately for the warmth newly lit in her heart. "Mike!" she whispered as she searched for his white hair.

She looked about the house, which consisted of one huge

room, like a reception hall. Everything had become unfamiliar in the five years she had been away, and yet she could still recall many things about it – the rows of Bukovynian tapestries upon the wall, over a horizontal pole, the clay stove on whose shelf she had often slept on winter nights; the sheaves of wheat and bunches of dried herbs hanging down from the rafters; the loom and spinning wheels; the deep window sills full of geraniums; the pearly ropes of garlic looped on the walls; the large gramophone with French horn.

There were children moving about, her brothers and sisters, creeping up to her bed to examine this newly-acquired sister whom they had forgotten, who had been sent from home before some of them were born. Whispers were heard, in a lisping voice, from a rosy-cheeked, bow-legged boy with yellow hair shaped like petals on his forehead: "Who is that girl?"

"She is your sister."

"Why is she so green?"

"She is sick with fever."

The boy looked longingly at the stove and sniffed:

"May I have a mushroom dumpling?"

"They aren't ready yet, Petey dear."

The boy gulped his anticipatory juices, his inner emptiness crying to be filled with the cosy bulk of dumplings.

"When will the party be?"

"There is no party."

"Then why is Granny cooking so many dumplings?"

"Hush, you will disturb your sister."

And now the sick girl's eyes fell upon two diminutive females, dressed exactly alike in flowered shawls and floor-length skirts. These were the twins, Masha and Tasha, but the girl, having been sent from home before they were born, thought at first the double vision was the result of illness. "Are they really two people?" she wondered, but her doubt was resolved when her mother made two gestures of wiping two noses. "They must be two."

The children, meanwhile, were holding a conference

concerning this sister, regarding whom they could obtain no satisfactory information, although they had been asking questions all day. Why was she so thin and small? Fialka, the eldest girl, a beauty, offered a solution:

"Uncle didn't want her so he sent her back."

"Why?"

"She is too thin."

"What is her name?"

"Gypsy."

"That's a strange name."

"She's a strange girl."

"She looks more like – "

"Like a monkey," said Fialka, and then regretted her impulse. "Sh, she's looking."

With a giggle, the children subsided, but the girl gave no indication that she had heard their jibes; she was looking away now to another part of the house.

Anton Landash, her father, sat in a corner called "Office," before him several small bags and a magnifying glass. He had been examining samples of grain seed and now, with the aid of his dictionary, he was composing a letter to the Manitoba Government. What an admirable person was her father, thought the girl, that even the government had heard of him!

Landash, meanwhile, was recalling, with some displeasure, the circumstance of the girl's birth. She was the third child, and after two daughters, Landash had set his heart on a son – a tall, handsome fellow who would inherit the farm and further Landash ambitions of becoming a great landowner. When Landash saw the puny girl child, he uttered a short laugh of contempt and disappointment. "Not much of anything," he said. "A gypsy brat."

On that same day, a band of gypsies had passed through the district, and Zenobia had taken it into her head that they had cast a spell on the child, or perhaps by some witchcraft had substituted their own brat for Zenobia's real child. Anton had been the first to apply the name of Gypsy to the girl and it had clung to her, so that her real name was forgotten. "The Gypsy will leave before morning," he jerked his head contemptuously in the direction of the child.

"Father," she whispered, trying to tell him that she did not want to leave. Anton, absorbed in his work, thought of the girl only as some odd, stunted plant which had to be pulled up to make room for another, healthy growth. "Father," groaned the girl. Sweat burst out on her forehead like globules on butter.

Anton Landash looked up with impatience. Not having had time to pull down the blinds over the naked dislike in his eyes, the full force of his hatred struck the girl across the face and she shivered, burying her face in the pillow.

Landash got up now and went out of the house. Some time later, he returned with a wooden box, which he placed on the floor beside the bed. "I made my old tool box over to fit her," he said.

"She should have a real coffin," objected Zenobia.

"Do you think we are rich people to buy a coffin?" asked Anton with a harsh voice. "We have to pay for the service and the lot in the churchyard."

"What will people say?"

Anton shrugged. "I'll paint the box white." He got out some paint and a brush.

"I hope people will not talk." Zenobia bent over the bed and mopped the waxen face of the girl with a damp cloth. "She is picking at the bedclothes, a sign of death."

"She is playing the fiddle," said Anton as he watched the nervous motion of the hands, plucking as at some instrument, an eerie rhythm, born of the chaos in the feverish mind.

The girl's feeling of despair and loneliness increased. She regarded the preparations for her funeral, and tremors shook her. The faces about her, coldly chiselled out of stone, betrayed no pity for the girl; they looked at her without emotion, watching her progress toward death with a kind of passivity, like spectators at a game. There was no help from them, nor from any human source. The only warmth in the room was the flame of the candles and toward these the dying girl directed a desperate plea: "Help me, candles," she implored. "Help me, help me." Tears glazed her eyes like glass marbles. The candles flickered and smoked, their flame appeared to become tarnished. Despair, with leaden fingers, pressed down her eyelids.

Granny was casting wax into water and murmuring incantations. She was convinced that some evil thing had caused the girl's illness and that the wax would take the shape of this evil and drive it from the girl.

Zenobia went about from guest to guest, serving poppy seed rolls and coffee. The guests relaxed and the talk assumed a melancholy suited to the occasion, being concerned with strange deathbed scenes.

Fearing the post-mortem vengeance of her fey child, for she felt guilty that she had sent her from home at so early an age, Zenobia began to extol the virtues of the dying girl, in a kind of premature keening, speaking not in extravagant terms, for she was a blunt person, but cautiously, being ill at ease in praising her luckless daughter. "She was very young, yet she earned her daily bread." This was the supreme peasant virtue, and Zenobia felt pleased that she could attribute it sincerely to her daughter. She went on, "Sorrow has ground her in its mill; she has eaten the bread of sorrow."

The mourners sighed, and alternated their rhythmically spaced lamentations.

"So young to die," wailed the crone.

"Fate did not plant flowers by her path," chimed in Tamara, she in the black robe. Her face, strong as death, reflected the sombre shadows of mourning.

"She will sleep a long night," crooned Zenobia. "Who will waken thee, my daughter?" The crone, whose every wrinkle was like the grave of some youthful hope, quavered, "The wind asks of death, for whom does the horn sound to die?"

"It sounds for the young to die," continued Tamara.

"It sounds for the weary to rest," Zenobia took up the refrain.

"It sounds for fate." Granny's voice was ominous as Fate itself.

Zenobia stitched her wailing into the shroud, "Who will comb your hair? Who will plait your wreath? Who will give you to the bridegroom?"

"Ai, ai," the lamentation went on. "Ai, ai, a . . ." The sound droned on and on, like a drill on the ear drums of the girl.

"If she dies tonight, we can bury her tomorrow," said Anton, who had now finished painting the coffin. It was near dawn, the children had long ago gone to sleep, and the candles, with tears thick upon each other, had shrunk into themselves. Anton felt the girl's feet under the blanket. "She is turning cold."

Meanwhile, a thick fog had descended over the sick girl, enshrouded her, drifted into her mouth and nostrils, choking her. Lost, she drifted alone, fighting the stuff that suffocated her, groping for a way out. A confusion of voices entered her delirium, engaged in a weird conversation, a mixture of the real and the imagined. "Where shall we put her?" A voice sounded through the fog.

"In this box. We must put her in this box. Then she will never get out again." Desperate, the girl cried, "No, no!" but the fog engulfed her.

A man's voice, her father's, sounded, exasperated: "The Gypsy has chosen a fine time to die. The seed must go into the ground and here we are waiting for her to die."

"I won't go," she tried to protest. "I won't go." She thought she was walking with a crowd about her, pushing her, exerting their strength to thrust her more deeply into the fog, disposing of her, burying her. She looked down and saw that she was wearing the long white garment which her mother was sewing. She put her hand to her head and felt a wreath of flowers. Walking thus, she felt disembodied. She was holding a candle in her hand, but every time she tried to light it, the fog put it out. A cold mist clamped down over her mouth and nostrils, strangling her. "Don't put me in the ground!" she protested. The wings of a crane appeared over her head and she reached out desperately. "Take me with you!" she begged.

Zenobia knelt beside the bed, hands over her face. "Why is this small flower plucked before it has bloomed? Why was it not permitted to grow and blossom?"

The girl became dizzy and faint; her pulse disappeared. When she recovered consciousness, she found herself in her father's arms. They had poured cold water over her head to revive her; it streamed over her burning face. As she opened her eyes there was a gasp: "She still lives." A tiny flicker betrayed life.

The fog had disappeared and faces swarmed all around her bed, but these faces appeared grotesque and huge, with fantastic features, like distorted caricatures of themselves. They swam about, closing in on her, shutting out the light. Darkness pressed, the final darkness.

"The spirit is leaving," said the father. Her face now assumed a mask-like appearance, as if life had fled. "We must let the soul out of the house."

Zenobia rushed to the window to open it, to allow the soul free passage so that it would not hold a grudge against the inhabitants and torment them by wandering forty days and nights about the place. She looked out into the starlit night and prayed, "Guide, O Lord, the soul of my daughter to walk through the bright gate of heaven."

All stood by, watching with awe the moment of death, but as the moments ticked away, they observed that the girl, while inert, was still quietly breathing. Halfway across the threshold of life and death she had stepped back and refused to pass.

"What a strong spirit the gypsy has!" exclaimed Anton, perplexed, yet admiring the unexpected strength of the frail body.

Zenobia continued sewing on the shroud. A sudden gust of wind tore the shroud from her hands and sent it gyrating across the floor in a kind of spectral dance. When the impetus of the wind was exhausted, the shroud flattened itself against the wall, and hung there for one ghastly moment before collapsing upon the floor. Zenobia, incredulous, watched this performance, believing the shroud to be bewitched. "This has never happened before to my knowledge!" she cried in agitation. "Is it a good omen or ill?" She hesitated to pick up the shroud which seemed to have a will of its own, and was bent on not being put to its assigned purpose. "A child who has no luck will not die, but live and suffer all its life."

Granny, imperturbable in the midst of the tumult, now stepped in to take charge of the situation. From the bags around her waist, she had taken an herb and was now scattering it over the bed of the girl, murmuring an incantation,

Sleep, little one, close your eyes,
Death, pass by this house tonight.
Go, illness, from this suffering child,
Come, sleep; come, health, come rest.

The old lady stood with a crafty smile upon her face. "I have fooled the Old Robber," she triumphed. From the oven she extracted a brick, wrapped it in grey flannel and placed it under the girl's feet. "She sleeps."

It was daylight now, and the square yellow candles squatted in their dishes like dowagers with their chins tucked into their dewlaps. The room, padded with slumber, had the stillness of a haunt. Only Zenobia Landash was moving about, bodiless as a shadow.

The girl opened her eyes and discovered that the aspect of the whole room had changed. The morbid presence of the guest no longer lingered about, and freckles of sunshine played tag on the whitewashed walls. Her body was scoured clean of the illness which had befouled it, and now her spirit stood poised on tiptoes, like a ballet dancer ready to make an entrance. "The light has come back," she said aloud.

"God in Heaven, she still lives!" exclaimed her mother. She hurried to the girl's bedside and stared down at the face, no longer waxy but betraying a faint blush. After Zenobia had washed the girl's face and braided her hair, she removed her sweat-soaked clothing and put on her a clean shirt made of bleached flour sack. Then she brought a bowl of broth.

As it appeared now that the girl would not immediately die Zenobia decided to embroider the shroud at the neck sleeves. To entertain the girl, she brought a number of skeins of bright embroidery thread. "Choose the ones you like best daughter." The girl frowned as she looked at the black thread and pushed it away. "Green and yellow and pink, like the flowers I'll plant in our garden," cried out the girl. She held a long hank of cerise thread and began to unwind it, singing to herself the childish rhyme:

Doctor, doctor, shall I die,
Yes, my darling. so shall I.
How many years shall I live?
One, two, three –

At each figure, she made a knot in the silk, which hung like the scarlet thread of life between her fingers. At last she finished knotting. "One hundred and two years!" triumphantly she cried, as she contemplated the life stretching before her, knot by knot. What would she do with all those years, she who was only eleven? "That is too long!" she exclaimed. "Mother, I shall live to be one hundred and two years!"

Her mother, who had been watching this performance with interest, immediately read a fatalistic significance into daughter's outburst. "God in Heaven has sent a sign!"

By this revelation, Zenobia knew that the shroud would never be used, and that she must get rid of it at once. Snatching up the garment, she tore it and stuffed the shreds into the stove. She shivered as she scrubbed her hands, trying to conceal her repulsion. The girl watched in horror. "Why did you tear my dress?" she inquired. "That was for my wedding."

Her mother dried her hands on a fresh white towel and gave her a long, peculiar look. Before answering, she took a basin of holy water and sprinkled it about the house to exorcise the spirit of evil. "You are too young for such a dress," she said finally. "I'll get you another, red with yellow flowers, better for a little girl."

"And red hair ribbons, too?"

"Yes, ribbons, too."

A red dress! The prospect was so exciting that the girl, thinking about it, fell asleep. Her dreams, this time, were all of flight and happiness. She was free, she was dancing in a red dress and on each of her four pigtails she had tied an enormous bow of satin. The pigtails flew out in the wind as she danced, and suddenly by her side appeared a blond boy in overalls. They clasped hands and danced together. Then he was chasing her around a hay wagon and they were both laughing and the sun was shining.

When she woke, it was noon, and the sun was indeed shining through the windows and all over her face, so that her eyes were dazzled. A kettle was singing on the stove. Granny had replaced her turban with a green and yellow silk shawl, and now, looking quite pleased with herself, was placidly sucking a peppermint and rocking.

"I'm hungry," announced the girl in a firm voice. She lifted her head from the pillow and yawned. Her eyes felt moist and she blinked them several times, like a flower shrugging the dew off its petals. When her mother brought her a bowl of mush, she noted with pleasure that it was sprinkled with brown sugar.

"Mmmm," she murmured.

The house and yard stirred with life. Petey, standing outside with a wreath of dandelions on his head, was playing with a puppy. Fialka, the beautiful oldest girl, her arms full of pussy willows, was approaching from the creek. Voices of children were heard, laughing and shouting. On the kitchen floor knelt Zenobia, sorting out seed for the kitchen garden. Through the open window the smell of smoke drifted from the bonfire which her father had built to clear the yard of rubbish. Vitality began to stir in the girl's limbs as she stretched out her legs and pushed her toes forward, urging herself to grow.

Suddenly she sat up. Anton Landash was approaching the bonfire with a box in his arms. It was painted white, and would have made a fine window box for flowers. As she watched incredulously, her father placed the box on the fire and allowed the flames to consume it. "Father!" she protested weakly. The contrary behaviour of her parents puzzled her. First the dress and now the box had been burned. Nevertheless, as the box disappeared in the flames, she felt an unaccountable lightening of her heart. The conviction came to her, "Now the spring has come."

3
THE FAIRY TALE SPINNERS
❦

THE HOUSE was still now, with the magic stillness of a spring afternoon, serene beneath the chirping of the kitchen clock. The girl was lulled by the sunshine into a peaceful mood of expectancy. Something marvellous was about to happen, born of that peculiar mood of childhood most receptive to fantasy. On such an afternoon, magic slippers commenced to dance, animals developed human personalities, golden mountains gleamed. . . .

In the few days which had elapsed since the crisis, the girl had gained enough strength so that she could be left alone in the house with Granny Yefrosynia, all the others having gone out to the spring work. The old lady sat now at the loom weaving a tapestry. Granny had one white curl, like a chicken feather, poking out from her shawl. Circling her throat, a necklace of many coins made music with every movement. Her features had once been clean-cut, as though sculptured by a chisel, but with age had become blurred in outline, like a melted candle. About her waist was a six-inch striped wool belt, from which hung numerous small leather bags in which Granny kept her treasures, such as tobacco, roasted pumpkin seeds, herbs. In one bag was a handful of earth from her native village. "What is it to be, then, a story?" questioned Granny.

"Yes, Granny, a story!" the girl clasped her hands with pleasure. To hear Granny tell a story – that was really something! Stories poured out of the old lady's mind "like grain out of a sack," as Grandfather Nestor used to say when the girl, as a small child, had visited the old couple in their house near the village church.

Granny now began to tell the story of the Cranberry Flute, which concerned the secret murder of a beautiful girl by her jealous stepsister. The girl was transformed into a cranberry bush growing by the side of the road. A couple of travelling merchants, as they passed through the country, noticed the beautiful plant and cut a flute from the branches. The traveller began playing on the flute and the flute sang out:

> Gently, gently, traveller, pray,
> Lest upon my heart you play,
> For a treacherous sister's knife
> Took from me my youthful life.

And so the dreadful secret was revealed to the world. When the father of the girl heard the song, he said, "What kind of flute is this? It plays so beautifully that it makes my heart ache. Give it to me and let me play it." And the flute sang out with a human voice.

As Granny sang, the girl listened critically. She knew by instinct that the quavering sentimentality of Granny's voice was not adapted to this particular song. She heard, hovering about her, another tune – a high, youthful cry of anguish reproduced musically, capturing the tone of a flute. When Granny sang the song a second time, she protested, "That is not the right tune, Granny."

Granny stopped abruptly. She did not relish interruptions. "Well, you sing it, then," she snapped.

The girl hummed the tune in her mind, a high note of youthful anguish and entreaty.

Granny listened appreciatively, tapping her feet. "Yes, yes, I forgot," she murmured. "That is the way it goes. Thank you for reminding me, dearie." Although Granny had never before heard the tune as the girl had sung it, she did not inquire into its origin, but accepted it, as all folk tale spinners accepted improvements on the original. The girl herself did not know she had composed a tune – she had heard the tune and knew it must be the right one. Stories, for her, were accompanied by melodies heard only in her mind – the running of a rabbit, the cry of a flute, the siren song of water nymphs.

It was this enchantment which lingered on that afternoon, which gave the girl the feeling that she herself, under its magic influence, was changing somehow, that some transformation was taking place in her. People sometimes imposed upon one an uncongenial personality which did not fit one, but which one had to wear, nevertheless, temporarily, like an unbecoming cloak, while another was being tailored for one.

"Now," said Granny, "I have something for you." She took a scrap of scarlet silk from a bag at her waist and gave it to the girl. "That silk," said Granny, "is from the dress of a gypsy."

"Who are the gypsies, Granny?" The girl rubbed the silk between her fingers.

"Folk who have no home, but wander about the earth."

"Am I a gypsy, Granny?" asked the girl.

"Lord forbid!" exclaimed Granny, but she seemed uneasy.

"Then why do the gypsies wander?"

"They were cursed by God."

The girl was struck by an idea. "Granny," she confided, "Granny, I would like to grow. I am too small."

"Yes," reflected Granny. "You could walk between the raindrops and not get wet."

"If I were not so small," continued the girl, "then father and mother would let me stay home, and I would not have to wander."

Granny regarded the girl with a shrewd look. "You will grow," she said positively. "You have many years for growing yet – one hundred and two years, haven't you? In that time, my dear, you might become a giantess."

Comforted by this logic, the girl leaned back on her pillow. She felt closer to the intense humanity of Granny than to her mother and father, and wished that Granny would always live with them, instead of staying as an occasional visitor, as now. Her mother was an alien person, enclosed between two boards of stiffness and morbidity, but Granny could enter the child's world of fantasy and create something new and beautiful out of scraps, whether of cloth, food or words. Who could be unhappy in the presence of Granny?

Granny believed intensely in her stories, and the tales she told formed a gigantic story book, rich and full of life. The legend of the Cranberry Flute had travelled the seas and continents, and yet had an immortal hold on the imagination, this story of the human voice transferred to a musical instrument on the death of a girl. Distilled through the primitive mind of Granny it opened the door for the girl to the magic of poesy and legend.

4
THE SPRING DANCERS
❦

"PEOPLE, SUMMER has come! People, summer has come!" The meadowlark spilled a golden cascade of notes upon the prairies, as he elaborated upon the immemorial call of meadowlarks in a new version which he had been practising that winter for his spring debut. Choirs of meadowlarks took up the call and relayed it far over the prairie: "People, summer has come!"

The girl stood by the road awaiting the arrival of her school mates. She felt the spring, like a peasant, with her body; her kinship with the earth was renewed. Smoothing down the folds of her red calico dress, she tossed her braids, tied with red satin hair bows. Her bare brown feet pounded to the rhythm of awakening life as she whistled through a blade of grass held between her thumb and forefinger. Like a robin moistly emerged out of an egg, she had had to make some adjustments to a new self which had begun to emerge in the weeks since her recovery.

"People, summer has come!" The prairie spring, with high exuberance, had rushed across the Manitoba prairie, blotting up the moisture and transforming the countryside with a haze of shimmering air, an enamelling of wildflowers. Tassels of the Manitoba maple tinkled like earrings with tiny beads of red, green and gold. "The tree is a gypsy," thought the girl. She looked up to see a robin and called to him, "Robin, robin, where did you spend the winter?"

Beneath her physical exuberance, she felt some fear at

meeting her schoolmates for the first time. Her throat was sore with suspense as she remembered that she could speak little English. Would the children accept her, or ridicule her?

Ta-ta-ta. Ta-ra-ta-ta. Ta-ta, ta-ta. She heard a noise from a distance and down the road a cloud of dust announced the arrival of her schoolmates. Arms full of marsh marigolds and pussy willows, a crowd of barefoot children advanced, tooting on whistles which they had cut from willow branches by the wayside. The girls, with buttercups in their hair, wore long skirts of red, green and blue calico almost down to their ankles; hair coiled in buns low down on the neck or braided in four braids with wool hanks and satin ribbons. The boys, with dandelions stuck behind their ears, or curled up like moustaches on their lips, wore overalls and white linen shirts embroidered at the neck and sleeves. They had rolled up one trouser to show their bare legs, and had pulled one overall strap off their shoulder, giving them an insouciant air. Dancing and singing, they came down the road to celebrate the rites of spring.

At the sound of their singing, the self-consciousness of the girl slipped off her like a garment. Music had always had that effect on her; it took her out of her shyness. She commenced running down the road to meet the crowd, jangling her lunch pail. Her feet, she noted, could give pleasure. Feet had formerly been for the purpose of walking wearisome miles after cattle, feet had been for treading up and down garden rows, feet had been for walking all night with a child in her arms. But now she realized that feet could give joy. Wonderful feet could run and dance, feet could jump and wriggle, feet could feel exhilaration as she ran with the wind.

As the cry of the meadowlark was heard, she stopped, and without thinking, imitated its song so exactly that all the children halted to listen. "Who's that?" they asked. Immediately the crowd of scholars, mocking the song of the meadowlarks, took up the refrain in,

TELL YOUR TEACHER ON YOU!
Your teacher on you!
On you! On you!

From all directions, in musical diminuendo, the intermingled call of larks and children sounded and resounded in a multiplicity of echoes all over the prairie.

Full of enthusiasm, the children swept the girl away with them as they marched on between the rows of trees, the poplars leaning eagerly over the road like gossips over a back fence. The wind stirred softly through the grasses, like a cat licking up cream.

One boy, dressed in linen shirt with embroidered gilet, had an orange cowlick jutting up at either side of his head, giving him the odd appearance of a juvenile satyr. He had devised Pan's pipes by cutting reeds in graduated lengths parallel to one another and joining them together with wax. His long limbs, gracefully functioning, as though on well-oiled pistons, marched to the ecstasy of his playing, as with arched torso he flung his head back and blew into his pipes. Running from behind, he took his place next to the girl in the calico dress and laughing, they clasped hands as he started off on a familiar song-game. "If I could run, I would run," he sang out in a husky voice.

The crowd, following after him, repeated, "If I could run, I would run," and suiting the action to the word, the children skipped forward.

"If I could skip, I would skip," continued the leader, skipping about.

"If I could skip, I would skip," carolled the choir, and forming couples, the children skipped about.

"If I could sing, I would sing, la, la, la, la," and the children sang with their leader, la, la, la, la, repeated over and over.

Spinning dizzily, the skirts of the girls billowing like enormous poppies on the road, the boys and girls advanced, singing, clucking, skipping, thumping, clapping. Joy lit up the landscape. Dogs accompanied the procession, barking and frisking and leaping deliriously. Meadowlarks skimmed along the telephone wires. Birds became excited and flew over the group to ascertain the causes of their commotion, as their excitement increased to a frenzy.

Now the children came to a tiny whitewashed house where they had a call to make. The leader stepped forward, and hanging a garland on the blue door, knocked loudly.

"Who is there?" a voice called.

"It's the Maytime. Open up!" chorused the children.

"Welcome, Maytime!" The door opened. Out bounced a roly-poly man with a cheerful turnip face, yellow thatch of hair above a purple countenance, and greeting the children, he strode across the yard with the crowd following close upon his heels. Suddenly he turned around to catch them unawares and laughing, ha, ha, ha, ha, he opened his huge fists and tossed fifty shining new coppers into the air. Like a golden shower, the coppers descended upon the children. The girl in the red calico dress was directly beneath the shower, and as the children scrambled for coins, she picked up her red skirt and caught six coppers.

The young coryphæus had seized four other coppers and these he now flung in her skirt with a lordly gesture: "For you. For Maytime. For be rich."

As the fat man watched the children diving and scrambling for coins, he quivered with laughter, ha, ha, ha, ha, well pleased that for fifty cents he had purchased so much of youth, spring and laughter. When all the coins had been gathered, the man with the golden money held up his hand: "And now I have a favour to ask."

"Ask, ask, we will do anything!" cried the children.

"Bring good harvest to my crops!" he requested.

"We will! We will!" shouted the children. Forming a long chain, the children twined in a circular motion about the fields, singing, "Around the field we have gone, calling on our brave St. George, to save these crops, from hail, from frost, from drought."

And so, like a procession of miniature bacchants, wreathed in flowers, drunk with spring, the rapturous throng approached the schoolhouse.

5
THE BOOK READERS

THE CHILDREN swarmed into the schoolhouse with disorderly enthusiasm, their bare feet swishing against the splinters. As they passed by the teacher's desk, they laid their floral offerings upon it, and then flopped noisily on the creaking wooden benches. Ian MacTavish examined each pupil, making a note of all those who had not appeared before. The settlers were prolific and each day some new pupil appeared, while others disappeared, never to return. Those who did come seemed almost scared, as if they had never seen people on their isolated homesteads. MacTavish recalled his first day of school, when one girl had come armed with a stick, for fear she might have to beat off the teacher like a wild animal. There were fifteen-year-olds in the first grade who had never seen a book.

The girl in the red calico dress, as she passed by, attracted him particularly, because of the curious way in which she regarded every object in the classroom. Pausing before the blackboard, she rubbed her finger across it stealthily. She touched other objects – pictures, desks, books. With a piece of red chalk, she scrawled on the blackboard. On her way to her seat, she sniffed the classroom air, a curious smell compounded of chalk, books, sawdust, lunches and bare feet.

"She's never been in a classroom before," MacTavish realized. He examined her more closely and discovered that this was the girl who had made the trip on the jigger with him;

several times since he had wondered what had happened to her.

"How alive she is!" he thought. "Who would think she'd been so close to death?"

Finding a seat near the window, through which she could see the creek and trees by it, the girl was attracted by the numerous charts and pictures with which the room was decorated. She scrutinized these carefully, made a note of her fellow pupils, and looked slyly at the teacher. Would he remember her?

MacTavish now turned to his flower-laden desk. "Are all these flowers for me?" At his look of astonishment, all the class burst out laughing. Pleased that they had "made a joke on the teacher," they felt kindly disposed to him, and he knew that he had made an auspicious beginning. As he arranged the flowers, he spoke casually about them, their colours, perfume, where they grew, their names.

The girl in the red dress swallowed the information greedily. She repeated to herself the names of the flowers – marsh marigold, crocus, violet, buttercup. With admiration, she noticed how many English words the other pupils knew; their poise in sharpening pencils and writing in their exercise books. They loved physical movement, drawing on the blackboard, handling coloured pegs and chalks, showing off their hand work. She opened her scribbler and looked at the clean white paper. How she longed to be a book-reader like all these others! Tentatively, she made a few strokes with her pencil.

"Let me sharpen your pencil," whispered the young lad of the cowlicks, who had somehow managed to get the seat next to her. Dumbly, she held the pencil out to him.

"Don't look so scared," he whispered, taking out his penknife.

"Who scared?" she smiled valiantly.

MacTavish, as he looked at his class, so full of joy and

vigour, despite their shaggy and untamed appearance, reviewed the goals he had set for himself: to broaden their horizons, to help the parents to adjust themselves, to develop every pupil by making each day a complete, creative entity. For some of his pupils, he knew, that one day might constitute their entire formal education. He was excited, therefore, to think that he was, so to speak, scratching on new ground. Having in him much of the pioneering spirit of his Scottish ancestors, he felt it was a challenge to him to make book readers of the descendants of the men and women in sheepskin coats.

"Now, what shall we do? Sing a song, perhaps? Yes, I think we can start off with a song."

"Yes!" chorused the children. "Yes, yes, yes!" One by one they held up their hands in agreement. All liked singing. They were in a mood of excitement and could not have settled down immediately to humdrum tasks. Accordingly, they were set to march around their desks, chanting, "Good morning, Merry Sunshine!" Some of the pupils knew English, but others, learning by example, tried to imitate the rich Scottish burr of the teacher, overlaying it with bizarre overtones of Swedish, Polish and Bukovynian.

"Good Morning" was followed by "Annie Laurie," which the class sang in harmony. The teacher, waving his arms with enthusiasm, was surprised at the natural ability of his pupils to harmonize; song seemed born in them. Above the noise of cheerful young voices MacTavish now detected one, a low voice overlaid with the velvety fuzz of a crocus petal, yet strong enough to dominate the whole classroom. Who was this singer? He scanned the eager faces one by one. The voice appeared to come from the direction of a big, glossy-eyed girl who was singing with mouth wide open to reveal all her splendid teeth. The teacher smiled appreciatively to her, but to his puzzlement the rosy mouth closed and the glossy eyes wandered to the window where a butterfly had alighted.

Meanwhile the velvety voice continued deep and true from

somewhere behind the girl. MacTavish walked unobtrusively up the aisle to investigate. He stopped short as he discovered that the unique voice was issuing from the scrawny throat of the little brown girl in the red and yellow calico dress. Her thin chest puffed out like a pigeon's, she was singing the song whose words she did not understand, but whose beautiful tune had aroused a flame of joy in her heart.

When the class had finished the song, there was a moment of silence, and then MacTavish motioned gently to the girl and said, "You, little girl with the beautiful voice, let us hear you sing alone."

The girl turned scarlet and hid her face in her sleeve. "She don't speak English very good," cried out the pupils. All stared at her. Where had she come from?

"She's shy and wild," thought MacTavish. "Now is the time to teach her self-confidence." He insisted, "Come, let us hear you. Let all the class hear your beautiful voice."

"I don't know words," gasped out the girl, and put her hands over her face as her thick accent betrayed her. She trembled with shame. Never had it occurred to her that she would be singled out for a solo performance.

"Then sing, la, la, la," MacTavish sang the first phrase and encouraged her to follow him. "Come, sing." She remained mute. "Look at me," he commanded. She looked up at him and he put into his eyes all his authority and compassion, willing her to obey him, to trust him. Suddenly her face relaxed and she began to sing the Scottish song, interpreting the unfamiliar tune with few errors. What caused MacTavish to marvel was that she created of it a strange new melody of haunting melancholy, quite unlike the original. It sounded like the song which the "sheepskins" had sung that memorable evening on the track motorcar. "Who is that girl?" the pupils whispered among themselves. MacTavish felt that he had made a step in the conquest of the girl's diffidence: the thick crust of neglect obscuring her personality had been broken.

As several new pupils were present that morning, MacTavish began to enter their names in the register. Having heard names with a plenitude of unfamiliar vowels and consonants, MacTavish had decided to call his pupils by their first names until he had mastered pronunciation, but was frustrated in this purpose by an unforeseen circumstance.

"What is your name?" he asked the girl in the first seat.

The girl stood up and replied, "Mary Khvalyboha."

The teacher smiled, "Good morning, Mary."

"And yours?" He proceeded to the next pupil, who sat looking at a butterfly which had plastered itself against the school window. The girl turned calf-like eyes upon the teacher. "Mary Bezkorovainy," she said, and looked back at the butterfly.

MacTavish frowned. He saw now that instead of studying Greek and Latin he might have better been employed learning modern European languages. Then he turned to the next girl who, with flaxen hair and blue eyes, turned out to be, "Mary Shakhnevych."

Was it possible that all his pupils were called Mary? An idea came to MacTavish. He singled out Mary of the calf eyes and suggested, "How would you like a new name?"

"A new name? Oh yes, I like a new name all right!" carolled the girl. "Everybody is Mary in this school. Never can tell who is calling!"

"You will be Marigold."

The girl beamed. Marigold! She nodded triumphantly to all.

"And you – " The teacher looked at Mary Khvalyboha. "You will be Rosemary." Rosemary! The children's faces were all alight. Marigold! Rosemary! They had never heard such beautiful names. "All like flowers!" exclaimed Rosemary.

MacTavish came at last to the girl in the red calico dress. "What is your name?" Everyone in the class turned to look at her. Stricken with panic, the girl sat dumb. How could she confess her namelessness, or admit to the names which her family called her? No name? Gypsy? Little Bit of Nothing? Then she had an inspiration. Rising to her feet, she announced in a firm voice, "My name Mary Landash." And without waiting for comment, she pleaded hurriedly, "Please, I like new name, too."

MacTavish regarded her thoughtfully, and despite her plain face, her singular personality reminded him of the tiger lily of the prairie. "Your name will be Lily!" he exclaimed. "That dress of yours is just the colour of our prairie tiger lilies."

"Lily!" The girl breathed with ecstasy. She made a stroke on the page of her scribbler, in order to inscribe her name there and thus give it permanence. Looking sideways with some childish coquetry, she whispered to her neighbour: "How you write it?"

The boy smiled a superior smile, seized her scribbler and wrote with scholastic flourish, "Lilli Landash." That was she, that was her name. She touched the letters with her fingertips, as if absorbing her new identity.

"Hello, Lilli." The boy extended his hand. "I am Vanni Karmaliuk."

"Hello, Vanni." They clasped hands. "How big and shining her eyes are," he thought. He did not know she was plain.

Columbus now discovered America in the classroom with the assistance of a globe and compass. Following the mariner as he progressed from one adventure to another, the teacher showed the pupils the countries and seas over which Columbus had travelled and invited each pupil in turn to examine the globe. Lilli, when her turn came, pored so long over the fascinating object that MacTavish inquired, "Are you looking for something, Lilli?"

Still Lilli would not yield her place. Standing with hands clasped around the globe, striving to express the many impressions which were thronging to her mind, she exclaimed at last in triumph, "I have whole world in my hands!" The class now exploded with the mirth of Maytime, and the long, lean face of the Scot relaxed in a smile. Lilli's remark seemed to him symbolical of his task – to put knowledge into his pupils' hands so that they might indeed possess the world.

As Lilli took leave of Vanni at the end of the school day, they stood looking at each other, inarticulate but conveying their interest to each other with glances.

"You sing beautiful today, Lilli," ventured Vanni at last.

"In Maytime everyone sing beautiful and be happy, Vanni."

The boy reached out and pulled one of her pigtails. "To grow."

"I think I never be big, Vanni," sighed Lilli.

"Never mind, Lilli," consoled Vanni. "Sometimes flower which is small is sweeter like big flower."

The beauty of the day overwhelmed them. "I think I never see such a day in my life again, Lilli," breathed Vanni. They swayed, moved by the rhythm of returning life.

Spring turned somersaults about them.

"Good-bye, Vanni, good-bye."

Lilli lifted herself on her toes and whirled like a leaf down the road. When she came to the railway intersection, she paused to look down the track and from a distance the sound of the jigger came to her. It was Mike the section-hand, recognizable by his white thatch and plaid windbreaker.

Lilli, in mad delight at seeing her Irish patron again, and striving to tell him in a few words the essential happenings of the day, as well as to reassure him about her health, flung her arms up and dancing, she shouted incoherently, "Annie Laurie! Christoph Columb! Lilli Landash!"

Mike brought the jigger to a halt, incredulous that this tornado of energy could be the dying girl whose pathetic fate had haunted him for weeks. "Well, as I live!" he exclaimed. "It's my little pee-wee, and how are you?"

"No more pee-wee!" shouted the girl. "One inch I grow!"

They both laughed. Mike reached over and pinched her cheek. "Are you from school?"

"Oh, yes, Mike, I go to school."

"And what did you learn?"

"Learn song, Annie Laurie. Go with Christoph Columb find America. Get new name, Lilli."

"Well, now, you're an educated lady."

Lilli preened herself complacently.

Seeing that vitality, Mike's conviction grew that her zest and originality would serve to enrich the country, and he felt grateful that he had had some share in preserving them. His investment in her was safe for life, and he felt a complacent pleasure, as if something had been added to himself; and if that small light would not shine always in his presence, at least he would know that it was glowing to good purpose, somewhere.

"Well," he said finally. "Good luck, Lilli. Good-bye!"

"Good-bye, good-bye! Oh, good-bye, Mike!"

Lilli ran down the track after the jigger, calling and waving her hands until Mike was out of sight, and singing to the wind, "Oh, how my heart full of happy!"

PART TWO
Songs of the Seasons

1
THE SOIL TILLERS
🌱

LIFE WAS returning to the prairies. The sound of wings preceded the appearance of a great wedge of geese storming the air. The earth breathed deeply as it emerged from the deep-freeze which had locked it for six months. From fence-post to fence-post, the roundelay of the meadowlark throbbed in a great, overwhelming burst of joy. Odours of burning green brush, of sticky poplar buds, of melting snow arose from the spongy brown soil. On the Landash farm, the spring work was beginning. From dawn, the figures of the children had dotted the fields as they piled twigs and rubbish, picked up stones, chopped down saplings and hauled them to the pyre. Zenobia in red skirt and green shawl was seated on the ground beside the house, sorting seeds for her kitchen garden. Each gesture was sure, as she was now working in her own element. Anton had set a tree stump on fire and now, like an enormous candle it blazed in a pillar of flame and smoke, crackling in the spring breeze. On an uncleared field, Lilli and Anton were breaking the land with an enormous plough that Anton had made in his smithy that winter. Anton held the reins of the horses while Lilli, dressed in boy's shirt and overalls, guided the plough. As the ponderous share cut a four-foot lap through the stubborn soil, a slow, burning ache began to make itself felt in her muscles. She staggered over the clods of earth which cut sharply into her bare feet. Searing pains crept up her back and legs. A red light glared before her eyes and tears trickled burningly down her face. Her mouth was swollen and dry inside and her eyes bulged with strain. She lifted her face to catch the gentle breeze which was stirring the atmosphere.

"O God, how it hurts!" thought Lilli. "Oh, let me stop for a minute to rest!" Sweat was beginning to drip down her cheeks, and on the back of her shirt a wet stain spread over her shoulders. "Father!" she gasped, trying to attract his attention, but he did not hear her.

Anton drove his horses on, noting the beauty of their plump, satiny sides. He looked greedily at his land, encompassing it, feeling the pride of ownership. "My land, my land," he murmured to himself. He felt as if he were holding in his hands that rich virgin soil, running it through his fingers with a pleasure almost sensual. He whistled as he walked, swaying his massive shoulders in rhythm. All around him, he felt the elemental craving of the earth, he responded to it with a strong physical reaction. He looked across to his neighbour's field, where a woman walked over the earth casting seed with her hand in a circular, primitive rhythm. Her gesture seemed futile to Anton, and he thought, "Better she had never left the old country." When he looked up into the skies, the clouds formed, or so it seemed to him, the pattern of a harvest field – they stood about like sheaves in the fall, and the words of an old peasant song ran through his mind: "O thou beloved harvest field, O thou earth from which I gather the harvest which springs from the soil and flourishes through bitter distress." The bitter distress of the old country had changed to the promise of the new, he thought, as he saw his son Petey run about the fields. He thought that he was building for the future of Petey, and he was pleased that future generations of his seed would benefit by his present labour.

Absorbed in his dreams, he did not notice the small figure guiding the plough behind him, and was not concerned when Lilli tripped over a clod of earth, panting as the plough nearly slid from her hands. The veins on her arms stood out, and her muscles pulled as though her arms were being wrenched from her shoulders. "O God how it hurts!" she thought again. There was only the will left to drive her undersized body. "Must do it, must do it!" she exhorted herself. She strove to divert her mind by catching at the many details of change which spring had wrought on the landscape – the shoots of green on the poplars, the moist, tender fragrance of prairies after winter, the songs of birds as they arose in the wake of the plough, the flight of some hawk across the great prairie sky. As the plough turned back, Lilli held up her hand to wipe off the sweat and dirt. Again the plough slipped from her arms, jerking in a zigzag. She stumbled in the furrow.

"Watch out there, Lilli!" shouted Anton. He jerked angrily at the reins, and the horses plunged on, dragging Lilli with them. The heat of the noon day was upon them, and Lilli's clothes, now soaking wet, clung to her like a second, wrinkled skin.

A meadowlark sang, rising from the earth like a shadow. The song gave Lilli momentary relief. She looked up from the furrow and thought, "The earth is full of music." It gave her strength to finish the row, to disregard the dirt which flew up over her arms and legs and face, bruising and scratching her skin. She envied the freedom of the bird, as she was released at last from the plough and staggered blindly to the water trough. She stooped over it to bathe her hot face and drew back in horror as she saw her reflection mirrored in the water, covered with scratches and dirt and blood. She splashed water freely over her face and hair and stood gasping and choking as the water dripped down over her face. Leaning back against the trough to steady herself, she could not control the shuddering of her body. Her hands were a mass of aching bruises.

"Lilli!" her father called out impatiently. "Come help with the horses!"

She bent her head once more to examine that face, with its frightful expression of strain, its huge eyes starting out of their sockets, the sweat rolling down, the mouth open in anguish, the features so distorted that she could hardly recognize herself. The breath seemed beaten out of her body. She grasped the lip of the trough and plunged her face down again and again. Streams of water ran over her face and figure. She thrust her hands into the water and gasped as the coolness gave her relief. Beneath the surface, she watched the enlarged veins writhing like snakes under her skin. The knobby muscles of her upper arms bulged out like balls.

"Lilli!" Anton Landash called out again.

Lilli could not obey the call; her limbs refused to take orders from her mind. Dazedly, she stood watching her veins writhe beneath the water. They seemed more like snakes than ever, especially when she regarded them through half-shut eyes. To close out the sight, she drove her head down into the water again.

Anton looked about and spied Lilli standing by the trough. He strode over and regarded her with incredulity while she went through this fantastic performance, like one demented. "Are you mad?" He seized her and dragged her to her feet. His pride was outraged by the spectacle of this half-drowned daughter, hair and face and clothes dripping, gasping and choking. Raising his whip, he struck her about the head and shoulders, then shook her violently and threw her from him. She lay sprawling on the ground. "When will you learn to come when I call you?" he exclaimed with exasperation. "Go into the house." She staggered over the steps into the kitchen and stood for a moment, the water running down her body, so that her shirt clung to her chest, revealing the outline of her small breasts. She took up a towel to dry herself.

As she stood near the window she could see someone approach on the road, a familiar figure riding on a horse, the teacher, Ian MacTavish, coming to visit. "Mr. Mac!" she thought in consternation. She did not wish to be caught in such a condition, and ripping her shirt and overalls from her, she began to put on clean clothes with trembling fingers. By the time MacTavish had come into the yard, she was completely clothed.

She ran out to meet him, so eager that she could hardly speak. As he dismounted, she said, "Come in, please." Her face and hair were still moist, but her shirt was clean, and she wore dry overalls rolled up from the ankles. MacTavish noticed the bruises on her bare arms and legs, but gave no indication that he had seen them. "Is your mother home, Lilli?" He made a few steps forward. "Mother is at Granny's," replied Lilli, flushing. "But Father like to see you. Wait here," she said. "I bring him."

She ran to Anton, who was in the stable. He turned around with a frown and made a step forward as if to strike her, but she forestalled him by saying, "Oh, teacher come. Oh, Mr. Mac here, father." He checked his impulse and made haste to leave the stable. He had already found the teacher a shrewd man with a practical knowledge of farming and welcomed the opportunity to talk to him. He strode over to MacTavish and gripped his hands. "Good that you have come. There is much to talk, much to learn." The two men, despite the dissimilarities of their characters, had a sound respect for each other. In the affairs of the community, MacTavish had learned to like and admire Landash, so as he returned Anton's welcome, he said, "I'd like to hear something about this irrigation scheme of yours, Landash."

Leaving the two men engaged in conversation, Lilli rushed into the house and began to set the table with a clean cloth and paper flowers. She brought the best food up from the cellar, and by the time the two men had entered, a platter of chipped beef with sour cream and horseradish stood on the table.

The men sat down while Lilli waited on the table. The teacher, although he spoke only to Anton, was aware of every one of Lilli's movements. He noted the bruises on her arms and her downcast, apparently submissive behaviour. Yet there was, in the glance of her eyes as she looked at her father, something like inner rebellion. He noticed that her legs were much longer than they had been when he last saw her; her overalls, rolled up to her knees, revealed a fine ankle and a slim, high-arched foot. When he caught her eye, she smiled, and the smile gave radiance to her sombre face.

"She's good around the house," said Anton, with a nod in Lilli's direction. She stood now by the window, humming a tune to herself.

"Don't you think she's rather young to do such heavy work?" asked MacTavish pointedly.

"She has to learn to work hard," said her father, as he cleared his plate of the chipped beef. "Better she should learn now. Besides," he added, as he helped himself to the last of the sour cream, "Lilli will never grow big. When she was born, I thought she was midget. Ha, ha," he laughed, not noticing the flush of shame on Lilli's cheek.

MacTavish, who had seen Anton strike his daughter, did not try immediately to interfere, since he knew he must not antagonize Anton, one of the most influential men in the Bukovynian community. Besides, he had other plans for Lilli, and so he said, only, in a mild voice, "Well, among us Scots, there is a saying that fine things come in small parcels."

The teacher had brought with him a sample of grain seed, which he now poured on the table while Anton ran the reddish kernels through his fingers. "This seed," said MacTavish "came originally from your own country, but has been much improved."

"Where did you learn all these things, MacTavish?" asked Anton, pleased. He thought that the teacher spoke in an intelligent manner and imitated it, using words which he had looked up in the dictionary. MacTavish was something of an amateur agronomist and described some of the experiments which Canadian scientists had made to develop superior seed.

He was surprised at Anton's shrewd comments. "If only you had an education, you might have been a scientist."

"What do I need with education?" roared Anton. "I get all my lessons from nature." Nevertheless, he was pleased. "I'm sending my boys to school," he said. "I want them to become real men – not, as we elder people, to kiss the hands of the noble, not to bow, not to say, 'yes, yes, your honour,' but to stand up straight, to look people in the eye and say, 'I'm a free man.'" He went on to tell the teacher something of his background in the old country and the motives which had impelled his people to migrate. MacTavish never admired Anton so much as at this time. A man who partook of the intolerance of the earth itself, Landash was possessed by that desperate compulsion of the "sheepskins" who had to skip centuries in a single generation, eradicating in themselves the deep traces of the serf. "The land is in your blood, I see," he commented when Anton had finished.

"From many years back," replied Anton, still caressing the grain on the table. "My grandfather, my great grandfather before him, all lived on the land." He sighed as he recalled his peasant ancestry. "We have a saying in our country, with fire, with water, with the wind, do not make friends, but make friends with the earth."

MacTavish chuckled. He had been keeping a notebook full of information regarding the life of these people, and already knew something of the language. "Do you mind my writing that down?" he asked, taking his notebook from his vest pocket. He opened the first page and read something he had written months back concerning these immigrants: "Their language is related to nature and describes with scientific accuracy the natural features of the landscape – animals, birds, conformations of land. It is concerned with herbs, sorcery, the song of birds, festivals, cloud formations, the market place, spinning and dyeing, with peasant wisdom. There is a beautiful word, *tyrlo*, which means the resting-place of birds at night. With a single word, they express such intricate conceptions as, "a piece of arable land ploughed by one pair of oxen during one day;" "an ox with a tuft of hair between his horns;" "a petticoat made of silk dyed with cochineal;" "an adorned candle used at match-making;" "a fidgety man shifting from one place to another;" and "an ochre brown paint used for decorating earthenware."

Every detail of the house and its furnishings interested MacTavish. He had already noted in other homes the rows of kilims or tapestries which hung over a long pole suspended from a rope about one foot from the ceiling, covering almost all the wall to the floor. Now he watched Lilli as, preparatory to baking, she opened the clay stove and scratched the bottom with a rake to test its degree of heat. The stove, six feet wide and eight feet long, was made of a basketwork of willow twigs coated over with the clay found in swamps, and was supported on a platform built on four posts. "The bread you bake in such an oven," he remarked as Lilli sealed the oven, "has a very good flavour. It seems to be evenly baked."

"The crust, too, is never burned," added Anton as Lilli brought tea with lemon. He put a lump of sugar in his mouth and sucked the tea.

Lilli, after she had tended to the men, returned to the window, looking out over the swamp, where a great flock of geese arose and headed north. Their barbaric trumpeting at first blared compelling like the noise of an orchestra, then gradually diminished as their forms faded in the skies. Anton frowned, scarcely noticing the geese. "It's hard to get the soil here under cultivation," he remarked, "because of the tangle of willow and poplar in that low swamp." As he pushed back his chair from the table, he suggested that Lilli take MacTavish around the farm, while he himself would attend to pressing work. "Take the teacher around the farm and show him everything," he said. "I have some work to do or I'd take him round myself."

The two walked out into the yard, beneath the archway of trees, which, interlaced over a ploughed road, formed a protected entrance. "Like a church," commented Lilli. As they came into the fields, MacTavish stopped to look at Lilli, wanting to see her apart from her father. Susceptible to the appeal of tenderness, Lilli looked shyly down, rubbing her bare feet together. This was her first opportunity to be alone with the teacher, whom she adored. Her heart thumped with ecstasy. How she longed to talk to him, to ask him about the great world beyond! She wanted to say something clever, but she was tongue-tied. "The earth is rich here, Mr. Mac," she pointed out. "Everything grows big here."

As they walked on, MacTavish tried to analyze his own feelings. Why was he so deeply moved by this girl? Why, of all his pupils, did she please him most? How strangely stirred was he by her! And how easily the onlooker might be deceived as to her rare quality! He asked, "Will you come to school, Lilli?"

She shook her head. "Father won't let me. I have to work on land."

"How old are you? You can't be fourteen." He stopped to look at her childlike form which formed a strange contrast to the premature knowledge of death written on her face. He knew that children living three and a half miles away from school were not compelled to attend, nevertheless, he longed to have her as a pupil. "She is not like any other child hereabouts," he thought, "nor, for that matter, like any child I have ever met." Lilli, meanwhile, answered his question, "Don't know how old I. Father say I am too old to go to school."

MacTavish could see that something was tormenting her. She had a thought which struggled like a captive bird for liberation from the dark recesses of her mind. He could tell by the swift change of colour, the upward glances which she directed quickly at him and as quickly withdrew. At last, in a choked voice, eyes cast down, in an agony of shyness, she exclaimed, "Oh, I like to learn talk like you. My tongue lame like old horse."

He considered her for a moment. "Would you, Lilli?"

She nodded. A smile lit up her face, displayed her wide mouth, beautifully curved, her small white teeth.

"Look at me."

She raised her eyes to his. How lovely was her defencelessness, he thought! Like a very young, wild deer – the big eyes, proud, shy, "as if in one instant she'd run away." When he said to her, "Anyone can learn," a light of hope gleamed in her eyes. "Teach me."

"I'll give you your first lesson now. Come, let's sit down here – " He indicated a log on the bank of the creek. They sat down, faces turned to each other. For a moment they said nothing, MacTavish deliberating where he should begin, then Lilli, eyes uplifted, pointed upward. "Look, Mr. Mac, how straight rows in ploughed skies."

"Ploughed skies?" He was startled by the figure of speech. "Look like field, all ploughed with golden plough."

MacTavish looked up at the orderly row of clouds in the sky and thought, "This closeness to nature is something we lose in the cities. We can't describe it, because we've lost it."

"I'm ready now for lesson, Mr. Mac," Lilli said demurely, reminding him of her presence. He came to with a start.

"Say after me, I think that I can learn to speak very well."

"I tink – " began Lilli. She stopped. "Wrong, isn't it?" He nodded. "Think, Lilli. Like this. Put your tongue up against your teeth, and say think – " He demonstrated the proper actions.

"Think – " she brought out with triumph. "Think!" she repeated.

"Good. Now go on."

"I think dat – that – " She smiled as she made a conscious effort. "Now I know how to say – that."

"Right." He was pleased with her progress.

She went on – "I think that I kin – " He stopped her. "Can, Lilli, not kin. Watch my face; watch the way my lips and tongue move. Where does the sound come from? In any language it is the same; when people are speaking a language you don't know, watch the muscles of their face, the lips and tongue; by imitating them, you can make the same sounds."

"Can!" Lilli brought it out with triumph. She looked at him for approval.

"Now, go on."

"I think that I can lorn – " She frowned. "Oh, that is hard, Mr. Mac!"

"Learn, not lorn." He demonstrated the positions of the two vowels. "Learn – like this." She watched him closely.

"I think that I can learn to spik – "

"Speak, not spik."

"I am so stupid!" she laughed. "All the time, mistakes!" At such times, glints of mischief appeared in her eyes.

"You are not stupid. How can you learn, without mistakes? Everyone makes mistakes. Take it again. Patience will do it."

"I think that I can learn to speak wery vell."

MacTavish smiled. "Those v's and w's are troublesome, aren't they? Let me show you how. For the v, the lip beneath the teeth; for the w, the lips puckered out. Like this, very well, very well – "

"I think that I can learn to speak very well." She paused, then clapped her hands. "Oh, Mr. Mac, it is all right, isn't it?"

"Say it again."

Lilli repeated the sentence. "Oh!" she breathed. "It comes out right again." She continued, with excitement, "You know, all the time I will speak like this. Everybody will be surprised. Easy when you know how!"

"Like anything else."

"I will teach you sometime our language, Mr. Mac," she offered as they scrambled to their feet and continued to walk about the farm. The children were still busy out in the fields. Petey, a red cap on his head – he was fond of red, and always wore an article of this colour – had seized a large stone and now, with a rope around it, was trying to haul it away by pulling and dragging. Finally, unable to make any progress, he sat down on the stone, and laughed with such a carefree air that Lilli said, "Petey loves the land. For him, life will be good. He will be a real Canadian, Mr. Mac." She was so staunch in her loneliness that MacTavish asked, in an impulse of pity, "Don't you play with other children?"

She averted her eyes and shook her head. Something of her solitude betrayed itself in her voice as she replied, "I like to go by myself, walk, look at skies, listen to wind, sing, make plan – "

"What plan?" MacTavish interrupted.

"What to do when I grow up." She lifted her eyes to his.

"What would you like to do?"

"Sometime I dream I am in city, free, happy, can live how I like." She looked into the distance while she described her ambition, as though all these marvellous things could there be seen.

"Each person," said MacTavish, "has a right to live, not as someone else wills him to live, but as he himself feels within his heart that he must live. Some day, your time will come."

"Oh, when that day will come?" whispered Lilli with sad desperation. They paused to listen to the wind in the grass. "Like girl combing hair," said Lilli. "Like whispering on silk." They strolled across the fields.

"Perhaps you can teach me something, too, Lilli."

"I can teach you?" She peered up at him. "You are joking, yes?"

"No, Lilli, I'm not joking. . . ." His face was quite sober as he asked, "Tell me, what song was that you were singing in the house?"

"Old song." She was flattered that he had noticed it.

"Who taught you?"

Lilli remained silent, reluctant to reveal herself. As she stood in the brilliant sunshine, dressed shabbily in men's clothing too large for her, defensive yet secret, she had a feminine allure, the beginning of womanhood. MacTavish could not look at her without a stirring of emotion, compounded of pity and something akin to excitement, a consciousness that here was something rare and undeveloped. He asked again, "Where did you learn that song?"

She spoke with head averted. "From old people. In winter, when snow come, all sit around and sing, fire in big stove and snowflake fall on window. Everyone sing, so sad, so far away."

"Do you sing often, Lilli?"

"Oh, yes!" she exclaimed. "All around me I hear songs." This singular moment of self-revelation was almost too much for the reticent girl, but suddenly she lifted her head and looked with strange intensity at MacTavish. "I hear now," she exclaimed. "Listen, listen!"

Wild music arose from everywhere around them – the church bells, the wind, the birds arising from the swamps, the insects, the trees. Lilli stood barefoot and bareheaded on a little knoll, head raised to the sky, watching intently the procession of clouds. It was almost like an attitude of prayer, prayer to the inanimate forces of nature. . . . Here in this land, scarcely redeemed from the wilderness, old legends lived on in the winds, the sunshine, the clouds. Lilli moved with the wind, not disturbed by it, adapting herself to its rhythm. Everything provided a background for her – the grace of her movements, the animation of her face and body, the expressiveness of her voice. So excited was she that MacTavish could see her heart throbbing through her ragged shirt. Standing thus, you did not notice her shabby clothing; she appeared a heroic figure; the rags in which she was clothed, part of the shaggy landscape.

"Listen!" She closed her eyes and began to sing. The wild

strains, supremely fitted to her surroundings, rose in a kind of ancestral chant, like the cry of women bereaved, and the wind formed a natural accompaniment. MacTavish was stunned by the deep emotion which welled up from that slight body, disturbed that a half-grown girl could sing with such great feeling. Out of what depths of racial tragedy had that song sprung; how many centuries of oppression had been necessary to produce that feeling? In all their traditions, how conscious these people were of their past, so that their music was like the cry of the soul for freedom. Little by little, MacTavish thought, he would piece together the past that had created Lilli.

"You sing with great feeling," he said when she had finished.

"Those who suffer most can sing most beautiful, my mother said once to me, Mr. Mac."

"It's strange that you, so young, should know how to sing these old songs."

"Oh, I feel it belongs to me!" Lilli exclaimed. "When old people tell stories, when granny tells fairy tale, when mother sings of old country, I get all excited; it makes me feel rich and warm." She turned to him and with eyes shining demanded, "Why *you* like such old song?"

MacTavish, a little disconcerted at having the tables turned, replied, "They tell me how people lived, dreamed, loved long ago. People of every country get to know each other by songs."

"Annie Laurie?" Lilli smiled and threw her head back. It was a sudden and unexpected gesture of coquetry which amused the teacher because of its very naiveté. Lilli, seeing that he was amused, laughed also, although she did not guess the reason for his amusement. "What are you thinking, Mr. Mac?" They had reached the limit of the Landash farm, marked by a windbreak, and they now stood ready for the trip back to the house.

"Some poetry I read as a schoolboy." MacTavish was

reluctant to return; he was invigorated by his contact with these people, as the giants of old became stronger by contact with the earth.

"Tell me about that poetry." The word was new to Lilli, but she divined what it meant.

"It's about a girl like you, Lilli."

"Like me? Then truly I must hear."

As they cut back across the fields, MacTavish in a vibrant, low voice – he was an excellent reader of poetry – began to recite:

Behold her, single in the field,
Yon solitary highland lass –

Lilli was enchanted. "Oh, that is truly like me, Mr. Mac!" she exclaimed when he had finished. "To sing without ending! Such beautiful words I never hear before!"

As MacTavish rode away from the farm, he looked back and saw the shaggy figure of Anton Landash silhouetted against the horizon, his sheepskin coat slung over his shoulders, and the big, home-made plough standing in the earth beside him, and these figures appeared to symbolize for MacTavish all the soil tillers who had worked upon the land to break the Canadian wilderness.

When he got back to his teacher's shack, MacTavish wrote in his diary: "Today I have learned something of the cost of settling our country. These sheepskins who settled here with little assistance from our government had little to sustain them in their pioneering life except their conviction, 'Free land and strong hands open the door to the future for our people.' As for Lilli, she is so much a product of nature at its wildest that I don't know whether it would be right to encourage her to leave this environment. Would she lose her original qualities, or discover opportunities for the free development of her talents? It is as though an anachronism of circumstances had produced a genuine folk poet in this isolated Bukovynian community of

Manitoba. I feel almost as though I were a spectator of history delayed; it's like seeing a film run backward." He paused while he struggled to find expression for the faith which he had in Lilli, then wrote: "I believe, however, that given a few leads, Lilli will stumble into the right path by herself."

2
VOICES OF THE PRAIRIE

THE SOIL which Lilli had broken to the plough two months previously was already covered with green when she arose one summer morning and ran, quick and light, to the garden, where her mother was already at work, although the pink smudges or dawn had not yet faded and the grass was still encased in silver dew. As Lilli's bare feet came into contact with it, she shivered slightly, a shiver of pleasure, for she loved the touch of it – it made her feel fresh and young. A red bandana which she had knotted about her blue denim trousers flew free when she ran.

The kitchen garden was Zenobia's domain. Vegetables, flowers, poppies, sunflowers, herbs – all were laid out in symmetrical rows, or in the case of flowers, in beds arranged to imitate Bukovynian embroideries. Early in the morning, Zenobia hurried out wearing a shawl knotted at the back of her head, a shirt made of flour sacks, with a bit of embroidery at the neck and shoulder, and a skirt of black wool stuff draped triangular fashion to her waist. Once in the garden, she knelt among the rows as some kneel in church, in a kind of earth worship.

On her way to the garden, Lilli paused to peer beneath a shrub where she had planted slips for her flower garden. Bending down, she examined the lady slipper she had hidden there so Zenobia should not find it. "That is an evil flower," she had told Lilli. "Never touch it. When you see it, walk around it." Could anything so rare and beautiful be evil? Like a gold pouch inlaid with rubies, the plant was an alien, as exotic a growth as Lilli herself. Every day she came to pay homage to it as to royalty, noting the gradual unfolding of the bud, and pondering upon its exquisite form.

The flower garden was close to the house and Lilli stopped there to visit her favourite flowers. She had her own names for them: pansies she called Little Girls; sweetpeas were petticoats; wallflowers she named Sunshine, and susans were Black Brows. Everywhere, colour in small torches – zinnias stiff and starchy, nasturtiums with orange satin petals, dahlias like grand ladies in wine velvet gowns. Lilli snatched up a nasturtium flower and took it into her mouth to suck the nectar.

As she came into the kitchen garden, a bee alighted upon her head. Zenobia looked up, beads of perspiration on her lip, her face grey with exertion.

"Lilli!" she exclaimed, getting up from her knees.

"What is it, mother?" asked Lilli, oblivious of her strange ornament. She took up a hoe and considered where she should start working.

"A bee on your head."

"A bee?" Lilli, unafraid, stood laughing in the sunshine, with the bee caught like a golden ornament in the brown net of her hair. "A bee? Ha, ha!" Lilli put her hands to her hair. "It thinks I'm a flower!" The bee circled round Lilli's head, as though tracing a diadem, and then flew off. Zenobia stood staring after it, incredulous. What did this portend? She recalled the old folk saying that a person on whose head a bee alighted was destined for a strange fate. Why was the girl laughing in that gypsy way? Lilli, excited by the beauty of the thing, ran to her mother and flinging herself upon her, kissed her. A look of distaste appeared on Zenobia's face. She rubbed the moist spot on her cheek with her hand, as though it were something obscene. "Faugh!" she exclaimed in disgust. "That is shameful, to kiss like a baby." She did not like physical contact with this daughter of hers; Lilli was too alien, too secretive in her personal life to be congenial. Lilli backed off, conscious that she had erred, that her feelings of affection were to be hidden and pushed out of sight like something disgraceful. She attacked a hill of potatoes.

As the two worked – Lilli with ambidextrous skill which made Zenobia's stolid movements appear graceless – Zenobia recalled the circumstances of Lilli's birth. The girl had been born at the twilight hour, and was clothed in a caul, for which reason Grandmother Yefrosynia had predicted that the child would have second sight. It was true that Lilli possessed many curious powers. Zenobia valued Lilli's assistance in planting; slips which the girl transplanted flourished, for she had the green thumb. When Lilli baked bread or made pickles, she always had success – the "lucky luckless one" her mother called her.

When the two had finished their work, it was near noon. Both were sweating, and the veins stood out on Lilli's hands like cords. Zenobia staggered to the bench by the house. "Bring some buttermilk from the cellar," she said to Lilli, "and something else for lunch. We'll eat here in the shade."

Lilli ran into the house and lit a candle which she placed on the floor in order to lift the lid to the cellar entrance. Here Zenobia kept sauerkraut, pickles, sour cream, ewe cheese, eggs, preserves, vegetables. Lilli stepped down the stairs and set the candle down on a stone crock, looking about with admiration at the yellow, red and green preserves glowing in their glass jars like jewels in the dim light of the candle, the smoked meats hanging down from the rafters and the wooden kegs of apple cider. Then she poured some buttermilk into a jug, selected a pickled lettuce, some cottage cheese and dills. These, along with a loaf of rye bread she took outside to her mother who was sitting now, fanning her face with her apron, as she rested on the *pryspa*, the wooden bench which ran all round the house. When they had finished their lunch, they rested for a while, Zenobia chewing some salted sunflower seeds while she wriggled her toes in the earth. She had a mint leaf on her head and over it had tied a handkerchief.

The still prairie had come to life. A myriad tiny voices sounded from every blade of grass as though hundreds of insect musicians were playing their after-luncheon music. "Listen, mother!" exclaimed Lilli.

"I hear nothing," replied Zenobia, shrugging her shoulders as she felt the warmth seeping through her.

"Listen, listen!" implored Lilli. A leaf turned; it was like a musical note. A caterpillar plopped from a twig; a robin swished his rump briskly in a bowl of water.

Petey was near the creek, tumbling in a pile of hay. He stood up, took a stone and splashed it into the creek. The noise plunked musically and Petey shrieked with delight. A stray breeze lifted the wig of an elderly dandelion. Petey, enchanted, cried out, "Grandfather is losing his hair!" He sat down on the ground and one by one examined his toes, which he appeared to find most satisfactory. He scratched his back, yawned, stretched, put his toe in the water, and withdrew it when he found the water cold. Joy was in every motion. He looked into the creek, saw a frog, and stared at him as though hypnotized. What a wonderful huge world of discovery was the child's! And how the world shrinks in maturity, as everything becomes familiar and dulled! Petey chuckled, rushed, charged, bounced, ran around in circles, battled with an invisible foe. Finally, in ecstasy, he fell down flat on his face in the grass, laughing.

Lilli watched him with wonder. The joy and freedom of childhood had been denied her, and they were all the more delightful to her as she watched Petey, now sitting on the ground, drawing a picture in the dust. "Everything is new for Petey," she commented. "He is fresh as a bird come out of an egg."

"He is a *molodets* like his father," replied Zenobia,

thinking of the youth Anton had once been. A *molodets*, Lilli knew, was one who possessed audacity, courage, a zest for life. To be a *molodets* was to have a special quality in meeting life, a quality which Petey would always have, if he lived to be one hundred.

Zenobia took up a handful of brown earth and ran it through her fingers. She loved the earth and contact with it. There was a solid earthiness about her that Lilli appreciated. She had an unchanging quality; one could depend on her to carry out all the rituals connected with living.

"Tell me something of your life in the old land, mother," requested Lilli, feeling that this was a good time for the old stories which she loved.

Zenobia pondered, thinking back to her own girlhood, to find some basis of comparison. She began to talk, trying to describe to Lilli, born on the prairie, the world of the Carpathian Mountains. "You wouldn't know me, Lilli, if you had seen me as a girl – I was proud!" She sighed at the recollection. "Skin rosy and firm, eyes bright, high bosom, trim legs. On Sundays, when I put on my red woollen coat, richly embroidered linen blouse and two-piece skirt with golden-woven stripes, all the other girls stared with envy as we rode on our small mountain ponies to church – the old folks with their umbrellas, the young people adorned with beads, gold thread, ribbons, belts, shawls – what beautiful colours, like a picture! In the summertime I would put flowers in my hair – what fine hair I had, glossy and fine as silk – and decorate it with shiny ornaments clustered on both sides of my head. Then, proud as a peacock, I would walk along the mountain paths through fields of poppies and chrysanthemums and other blooms – a thousand colours, such as you never see on the prairies!" She paused as she regarded the flat prairie around her, then resumed, "The whole mountainside was as if on fire with flowers. Everywhere, medicinal herbs which women and girls gathered to cure ailments. As I walked, I thought of tales which the old folks used to tell of mountain nymphs – how anyone who is caught in the forest and meets a nymph must give her a shawl or a piece of clothing, otherwise she will do him mischief. I remembered the travellers who used to come to visit us – yes, even in our village up in the mountains we had visitors – gypsies in velvet coats with silver buttons; traders who came to buy the heavy woollen greatcoats we made for the fairs; saffron merchants who arrived in the autumn and sold us caraway seeds – and above all, the *olyikari*, oil merchants – the women used to buy love philtres from them. One of them told my fortune, said I would travel to a distant country and live on a great piece of land – that story has certainly come true."

Lilli, during this narration, had her eyes fixed with curiosity on her mother. It was a revelation to her that beneath the placid exterior, her mother could have nourished this recollection of her youth which now sparked out in poesy. It was always difficult to imagine a woman as she had been before she had borne her children, for she was much more attached to them than was the father, and they were more a part of her life. "It must have been very different from the prairie, mother," she commented as she tried to conjure up a picture of the old country.

"So different, Lilli, it's hard to tell you," replied her mother. "That mountain river, so fierce it seemed to boil, but the water was as cold as ice. Sometimes I stood on the banks and watched the timber rafts come down the stream and called out to the young men. . . ."

"You did this when you were a girl, mother?" queried Lilli, as she tried to convert her present mother into the high-spirited mountain lass.

"Yes, I did," affirmed her mother and there was a softness and slyness on her face which Lilli had not seen before. She continued, "As I walked, I looked up at the clouds, always changing, steaming like vapour above the Black Mountain, the air clear as tears! And from the distance would come the sound of the flute played by some shepherd lad as he sat in a meadow of glorious flowers watching over his flock. How bright was the Paschal Night with its thousand candles lit like stars against the black mountain side! You cannot think, Lilli, how splendid it was to watch the thunder clouds ride on the wings of a storm, above the black heights of the mountains!"

Where had that girl gone, thought Zenobia, as the scenes faded from her mind, and with a sigh she found herself beside this strange girl who was her daughter, and yet not her daughter. Was this what she was preparing for when she had danced with that handsome, dark-haired youth named Anton Landash, and he had spoken of Canada, where one might acquire a great estate like one of the Austrian nobles?

Lilli wondered at this untold chapter of her parents' history. How had her father, so adventurous a person, married a woman placid and resigned as her mother? Without thinking, she blurted out, "Mother, how did you come to marry father?"

Zenobia reddened unbecomingly, since she did not confide easily. How had Lilli divined what she had been thinking? She shot a suspicious glance at the girl, but Lilli's face was impassive. How could she explain herself as she used to be, draw for Lilli the portrait of the girl she had been? She knew only too well what she had become, how the flesh had betrayed the spirit of that exuberant girl. Nevertheless, she decided to tell Lilli the truth: "Your father married me because I had a new pair of yellow boots."

A pair of yellow boots! Zenobia saw them now, as they appeared to her delighted eyes when her father had presented them to her to wear to a dance in a neighbouring village. "Yes, a pair of yellow boots," she continued defiantly. "Oh, they were of the finest leather, soft as a stocking, tall as my knee, yellow as gold. . . . They were made by my father; he was an artist – people came from miles around to have him make boots for them, but nobody had yellow boots like mine!" She spoke with passion, feeling that perhaps as long as she had the yellow boots, she would not lose contact with the girl she had once been. "Girls nowadays speak of freedom," she went on with a touch of spite, for she was opposed to the talk of young people concerning the new ways, "but the mountain lasses had freedom then! Freedom to walk, as I walked, twenty miles to that village, to be at the dance, and those yellow boots of mine attracted many eyes, I can tell you! Bounding, leaping, whirling, they sang out as I stamped and glided about the room, and seemed to say, 'Look at my new boots! Look at my boots!' Who could resist such boots? And then" – Zenobia sucked in her breath at the memory of it – "then my boots caught the eye of Anton Landash, a handsome young man of the district – " She stopped, and did not appear willing to continue. "What happened then?" Lilli was jumping with excitement. Zenobia bridled: "He came to me, seized my wrist and whirled me off – my yellow shoes dancing all the while. . . . It was the beginning of our courtship, for we were married six weeks later. Yes, Lilli, when I put on those yellow boots, I never dreamed how far they would take me. . . ." Her voice faltered to a whisper.

"A pair of yellow boots!" breathed Lilli. What things of beauty! They appeared to her like a magic talisman in a fairy tale. How long would those boots dance, thought Lilli, feeling that they were symbolical of peasant craftsmanship. All those old things – which she felt belonged to her somehow – were passing, relegated now to the obscurity of an immigrant's trunk. Her mother, that sombre peasant, must have felt this special quality in Lilli, for her daughter's appreciation of the old beauties was the one point of intimacy between them. She was pleased now when Lilli inquired, "Were those the boots which you have in your trunk, mother?"

"Yes," replied Zenobia with a sigh. She stopped as her eyes fell upon the cracked skin of her hands. It was as if the sight had brought her back to her present status. "You live life not as you want to," she commented, "but as you must. Yes, in youth you think you'll fashion life as you wish, and wear it like a golden garment, but in age when you look at this garment, you see it's made of a sack all covered with patches."

Zenobia loved these peasant saws, such as, "Truth is a thorn, it pricks from all sides;" or, "Sprinkle a pig with holy water, and a pig remains a pig." For her, they embodied the harsh truth of peasant experience. "Anything that blooms true from peasant seed must live," she was fond of saying. At the moment, she might have lapsed into moroseness if she had not spied Petey, trying to clamber upon the back of a black and white calf, engaging the slippery sides with a stubbornness which did not doubt his ultimate victory. "Did you ever see such a child!" she exclaimed fondly, and all her regrets for her girlhood vanished.

"Do you remember when I bought Blackie from you for two cents, mother?" asked Lilli. It was only a short while ago that Blackie had been sick, and according to an old custom Lilli, as a member of the family, had purchased the calf from her mother, in the belief that this transaction would help the animal recover. "From that day," recalled Zenobia, "Blackie began to thrive." Lilli laughed: "He's Petey's now, mother . . . I sold him again for two cents, no profit. . . ." Her mother replied: "Petey is early getting into business."

Lilli inhaled deeply the scent of prairie grass, and it made her long to get away by herself in the country. "The berries are ripening, mother," she suggested. "Just right for picking. . . ." "Your father likes berry dumplings," considered Zenobia. "Yes, we could have some for supper. Take Petey with you." She added as an afterthought. "And pick some wormwood – I must have some to make a brew. A little of it, in whiskey, is the best medicine for stomach trouble . . . that way, you hide the bitter taste."

The prairie flowers were thick around the berry patch,

which nobody had yet discovered. Before Lilli began to work, she sat Petey down in the shade and gave him a rhubarb leaf for a fan. All the affection pent up in Lilli's heart was lavished upon her small brother Petey, with whom she had a closer bond than any other member of the family. As he grew, she devised many amusements for him. She wove wreaths of flowers for him. Red was Petey's favourite colour, and she had made him a red wool jacket and cap, trimmed with gold buttons. He was fond of this outfit, and would not consent to go for a walk unless he were wearing it. "He looks like a little king," said Anton, pleased with the appearance of his son.

Petey early displayed the quality of curiosity concerning his surroundings. He followed Lilli about making royal demands upon her, and she endured his tyranny lovingly. He would not permit any one else's ministrations and if Zenobia attempted to perform some service which Lilli was accustomed to do for him, he flew into a rage and demanded, "Liliana!" He thrust his hands into the sleeves of his jacket and stood like a miniature Buddha, awaiting Lilli.

She devised for the little boy many song-pictures in which she described people, things, tastes, sounds. He liked songs with onomatopoeic sounds, or songs describing colours and tastes. Lilli instructed her little brother how to put his ear to the telegraph pole so that he could hear the singing of the wind through the wires; she made a flute and played for him, or blew through a grass stem. Together, they watched the ripples of light and shadow pass over a field of oats; they saw the dance of clouds before rain, they felt the satin texture of flower petals. Petey was a thoughtful child, given to large reflections and deep ponderings. His was not a passive nature – he rushed at life, grasping with eager hands. He pulled up handfuls of flowers which he sniffed with moist, loud sniffs. His favourite expression was, "What is this?" and his reaction to the external world of sensation was one of continual discovery.

Lilli now turned to him, as he sat languidly fanning

himself, listening to the plunk of berries as they dropped into the pail. "Look, Petey, a gramophone flower." Lilli picked a wild morning glory and showed him how its shape resembled the huge horn of their gramophone.

"Will it make music?" Petey stretched his hand out.

"If you sing into it," replied Lilli, and she hummed with her mouth close to the trumpet.

As Petey grew sleepy beneath the summer sun, his limbs relaxed and vagrant bubbles came from his mouth. Drowsily he heard the murmur of Lilli's voice as she related the wonders of sleep. Sleek was a beautiful fabled land. There from a tree grew golden apples; birds with golden wings flew in the air; the scent of petals dropping from flowers was languorous upon the mind of the sleeping child. Clouds, rose-tinted, grazed peaceably in the wide meadows of the sky. The goddess of summer, clad in coral muslin, walked gracefully through the land, scattering gems from her rosy fingers.

While Petey slept, Lilli sang a lullaby, composing the words and tune simultaneously:

Sleep, little one, sleep, brother mine, God give thee joy, my little apple! I will give thee a sugar lump, I will give thee a cup of milk. Thou wilt have a cake of honey and rye. Thou wilt ride upon a sheep, thou wilt run over the prairie, and flowers will bloom in thy steps. Sleep, little brother, for the dream man comes with his bag past the window. He will bring thee a pink and gold dream, he will wrap thee in a blanket of sleep.

She stretched out beside the boy and watched the clouds overhead. It began then, the music which haunted her, a tune which she had never heard played or sung. It came out of the air and followed her. Each time a shadow passed the trees, it was like a note. Leaves rustled, animals ran through the bush, birds flew by, a partridge exploded from the underbrush. Lilli realized that this was the raw material of music. Flowers opened, the dew fell off; bees glittered in the sunshine, the wind blew the underside of a leaf, the whole world was speaking with her. Rhythm was felt in the swaying and bowing of trees to each other. The leaves turned, half silver, half green on the silver maple. The quickly moving clouds of the Manitoba sky made her want to sing. She could hear music at a distance, as if a violin or pitched voice, but she could never reproduce the tune.

It was sounds which intrigued her, the infinite variations of sound in nature. The wind whispered through pine needles as if hissing through its teeth. The wind as it struck the large, coarse leaves of the poplars jiggled the round, flat discs and set up a clatter like raindrops in a tin pan. The long, thin leaves of the willow had a quick, light sound like the scraping of a bow across the strings of a fiddle. Every sound of nature was music to her ears, the chords through telegraph wires, the wind through wheat, the song of the meadowlark as it arose from the ground, the whirring and beating of wings, the horns, throbs and whistles of prairie songsters.

They inspired her to song, and this song was in imitation of the distant music which she heard, but could not capture. It remained always just beyond her, calling her, arousing her to wonder and mystery. So insistent was the melody that Lilli sometimes walked for hours in pursuit of it, led on and on, and hearing everywhere the song of enchantment. Yet it always eluded her, and vanished in the end, leaving her dissatisfied and wondering.

3
THE HARVESTERS

❦

IF THE songs of summer had enchanted Lilli on her prairie walks, then the voices of the wind in the fall were even more compelling. Lilli, brown and wiry after a summer in the fields, lay on a haystack, her bare feet stretched out, and watched the swiftly-moving clouds of a Manitoba autumn day. "Gold, gold!" she murmured. The land was relaxed like a mother after childbirth. Lilli, too, felt a voluptuous yielding in her limbs as the sun caressed them with its golden film.

At this moment, Anton appeared on the doorstep of the house, dressed for town in his fawn gabardine trench coat, felt hat and camera slung over his shoulders. He was an amateur photographer, developing his own prints in a dark room which he had set up for the purpose. Birds, rare plants, fields of wheat – these were his favourite subjects. Full of confidence and some vanity, he squared his shoulders as he reviewed the business he had to transact in town.

A few weeks back an itinerant photographer had stopped off at the Landash farm, and Anton consented to have a photograph made of the entire family. Accordingly, after a family consultation, it was decided that the family should sit around a table, and all engage in some cultural activity to show themselves off to the best advantage. The table was spread with flowers, artificial and real, and at the head sat Anton, his dictionary before him, as though in the midst of study. Beside him, on either side, sat Zenobia and Fialka, with needlework in their hands, and then Petey, his blond hair in a curl like a question mark, blowing into a tin horn, Masha and Tasha with half-sized violins tucked under their chins, and all the other children with books or musical instruments, except Lilli, who was not deemed to have musical or scholastic talent. By the time she had finished disposing the children around the table and supervising their activities, Lilli had little time to provide herself with something to do, so that when the photograph was taken, she was caught unawares with her hands clutching the table, and mouth wide open.

When the photograph came, some time after, all the children rushed to their father to see it, crowding about him with exclamations:

"Look at Petey's curl!"

"And the violins!"

"And the books!"

"And the flowers! Like real!"

"And look at Lilli! Ha, ha, ha!"

As each one seized the photograph, he burst into laughter, for Lilli appeared like a dark blotch, with her mouth gaping and her hands, huge, grotesque, upon the table.

"Give that to me, I'll fix it," said her father, and he took up a pair of scissors to cut Lilli out of the picture. He was proud of his good-looking family, and did not wish to acknowledge this gnome.

"But you are cutting me off, Father," cried out Lilli heartbroken. "I'm part of the family, too, let me be there."

Anton, as though he had not heard, took up the scissors and snipped off the end where Lilli sat, and as the tiny piece fell to the ground it was not noticed by anyone except Lilli.

Apart from all the others, in her hand the bit of paper Anton had cut off, stood Lilli, thinking that never could she re-unite that scrap to the photograph, that always she would stand on the outside of the family circle, trying to get in, yearning to share their joy. . . .

While Anton was getting out the horse and wagon, Lilli,

seized by a desperate resolve, slid down the haystack and ran into the house. How could she dream that he would take her with him – the least favourite one, she chided herself as she scrubbed her face till it shone like an apple. He would never ask her, she told herself brushing her hair like mad. But if he did? If he did? Her mind countered as she clambered into the new plaid pantaloons which her mother had made for her, and then scrutinized her bare toes to see if they were clean. She came out of the house and stood on the doorstep, not daring to express her wish to accompany Anton, but putting her desire so forcefully into her eyes that he must surely notice it.

"You like to come to town with me, Lilli?" he asked her on a sudden generous impulse, his peasant dislike for the unlucky one dissipated at the sight of this so eager, so shining girl. Then, too, he had a feeling of guilt regarding the incident of the photo, for he had seen the girl standing apart.

"Oh yes, father!" exclaimed Lilli. "Oh, I like to go." She rushed out to the wagon before he could change his mind and scrambled into the front seat beside her father, thinking how the other children would envy her. A person who had been to town always came back laden with news, mail and gossip.

As they passed a neighbour's fields, which contained wheat not yet harvested, Anton stopped the horses and sat for a moment looking at the fields. "Listen, Lilli," he said. They were still as waves of sound came from the tossing and shuddering of the heavy wheat ears; the slightest tremble of wind magnified the silken rubbing of ear upon ear. "Sh-sh-sh," whispered Lilli, trying to imitate the sound. "Do you think it sings any different than our wheat?" he asked her with a smile. The autumn wind seemed to sing in four-part harmony, rising now from one direction, then another voice joining in, and so on, until the four winds were all singing together. "I must see that wheat," said Anton. He threw down the reins, leaped out of the wagon, and strode into the fields, returning almost at once with a handful of kernels. "See, Lilli?" He showed her the wheat as he got in again. "This is a new wheat which Karmaliuk got from the city. I'm going to write to the Government for wheat seed like this."

He took out a box with several compartments, and placed the Karmaliuk specimen within. "I don't think this is as good as the wheat which I grew in our garden from my own seed," he went on. "Look in this box, Lilli. I grew this from wheat which I brought, long ago, from the old country. These seeds were immigrants like myself." The simile pleased Anton, and he repeated it. "Yes, seeds, too, can be immigrants." He poured the grain from one hand to another, recalling those kerchief-wrapped seed bundles which the Bukovynian immigrants had brought with them to Canada, along with the rest of their worldly goods. Lilli took the seed in her hand and rolled it between her fingers. In those hard, red little bodies was contained the magic of life, the power which would one day cause them to shoot up and grow in gold-crested waves under Canadian skies.

"Some day our farm will look like that," Anton pointed with his whip to the farm of Jensen the Swede, where stood a white house with green gables and a modern barn. Jensen was one of the wealthiest farmers in the district; he had been farming since the turn of the century.

"That kind of farming," said Anton, "is done, not by scratching the earth, as our people do; it is brought about by science."

"Science – what is that, father?" asked Lilli. The word was new to her.

"Science," deliberated Anton, "is to know how to do things with learning and skill, to be of the new country, not of the old. Science is to live in the light and not in the dark."

What a fertile mind her father had, thought Lilli! How everything came to life as she listened to him – the earth, the fields of wheat, each plant! He knew their properties as a peasant knows them, and now he was reaching out to another kind of knowledge which came out of books, no less.

As the wagon passed the swamp, Lilli's eyes darted from side to side. The life of the swamp excited her – the sounds and motions of the wild life within, its swarms of insects and birds, the willows bending over the edge, the long grasses bordering it, the cat-tails, rushes and big-leaved swamp docks growing in it. Above them, the clouds drifted like tufty white polka dots on blue calico. Anton, too, found the life in the swamp worthy of study. "Everywhere," he said, "you can see stories. There is hardly a plant, a bird, even a rock which does not have its story. Look there – " His sharp eyes had discovered something, and he stopped the horses and got off. "Jump off, Lilli," he said. "I want to teach you a lesson in science. Today we are two scientists, yes?" He held out his hand and helped her down.

"See this?" He picked up a stone lying by the road, and scratching at its surface, showed her the pattern of a fern leaf on its surface. "This was once a real leaf, Lilli, which was buried in the earth and became a stone." Lilli ran her finger over the inlaid pattern. "Who told you that, Father?" she asked. "I heard it from Mr. Mac," replied Anton. "This is called a fossil." Anton had some difficulty with the word, which he pronounced "possil," since the letter "f" was not common in his language.

They got back into the wagon, carrying the stone. "Oh, how beautiful the prairie today, father!" exclaimed Lilli, stirred by the sight of all those harvest fields, with threshers busy everywhere, the chaff flying about, the vast perspective due to the clear air of autumn, the neighbours calling out as they passed, the women in their draped Bukovynian skirts and coloured shawls standing in the fields, the children by the roadside with handfuls of autumn flowers, the dark red elevators piercing the Canadian skies.

"Yes, the new country is far better than the old," agreed Anton, "for all your mother's stories. . . . I could tell you how our people suffered in the old country." His face became hard with the memory. "On Sunday morning," he related, "when church bells were ringing, and all good people were riding off to church, the servant of the baron came with a big whip to chase me to work: 'Get up and herd the oxen,' and go I must, for people had no choice but to work on Sundays as on every other day." Anton's voice had a bitter edge, bitter with wrongs suffered. "I was seventeen years old then, a hardy lad without fear. . . ." And without affection, he might have added, for the children of the mountaineers grew up early in the pitiless struggle for existence. He continued, "Well, I worked a whole week herding cattle all day, with no chance to wash my face or to go to sleep. . . . In the morning I arose and without breakfast, without shoes, I left for work. The snow was falling, my feet were freezing. . . . It was like lifting two lumps of ice to walk. . . ." So realistic was his narrative that Lilli shuddered, although the autumn sun was warm on their shoulders. Anton went on: "When I came back, I was so tired that I fell upon the doorstep of the baron . . . and the cook called out, 'Here's a drunk lad, let's beat him up to teach him a lesson!' So they brought in the servant again and with his great leather whip he gave me the payment for my week's labour – twenty lashes on my bare back. . . ." He turned to Lilli, and for once Lilli caught a glimpse of the circumstances which had moulded his harsh character. "And thus was spent my boyhood, Lilli – and that of all our young men." Lilli frowned. "How could you endure such a life, father?" she asked. Anton shrugged as he replied with a folk proverb: "They hanged a gypsy – he kicked for a while, and then got used to it." Still, he conceded, as he recalled other incidents of his youth, "We had many free, happy days, and especially when I went as a sheepherder along with other shepherds to the mountain downs. . . . In the evenings, we took our meals about the bonfire, the mountains standing up around us, clouds about their heads. . . . We sang and told stories, and about us, the shooting stars, like rain, fell from the heavens. In the fall, there was dancing about the bonfire. We'd take our scarlet capes and move in a long line about the fire, always dancing, leaping, stamping – thus we kept ourselves warm."

How, wondered Lilli, had the news come to them of the new country? She asked: "How did you hear about Canada, father?" He laughed as he replied: "Men came, agents, I know not what, all dressed up in fine clothes, and told us a story as we sat around in a cafe drinking tea. What stories!" Anton threw back his head and guffawed. "Sausages grew on trees, all the women had silk hose, push a button and you get everything you want. . . . And we sat, open-mouthed, drinking it all in. Could this be true, we asked each other? Canada, what a country!"

Landash's laughter had a free, robust quality; his sense of humour was coarse but exuberant. Once he started to laugh, he infected all his hearers, and Lilli, certainly, could not resist; they both laughed, and there was a similarity in their laughter, Lilli's being like a junior echo of her father's. Anton's mood of laughing was generally followed by a spell of singing. He boasted he could sing three or four days and never twice one song. One of his favourites, which he sang now, concerned the life of a Carpathian mountain outlaw. He was none of your passive performers; rather, he brought vigour and action to his role; he swayed his shoulders, pounded his feet, tossed his head, so that the song of the outlaws, as it rang over the Manitoba wheatfields, was not only something to hear, but to see – as though the Canadian farmer had suddenly been transformed into a mountain brigand:

Hai, brother outlaws, fill the cup and pass it around! Heap more wood upon the campfire. Let the song burst from our throats as our musician plays softly upon his pipe. Hidden in the bush beneath the green pine trees, even devils could not find us here. As the sky is for the birds, so for us are the caves, our retreat in these Carpathian crests. We sleep till the stars light the skies with their lamps, and then we emerge by stealth. Rejoice, brothers mine, for each day that is ours, since a life such as ours can't last long. With the first fall of snow, our heads will hang down like flowers, no more shall be heard our glad song.

The wagon bounced and jiggled its great five-foot wheels, as though in eager rhythm, Anton sang and cracked his whip at the end of every line, calling, "Hai, hai," drawing out the "ee" as was the custom of wagoners to the curl of their whips, and the girl beside him echoed "Hai, hai!" Then, song finished, Anton reached into the back of his wagon for a sack of musk melons and split one with his knife. The melon cracked open with a popping smack, revealing a bright peach-coloured interior lined with rows of seeds. "These are better in the old country," he commented as he cut the melon into slices and gave one to Lilli. The juice trickled out of their mouths as they ate with not too much delicacy. "Save the seed, Lilli, I want to give it to Jensen." They took the pips out of their mouths one by one and carefully put them away in a paper bag. "The seed which grew this melon came from the old country," said Anton between bites. "Yes, Lilli," he went on, "the great grandfather of this melon – how many great's, I can't count – was a Bukovynian melon."

As she ate, Lilli thought of that granddaddy of all these melons, basking in the sun, accumulating all those warm juices, growing plump and succulent under Bukovynian skies, little dreaming that his descendants would multiply so profusely over Canadian prairies. "I'll bet that great grandaddy never thought that his grandchildren would grow on Canadian prairies," she chuckled. She had seized half a melon and had plunged her face into it, so that only her big eyes stuck out, like beetle lamps above the rim. The sight and the remark struck Anton as so comical that he burst out laughing, and pieces of melon flew round about.

"Look, father, the village!" Lilli called out in joy. Two

rows of whitewashed houses ran in old country style on each side of the street, big-wheeled Bukovynian wagons were arriving, farmers in sheepskin coats or plaid mackinaws bustled in front of the general store, women thronged inside to purchase fall clothing. Even before Anton got off the wagon, people called out to him and approached him, since they had been waiting for him to write letters for them. "Go play with the children, Lilli," said Anton carelessly as he jumped off and went to join a group of farmers.

Lilli, left to her own resources, stood awkwardly looking at the other girls and boys. They were dressed differently than she was and stared at her clothes. She wanted to make friends with them, but she did not know how to go about it. Going to the store window, she peered in. What a wealth of things! Children were looking at the candy counter, admiring the striped sticks, licorice and toffee.

Lilli opened the door and walked in. The store smelled of mucilage, sawdust, leather jackets, calico, herring and pipe smoke. A crowd of people, Swedes and Bukovynians, Icelanders and Scots sat about or stood in groups. The women crowded about the counters, looking over bolts of calico for new dresses, sniffing the sweet, dusty smell of the cloth as it was ripped off the bolt by the clerk. The men discussed the harvest, grain prices, machinery, future plans. They were good to look at, these immigrants, their faces weatherbeaten by years of struggle on the wild prairie, with wrinkles like furrows ploughed in their faces by time. Some were poor farmers from sub-marginal farms, others owned substantial property, but already a similarity existed among them, the beginning of a national spirit.

Lilli gazed covertly at the other children. One Swedish boy was stiff in his new braces; a little Icelandic girl of twelve strutted about in a blue velveteen costume, very conscious of her good looks with her fair hair in curls. Somewhat apart stood a Finnish boy wearing a jacket too small for him, and trousers from which his thin legs stuck out like sticks. He was whittling at a willow branch. For these children, the store appeared larger, more glittering, more crowded than it did to the adults, so full of sights that one might spend months examining them all.

"Look at the girl – " the Icelandic girl pointed Lilli out to the Swedish boy and they laughed. "She's wearing pants." The boy, who wanted to win the favour of the beauty, giggled nervously, encouraging the Icelandic girl to go up to Lilli and say, "I think you can't talk, ha, ha." One old lady disapproved of this display of girlish vanity and said, in a tone of rebuke: "The flower which blooms latest is sometimes the fairest."

Her remark, however, did not reassure Lilli, who backed away from the children and sought refuge in the crowd about the post-office, where a group of people were standing at the wicket to get their mail. They were opening envelopes, licking stamps, sending and receiving letters from far away. Most, as they turned from the wicket, carried big bundles of circulars, catalogues, parcels, letters from the old country and newspapers in various languages from the city press. Lilli stood at the end of the line, patiently waiting her turn. When she came to the wicket, she asked the postmistress, "Is there a letter for me?" She peered into the cage and saw an assortment of mail neatly arranged in pigeon holes. It was the first time she had ever seen how letters were distributed.

"What kind of letter, little girl?" the postmistress asked kindly. The rosy face of the Swedish woman bloomed like a pink dahlia above her blue gingham apron. So there were many kinds of letters! Lilli pondered what kind she would like to receive. Eagerly she peered over the top of the counter into the cage, scrutinizing the hundreds of letters within. "A letter from China," she whispered excitedly.

"From China!" exclaimed the postmistress and she bent forward to examine the girl through her thick spectacles. She had never seen this child before. "Yes, from China!" Lilli spoke in a loud, firm voice. "A letter from China." She had made up her mind. A letter from that country would be something, indeed, to receive! To travel all that way over the top of the globe with its countries like coloured patches – red and green and yellow and blue, and finally arrive in a country where, she had heard, people walked on their heads. To hold in her hands such a letter, which had been written by a Chinese girl or boy and think of its contents – how would she hold it to read it – upside down? She could keep such a letter for a whole lifetime, yes, if such a letter had come to this post office, wouldn't she have the right to receive it, she who would treasure it more than anyone else?

Years of dealing with people in relation to letters had taught the postmistress wisdom. What was there in a letter – wishes, dreams, hopes, all human tragedy and comedy were contained in the mail. How did she know, when she handed over a piece of paper, what it might contain, how it might change the life of the recipient? So, she did not find ridiculous the request of the girl, for, after all, what was she asking? Simply for a touch of adventure, what each person, in his heart, really hopes for when he receives a letter.

So, in a kindly tone, she inquired, "What is your name, little girl?" Her eyes took in the plaid pantaloons, the shyness of the girl, the big pleading eyes.

Lilli replied, in a faraway voice, "Lilli Landash."

"I know your father," said the Swedish woman, bringing the girl back to reality. "He comes here often. We have a big bundle of mail for him. Wait, I'll see what there is for you, Lilli." She made a great display of hunting through the piles of letters. So many letters and parcels – surely there must be one for her! "I can't find your letter from China, Lilli," she said finally, "but here is something just come from the city, that I think you'll like. Maybe another time you'll get your letter from China." She held out a travel circular, full of coloured pictures.

"Oh thank you!" exclaimed Lilli. Heart beating rapidly, she went over to a cracker barrel and sat down on it to examine her mail. When unfolded, it became a big sheet, like a map, and on it were pictures of countries all over the globe. "See the World," the caption urged. Lilli spelled out the names one letter at a time, for she could not read very well. Here was China, indeed. Pagodas with roofs curved like wings were there, houses of a shape nobody in the village possessed, cherry blossoms, and a boy and girl dressed in flowered kimonos, not walking upside down at all. Chinese symbols in a row beside them, those were letters like the letters of the alphabet, though they looked more like pictures of tiny houses. Where was Bukovyna? Nowhere on that sheet could she find it, but here was Sweden, that was where Mr. Jensen came from. There he was now, a man of over sixty, his face all lean, hard angles under his sunburned blond hair. The Swedes no longer wore costumes in Canada, as the Bukovynians, because they had been longer in this country and had become more Canadian, more – with science, as Anton had expressed it. "See the World." Lilli repeated the phrase to herself as she tried to visualize how one would travel to those distant countries. How many days would it take to get to China if one set off in a horse and buggy? what language would the people speak? Their country must be strange and beautiful. In this store, reflected Lilli, were people from many countries, Sweden, Iceland, Bukovyna, Poland. If one were to hear all their stories, what a fine tale it would make! What the nature of their country was, how people dressed, what language they spoke, what songs they sang, what kind of children they had been, what dreams they had dreamed of in the new country.

The big, shaggy farmers in their speech still retained the rhythm and natural poesy of those who live by the soil, and Lilli, perched on her barrel, listening to their talk, absorbed those rhythms, felt how much of their daily struggle with the soil was revealed in those earthy words. They told stories, the history of each piece of land, the epic of wheat, yarns of the old country, where they had come from, what it was like, how it was better here. The stories were punctuated by long silences, as if they felt they had time to spare, they were not rushed as people are in the city.

Lilli's father was now sitting at a small table writing and interpreting letters for the other Bukovynian farmers, official letters dealing with grain, taxes and voting. He had his spectacles on, more to impress his neighbours than to assist his eyesight, which was good. Lilli approached him now and held out the circular, saying, "Look, father, what I have – a letter from China." Anton pushed up his spectacles and laughed. "From China, ha, ha." He peered at her folder. "Listen to the girl making jokes." He pushed her away. "Go play with the children."

She went outside and approached a group of children. Standing a little distance away, she looked at them with longing, but said nothing. One of them, a thin, spiteful girl wearing a red dress, came over to her and stared, then burst out laughing. "Come and look at this girl – she's wearing green striped pants." The others came over and formed a circle about Lilli, ridiculing her clothes. One child, more insolent than the rest, ran at her and gave her a push. She staggered back a few paces, then recovered and tried to smile. "Hello," she said uncertainly. She wanted so much to be friends with them, to share the treasures of her letter and tell them so many things – about the grandfather melon, about the stone picture of the leaf, about the wheat seed. "I have a letter," she said diffidently, and held it out like a peace offering. One boy snatched it from her and tearing it to pieces, threw it down and stamped on it with big, noisy stamps. "Letter, ha," he shouted. "That's not a letter." The gang of children increased and became more aggressive, their faces hostile. Fear suddenly betrayed itself in her eyes and this was the signal for an attack. "Onion Eyes!" shouted one tormentor. He spat on her.

"Green Pants!" jeered another and he gave her a shove from the other side. "Snake Hands!" called a third. They began to dance about her, pulling at her clothes and jeering, while Lilli stood helplessly in the centre, looking from one to another with growing terror, trying to break through the circle, but stopped at each point by her tormentors. "Let me out!" she screamed, afraid of being trapped. The children laughed, enjoying the spectacle, sensing their power. A couple picked up clods of earth and threw them at her, laughing as they struck Lilli's face and throat. "Look how black she's getting," called out the Icelandic girl. "She never washes her face, I think." Her own white complexion contrasted with Lilli's tanned, mud-streaked skin. Lilli turned from one to another, imploring, and each greeted her with a jibe. She had a sticky feeling in her fingers, her stomach was tied in knots, her voice was thick with fear as she croaked, "Let me out!" Desperately she broke out of the circle, and ran down the road, pursued by her tormentors. Her mouth was dry inside and sweat poured down her face. She had never run so fast, and the children, seeing themselves outdistanced, one by one abandoned the chase. Lilli kept on running, kicking up the dust with her heels, her eyes stinging with the burning brilliance of the road, past the houses, past wagons, past the store, past people who turned to look and laugh at her, thinking this was some childish game they were witnessing, until at last she had left the village, and came to a haystack into which she dove head foremost, sobbing frantically. She lay hidden in the hay while people passed to and fro, wagons rumbled by, cows ambled down the road, tinkling their bells. What if her father had seen! He would never again take her to town! He would never sing and tell stories to her, instead, he would place her on a stool in a corner and make her peel potatoes all day, like the fool in the fairy tales. And if she had a blue velvet costume? Some day she would have! Her hair would all be in ringlets, and her skin, white as paper! She sat up and rubbed her eyes, picked the hay off her clothes, spat on a hanky and cleaned her face. What was so disgraceful about pantaloons! They were made of good material, and one could run swiftly in them. Resolutely she got up, smoothed her pantaloons, patted her hair again, rubbed her face. She peered around the haystack. The children had disappeared. Head up, she marched down the road, thinking, she should have stayed, she should have fought – better to stand one's ground than run!

When she opened the door of the store, she found her father the centre of a circle of farmers, talking about his grain seed, which he had poured out of its box onto the table before him. All listened intently as he expounded his theory. "Seeds are immigrants, too. . . . " Anton was pleased, because he could see that he had made an impression on Jensen, the Swede. He had not noticed Lilli's discomfiture, and as she stood by him, touching his arm, he turned and said, "Well, is it you, Lilli?" Her face was composed, her hair slicked. "We'll have to go home now."

The ride home was glorious, Anton singing boisterously a rowdy song, "Who will take the widow home from the ball?" He was in rare good humour. "So – you enjoyed town?" he asked his daughter. "Oh, yes," agreed Lilli with enthusiasm. Forgotten, her humiliation, forgotten the ridicule of the children, only the wonderful remained, the ride across the prairie, the sight of the men in the store, the travel poster with pictures of China.

As twilight came on, the whole countryside was lit up as one straw stack after another was fired, until the fields glowed for miles around. "That's Jensen! That's Karmaliuk's! That's Johannesen!" they exclaimed in turn, identifying the source of each fire. "It reminds me of the old country," said Anton, for so many peasant rites were connected with fire. The defeat which she had just endured seemed to make Lilli even more receptive to sensation, and she could not get enough of the marvellous spectacle. One thresher, still humming in the fields, stood out in a huge black silhouette against the horizon. Occasionally the figures of harvesters could be seen scurrying in the dark. As the wagon moved across the prairies, Lilli was filled with a strange exultation, engendered by the rhythm of the harvesters, the throb of the threshing machines, the great torches of burning stacks, the shaggy figures of the immigrants in the store – all united to form in her mind the picture of a rite as ancient as the human race.

4
THE IMMIGRANT CAROLLERS

THERE WAS little enough left of that autumn glory on the December afternoon when Lilli snuggled on a pile of sheepskins near the window, scratching off the frost with her fingernail so that she could see outside. A light fall of snow whirled through the yard, covering the ground in sculptured contours. The flakes were large, sleepy, revolving in a kind of charmed trance, each shape, each motion, creating a fresh pattern in Lilli's mind, like a succession of musical notes. It was cosy to be within on this day before Christmas, to feel the heat of the great clay stove, to smell the cinnamon rolls as they came out of the oven, and to think about the transformation which each month brought to their prairie country. In the peasant dialect which these Carpathian mountaineers spoke, December was called *hruden*, the month when the earth turned to frozen clods – an appropriate name, thought Lilli. November, which had just passed, was the month of falling leaves, *lystopad* – and how stripped and bare was the Manitoba landscape at that time! One by one Lilli enumerated the months: January was *sichen*, when trees were cut down for firewood; February was *liutyi*, or the fierce month of winter gales, and March *berezen*, when the birch trees showed the first signs of budding. April was *kviten*, the month of blossoms – a lovely name. May was *traven*, the month of grass. Following spring, came the summer months: June was *cherven*, the red month, when fruits and berries ripened; July was *lypen*, when the linden tree bloomed; August was *serpen*, the month of the sickle. September was *veresen*, the month of threshing grain, and October *zhovten*, when the leaves turned yellow. What lovely names! Each a picture! The poetic peasant fancy which had bestowed on each month its special quality pleased Lilli. She was even more pleased by the sight of Petey sitting beside her, his golden head bent over a Christmas card depicting an angel dressed in embroidered white smock, high leather boots, sheepskin cap and pale green wings. The makers of these cards, thinking properly that man had been created in the divine image, had endowed these heavenly beings with their own peasant accoutrements. "This angel looks like me," Petey concluded after long deliberation. "Except I have no wings." There was some dissatisfaction in his voice. "Little boys have no wings," explained Lilli, and the boy's face dropped. "But I'll show you how to make angel wings in the snow when we go out."

Zenobia at the kitchen table was busy making cabbage rolls filled with rice. These were very tiny, about the thickness of a finger, and two inches long. After washing the rice, she boiled it for twenty minutes and then fried it with onions, parsley, dried dill, salt and pepper, rolled it in cabbage leaves and baked it for two hours. "Have you ground the poppy seed for the *kutia* Lilli?" she inquired as she looked up from the work. *Kutia* was a ceremonial Christmas dish eaten in thanks for the grain harvest: it was made of boiled whole wheat sweetened with honey and flavoured with nuts and poppy seed ground to a paste. "Mix it well with the honey and wheat," directed Zenobia, "and add a pan of chopped nuts." Lilli got up from her seat by the window and began grinding the poppy seed in the grinder, eyed hungrily by the children, who had been fasting since the previous night. Nevertheless, their eyes shone with eagerness, for Holy Eve was approaching.

Zenobia believed that Lilli possessed fey powers – to make bread rise, to supervise the planting, to devise new designs; and although this belief increased her mother's feeling of alienation from Lilli, nevertheless the older woman always called upon

Lilli's help when there was a ceremonial cooking to be done, or pickling or sowing seed. Plants sown by Lilli grew and flourished; a batch of bread which she made always rose and had good flavour; jars of pickles which she put up always proved sound.

Now, in the midst of Christmas preparations, with odours of honey, cinnamon, spices and fresh bread around him, Petey was in ecstasy.

"If you keep on sniffing, Petey," warned Lilli, "your nose will turn into a corkscrew."

At this dreadful warning, Petey ran to the mirror to flatten out his nose, while the twins took advantage of the distraction to run their fingers over the syrupy backs of the cinnamon rolls and gouge out the nuts embedded in them.

"Now who will take the *koliada* to the widow Fermenyk?" asked Zenobia, for this gift of food, taken by tradition to the grandparents, she wished to send to a poor woman of the district, since in any case the grandparents were coming to dine.

"I'll go," Fialka offered hastily, as she yearned for a chance to wear her new white brushed-wool coat and scarlet beret. In addition, the road to the widow's house passed by the home of a certain young man in whom Fialka was interested. All the children admired her as she stood, happy and laughing, in the doorway, before setting off.

"All the boys will like Fialka in that white coat," observed Petey sagely as he watched her leave.

"How was Christmas in the old country, mother?" Lilli asked when she had prepared the *kutia* and placed it on the window sill to cool, the swollen grains of wheat bursting out of their skins like pearls out of an oyster, while the faint fragrance of poppy seed mingled with the amber stream of buckwheat honey. She loved listening to Zenobia's stories of life in that faraway land; it gave her a sense of continuity with the past, as if informing her where she had come from.

"Well," began Zenobia as she paused to collect her

memories. "On Christmas Eve the boys prepared costumes for the Bethlehem play. There was a Devil, angels, three wise men with crowns, shepherds, musicians, and so on – also a stable made of wood and paper to signify the birthplace of the Christ child." She began to mix the batch of honeyed waffles with which the Christmas supper would commence. "All this they take from house to house and perform a play, to show the first night of Christmas. The shepherds are shown watching the skies, the three wise men appear and the musicians play a joyous song for the child in the stable." She interrupted her narrative to move Petey's fingers from the batter, and then continued: "But the children – they have a time of it, I can tell you – the morning after Christmas, before sunrise, a bright bonfire is burning in the street before each house. The boys take straw from out the house and burn it outside the gate, spread the ashes in the shape of a cross, symbolizing the cross of Christ. The street is marked with black crosses in the white snow the length of the village. All boys and girls take turns jumping over the burning cross as it is thought this will ward off sickness for the coming year." Lilli, who had been following her mother's recital intently, remarked, "Some boys and girls in the village here jump over fires, mother. . . ." She exchanged a look of conspiracy with Petey: "We'll make a fire, too, after Christmas."

The door opened abruptly and Anton came in from town, where business had called him. His coat was encrusted with snow, which smelled frostily as it came in contact with the steaming air from the oven. "You are a snowman, father!" exclaimed Petey, pulling at Anton's coat so that the snowflakes fell off in a shower upon the kitchen floor.

"A company of immigrants arrived in the district today," Anton announced as he took off his tall fur cap and shook it.

"Who are they?" queried Zenobia, spreading the coat on a chair before the stove to dry.

"Three big fellows to take up homesteads." Anton stamped

his high leather boots, clapped his hands together and went over to inspect the fuel bin. "I'll have to fill this soon."

"From where do these immigrants come?" persisted Zenobia. She had a natural curiosity about people and was forever asking questions concerning origins, ages, deaths and marriages.

"From the old country," replied Anton. "I interpreted for them at the station." He added, as an afterthought, "They will be here tonight to sing carols."

"Good!" exclaimed Zenobia with satisfaction. "To welcome strangers on Christmas Eve is the same as welcoming Christ." She hurried to check on her supply of apple cider, buckwheat gruel and pumpkin seeds, traditional fare for carollers. "Married?" she asked as she brought out a cask of cider.

"They brought no women with them," replied Anton. "Perhaps they can take one of the girls in our district." He yawned as the heat from the stove made him sleepy. He removed his boots to the floor.

Immigrants! From a strange country! From a distant land! Lilli, as she darted about the house to make sure that everything was in order, teemed with questions. What kind of immigrants? Were they perhaps something like the Three Wise Men? It was surely significant that they had arrived exactly on Christmas Eve. Like her mother, she was concerned with appearances, and bustled about, lighting candles before the holy pictures, getting out fresh linen, and inspecting the dumplings on the stove. They looked, she thought, like mother-of-pearl, with their filling of cherries and plums glowing rosy through their nacreous coats.

Petey, trailing after Anton and imitating his every action, tugged at his father's coat: "Father, will our cows talk tonight?"

Anton looked down with indulgence at the red-cheeked boy and chucked his chin. "Yes, Petey, they will. They are permitted to talk on Christmas Eve because they kept the little

Christ warm with their breaths when they lay in the straw." He took up his coat again. "Do you want to come to the stable with me?"

"Yes, oh yes!" shouted Petey. He scurried about, trying to get dressed, stumbling in his anxiety, tangling himself in his clothes, and finally in despair ran to Lilli. "Put on my coat, Lilli." His short fat legs beat an impatient tattoo as Lilli pulled on his coat, cap and mittens.

Together, they followed Anton outside, Petey wearing a sheepskin cap exactly like his father's, only smaller, and a pair of tall red leather boots. Lilli had wrapped a flowered woollen shawl about her head. Outdoors, the snow had stopped falling, the trees were laden with diamond dust, sleighs were dashing by with bells jingling, the skies were blazing blue. The intensity of the white snow blinded their eyes momentarily, and all three stopped, blinking until their eyes had become accustomed to the glare. The air, too, had a crust of frostiness like the icing on a cake, and Petey gulped it down in big gulps, licking his lips and explaining to Lilli, "I like to eat the air. It makes me feel good inside." As they walked into the snow, Lilli showed Petey how to fall into it to make angels by waving his arms against the soft, fine stuff. The puppy, who was with them, dove in and out and swam around as if in water, his black eyes gleaming like buttons.

Anton made the round of the household, following the direction of the sun. "Are you content?" he asked each cow, ox and calf as he fed it, for it was believed that cattle acquired speech on Christmas Eve, and could speak of the past, present and future. Each animal was given special food, sweet clover for the horse, something green for the cows, so they would know Christmas had come.

Lilli held out a dish to summon evil spirits, wolves, winds and storms to share their supper, and thus to protect them against evil influences in the coming year of soil cultivation. Behind her trailed Petey, puffing and red in the face, anxious to be of service. "Frost, frost, come to dine with us, but do not freeze our grain," he called out. As the two stood with faces upraised, Lilli experienced a strange feeling: would the spirits of the winds and storms really hear her? She felt a stirring of the air as if her cheek had been lightly brushed, and she trembled. The wind stirred the snow up around her so that it touched her body in a light whirl.

Meanwhile Anton had piled a bundle of rye straw and fragrant hay on a sled and directed Lilli, "You bring in the sheaf with Petey." This sheaf was called Old Man, and was placed in an honorary corner behind the table under the holy pictures, to symbolize God's gift of a bountiful harvest. There it would remain until New Year's Day, to invoke the blessing of the spirits which were thought in olden days to haunt the grain fields.

When they returned to the house, Zenobia and Lilli set the table for dinner, which commenced traditionally with the appearance of the first star in the sky. First, Zenobia spread a white cloth over hay and as a centrepiece she placed a *kolach*, the white Christmas bread, flanked by two loaves of dark bread. There were twelve dishes, one for each Apostle – beet soup, honeyed waffles, stuffed dumplings, fish jelly, cabbage rolls stuffed with rice, fish fried in oil, fruit compote, poppy seed buns, honey and wheat mixture, braided bread, apple turnovers, prunes, and a drink made from the juice of boiled dried fruits. All had been laid out on the table in decorated dishes and wooden bowls. One large wax candle was lit on the table to symbolize the Star of the East.

Lilli went over to the wooden chest and began to take out their holiday attire – new ribbons, kerchiefs, woven belts and fresh white smocks. She caressed each garment, for she loved the feel of clean, starched linen and soft silk. "A belt, a red belt for me!" exclaimed Petey, prancing about in his white trousers and white shirt, his yellow hair slicked back. "You look like a buttercup, Petey!" exclaimed Lilli, hugging him.

When she had dressed her smaller brothers and sisters, tied their ribbons and combed their hair, she arranged them in a row on a bench to wait for dinner. She looked outside. The sky had darkened and now the first evening star was faintly visible far over the church. "I see it! I see the star!" she cried. A feeling of holy quietness came over her as she looked into the beauty of the night. In the distance, she could see the lights in other farm houses. Turning from the window, she contemplated the food, the candles, the *kolach* on the table and all these gave her the feeling that Christmas Eve had really begun. At this moment, her grandparents arrived, and supper was announced.

The children shouted for joy and all came to the big round table, which had been expanded for the occasion. Granny Yefrosynia and Grandfather Nestor were in the places of honour, the rest seated according to age. Faces around the table glistened rosy and bright; here Grandfather Nestor with long white hair and fluffy white whiskers; here Granny Yefrosynia like a russet apple in contrast to the tender baby faces of the smaller children, who, like cherubs, were all wearing their haloes that night; invisible wings sprouted on Petey's shoulders, for Christ was at supper with the family.

It was almost nine when bells were heard to jingle, the snow crunched beneath the sound of footsteps and voices rang clear in the outdoor frost. Faces appeared at the window, looking fantastic in the light of the kerosene lamp. Lilli cried out, "The carollers are here!"

A voice boomed from without, "Is it permitted to sing?"

"Sing, sing!" cried Anton unbuttoning the top of his vest, as the air was now very warm with the scent of candles, human breaths, hay, incense, food and pipe smoke. Lilli, followed by a swarm of children, ran to the window and placed a candle on the sill as sign of consent to the carollers. In the light of the candle, faces and shapes were seen – first of all three bearded strangers appeared, and behind them a throng of neighbours pressed, their sheepskin coats familiar, but their faces transformed by the radiance of the night. Bowing low, the three strangers approached the house and soon the majestic strains of the first carol were heard: "Rise, O David, with your harp," in which not only men and angels were asked to join in the rejoicing, but also sun, moon, rain, fire, hail, wind, earth, rivers, serpents and wild animals, until all that breathe on earth echo the praises of the Christ Child:

The first to come is the bright Sun in Heaven,
The second guest is the Moon in the skies,
The third one to come is the small rain pattering.

Sacred thoughts filled Lilli's heart as she listened; she brooded deeply upon the meaning of this night. The three immigrants had invested the occasion with peculiar significance, as though they were important ambassadors who had travelled from a far country that very night. At the end of the first carol, Anton went to the door and flung it open. "Come in, come in," he invited the carollers. As the people crowded in, they brought a fragrance of snow, leather coats and sheepskin caps. There was much stamping of feet, shaking of coats and clapping of hands as they piled their sheepskins into a corner and seated themselves on the straw-covered benches. One by one they greeted Anton, "Good-evening, master of the house; set forth candles and three loaves of bread upon your table, for Jesus Christ is born in Bethlehem."

"God be with you," replied Anton.

Zenobia came forward to greet the guests, and close behind her came Lilli. She approached the tallest of the three carollers and bowed low. "May God give you health," she said. The man took her hand in courteous fashion and bowed.

Zenobia could not conceal her pleasure. "It is a good omen," she thought. "These three men are like the sun, moon and rain."

The neighbours whispered among themselves: "Who are

these men? They are not from hereabouts." The whisper went around: "Immigrants. From the old country. They have just arrived." Partly Canadianized themselves in manners and speech – most spoke a few words at least of English – they recognized in these strangers men who had not yet departed from the old ways, who still kept intact from foreign influence the native tongue and habit.

Divested of their sheepskins, their tall furry bonnets shaken free of snow, the immigrants sat down together on one bench, and as though of one accord, smiled.

"And how do you write yourselves, friends?" inquired Grandfather Nestor. He tried to subdue the curiosity of the children, who were staring openly at the foreign clothes of the immigrants and whispering.

"We are Matthew, Mark and John," replied the biggest of the three. An exclamation of delight arose from all. "Like the apostles!" They crowded in a circle about the three immigrants. One had the simple face of a child, with a halo of shaggy blond curls, shining red cheeks, slightly crooked smile and tilted nose. The second was a gentle giant, bearded, with strange violet blue eyes above his black beard. The third was scholarly in appearance, with white skin, pointed red beard and reddish hair, which hung low about his neck. He wore spectacles and had a signet ring on his long white hand. The clothing of the three men was cut European fashion, dark blouses with high necks, trousers tucked into high leather boots.

"Of what family are you?" asked Grandfather Nestor, when all had completed their inspection. "We are cousins, all of one name, and call ourselves Moroz," replied the dark one, who acted as spokesman for them. This surname, indicating Frost, aroused further quips: "Grandfather Frost has certainly come with his family to visit us on Christmas Eve."

Lilli looked hard at the red-headed man. His expression, as he regarded each person, was grave and tender, as though he bestowed on him a kind of unspoken blessing. "He looks like Jesus," thought Lilli. The three men appeared to her deeper in thought, and expressed themselves more profoundly than the farmers in the district.

"How is it in the old country?" inquired Anton, when he had seen to it that all were comfortably seated.

"Bad," replied the giant. "The peasants are losing their land and moving into the cities," explained the red-headed immigrant. "The end is starvation or immigration," concluded the one with blond curls.

"What was your business in the old country?" inquired one of the neighbours. "Teacher, secretary, deacon," enumerated the giant, Matthew. "Aha!" Heads nodded. "You are scholars."

"Well!" laughed Anton, waving his hands as though to distant horizons. "You are welcome to settle here with us. Here is land for all. We need educated people. As you can see, we have few among us with book learning."

"Yes, yes, here is land for all," murmured the neighbours. Whispers circulated concerning their trunk: "A trunk, a whole trunk of books – could it really be possible? Anton saw it with his own eyes! There must be much wisdom in such books. And it is time for us to be wise!" Much satisfaction was felt by the homesteaders at the advent of the immigrants and their trunk of books; they felt that a new era of culture was now at hand.

Now the giant with gentle eyes, having heard Lilli's voice in the chorus, beckoned to her and suggested: "Let this little one sing for us. It is good to hear the voice of a young one on Christmas Eve."

Lilli, proud at being singled out, was about to comply, when she was prevented by her father. "Lilli has a low voice like a boy," he protested. "Let Fialka sing, high and sweet, as a girl should. Come, let us hear you, Fialka."

Fialka stepped forward and sang an odd little carol of

ancient origin:

> The Saviour was born but He had neither babe clothes nor
>   bedding,
> Halle-Hallelujah,
> There was only straw, knee deep, on which to sleep,
> Halle-Hallelujah.
> The fish brought Him water, and the mermaids gave Him milk,
> Halle-Hallelujah.

All laughed and clapped when she had finished, then called out that the three immigrants should sing once more.

Now the voice of the red-headed man, like the sound of a distant bell, was heard, and shortly the two others joined in like a carillon, each carrying a different tune, the first meanwhile singing monotonously and shrilly, the giant in deep, slow clangs, and the third in a strong baritone, as though they were bells summoning people to worship. Finally all three were chiming furiously, the bronze bass chimed lower and lower, the shrill tenor more and more piercing, and the baritone weaving an intricate pattern of melody. Then the neighbours joined in to swell the music to a mighty climax, until the house could hardly contain it.

Then Grandfather Nestor inquired, "Who will relate the birth of the Christ Child?" Without exception, all the guests looked to the three immigrants, thinking it fit that, since they had come tonight, this important function should be performed by one of them. With modest grace, John, the red-headed immigrant, offered: "If you will permit me, I will." The voice of the tenor began to relate the story of the Nativity, and it was to the simple hearts of the farmers present like the first night of Christmas:

> All over the world there came the news
> To Virgin Mary a Son was born.
> On hay in the manger she laid the Son Of God.

Virgin Mary to God prayed, "In what should my Son be robed?"
O King of Heaven, send gifts through the master of the house.
Then came angels from Heaven to earth, bringing gifts,
Three candles of wax and robes of silk for the infant,
In Jordan River, where quiet the water stood,
O there the Virgin Mother of the Holy Infant bathed Him,
And when He was bathed, in robes of silk she robed Him,
And near the manger grey oxen stood,
On the Holy Infant their warm breaths they breathed.

Each phrase created a picture in the minds of the listeners, as if they stood in the real presence of the infant Christ, heard the song of angels, felt the warm breaths of oxen, and smelled the hay in the stable. The lines ploughed by harsh labour on their faces were obliterated and in their place were looks of gentle piety; memories of their squalid, monotonous life on the Canadian prairies were superseded by deep ancestral memories. Faces had become gentle, full of humility. Here and there, a tear glistened, rolled down a leathery cheek, and was flicked off with a finger. A sigh, an exclamation, a word of prayer came from moving lips. Lilli sat pensive, deeply moved by this story which she was hearing now in its primitive beauty for the first time. Each Christian present reviewed his life during the past year; all misunderstandings had to be cleared away; all broken friendships restored.

In the general conversation which ensued, the black-haired immigrant beckoned to Lilli, and drawing her to him, enquired, "What is your name?"

"Lilli."

He stroked her hair with his huge hand. "Lilia." He accented the name on the second syllable. "Lilia, little daughter, listen to me." He looked deep into her eyes, thinking, "This child has known sorrow." He enfolded her hand in his enormous one, and scrutinized her for a long while. "With your voice, you can express joy, sorrow. You can give people ease of their pain. You can make real for them all that is in their hearts." When he had finished speaking, the two continued to gaze at each other, drawn together by a complete mutual understanding. Lilli's eyes glowed with rapture, and yet beneath it all, the big immigrant could sense her pensive mood. Presently he spoke: "The one who sings need never be lonely. Remember that, Lilia." He realized, from the tremor of her hand, how deeply he had touched her impressionable heart.

How did he know that she was lonely? Lilli slipped away from the crowd unnoticed. The carollers continued to sing and the sound was carried out of the house and far across the snow. The night was frosty and peaceful. Swarms of stars glittered jubilant in the dark blue sky. Lilli stood on the snow where the light streamed down like a banner and looked up. The stable was illumined by the light of the stars; sleighs dashed over the powdery snow; bells rang from the church. When she had looked deep into the giant's eyes, she had felt the sacred nature of song. Thus it must have been on the first night of Christmas. An intense longing and joy filled Lilli's heart. "Oh, I will never be lonely again!" she thought.

PART THREE
The Wreath Plaiting

1
BIRTH OF A BROTHER

LILLI HAD been out on an expedition to gather the seneca
snake root which was dried in the sun, sewn up in sugar sacks
and shipped to the drug companies in the city. Every spring,
when the tiny white flower of the snake root bloomed, the
Bukovynian children went out to gather it on government
land. They depended on it for spending money, since ready
cash was scarce in the homes of the immigrants, and it was
necessary for them to supplement it in some way. All summer
long, the children saved, and in the fall, when the new mail
order catalogue arrived, each child was permitted to make up
his order. Lilli had long ago decided what hers would be: fine
blue cotton material with confetti dots, which she planned to
make into dresses for herself and the twins.

Early in the morning, with the rising of the sun, she had set
off, carrying her lunch, a sack and a knife to dig the roots. The
grass was hoary with dew, each blade as if dipped in
quicksilver. Like quicksilver, too, was Lilli's blood; it danced,
shook, tumbled joyously in her veins as she hastened across
the steaming prairies.

Now, as she returned home dragging behind her the full
sack, weighing forty pounds, Lilli stopped to watch a flight of
wild geese over the swamps. Spring, like a mischievous boy,
had certainly played tricks, thought Lilli, as she looked at the
prairie and saw a petal unfold here, a catkin swing there, a

courtship conducted in mid-air. "You can see life happening," thought Lilli as she listened to the rumbling chortle of a bullfrog.

Overhead, the geese stretched in an immense V across half the sky, calling and answering and blending, their undulating wings illumined from above by the morning sun. Another great wedge appeared, until the sky was traced in two great moving silvery V's, impelled on and on northward with the spring.

When they had finally disappeared in a scattering of black dots, Lilli heard church bells ringing in the distance, and the question came to her mind, "Who has died?" People spoke in low voices of deaths which occurred at this time of year, when packs of hungry wolves roamed the prairies, when the spring floods filled the great pits burned by forest fires, so that men who had lost their way were sometimes drowned, and not until the heat of summer had dried up the waters were their bloated stinking corpses discovered in the hollows.

When Lilli arrived home, she met Fialka, hair flying, face distorted as if in panic. "What's the matter, Fialka? Is anything wrong?" asked Lilli, but her sister rushed past her so rapidly that she almost knocked Petey over. On the doorstep stood Masha and Tasha, button-eyed, panties askew, pointing within and trying to tell Lilli something, as though fear had nailed down their tongues to the roof of their mouths.

"What's the matter?" asked Lilli, dropping her heavy sack, but she received no answer. "What's the matter?" she asked again, shaking each twin as though to shake out some information, but all she accomplished was the collapse of their undergarments. Pulling them up hastily, she sat the twins down on the steps and then ran into the house.

The room was in disorder, as though someone had been overtaken in the midst of preparations. Preparations for what? The chest had been opened, a basin of water stood on the stove, there was a little pile of linen of the table. But it was the cradle, handcarved by Lilli's grandfather, which provided the decisive clue, for she knew that Petey and the twins had long since outgrown it.

Even before Lilli saw her mother's figure prostrate on the bed, one hand grasping the post, instinct had already instructed her. Generations of women, caught in the rhythm of childbirth, had passed on this knowledge to her, and also, as most children born on a farm, Lilli had often observed animals give birth to their young, and it seemed a natural rite to her. Nevertheless, she felt awe that she was about to witness the birth of a child, awe and shyness, for she was a modest girl, and she stood, limbs almost paralyzed with terror, thinking what she must do to help her mother. She would have prayed, but no words came to her.

Was that her mother's face, features so bloated as to be almost unrecognizable, with the colour squeezed out of the skin till it looked like an old lemon? Was that her voice, uttering those moans of a woman in labour, so hoarse and grotesque, and yet so soul-stirring; were those her eyes, straining as though ready to burst through their sockets?

"Everything is ready," said Zenobia as she saw Lilli, in an interval between pains. "I have sent Fialka for the midwife, but as she will not get there for some time, you will have to help me, Lilli. If you do as I say, we will see it through."

Lilli, when faced with an emergency, never ran away; she had never had a place of refuge. So she moved mechanically in obedience to her mother's direction, watching the drama of human birth, not quite believing what she saw, and yet knowing that this indeed was how one came to be. She tied a towel to the bed post and gave the end to her mother to pull on while the rhythm of labour pains accelerated and her mother pushed, grunted, twisted, writhed and bit her tongue until blood ran out.

Meanwhile Lilli prepared clean sheets, hot water and clean rags and set up candles to smoke out evil spirits, thinking, who was this stranger who was coming to them out of her mother's womb? What destiny would he have in the life which had not even begun for him? She hurried back to the bed and watched as her mother, exhausted by the convulsions of her body, gasped and struggled for breath. Excited, almost beside herself, Lilli assisted her, guided by blind instinct while her mother, a peasant woman of great strength and heavy build, strove to deliver herself. In threshing about, Zenobia by accident struck Lilli so powerful a blow that she staggered, and as her fist came into contact with Lilli's cheek, Zenobia cursed in peasant fashion, directing her cursing, not so much at Lilli as at her own agony, "Akh, cholera!" Then, as her eyes followed Lilli, she cursed again, crying out this time, "*Akh, tsyhanka*! (gypsy)," and the use of the old nickname stabbed Lilli to the heart, although she did not pause for a moment from her work.

The drama of childbirth had now reached its final stage, and Zenobia, face streaming with sweat, gasped, "Press down hard," and Lilli pressed with force. With a great triumphal cry, Zenobia expelled the infant, and Lilli stood in the presence of a new world citizen. "The Lord be thanked!" exclaimed Zenobia in a shuddering sigh of relief, and then said, "Get me the scissors," and Lilli reached under the mattress for the scissors, which had been placed there, as was the custom in childbirth, and cut the cord, then rolled the baby off on to a diaper. He was slippery as a sausage skin, with a puckered face and big mouth, but Lilli found him quite endearing, rather like a pretty frog. What a perfect tiny mannikin he was, everything complete to the toenails, and a thatch of dark hair upon the top!

"Hit it across the bottom," gasped her mother, and Lilli, holding the fragile infant, feared to injure it, and so slapped it lightly at first. The contact of her hand upon that bare skin made her realize, more keenly than anything else, that this was life which had only recently been created, that she was the first to touch this living thing.

"Harder," said her mother, whose face by now was

beginning to assume a gentler, more normal aspect.

Lilli gave a hard spank and the infant emitted a yell, its first voice in the world. When she felt the warm, breathing child in her arms, she knew the awakening of maternal instinct, and thought, "This is one of the most wonderful things that ever happened to me."

As she bathed the baby in the bath, the child bellowed mightily for the water was too hot, and she hastened to cool it off, then she anointed it with olive oil and swaddled it in a blanket, watching with wonder all the while each motion of those tiny muscles. When she looked at the clock, Lilli saw that only half an hour had passed, yet it had seemed like eternity.

"An easy delivery," Zenobia whispered. "Lilli is indeed the lucky luckless one." She closed her eyes. "An easy delivery!" repeated Lilli, thinking of the anguish she had just witnessed, and wondering what a difficult delivery might be.

Now that it was all over, she stood gasping. How had she ever done what she had done? She put her hand to her face, and it came away wet with perspiration, as though she had plunged it into water. Only now, with the child in the cradle as inconvertible proof of what had occurred, could she grasp the reality. O miracle of birth, that there now existed a human creature, which only an hour ago had been a senseless part of her mother's flesh! "Never can I speak to anyone of this," she thought. A holy joy flooded her, like the feeling she had in church when the choir began to sing and the clouds of incense drifted everywhere.

Stillness now succeeded the former tumult, and in that stillness, outside noises became distinct – the cheeping of an insect, the cry of children at play, a swift breeze tossing a leaf. . . . Shadows on the wall, the interplay of light and dark, everything assumed a larger, sharper significance. Surely, she mused with a choking in her throat, this great experience would bring her closer to her mother, surely this wondrous intimacy shared would bridge the hostility between them and give her a rightful place in the family!

Moving back to the bed, she looked down at her mother, whose face was now rosy, and whose brown hair was becomingly disordered around her face. "Mother looks beautiful," she thought, and this was the first time she had considered Zenobia so.

"Mother," she whispered, but there was no response. "Mother," she said again, with great urgency. Zenobia's eyelids fluttered open, and she looked at Lilli as though she had been expecting to find someone else.

"Where is Fialka?" she inquired fretfully.

Lilli felt a chill of repulse as she answered, "She has not come back yet."

"Prepare the house for visitors."

Lilli, who had not yet recovered from the shock of her experience, would have wished time, a few moments, a few words shared with her mother, to indicate the warmth of a new bond, and now she hesitated, trying to express her feelings. "Mother – " How could she tell what was in her heart?

"Did you hear me?" reproved her mother with some harshness. "Make haste as people will soon be here."

To her mother, birth was a commonplace event, for this was her eleventh child, and she could not imagine what the event might mean to Lilli, but the girl, whose emotions had suddenly burst forth from the tight bonds in which they had been held during the actual birth, could not bring herself back so quickly to the commonplaces of existence: her soul was in a ferment.

Going over to the cradle, Lilli stood looking at the infant, her heart swollen and sore as a boil.

"What does he look like?" Zenobia asked.

Lilli hesitated. She did not wish to tell her mother that the baby resembled a frog, especially after her mother had exerted so much effort on creating him, so she said merely, "He has a great forehead."

Her mother was pleased. "He will be a scholar," she said. "Your father wanted one of his sons to be learned. He will read many books."

As her mother closed her eyes and dozed, Lilli made the house presentable for visitors who would shortly arrive with gifts of bread, cheese and honey. After she had tidied the place, Lilli went to the carved wooden chest, took out several articles and hung, on a cord suspended on the wall over her mother's head, Zenobia's bridal bedspread, with its wide border of varied colours, also the blue silken scarf which had been attached to her maiden's wreath.

Shortly afterward, Fialka arrived with the announcement that visitors were on their way. At once she took up the baby and commenced to coo over it, tickling it, exclaiming, humming, cuddling. She looked like a madonna, thought Lilli, standing neglected beside her mother's bed and envying Fialka's free nature. Why could she not have acted so, why in the presence of her mother did she become stiff and curdled? She had words, too, and feelings as warm as Fialka's but they were frozen like icicles, and stabbed her within, instead of melting and flowing out in a warm stream.

"You will make a wonderful mother, Fialka," approved Zenobia. She felt more relaxed in the presence of her oldest daughter, whose spontaneous nature had no difficulty in expressing itself, unlike Lilli, who was tongue-tied in speech with her mother, "as if," thought Zenobia, "she had knobs all over her tongue." Mentally, she pushed Lilli farther away from her, made of her even more of an alien, and frowned as she noticed that Lilli had neglected one aspect of her cleaning-up. Pointing to the parcel which had been wrapped carefully in paper and laid on the floor, Zenobia said to the girl, "Take that outside and bury it."

It was the last acknowledgment Zenobia made of Lilli's presence that day, for now visitors arrived and the house, from then until evening, was filled with congratulations and laughter.

2
THE PICKLING

THAT had been spring, and now it was fall, and the baby, a stout fellow, had long since lost his resemblance to a frog, and had developed an entrancing asset, a pair of dimples such as no other member of the Landash family possessed. The twins loved to lean over his cradle and make him laugh for the purpose of enjoying his dimples, into which they poked their fingers. Lilli, having observed their antics with a dubious eye for some time, decided that the baby had produced his quota of dimples, so taking the twins by the scruff of the neck, she removed them, saying, "The baby can't make dimples for you all day. Now, out."

"What else baby got to do, Lilli?" asked Masha cleverly.

"Eat, sleep, grow, make bubbles," snapped Lilli. "Baby has plenty of work." She deposited the twins on the doorstep. "Now, stay there until I call you."

She returned within to assist with the pickling. For her mother, the pickling season was a delight. Working with her hands, according to the seasons, kept Zenobia from feeling uprooted. There was always something drying – vegetable, root or herb – in the sunshine outside of the house, or hung up in bunches from the rafters. Sunflowers, their bright crowns shrivelled, hung over the fence, the last glory of summer contained in their yellow leaves. The children had been mushrooming the previous day, and the results were now being pickled, dried and converted into soups and sauces. The floor of the house was littered with small green cucumbers, watermelons, lettuces, green tomatoes, beets, horseradish, dill, apples, herbs, sunflower seeds.

Now, like an animated potato peeling withered by age to a snuff-brown colour, Granny Yefrosynia was supervising operations. She had her head tied up in a flowered turban; her pockets bulged with spices in knobs all around her person, giving her an odd shape, like a gnarled tree trunk overgrown with strange protuberances. She sang, as she worked, somewhat off-key, but with resolution. Granny's motions were a joy to watch, thought Lilli as she observed her grandmother putting down dill pickles into a small wooden barrel: whether shaping a dumpling or placing a patch, Granny had that infallible mastery of her material which betokens the artist. When the old lady had finished filling the barrel, she placed a wooden lid on top, anchoring it down with a stone.

She looked at Zenobia with an air of conspiracy: "Shall I make the *maritura* now?" *Maritura* was Granny's pickling specialty, reserved only for great occasions such as weddings. The pickles were made of string beans with carrots, oil and onions, and were fermented by a pound lump of dough placed in the pickle and allowed to ripen for ten days. There was a special technique involved which only Granny knew, and the old lady never gave this secret away.

Zenobia, in replying to Granny's question, feigned indifference, but Lilli sensed an undercurrent of excitement as her mother said, "Perhaps it would be as well." She knew there was some great event impending; that was why Zenobia had asked her to keep the children busy outside and why Fialka had been sent away to the neighbour's. Anton, too, was away at a building bee for the three immigrants. He had left early, carrying with him a *kolach* sprinkled with caraway seeds, a bag of dried mushrooms and a cottage cheese, all wrapped up in a white cloth.

Lilli went out now to supervise the children, directing them to turn the mushrooms drying in the sun "so they shouldn't worm." She stood for a few moments in the fall sunshine, admiring the birches with their white bodies and blond heads, like abashed maidens, and the poplar trees dangling their round golden leaves like coins. The wind billowed Lilli's calico skirt, blowing it up like a scarlet balloon. From the house, the smells of pickling came in tantalizing steam, and Petey, dragging a pumpkin to Lilli, stopped for a moment to snuff at the air, remarking, "Something good is making to eat in the house."

He looked so delightful that she stooped to embrace him, saying, "You look like a flower, Petey," but the truth was, every day more and more Petey was losing his halo as he struggled manfully with temptations of the devil to perform various mischief.

While Lilli was outside, Granny Yefrosynia remarked to Zenobia, "I advise you, Zenobia, to be kinder to Lilli than you have been, for you cannot carry out this business of Fialka without her assistance. Try to make her one of the family." The old lady, who was fond of her granddaughter, was not satisfied to see Lilli relegated to the position of slavery in the house.

"Fialka must spend her time preparing her linens, and who else is there to help?" said Zenobia, but she recognized the truth of Granny's observation.

When Lilli returned inside, she found the baby loudly bawling, and going over to him she fixed him with a stern eye: "Keep quiet, baby," she admonished. "You're too small to make such a big noise."

Meanwhile, as Granny began preparations for her pickle, she asked Zenobia, "Is Fialka embroidering a shirt for Marko?" Lilli pricked up her ears and looked out of the corner of her eye at her mother. The question of Fialka's courtship had been on Zenobia's mind for weeks and it was only now that she had the chance to talk the matter over with the old lady.

Fialka was now eighteen and "under the wreath," or ready to be affianced. She was a beautiful girl, white-faced as the moon, with black brows like crescents, and eyes grey as a dove's wing. The matchmakers had been buzzing about her betrothal; suitors had come from distant towns. All that spring and summer, Lilli had watched the wooing of Fialka by all the local youths, but up to now, the results had been the same; the suitor had been repulsed. If Fialka did not like the boy – and such had been the case up to now – she went out of the house. If Zenobia was not satisfied with her proposed son-in-law, she turned things upside down, complained that the stove wouldn't burn, and told the suitor, "I haven't a girl to give away." In this event, the suitor did not stay long, and the whole district knew that the boy had been "given the pumpkin." Recently, however, Fialka had acquired a suitor who appeared more likely to win the beauty than any other aspirant. She danced most often with him; he had escorted her home from every dance for the past month. The young man was Marko Molodets, who was an eligible bachelor, having a farm of one section. He was a good-natured, healthy young man with blond hair, sunburned face and spectacles. These spectacles endeared him to Zenobia, who thought they signified that the young man had superior intelligence. Fialka, however, had refused to be sounded regarding her feelings for the young man; she continued her flirtation with other admirers and permitted one of them to escort her to church.

"Well, is Marko to be the one?" demanded Granny with some impatience. She was conducting her operations in a corner of the house, so that even Zenobia should not witness them.

"This I will say," confided Lilli's mother to an eager Granny. "Fialka acts like a girl in love, goes into a dream, does not answer when spoken to, goes off for walks by herself." She frowned as she took a sip of apple juice. "One thing I am determined on," she said, "the wedding will be in the old style.

Too many young people are forgetting the old ways."

"Many wish to celebrate in the new fashion," suggested Granny with caution. "Perhaps Fialka – "

"Fialka will do as I tell her," snapped Zenobia. "Besides," her voice lowered to a whisper and she looked about with caution, "I have a thing, something which will persuade her."

"And what is that?'"

"A veil in the new style for Fialka. Yards of net and orange flowers, like a cloud on a summer day. This I got from the mail order catalogue. No girl around here ever had such a veil. I saved for months to buy it, a real Canadian veil. When Fialka sees it, she will agree to anything."

"Does Fialka know the wedding songs?" asked Granny.

"She will learn them."

"From whom?"

"I shall send her to the widow Tamara."

Granny paused in the act of placing the beans in the stone crock. "There is some strange talk about that woman. It is said that she speaks with evil spirits in the swamps."

Uneasiness flickered over Zenobia's face. She tasted the green tomato pickle and her eyes widened with pleasure. She dipped the spoon back into the mixture and tasted again. "Sharp and sweet," she commented. Then she wiped her mouth with her apron. "I don't put much trust in the talk of people. They will invent stories about a woman who lives alone. In any case, who else is there to teach Fialka these things?"

When the pickling was finished, the three sat down to a lunch of cabbage rolls stuffed with meat and rice, preserved cranberry sauce on potatoes, and cooked plums. The children ate outdoors on a bench beneath the trees.

"And now," said Zenobia as she disposed of the last of the dishes, "now we'll look at Fialka's linen chest." The three went over to the wooden chest which was covered with a tapestry and placed on a raised platform, away from the children. Tall, on carved legs, it was covered on every inch of its surface with carvings and inlaid work in mother-of-pearl, beads and brass rings. "Have you everything prepared for her – sheets, blankets and so on?" asked Granny bending over and peering into the chest, which was filled to the top, with not an inch to spare.

"Everything." Zenobia took the articles one by one from the chest and enumerated them: "Fifty yards of cloth, linen, cotton wool, so that Fialka should not go from her home with naked hands; three pillows and slips, all hand-embroidered, in finest work; six embroidered linen towels, two silk cushions, two blankets, a comforter, embroidered table cloths, a tapestry, a black woven wool bedspread of heaviest wool, which I made myself – "

Zenobia now dove down again into the chest, and came up with something that glittered like a sudden glow of gold. "And these – " Her wedding boots! Lilli pressed close to have a look at those fabulous boots. "Mother, let me see those boots." Eagerly she stretched out her hand for them. "Are those the boots you wore at your wedding, the boots you danced in when you met father?" Zenobia held the boots for a moment in her hands, caressing the leather, her eyes full of memories. "The very boots." She handed them to Lilli.

The boots were of finest orangey-tan leather, knee high, with a slipover of scarlet leather in scalloped design covering the toe, instep and lower part of the heel. They were shoes to dance in, fairy tale shoes, wedding shoes. "No woman in this whole district has such boots," Zenobia observed with satisfaction as she replaced the boots. "Fialka will dance at her wedding in them, and then I'll put them back in the trunk until the time comes for Lilli to have them."

3
THE MATCHMAKING

ON SATURDAY night of the same week there was a dance at the community hall and Marko had called to take Fialka with him. An hour later, Zenobia summoned Lilli to her and said:

"Give this lunch to Fialka and Marko," and she handed a heavy basket to Lilli. "And watch who dances most often with her. If it be Marko, stand close when they are talking alone and find out what he is saying to her. If he speaks of marriage, watch how Fialka receives him. And do not tell anyone what you are about, but come straight back home and report to me." Because of her small size and exceptional lightness of foot, Zenobia knew that Lilli would be able to slip in and out of places unobserved.

Lilli raced over the fields, pleased with the mission she had been charged with – as it gave her the feeling of being part of the family group – and thinking of the good things which the basket contained – roasted chicken, a bottle of wine, cake.

As Lilli approached the hall, which was all lit up with kerosene lamps, the music burst forth joyous, impetuous, and the sound of dancing feet pattered on the air like rain drops. She walked around to the side of the building and spied a large box which was conveniently placed beneath a window, and on this she climbed and found herself looking right on to the dance floor. There was a long line of dancers doing the heel and toe dance and there seemed to Lilli to be hundreds of heels and toes moving rhythmically as the dancers passed around the hall.

"How beauty! What a wonderful!" she exclaimed aloud. "How people, full of music, make dance go round!"

She pressed her nose flatter against the window and was stretching out her arms to get a firm grip at the sides to maintain her balance when a voice called out behind her:

"Young lady!"

Lilli turned about and gave a startled glance at a huge jolly person who was standing by watching her. He had in his hand a garlic sausage which he bit into and chewed for a while before asking her.

"You are holding up building so it should not fall down on dancers?"

Lilli looked abashed and shook her head, unable to move. She recognized the man as the local fiddler, much renowned for his skill in playing at weddings.

"Come down off box."

Lilli descended and stood looking at him speechless.

"What that is?" He pointed to the basket.

"Lunch," whispered Lilli.

"Lunch?" The fiddler stared at the basket and then at the figure of Lilli, comparing them. "Hm. Big lunch for small girl. You think you will get outside that?"

"For Fialka and Marko," explained Lilli. "For to see if they get married –" She stopped, remembering Zenobia's admonition, but the fiddler had taken in the whole affair.

"Aha!" he exclaimed, his red face beaming like the morning sun. "Aha!" he repeated and winked at Lilli. "You come to spy on them, to tell mother how is situation."

Lilli hung her head in shame at being discovered, but the fiddler reassured her. "Come, I will take you to them. It is right mother should know if girl is planning to marry. We will watch quietly, and make report."

They tiptoed up to a bush behind the dance hall and there, standing with hands enfolded and eyes intent upon each other, were Marko and Fialka, engaged in serious discourse. As they listened, they heard Marko say, "Fialka, I do not wonder at your beauty, for a morning star fell streaming upon you at birth."

It was Fialka's face indeed, thought Lilli as she watched her sister, but so transformed with bright eyes full of tears and laughter at the same time, with a look of tenderness which quite effaced any girlish giddiness she might ever have displayed, that Lilli's lips trembled at the beauty of it, and she wanted to cry out. The fiddler took Lilli by the hand and led her gently away, so they did not make a sound to disturb the lovers.

"Tell mother it will be very soon," he whispered, but Lilli, still entranced by the spell of what she had just seen, turned her face to him, still full of wonder, and asked,

"Tell me what that love is, which make girl shining like star."

"So?" smiled the fiddler. "You want to hear about love? Come here, sit down." He drew her over to a bench and placing his arm about her shoulder, began to talk, his blue eyes like those of a young man again as he recalled the days of his youth.

"Listen, Lilli, and I'll tell you how in my village in the old country, young people made love. In the moonlight, when the nightingale is bringing music from his soul, a wonderful pale night, the sweet songs of the maidens are heard. The young people go down into a valley and there stay all night, singing and making love. All over, boys and girls are kissing. Kissing! Like hail!" The fiddler made juicy, smacking sounds with his lips, as though recalling all the girls he had ever loved and kissed. "That, Lilli, is love." He sighed with gusto, an enormous, soul-shattering sigh.

Love! Lilli mused. Would the matchmakers ever come for her? Excited, she began to dream – that some day she herself would be the centre of similar ceremonies, and beside her would sit a youth with blond hair swept up in two peaks at each side and he would be saying – what? Breathless, Lilli waited upon life.

"Some day, little one," said the fiddler pinching her cheek. "You will find out for yourself, and it will be better, much better than you dream."

The fat man now stooped down to the basket, and before Lilli's horrified eyes, severed a whole leg off the chicken and proceeded to devour it. Seeing her hungry eyes upon him, he removed a delicious morsel and popped it into her mouth. That was all very well, thought Lilli bitterly, swallowing the bit, but how was he going to replace the missing leg before Fialka arrived?

But when the time came to deliver the basket, Lilli found Fialka in such a state that she would not have noticed whether the chicken had one leg, or three or five. . . .

Nobody was much surprised, therefore, although, according to custom, they pretended to be, when Marko, accompanied by two elders, called shortly afterward at the Landash home. The house had been scrubbed and whitewashed, all the linen freshly laundered, and many pastries baked, so when one evening after the harvest a wagon stopped before the house and three men, Marko and the elders, got out with great ceremony, the family was prepared and all dressed in their best. The elders, who were accounted two of the shrewdest men in the village, approached with the excuse: "We were passing by, and stopped to pay our respects." Zenobia stood in the doorway, dressed in skirt of maroon and black striped satin and white linen blouse.

"God give you health!" she greeted the matchmakers, and invited them into the house. Marko remained outside to await the verdict, as it was not proper for him to participate.

"The weather has been golden," said Anton, coming up from behind to shake hands with the elders. "Fine weather for harvesting, courtships by moonlight, and marriages," quipped one of the matchmakers.

Phillippe Fuyarosh was a pompous, tall, red-faced personage, fond of good food, with a formal manner of speaking. He wore a long black frock coat, and had once been a schoolmaster. His companion, Emilian Putnyk, was the exact opposite – a great comic, round as a ball, with drooping salt and pepper whiskers and a bald head. As they came in, they paid little attention at first to Fialka, and pretended instead to find Lilli most attractive.

"Are you preparing to give her away?" joked Putnyk, as the two men sat down, having delivered to Zenobia a package containing two bottles of whiskey.

"She is not ripe for picking," replied Zenobia, unwrapping the package and preparing the glasses on the table. For once, she was pleased with Lilli's behaviour and appearance, so expert was the girl in catering to the guests. Lilli had a new dress of blue cotton, sprinkled with small coloured dots like confetti. The twins wore blue dresses made in miniature editions of the same style.

"Ah, well," sighed Fuyarosh, drinking his whiskey in one gulp, "perhaps we shall leave her to grow a little while yet in the garden." He flipped up his coat tails and brought forth a fine white linen handkerchief with which he carefully wiped his whiskers.

Fialka, meanwhile, sat meek and demure, looking like a picture in her black satin gown, a string of pearls around her throat, and her black hair up in a coronet, with a rose tucked behind her ear. She had gathered her belt in her hands and plaited it continually.

Now Fuyarosh plunged into the conventional speech:

"We are hunters from a far country, who travelled through many lands, in the face of blizzards, over rough trails, pursuing game in all the countries through which we passed. Then one day we met a prince who was out riding in search of game. We made his acquaintance and he informed us that he was seeking game – a rare fox which was not really a fox, but a beautiful girl, whose peer had never been seen in any princedom. For many months he sought to capture this fox, but it always escaped. Would we help him to seize it? He would give us our heart's desire – a wagon of grain, a fine horse."

Fuyarosh paused as he set down his empty glass. He appeared not to notice as Lilli filled it, but smacked his lips nevertheless. Zenobia kept on nodding throughout the speech, as though convinced that the men before her were indeed hunters. Punctilious in matters of custom, she knew exactly the symbolism of every phrase. Anton, dressed in his town suit, was stiff and formal; he cleared his throat often, adjusted his tie and frowned. The function of father was somewhat relegated to the background, and he felt awkward, as if a bone had stuck in his throat.

The elder continued, "In pity for his passion, we helped him with his search, and the trail led straight to your house. So we have entered to find the fox, which we see now is this beauty Fialka. Thus we come to the point of our visit: are you willing to give to this prince your lovely daughter, or is it your will to keep her beside you for a while longer?"

This whole scene, staged according to custom, was not as spontaneous as it appeared, as all the symbolism was ordained by use, but the method of delivery was left to the imagination of the speaker.

Fialka, through all this, remained calm, not betraying her feelings except for a slight smile. When Putnyk addressed himself to her directly and asked, "What do you say, Fialka, do you love the young man?" she feigned indifference and answered,

"I don't know – ask mother."

This apparently noncommittal answer was taken by all as a sign of consent, for if Fialka were unwilling, she would have left the room. Zenobia took the matter into her hands: "We must be sure that our treasure will be properly taken care of: what guarantee does the prince offer of a home?"

"Guarantee?" The matchmakers looked at each other in glee. There was to be no sordid haggling at this affair, as in the case of some niggardly farmers. Fuyarosh spoke: "Land, a whole section, with a house and buildings." At this magnificent offer, Anton responded with a handsome dowry: "For Fialka, a cow and a pig." The matchmakers shouted, "Bravo!" and another round of drinks was called for. Then the bridegroom was summoned from outdoors, where he had been shivering in the cool autumn air. As soon as he heard the news, he rushed into the house and cried out:

"This I know – I can't live without her. Day and night the thought of her burns my soul. Without this beauty, life won't be worth living."

Anton burst out laughing at this eloquence, and said: "Our future son-in-law is a poet, I see." His remark was interpreted as sealing the bargain, and Fialka went out of the room, returning with a dish containing two embroidered scarves. The two young people, standing side by side, bound each other's arms with the scarves, and the engagement was sealed.

4
THE WREATH PLAITERS
❦

THE WOMEN had been working for days to prepare the wedding feast, and now a great table was spread along the entire length of the house, where the food was laid as it came from the pots and oven: pastries, tarts, rolls, strudel stuffed with cherries or figs, honey cake, cookies in animal shapes, prunes, cottage cheese, pickled herrings, nuts, rolls with poppy seed and honey, jars of preserves, garlic sausage, dumplings, cabbage rolls, and three fancy kolaches for the bride's table. The previous night Zenobia had made preparations for the chicken and pork stew by cutting the meat in small pieces and salting them overnight, then cooking them in the oven until brown with onions, fat, garlic and parsley. With this she served *dushynyna*, made of roasted cornmeal which had been mixed with fat, fried onions, hot milk, eggs, salt and pepper to form a thin batter which was baked in a dish until brown. As an appetizer, she had small pickled mushrooms which she had put up a few weeks before in vinegar, spices and cinnamon sticks.

The interior of the house had been whitewashed and decorated with tissue paper designs on every empty space; benches had been placed against the walls and the central floor space cleared for dancing. At one end was the bride's table, with a tapestry and linen towels draped like a canopy behind it. The red rag of virginity had been tied before the door, to signify that Fialka came as a chaste maiden to her groom.

On the evening of the maiden's farewell party, which

Marko was not permitted to attend, the children were all dressed in white, and propped up against the wall like a row of stiff hollyhocks, their legs stretched out before them in a graduated row, from biggest to smallest. Granny Yefrosynia put the last touches to her costume, which was composed of a black woollen skirt striped in blue and red, the end draped diagonally across the front to the waist and kept in place with a wool belt woven in orange, blue, green, red and black with an eight-inch fringe. Her shirt was of white linen, embroidered with openwork and hemstitching. On her head she wore a blue silk shawl with floral embroideries. Lilli was splendid in a black satin jerkin, blue accordion pleated silk skirt, shirt embroidered in red and blue beads, coral necklace and bracelets. Zenobia, more sombre in hue, wore her striped satin skirt with a white linen blouse, and over the two horns of her headdress she had draped a white shawl in the old style of Bukovynian women, a relic of the days of the Tartars, to signify the married state.

First to arrive were the old ladies, gossipy and curious, anxious not to miss a thing, for their lives having been emptied by the inevitable passage of time, they filled their days by a vicarious interest in the lives of other people. Then came one wagon after another, rumbling up to the front gate and disgorging the wedding guests. Lilli was kept busy running to the door and helping the guests with their wraps. A chorus of laughing voices signalled the arrival of the bridemaidens, tumbling out of the wagon in a rainbow of ribbons, flowers, satins, velvets, heels clicking, beads jangling, voices ringing. Lilli thought she had never seen so much beauty before. The girls crowded before the mirror, chattering and arranging their hair, posing and turning around to display their dress.

"Youth is like flowers!" exclaimed one old lady to another.

"I was a beautiful girl in my youth," sniffed one old crone with a pulpy red nose. "The best dancer in our village."

The young girls came out in a throng and found Fialka

sitting before the table on which were three large kolaches topped with lighted candles. On her head glittered a two-inch band of beadwork trimmed with flowers, peacock feathers and silver coins; her white linen shirt, modelled after her grandmother's, blazed with yellow and red weaving and embroideries of golden wheat ears; her knee-length wine velvet tunic, with its tight bodice and full skirt, was trimmed with gold and silver sequins and fastened with gold braid frogs; her accordion-pleated satin skirt was striped with bands of scarlet, green and yellow and three rows of metallic braid; on her neck, were strings of corals and coloured pearls; around her waist, a golden girdle; on her feet, the yellow boots.

"The most beautiful bride we have ever seen!" exclaimed the guests as they formed an admiring tableau around her. Fialka did not appear to Lilli to resemble herself. The emotion which she was experiencing had cast an unearthly radiance upon her, and although she smiled, there was a thoughtful expression on her beautiful yet melancholy features.

"Bless, O Lord, the father and mother who are plaiting this wreath for their daughter!" the guests sang out in a wild, impassioned outburst. As Fialka sat on her silken cushion, the bridemaidens approached her to unplait her hair, singing the while. The widow Tamara, as the matron, now appeared with a knife in her hands and made as if to cut Fialka's hair, the bride defending herself the while. Finally, she permitted the matron to cut off a little hair, and the girls sang out again, "Comb my hair, mother, with your white fingers, with tears. Light may your hands be on my tresses! I did not ask this favour of you when I walked free as a maiden; now grant me my request."

The plaintive notes of the violin, weeping and rejoicing in turn, resounded while Fialka and her mother kissed each other. As the men's and women's voices combined in harmony, the pathetic music tore at Lilli's heart strings. The ceremonies were wedding poesy, handed down from generation to generation, and sewn into the wreath, for there was a song for every leaf. Each scene of that wonderful drama was imprinted on Lilli's mind. She watched with mounting excitement the motions of the bridemaidens' hands, as they wove the ribbons and leaves into a wreath, singing as the wreath grew into a thing of beauty, took on a symbolic meaning, the farewell of the bride to her maidenhood.

Now Tamara stepped forward from the throng and as she placed the wreath on the head of the bride, the guests sang out:

"The white blossom of the cranberry has flowered; the wreath glistens in beauty; let us put it on the head of the bride."

5
THE MARRIAGE RITES
❦

AMONG THE guests attending the next day's ceremonies was Ian MacTavish, who was still teaching school in the district. "Oh come, Mr. Mac," Lilli had urged. "You will see something wonderful," and Fialka, bowing low, had extended the formal invitation: "My parents and I invite you to my wedding." She was charming in her silk shawl and flowers, thought MacTavish. "I wouldn't miss it for the world," he said. He had long desired to witness such a ceremony, but more and more of the younger generation were being married in the new Canadian style.

He stood now, an incongruous figure in his tweed suit and red hair, among the costumed, rosy-faced Bukovynians, watching the crowd of guests who had assembled to see Fialka off to church. About a dozen wagons were lined up in front of the Landash home and within, young and old swarmed in the big room around the bride.

Lilli stood out as a unique personality, thought the teacher. Face, expression, gesture, were all marked by a peculiar delicacy and sensitivity.

One other person he noted – this was Tamara, a woman whom he had never seen before, because of her isolated way of living. The tall, sombre woman, so richly dressed, so tragic in expression, arrested the attention, and some of the women spoke of her in low, hostile whispers.

"I am surprised," hissed Lizzie Schwartz, "that Zenobia

should invite this Tamara for Fialka's wedding, for many have cursed her as a witch."

"I hope," said Ahapia Honchar with a vicious leer, "that Fialka may not live to regret it some day."

The time had come for Fialka to depart from her home and she stood now, pallid beneath her long white veil and flowered wreath, before her parents, who were sitting on a bench outside the house, holding the wedding loaf in their hands. The guests, accompanied by the musicians, filed out of the house, singing as they came, a prayer to the parents to bless the young bride beneath the "royal golden wreath." This poetic utterance was sung with such free abandon that MacTavish was stunned by its power. The entire scene seemed to him like a drama created by the people – the songs, scenes were all their invention, acted with spontaneity, as if springing that very moment from their hearts.

Tamara stepped forward now as matron and counsellor of the bride and exhorted Fialka: "You must now thank your mother and father for bringing you up. You have grown like a beautiful rose in the garden, in favour of people and of God; you have not lost your chastity. Fate awaits you at the altar. You must promise now to obey your husband. We pray God to cover your road with happiness."

Standing on a white cloth, Fialka bowed to the guests and to her parents, taking leave of her girlhood home. Overcome with emotion, she wept as she sank down on her knees before her mother to receive her blessing:

Mother mine, keep well! For now we two must part.
Say not that I've taken all, I pray you, have no fears.
Lo, upon the table I am leaving – tears!

Anton extended the loaf and touched Fialka's head with it lightly, as if saying in effect: "By the sweat of thy brow shalt thou earn thy bread. May'st thou never be wanting for bread." These bread ceremonies contained all the wisdom of the peasant and his philosophy of life, his love of the earth which is the mother and gives bread in return for hard toil.

All were deeply touched as Fialka, still weeping, kissed her mother's hands three times, and the musicians played the song of farewell in a minor key. Then Zenobia, with a flask of holy water, circled about her daughter, blessing her and the doors through which she had passed to begin a new life.

The wedding procession now got under way, as the guests clambered into the wagons and set off for the church, where the bridegroom and his retinue were already waiting. The countryside was beautiful that fall day, painted in the absolute blue and gold of a Manitoba autumn, as though decorated by a gigantic brush dipped in gilt and splashed over trees, grass, shrubs. In some fields, the stooks still stood about, like enchantresses in a circle. There was only enough breeze to fan the cheeks of the bride and lift her veil in a cloud of white net about her. Lilli, who had been left behind to help Zenobia with the dinner preparations, stood at the gate listening to the voice of Tamara as it came back to her, with such power that it could be heard by all the neighbours: "Blow, wind, on our young bride, let her hair fly free today beneath its scarlet band, because this night a shawl will hide it."

It did not seem long to Lilli before she heard the music of the returning procession, and she dashed out to meet them, tearing off her kitchen apron as she went. When Fialka stepped from the wagon, her younger brother Basil, with a wand in his hands, led the bride over the white cloth into the house where Zenobia had already seated herself, with a loaf in her hands. Fialka circled the table three times, then sat down to eat. The guests followed her example, while the musicians continued to play.

Lilli ran about with platters of pickled herrings, beet soup, stuffed cabbage, mushroom dumplings, poppy seed torte, beet relish and fig-stuffed rolls. There was one man, big, high-coloured, who sat at a table devouring a platterful of cabbage rolls as if afraid that they would disappear when he stopped. Beside him sat a pale, frightened girl of seventeen, whom he caressed with his greasy paw from time to time. Lilli watched this ill-matched couple for a few moments and then going up to Fialka asked,

"Who is that man, Fialka, eating so much cabbage?"

Fialka made a grimace of dislike and shrugged: "That is Simon Zachary. He does well by himself at weddings."

"But why does the girl look so frightened?" persisted Lilli.

"He wants to marry her."

"But you don't look like that."

Fialka gave her sister a pitying glance. "You see, Lilli, it is bad when the girl doesn't like the man. This Zachary has a bad reputation with women."

As Zachary suddenly pulled down the girl and forced his wet red lips upon her, Lilli shivered in the midst of the gaiety about her, and she thought, "What if for me, too, such a thing might come to be?"

From then on, the tempo of ceremonies accelerated. Led by the elder, one guest after another burst into song to wish the bride happiness, good health and prosperity, while in a recurrent refrain, the guests in chorus sang, "Many Happy Summers!" They mingled the querulous voices of old women with the gay voices of maidens, the shrill voices of children and the hoarse voices of old men. Some of the songs were traditional, some improvised, and there were dozens, in a kind of continuous performance, the elder interposing hi's, calls, good wishes at every interval.

The guests now stood in line to present their gifts, with Fialka's grandparents offering treasures – a marriage coffer of carved wood, porcelain in turquoise and brown design, and most admired gift of all – a gigantic coffee maker from Mr. MacTavish.

Fialka now came up to Lilli and said, "Lilli, I want you to have something; choose what you like best." Lilli looked at the gifts which Fialka spread before her and her eye was caught by a pair of coral earrings.

"The earrings?" asked Fialka, holding them up. They dangled, rosy-red, carved and beautiful with gold fastenings.

"Yes," whispered Lilli, her eyes glistening. "But what will Marko say?"

Fialka laughed, full of confidence: "He wants you to have something," she reassured her sister. "Here," she urged, fastening the earrings on Lilli's ears. "Come, look at yourself."

Lilli, feeling coquettish, stole a glance at the mirror and was amazed at the transformation in her appearance. Her face was flushed with the bloom of adolescence, her eyes appeared dark and enormous, her mouth fuller and of a richer colour; her hair, braided and twined with flowers, shone with a new gloss. Slowly Lilli passed her hands over her costume – her white linen blouse, her pleated blue skirt, her satin bodice. She looked down at her patent slippers; they were the first real shoes she had ever owned. On her face was an air of breathless expectancy, which had never been there before. "What has happened to me?" she wondered aloud. "You're growing up, Lilli," laughed Fialka. As the girl stood bemused before the mirror, she felt a light touch on her arm. It was Tamara. She smiled and whispered as she touched the earrings, "These are right for you, Lilli. They are your style."

As young girls suddenly in one day bridge the gap from childhood to girlhood, so too Lilli on this wedding day. She was partly puzzled, partly delighted at her new powers, scarcely knowing yet how to handle them. If she could only stay where she was, at that delightful age, and prolong for a while the day of awakening and self-discovery!

Meanwhile, the colours of the costumes – wine, green, yellow, scarlet, blue, swung like a rainbow before MacTavish, the pattern changing constantly at every moment against the background of tapestries, towels and pictures on the walls. The wide accordion-pleated satin skirts of the girls undulated in spirals according to the dance, and the recurring note seemed to be a bright blue shade. There was a great deal of this bright blue – in Granny's shawl, in Lilli's skirt, in the bead embroideries on the women's blouses. Another brilliant note was the breastplate of gold coins worn by the woman Tamara. Her entire chest was covered by coins, about seventy-five of them, and great hoop earrings of gold dangled in her ears. The third strong colour note was provided by the yellow boots of Fialka, which attracted the attention of all, since no other woman possessed such a pair. The hand-made boots symbolized for MacTavish a vanishing world. It was possibly the last time these boots would dance in their proper surroundings; they were like actors playing their last role. Each guest had some article of dress which indicated the intrusion of the modern world – store-bought shoes, or silk stockings, or machine-made shirts, or mail-order dresses. The schoolteacher stood beside the window and looked out at a neighbouring field where he could see a thresher as it hummed through a field of wheat. This was a new rhythm which was making anachronistic the rhythm within, and in a sense, the rhythm of Fialka's yellow boots. "For these embroideries," thought he, "they will substitute the machine-made variety; for the hand-made costume, the dress from the mail-order house; for the peasant poetry of their ceremonies, the cut-and-dried responses of a civil ceremony."

Matters were reaching a giddy climax when the rumbling of wagon wheels outside the house announced the arrival of the bridegroom and his retinue. The ground quaked as the guests rushed from the house to meet the party. As they dismounted from their wagons, the groom and his attendants sang:

The golden feather has fallen,
And we are full of joy.
The young bride has won our hearts,
Come out, dear one, come out.

Marko, splendid in an embroidered sheepskin bolero, white shirt, dark trousers, and six-inch scarlet wool belt, rushed to the doorway where Fialka stood, but she eluded him and tried to escape, defended by the members of her own party against Marko's young brigands from a far country. Some of her friends urged her to surrender, but she still fought, protesting, "No, I won't leave my home." This act of the wedding ceremonies was viewed by MacTavish with particular interest, as he knew it was a relic of ancient times when kidnapping of the bride – to avoid paying a ransom – was an accepted tradition in courtship. He was not surprised when the strength of Marko's party finally prevailed over the protests of the bride and she was borne, still struggling, into the house and placed on the knees of the seated bridegroom. To placate the bride's family, a "ransom" of a hunting knife was paid to Fialka's younger brother.

The time had come for Fialka to surrender the wreath of her maidenhood. When the bridemaidens had removed the wreath, they put on her head a flowered blue wool shawl and tied it behind her head in a knot. Fialka covered her face with her hands, as if overcome with modesty while the married women jeered, "You are now a married woman; you belong to the women's union. No longer may you wear flowers in your hair, as a young girl wears them." Once Fialka had assumed the shawl of wifehood, the maiden's wreath became the property of the bridemaidens. One by one they stepped forward and donned the wreath with such remarks as, "How do I look, girls?" or, "Do you think the bride's wreath will become me?" Each was seized by Marko and twirled about on the floor for a few turns, while the elder called out, "Play, musicians, play, and you, black-browed maidens, dance and sing for us. Play lightly, musicians, until the feet of our maidens ache from dancing."

The bridemaidens had all danced when a new candidate appeared for the wreath. This was Lilli. "Let me try it on," she begged, stretching out her hand for it. "You are too young," demurred Zenobia, but public opinion was against her. "Let the young sister have her chance, too!" Wearing the wreath proudly, she began to dance with her head high, shrugged her shoulders, winked at her partner, clashed her heels with a firm click, pointed her toes and stamped with authority. The tickle of Marko's moustache against her cheek gave her a funny kind of thrill. "Look at her dance!" commented the guests as they made way for her whirling figure. "The fiddler will have to give up sooner than she." The young men exchanged compliments: "Small but fine," others asked Zenobia, "Where have you been keeping this one?" and still others admired her spirit, "That one is full of life – she needs a young man to tame her!"

At last the hour had arrived for Fialka to be taken to Marko's home, and his attendants gathered around him and sang:

The maiden, wearing on her brow,
The wifely shawl, comes with us now.

Going up to her marriage coffer, they lifted it and carried it out to the wagon, which was outside. "Come with us," urged Fialka as Lilli appeared. She hesitated, but when the musicians cried out in protest, "We must have the little singer with us," she could not resist, and climbed into their wagon.

The whole procession moved off down the road, the lanterns on each wagon flickering in the dark countryside like a convention of glowworms, while the sky was lit with stars and a big copper moon hung low and full. The laughter of the young people mingled with the rumble of the wagons and the music of the players, while in some wagons the guests still sang and pounded their feet, and clapped. The great eyes of the widow Tamara gleamed by the light of the lantern which fell upon her face and on her breastplate of coins. Unconscious of the stares directed at her by the men, she sang on, as if she were trying to express something, or re-living the days of her courtship and marriage. "How she sings!" murmured the guests as they followed her lead and sang out with great intensity:

Light up the road, O moon,
So that we shall not lose our way,
So that we may not lose the bride.

PART FOUR
Dancing Boots, Peasant Boots

1
WATCHERS OF THE
PASCHAL NIGHT
❧

IT WAS some months later, in spring, with the memory of
Fialka's wedding already faded from the minds of village
gossips, when Lilli hurried across the pied fields, carrying a
basket of eggs in one hand and a bunch of pussy willows in the
other. The church bells were ringing, new bells which had
arrived only a week ago from Europe, and already they had
been christened by the priest, Michael, Mary and Matthew, and
a plaque placed beneath them reading, "Let them ring to the
glory of God." This Easter would be different, thought Lilli,
this Easter she was fourteen, she would be admitted to the
company of maidens at the spring games, she would wear the
yellow boots.

When she entered the house, the kitchen was all in a
bustle, Zenobia was baking the Easter loaf, which smelled of
saffron, spices, raisins, and the sixteen eggs which she had put
into it. Granny Yefrosynia sat at a table decorating Easter eggs.
She had before her pots of vari-coloured dyes, including a
beautiful russet dye made from the skins of Spanish onions.
There were also pens, a candle, and a pan of melted beeswax.

Lilli put the pussy willows in a porcelain vase which she
placed on the table for the Easter meal, then came over to
watch her grandmother. "Like a little carpet," she said as she
picked up one of the eggs. "How do you make such beautiful
designs, Granny?"

"Watch me as I work," replied the old lady. She inspected the eggs first to see if they were white and unspotted, then she washed them and put them in a warm spot, for wax does not cling to cold eggs.

"You read an egg like a book," said Granny, picking up the pen and dipping it several times into the wax to try it. "Into your design you put your wish – love, luck, good health." Holding the egg lightly in her left hand, so that she could turn it round, she wrote the design, working away from herself. As she worked, Granny related to the children some legends regarding Easter eggs. "An egg – that is new life. When spring comes, everything awakes. The egg breaks the shell and brings a new creature to life. Mother Earth is free from the chains of Old Man Frost. The sun dances and brings new warmth."

Granny placed the finished egg into a warm oven to melt the wax, then continued talking as she selected another egg: "The Holy Mother painted beautiful eggs for Pilate to redeem her son. The Three Marys, when they went to visit Christ's grave, brought eggs for the guards, to gain entry."

When Granny had finished several eggs, she spread them out on a plate so that the children could admire them. There were steeples, oak leaves, windmills, rabbit's ears. "What do all these signs mean?" inquired Lilli, as she examined one. "A horseshoe or oak leaf denotes good luck," replied her grandmother. "Sickles, rakes and windmills stand for the work in the field, which commences with spring." There was not a question Granny couldn't answer! "And why do people exchange eggs?" persisted Lilli. Granny winked an eye: "A young girl who wishes to marry gives a boy an egg. If he likes her, he will give her one. Otherwise, he must return it, for the egg might be bewitched." Remembering that this year Lilli would have the privilege of exchanging eggs with her sweetheart, she offered: "Here, I'll pick an egg for you – you can give it to your chosen boy."

For the Paschal Night celebration at the church, Lilli was

permitted to wear the peasant holiday costume which her mother had brought over from the old country, and which was taken out for display only on festive occasions. The jumper was of heavy rainbow-striped satin in wine and black; the shirt was heavily bead-embroidered, and the white sheepskin bolero embroidered with great scarlet roses and decorated with small tufts of black wool and metallic discs. She wound the wide hand-woven woollen belt, yards long, several times about her waist, with the ends dangling in tassels, and put on her head the tiny black satin pillbox above a wreath of flowers with long ribbons streaming to her waist in back. Last of all, she pulled on the yellow boots which Fialka had worn at her wedding. As she looked into the mirror to adjust her cap, she was well-pleased with her appearance.

The Paschal Night had arrived, beautiful, radiant. Stars lit up the great dome of prairie sky. As the Landash family approached the church in their wagon, Lilli could see a circle of wagons outside and oxen lying down before them. People from the village, people from miles around were arriving in throngs, and alighting from the wagons. There was a clatter of wagon wheels, lowing of oxen, ringing of high young voices. A bonfire had been lit on the grounds of the church, as the early spring night was cool. The worshippers gathered in small groups in the churchyard and about the bonfire, forming a brilliant picture as the flames lit up the scarlet embroideries and glittering wreaths of the young women, shone on necklaces and coin breastplates, illuminated the white linen smocks and shining leather boots of the young men.

"How beautiful it is!" exclaimed Lilli, catching her breath. She jumped down from the wagon, and ran to join one of the groups, determined to be on her own this night. A line of choristers bearing candles moved across the churchyard and circled about the bonfire, chanting a song of resurrection. From the moving throng, constantly shifting about the flames, arose a glorious Easter hymn:

Christ has risen! Rejoice, children,
Run in the field and meadow,
Gather herbs and flowers,
Weave a wreath for Christ.

The excitement increased almost to a frenzy as the throng, caught in the spell of the music, shouted, "Alleluia! Alleluia!" Then, dividing again into groups, each sang its own song, every song different, like so many choirs, all singing a different hymn, yet all blending together. As they moved about with their long candles, they appeared like clusters of fireflies in the darkness outside the great central blaze. Alleluia! Alleluia! The great colourful mass, moving constantly, created patterns, never the same, subject to light and shade, as the flames lit up faces, costumes, oxen and wagons, and the laughter of children resounded in the chill spring air.

Lilli was everywhere, singing her heart out, everywhere welcomed as the crowd caught her up, made her one of them, impelled her through the tumult of worshippers. "Like bird singing all night, she does not tire," admired one granny as she gazed into Lilli's enraptured face, but Lilli had already moved away, following the crowd, singing with them, mingling with people from the farms and village, like old friends.

Now she entered the church and caught her breath at the sight. Hundreds of tapers, at the altar, in the chandelier, in the hands of the worshippers flickered in points of light to illumine the way to Jerusalem. The altar was naively and joyously decorated with paper flowers, embroidered linen towels and sacred pictures. A representation of the tomb had been built, with three Easter loaves upon it, each embellished with a paper rose. Before the tomb were two soldiers on guard. An old grandmother was painfully crawling in the direction of the wooden cross, dragging herself to the holy crucifix to kiss it. Through the thickly packed crowd, all standing and singing, clouds of incense drifted from the candelabra in the hands of the priest. Lilli could see through the mist of incense the gold and blue embroidered vestments of the priest as he passed solemnly from the altar and then back, chanting to the response of the people. The choir singers in the loft were tirelessly relating the story of the crucifixion, led by the falsetto of the tenor, while the audience, with bowed heads, joined in the harmony. At first the tempo was slow, mournful, dragged from the hearts of a people who had known centuries of oppression; at the same time, it had a kind of healing effect on the hearts of the congregation. They seemed borne into a trance-like state, where the emotions were elevated into ecstasy, and there was evidence of actual suffering as the crowd sobbed, dropped to its knees, groaned in their search for the crucified Saviour. The torments of Christ were shared by the people; they mourned as if for someone newly dead. The feeling of drama was heightened by the constant motion – the crossing of head, shoulder and chest at the mention of the Holy Trinity; the rising and falling of the audience. Everywhere faces reflected this primitive emotion: the multicoloured shawls of the women, scattered throughout the church, moved constantly in a shifting mosaic; the faces of the children, at first fresh, became drooping and wilted as the evening wore on.

Beside Lilli stood an old man, wistful in the midst of the throng, regarding with age-bleared eyes the blazing scene. He turned to Lilli, and the pathos in his glance touched her heart. "I was thinking, little daughter," he confided to her, "Whether I would see another Easter on this earth. Already I hear a voice behind me, 'Why do you delay, why do you delay?'" Not to see another Easter! To have this beauty blotted out of one's consciousness! How glad she was to be young!

Then gladness and excitement swept in waves over the throng. Bowing as the worshippers did, Lilli prostrated herself, touching her forehead to the cold hard floor, rejoicing or weeping as the crowd rejoiced or wept. Something greater than herself, something incredibly ancient had entered Lilli's spirit and filled it with a sense of mystery old as the human race. Light and spring had returned to the earth, the fields awaited the plough, all life was resurrected.

The souls of the worshippers shed their guilt, fears and sorrows in this mass purification. Lifted above themselves, they forgot their days of black labour. Faces about Lilli gleamed in unearthly exultation; the traces of serfdom were obliterated in a sudden access of freedom. "Forgive, neighbour," each approached the other to ask forgiveness.

What had been closed up in Lilli, now suddenly burst forth: her body trembled, her singing swelled in a crescendo, and the people about her caught fire from her. She was transported, so that even Zenobia could hardly recognize her own daughter.

> Lord have mercy,
> Lord have mercy,
> Lord have mercy!

The chanting voices rose and fell like the raising and lowering of the cross, and above them arose one, Lilli's, throbbing with grief so intense that all the worshippers were drawn after it. Alleluia! The swelling chords thundered. Eyes alight, singing rapturously, Lilli advanced to the altar, her voice increasing in a fortissimo, she herself intoxicated by the lights, incense, music, colour, until ecstasy shook her limbs.

Outside, the tolling of bells reminded the worshippers that the body of the dead Christ reposed within the tomb.

"Christ Has Risen!" the signal was given at midnight for the resurrection. Cries broke out from all, "He has risen indeed." Kisses were exchanged as the worshippers greeted each other with the news of the resurrection. The polyphonic chants rose and fell like the waves of the sea.

"Christ has risen!" exclaimed Lilli. She turned to her neighbour and they embraced. Then through the throng she went, moving from one to another, embracing and exclaiming as she went, "Christ has risen!"

Suddenly the attention of the congregation was distracted and the singing of the choir faltered. The door opened and framed in the doorway stood the majestic figure of Tamara. She was dressed in a gown of dark red silk, with gold earrings in her ears. Her exotic appearance astounded the congregation and the service almost came to a halt as all gazed incredulously at this woman. Tamara glanced proudly, almost arrogantly about her, and then advancing a few steps, she made the sign of the cross and fell to her knees. The choir hurriedly took up its song and Tamara joined in, her powerful voice dominating the whole assembly. From all over the church, an audible murmur of protest was heard, mostly from the women, as rumours had been growing over the countryside that Tamara by witchcraft had recently caused a pregnant woman to abort.

"What is such an unhallowed one as she doing in this holy place?" a woman's voice demanded shrilly, so that all heard.

The remark reached Tamara's ears, and she turned white, but maintained her stand defiantly until the end of the service. As she turned to go, Lilli came up to her and bowing, greeted her, "I hope you are in good health."

Tamara turned, the gaze of her strange eyes on Lilli, and said, "And you, little one, don't you flee from me, also?"

"No," replied Lilli, "for at Easter time we seek fellowship of our neighbours, we do not flee from them."

"Brave heart!" sighed Tamara, and her dark eyes were filled with bitterness as she noticed, without acknowledgment, the looks of scorn cast upon her by the women. "With this heart, Lilli, the world will one day be yours."

Meanwhile all the candles in the church blazed up and the congregation, as though with one accord, were swept outdoors. "Christ has risen!" shouted the people as they swarmed out of the church bearing crosses and banners, led by the priest and his acolytes and deacons, bearing crosses and banners, and circled in a procession three times about the church, as if searching for the risen Christ. The fresh air touched their faces and the stars gleamed like huge lamps.

As the night waned, and a silvery streak in the sky heralded the approach of dawn, the women spread embroidered towels outside the church, and placed their Easter baskets upon them. These baskets, arranged in two rows, were filled with apples, sweet ham, garlic sausage, horseradish, eggs. The women bent over them, arranging the embroidered linens that covered them, showing the food to the best advantage. There were small straw baskets filled with candy eggs for the children. It was a beautiful sight to look down from the end of the row and see the baskets, pink, green and yellow straw, heaped with various colours, like a border of flowers forming a path down which came the priest to sprinkle the food with holy water.

Lilli helped Zenobia spread their basket on its embroidered cloth. She looked eagerly at the displays of other families. One woman in particular aroused the envy of all by uncovering a little suckling pig, all nicely browned and glazed, with his tail twisted into a curl, and a horseradish stuck in his mouth. "Look, mother, the little pig," Lilli pulled at Zenobia's sleeve. Petey, awestruck, regarded the pig with popping eyes. "Where did she get that little brown pig?" he cried, but Zenobia rebuked stiffly, "It is not seemly to examine the food of other people." Nevertheless, she stole a glance at the little pig. She was well-pleased, however, with her own display, which included a cottage cheese mixed with cream, sugar, butter and raisins, in the form of a pyramid with the top cut off and with crosses moulded on each side.

In the morning, after a sleepless but glorious night, the worshippers hitched their oxen to the wagons, and set off, their exclamations of delight and shouts of "Christ has risen!" re-echoing over the prairie. Lilli, sitting half-buried in hay at the back of the wagon, the basket of food between her feet, and still holding in her hand the stub of a candle, turned her face up to the morning, not sleepily, but glowing from within. Everything was etched with brightness on the prairie landscape: the trees, lightly rimmed with spring frost, the skies as though re-created for the resurrection, the earth bursting from its snowy prison, dotted over with small green shoots. The air had a faint fragrance of flowers imprisoned beneath the ground, of pine tree needles, of crocus blooms ready to burst.

"The sun has painted the world pink and purple like an Easter egg!" exclaimed Petey, as he gazed with chin propped over the edge of the wagon at the gaudy splotches of sunrise. He chirruped happily, now imitating the bird calls which arose from fence posts, now the creaking of the wagon wheels.

"How pure the soul feels!" observed Zenobia, as she pulled Petey down by the smock.

Lilli turned her head back to look at the small church on the hill, her eyes almost blinded as the silver dome glittered in the morning sun. On the road leading from the church she caught glimpses of other wagons, filled with men and women in costume, like great loads of flowers going off to market. In the distance, a tenor voice was still singing, tireless, and it was like a hymn to the rising sun, while other voices here and there merged into an accompaniment, as though greeting the advent of the spring to the prairie. Lilli leaned her head against the side of the wagon and hummed to herself, tears streaming down her cheeks, tears of fatigue and joy, tears at the beauty of the man's voice which still, as they rode away, could be heard in faint snatches on the wind, as though it had risen from the earth, like the voice of nature itself.

When they reached home, all sat about the table for the Easter breakfast – eggs, cottage cheese with raisins, ham, fruit compote, tea. Zenobia placed a piece of consecrated Easter loaf at each place. As Anton blessed the gifts of God, all crossed themselves, making the wish, "To live in happiness and health." There was little conversation, for all were tired and soon left the table. The children washed in a basin of water into which Zenobia had put coins and an Easter egg, for luck. Lilli stood by with a clean linen towel and wiped each face as it emerged like a rose from the cold water.

Now all lay down to sleep, and a quiet, golden peaceful time ensued, not a living soul could be seen anywhere. Only Lilli remained awake, to clean the table so that not a crumb was left. She stood briefly at the window, looking out at the sparkling landscape, to which the Manitoba spring had come with such a rush. "I shall never forget this night as long as I live," she thought. Her mind burst into pictures, always changing, like a kaleidoscope. She was excited, and thought she could not sleep, but when she lay down, the feather bed of sleep soon covered her mind.

2
THE EASTER GAMES
❦

HOURS later, she was awakened by the ringing of bells. "The Easter games!" she thought and arose quickly. This time was devoted to young people. She wrapped a few Easter eggs in a towel along with an Easter loaf and set across the fields, meeting on her way many girls and boys in their bright costumes. They greeted her, "Christ has risen!" and she replied, "He has risen indeed!" Already, she thought, she was accepted in their company. When she arrived at the churchyard, the young people were streaming in for the Easter games, the girls with flowers in their hair, the men with wide embroidered belts. There was some modern finery, also, purchased through the mail-order catalogue – straw hats with ribbons and flowers, red and blue coats and patent high-heeled slippers. All the young people milled about, dancing, talking, exchanging eggs, admiring each other's hats and frocks. Song arose, but this time it was a song of spring, sung in the fresh young voices of girls and boys.

The sight of all these young people in the yard, dancing in a circle like the sun around the earth, excited Lilli. She looked about for a familiar face. From behind, a hand nudged her. "Happy Easter, Lilli."

She turned around to face Vanni Karmaliuk, radiant in a white blouse. Fresh, with hair so gold and slick it gleamed like a freshly-applied coat of gilt, his smile aroused a tremor in Lilli's heart. She was speechless with admiration.

Vanni held out an egg. "My egg against yours."

"Be careful!" Lilli warned. "I have only big, strong eggs." She danced happily from one foot to another. Now she was really part of the crowd, now she, too, had a partner.

"Pouf!" sneered Vanni. "Your eggs are as small as you."

Lilli took from her napkin her biggest egg, on which some hen had expended a mighty effort. Vanni blinked. His mouth dropped open. "Out of what chicken came that egg?" he demanded.

Lilli's eyes danced. "You are afraid you will lose?"

"No," faltered the boy. He looked again at Lilli's egg, and knew beforehand what the outcome would be, in the battle of her giant and his pygmy. Each grasped his egg firmly and waited.

"Now?" asked Vanni. He shut his eyes as he prepared for the blow.

"Now," agreed Lilli, and struck her egg firmly against Vanni's, which cracked.

"I win, I win," exclaimed Lilli with glee. "You have to give me your egg."

Vanni pretended to be angry. "You have a stone in your egg, I think." He went on, with assumed malice, "That egg is a *smolianka*, a tar-filled egg."

"Only bad boys have tar-eggs," replied Lilli. Then she softened, became coy. "I have something for you – a special egg. Granny Yefrosynia made it. Wait till you see! You will not be sorry about your miserable little egg."

Vanni brightened all over his face like a new copper. He held out his hand. "Let me see." Granny's reputation as an Easter egg painter was well-known.

Lilli brought out her choicest specimen, which had a tiny, intricate design stippled on it, making it look like a miniature Persian tapestry.

"So beautiful!" exclaimed Vanni, as he took it in his hand and traced it wonderingly with his finger. "What is this design, Lilli?"

"Pine tree with star and moon, Vanni," explained Lilli. "That means that spring has come, and you will have good luck this year."

The two stood looking at the egg, turning it round and round and admiring it. "Granny is an *artiste*, Vanni. She makes only ten eggs every year. This one took two days to make."

"I will keep it always." Vanni hid the egg carefully in his pocket. Then he put his hands on Lilli's shoulders and looked into her eyes. "You know what that means, Lilli?"

"What?" Her eyelids were lowered. As if she didn't know!

"That you are my girl." Vanni's voice was husky with emotion. Lilli traced a circle with her toe in the earth. She said nothing, but her heart beat in big thuds. Could Vanni hear them? She put her hand to her heart to muffle the sound.

"That maybe we will marry some day," Vanni continued softly. He pressed Lilli's arm, and she withdrew. "Do you turn away from me, little one?" There was a note of reproach in his voice.

"No."

"Then what have you to say?"

Lilli gulped. "If all the others do it, we must, too."

They laughed, ha, ha, ha, at first with some timidity, then as new courage entered their hearts, their free, wild laughter rang out and could be heard all over the churchyard, so that many stopped to listen to them. Vanni seized Lilli's hand and squeezed it. "Don't forget, Lilli. Now you are mine."

The compact sealed, they stood, rocking their joined hands in a semi-circle. About them, boys and girls were holding hands dancing, merrymaking. Some youths had water sprays and wooden baskets holding water which they sprinkled on the girls' necks, as though watering plants and encouraging them to blossom. "Now, what shall we do?" asked Lilli at last. There were so many possibilities – dance, walk about the church, admire the eggs of others?

"Let's ring the bells," suggested Vanni. Lilli's eyes lit up. "Oh, that would be wonderful, Vanni!" she exclaimed, and they ran over to join the line before the belfry. All afternoon, people had been going up into the belfry to ring the bells, so that they had been chiming over the countryside for hours. When they had climbed to the top, Lilli looked out of the belfry window and saw far out over the countryside. "People can hear us way down there," she said, pointing into the valley. Vanni, who had seized the ropes, exerted himself until his face was red, then he collapsed on the floor, panting, Lilli beside him, breathing deeply. The ropes were seized by two other youngsters. When they had recovered their breath, Vanni and Lilli climbed down the stairs, to find that they were in the midst of a long chain of dancers, who seized their hands and dragged them along, interweaving in a crooked dance, like the disorderly movement of the clouds in the heavens, moving in the direction of a solitary poplar, around which they wound in a continuous line. As they danced, they sang:

All is blooming everywhere,
Beauty in the meadows lies,
Joy is in the fields and air,
In the woods is song.

As Vanni and Lilli finally broke away from the circle, the boy noticed a lonely figure walking slowly in the direction of the cemetery. "Look, Lilli, the widow Tamara," he said, calling her attention to the woman. "Father says she is witch, but I think she is only a lonely woman."

"So I, too, think," agreed Lilli, and her eyes were full of sympathy as she looked after the woman.

Before they parted, Lilli extracted a promise from Vanni to meet her early on Midsummer morn. "Don't forget," she warned him, "I have something to give you that day."

After Vanni left, Lilli looked across to the cemetery, where Zenobia was kneeling at the grave of Lilli's older sister, dead in childhood. She noticed almost at once the widow Tamara, a solitary figure in black, kneeling before the row of crosses beneath which were buried her dead. She prayed in great agitation of spirit, making the sign of the cross many times, and prostrating herself with each sign. Due to the malicious stories which had circulated concerning her among the people, most of the farm women withdrew from her and made spiteful remarks in whispers not too low for her to overhear.

When Zenobia was otherwise occupied, Lilli took the opportunity to run off and head in the direction of Tamara. She touched the woman lightly upon the shoulder as she knelt before her graves. "I have brought a candle for the soul of the dead," she whispered, and placed the candle upon one of the graves.

Tamara's face lit up. "Are you here, little one?" she asked with unaccustomed tenderness. "I always come here at spring," she confided to Lilli, her face resuming its burden of grief. "For it is at spring that the souls of the dead are closest to us, and it is then that we may communicate with them and make intercession for them."

The loneliness of the woman made her appear strangely defenceless, despite her pride and courage, and Lilli watched with sombre, pitying eyes as Tamara bowed and prayed over her graves while the other women directed hostile glances at her. Dropping to her knees, Lilli prayed fervently, hoping to alleviate the torment of the woman. She was stricken by the sight of the three small graves. So young to leave the earth!

When the two finally arose to go, the cemetery was almost deserted, and the clouds had deepened to a leaden hue. As Tamara went off across the prairie to her home by the swamp, Lilli stood looking after that solitary black figure, wishing to call after it, regretting that she had no word of consolation for that desperate, insatiable grief.

3
ENCHANTERS OF
MIDSUMMER EVE
❦

ON MIDSUMMER NIGHT, Lilli was awake long after the family had gone to bed. When she saw that all were asleep, she arose quietly and tiptoed out of the house, carrying a lantern. Walking in the direction of the creek, her footsteps scarcely disturbed the stillness of the summer night. Her body, lithe as a young birch, quivered with anticipation, her bare legs shone white against the dark grass, her eyes gleamed. She felt the magic of midsummer all around her. Overhead the moon, like a white enchantress, glimmered in the star-swept Milky Way, while in the slough the frogs, sitting in the soft warm mud, poked out their heads and sang – one always on two notes, as if chording an accompaniment, the others elaborating on the melody like a song. "Those frogs know what they are doing," thought Lilli as she listened. The woods seemed full of eerie voices, singing songs created by shadows of long-forgotten ancestors, as if to the high pitch of the *tsymbaly*, thrumming its primitive tune while the forms of young people flitted among the trees. In the old country, her mother had told her, boys and girls on this night had sought the magic blooming fern which would bestow a special virtue on the finder for the coming year. "And then, Lilli," her mother had related, "we would light bonfires and sing all night until morning." Was that a shimmering echo she heard now of those old songs, not merely the creak of the wind in the leaves, or the scream of a bird?

At the bank of the creek she stopped and put down her lantern, then began to look for flowers, which grew thick there. Her pupils dilated, she loved the night and felt at home in it. When she had a handful of blooms, she pressed them to her face breathing in their fragrance, then flung them into the creek singing, "Float, my wreath, with the wave's swift flowing, straight to the window of my love! Float to the heart of the one I love and bring good fortune with thee." To the rhythm of the dreamy music, she watched the flowers as they floated down the creek, in the direction of Karmaliuk's farm. When they were out of sight, she felt in her pocket for the lump of sugar which she had placed there. Kneeling by the creek, she held the lump beneath the current, speaking the words which would charm it, and then removing the sugar, she placed it in a piece of paper.

In the morning, Lilli arose early and placing some food in a basket, she then wrapped up the yellow boots in a parcel and went out to meet Vanni. Fleecy clouds, like pink cotton balls, rolled over the skies. From somewhere on the fields, the song of the meadowlark burst forth, the bright, sunlit phrase followed by a descending cascade, "like sunshine and rain," thought Lilli.

She met Vanni by a poplar bluff and they stood for a few moments looking down into the valley, which was shaped like a natural amphitheatre. "You look fresh in that white blouse and red skirt, Lilli," said Vanni, "like a gypsy."

"And you, too, Vanni, are fine today in your new trousers." She brought out a gift she had prepared for him, an embroidered red belt which he put on immediately over his navy trousers. Then she greeted him as "John," for this was the day of St. John the Baptist. "Because you, too, are an Ivan," said Lilli, "and this is your name day," referring to the fact that Vanni was simply a childish corruption of Ivan.

"I have something for you, too, Lilli." Vanni gave her a jar of buckwheat honey, a curious plant, and a transparent green stone which he had found on the banks of the river. "This stone reminds me of you," he said as they examined its curious brown spots; it was like looking into the depths of a pond.

"Why, Vanni?"

"Your eyes are like that, Lilli – green at the bottom, with brown specks."

They sat down in a nest of thick green grass, all covered with clover, beneath a poplar tree, and Lilli opened a basket which she had brought, containing poppy seed loaf, hard-boiled eggs, and cottage cheese, all wrapped in a white cloth. Vanni disappeared into the woods and came back carrying a dozen strawberries in a plantain leaf. He had dipped them into the creek and they were cool and moist. Lilli broke the poppy seed loaf, spread it with honey, shared the hard-boiled eggs. As they ate, Vanni reminisced: "I remember the day Mr. Mac gave you a new name, Lilli." He bit into an egg and went on. "You sat, big eyes happy, everything new, you were making voyage like Christopher Columbus to America. That was first time I liked a girl, Lilli. When I saw you, I knew you were for me. . . ." He reached over and helped himself to the cottage cheese.

"There was never such a spring!" sighed Lilli as she licked the honey off her lips. School was now, she thought, a closed chapter; she would never become a book-reader, as she had hoped. They watched as the breeze tore off the curly grey mops of dandelions, leaving them bald and shuddering.

"This is for you, Vanni." She took out the sugar lump and gave it to him. "Be careful how you eat it," she teased slyly. "There's magic in it."

"I know how you girls put sugar under water," replied Vanni, holding the lump to tease her. "If I swallow this, will I fall in love with you?"

"You are afraid?" challenged Lilli.

"Look – " He opened his mouth wide and popped the sugar in. "Now, you see, I am yours, all yours."

They stretched their limbs, yawned, smiled. Their souls were sunlit. They listened, breath sucked in, as if to catch the processes of nature in the act. "You can almost hear the petals open on the flowers," said Lilli. She wrinkled her nose in the sun. "Sometimes I wish I could walk around all day, doing nothing, only looking at the clouds and trees."

"All that is in you, Lilli," replied Vanni. "Oh, the clouds fast hurrying across the skies, the wind jumping and dancing like kid playing tricks, sometimes hiding in big bunches of foxtail grass which wave with light in their hairs, all shiny, different colours, green, pink, gold, and then a meadowlark flies to fence post and all of a sudden he is singing and I feel he is singing for me alone. I stand there, all around me the whole prairie is full of life, each tiny thing is busy, the earth is making music, the grass is moving, moving, as far as eye can see, and I feel that is my prairie – my prairie and my meadowlark." He turned to her and looked down into her eyes, continuing in a voice husky with emotion, "Such feeling I have when I hear you sing, Lilli."

She listened to his words, a dreamy smile on her face.

"Exactly how I feel, too, Vanni. That prairie is me, and I am prairie, and everything sings with me."

Lilli now took out her yellow boots and put them on.

"What beautiful boots, Lilli, yellow and red. Where did you get them?"

Lilli told Vanni how her mother had danced in those boots in the old country. "And that is how she met father, and they danced all night together. Think, maybe they would never come together, except for these boots."

"Let's dance in them now, there's room to go as far as you want."

They jumped up and began to dance, singing the while:

Boots, boots,
My yellow boots!
How are you charming me,
Where are you spinning me,
My yellow boots!
When music gay begins,
Squeaking like violins,
Singing like mandolins,
My yellow boots!
Over the streets you go,
How far I do not know,
Dancing both high and low,
My yellow boots!

Tired at last, they flung themselves down on the earth and panted with happiness. "Do you think we will always be so happy, Lilli?" asked Vanni.

Lilli's face was troubled as she turned to him. "I don't know, Vanni," she said slowly. "Your father and my father have bad feeling. Father say last week he is going to law with your father, something about land."

Vanni seized her hand fiercely and squeezed as though he would not let go. "Let the old people have their quarrels. You and I, Lilli, will make a good life together in this new country."

They sat for a moment, cheek to cheek, hardly daring to breathe. "Let me play your pipe, Vanni." Lilli reached into the boy's pocket and putting it to her lips, blew notes to create musical portraits of people.

"How is the deacon?" Vanni demanded.

Lilli played bizarre phrases, pompous droll notes, until Vanni laughed. "Exactly the way he walks and talks, in big, fat tones, as if he wanted to say, "How important I am! Look, everybody, at me! ha, ha!" The two rolled on the ground with merriment.

"Here is Lizzie Schwartz." Lilli named a notorious shrew. The shrill, peevish notes were repeated over and over. "Lizzie sounds like a mad hen," commented Vanni. "Now, let's hear Petey."

A merry lilting song poured out, followed by a march, then a short spurt of rough little barks, as of bravado.

"And me?" demanded Vanni. "How do I sound to you?"

Lilli hesitated, then played first an air like the tune of a shepherd, followed by a few notes of boyish laughter, and ending in a tender phrase, as of a love song. Vanni smiled. "Yes, that is me," reflected the boy, chewing on a blade of grass. "And you, Lilli?"

Lilli played the song that tormented her, a questing, a reaching out, ascending, then ceasing abruptly, as on a question mark.

"You are looking for something, Lilli, what?" Vanni touched her hand.

Lilli turned her head aside. "I don't know, Vanni. . . . Something. . . ." She stopped, then sprang up and cried, "Let's go find it."

Vanni ran after her, half humorously wooing and beseeching. Lilli, fleet of foot, eluded him, mocking and enticing. It was like a dance, the two racing about the valley, Vanni playing on his pipe, Lilli answering with a snatch of song. The prairie roses, crushed underfoot, made the air fragrant with perfume; the sunshine glittered on the striped gold coats of bees; the clouds drifted like feathers over the sky. Vanni played on his flute and Lilli replied, "Here I am, here I am." She took up the air and developed it, teasing him, enticing him over fields of clover and around haystacks, through fields of grain, feeling the silken swish against their bodies as they ran.

Then they stopped and laughed and Lilli approached the boy. Vanni laid his two hands tenderly on her hair and drew her to him and kissed her. They stood thus for a moment, hearts thudding with rapture, then separated, shyly and silently.

4
SWAMP FIRE
❦

DURING the months of July, August and September of that year Lilli was hired out by her father to work for a Swedish farmer of the district, as Anton required ready cash to assist in the purchase of a horse.

It was late in September, while working for the Svensons, that Lilli was sent some distance to summon a doctor, as the woman of the house had suddenly taken ill. On the way home, after her mission had been accomplished, a sudden storm arose and Lilli was driven out of her way into a desolate country near the swamp known as the Dead Land, because it was pocked with huge holes like craters, half-filled with water and the black ashy remains of forests.

As Lilli rode bareback through the storm on her pony, seizing his mane to prevent herself from slipping off, she knew she was in constant danger, for any slip might mean precipitation into a hollow of water eighteen to twenty feet deep. Whenever the pony bucked she cried aloud, scarcely able to see her way through the sheets of driving rain and the grey shadows obscuring the landscape. Water was all around her, and land so awesome in its wildness and immensity, that she felt her own smallness and insignificance, realizing that she might disappear that day without leaving a trace and nobody would ever know what had happened to her. A rising fear swelled in the girl's heart, but also exhilaration in the scene around her – the shuddering and lashing of tree tops as they bowed down and clawed at her; the rubbing of branches together, with their "skree-skree-skree" like an amateur fiddler playing a funeral march; the hissing of pine needles; the hoarse scream of the wind as it tore at leaves and scattered them – all this excitement of nature swept her along like thunderous music, and her heart pounded in rhythm. She exulted as she lifted her face to receive the pelting raindrops; she gasped and sobbed and laughed as the harmonies of the storm swept through her; she responded to the wild movement about her, so that she was one with the wind and rain and lightning, she was part of nature itself.

As she recognized the country in which she was lost, she recalled the stories she had heard concerning the will-o'the-wisp. On one occasion, a group of boys and girls were returning from a party, all happy and singing when all of a sudden a dead silence fell upon them and the horses stopped. The swamp fire appeared and the crowd sat motionless, not daring to talk, as the lights increased in size and seemed to approach them. Then the leader, aroused to action, whipped up the horses and raced furiously across the countryside. Behind them the swamp fire, like a gigantic jack o'lantern, bumped and danced and ran around the sky, then finally, as it reached the ground, evaporated into the night air.

The first time Lilli herself had seen the swamp light, it had appeared only as a small heart-shaped ball, like a lantern swung from the hand of some ghostly presence. Lilli, rooted to the spot, made the sign of the cross and began to repeat her prayers. The light faded to a dim glow and then vanished.

Thinking over these stories, Lilli rode on through the storm, until she saw ahead of her the dim light of a solitary cottage which she knew must be the home of the widow Tamara. Dismounting from her pony, she led it to the stable, and then knocked at the door of the cottage.

The door was opened by a woman tall as a man, with thick ropes of black hair coiled in a knot at the nape of her neck and a complexion like thick cream. Her black eyebrows met over her enormous dark eyes, a sign of witchcraft, according to the farm women. She had a sombre expression, as though she never smiled, and this was heightened by the dress of black wool whose only ornament was a heavy gold Byzantine cross. Her face was full of the sensuality one sees in beautiful women who have grown up in primitive surroundings. A wild imagination flashed from her eyes, was revealed in every motion of her body and every tone of her voice, which was not coarse as that of peasant women: there was a delicate modulation in it pleasing to the ear. Her manner, too, was gentle as she held out her hand to her guest: "Come in."

"I was riding home and got lost in the storm," explained Lilli as she stood within, her garments dripping. When the woman had helped her off with her wet clothes and given her a warm robe, Lilli looked about the house in amazement.

Although the widow lived alone, the table had been set for five persons, and candles were burning before the holy pictures. Every corner, every object was covered with some kind of embroidery or decoration, as Tamara was an accomplished seamstress. On the wall hung a tapestry: on the floor were woven tugs: the chest and furniture were of carved and inlaid wood. Beneath a glass globe on the sideboard was a curious object – a veiling of net intertwined with flowers. "So beautiful!" murmured Lilli, wishing she had liberty to examine every object there.

The two regarded each other for a while, Lilli trembling beneath that penetrating gaze, and yet her fear had something pleasurable in it, the premonition of a disturbing experience to come. At last Tamara exclaimed, "The same eyes as Dunia, the very same eyes!" She seized Lilli's arms and looked hard at her, examining her features as though trying to identify them, trying to convince herself that Lilli had been sent to her to compensate for the loss of her child, now dead these many years.

"You are afraid of me?" she demanded, pressing the girl's

arms with such strength that she winced.

"No, no!" protested Lilli with warmth. She did not try to free her arm: instead, she looked up at the woman's face, trying to convey something of the pity she felt. Tamara in turn recognized that Lilli was not a common farm girl, she discerned in Lilli taste and instincts of an unusual sort; there was pride and sensitivity in the girl. It was this sympathy that made her even more desperate in her attempts to make friends with Lilli.

"People have spoken ill things of me?" the widow persisted, bitterness eating into her face like acid. Due to the gossip to which she had been recently subjected, she had lost much of her poise. Recalling her majestic appearance at Fialka's wedding, Lilli was shocked to see how her face had been stripped of pride, leaving it like a wilted rag. Witches in all times, thought Lilli, might have been superior women such as Tamara, amateur doctors or poets who, denied natural outlets, turned to perverted hatred of the community.

"What do they say of me?" queried the woman, and as Lilli still could not reply, she went on, "Do they say I am a witch?"

Lilli shook her head, knowing that this was a great disgrace to the woman. But she thought of the gossip she had heard: women of the district said that Tamara tied up cows' horns with cobwebs and prevented them from giving milk; that she had looked upon a pregnant woman and caused her to abort; that she held conversations with evil spirits from the swamp. People distrusted her because she had a deformity of the foot, because of her overgrown eyebrows, her house by the swamp, the deaths of her three children in an epidemic and the mysterious death of her husband. A woman who had suffered so much must surely be accursed!

Tamara's personal history was a tragic one. A worker on an Austrian estate where she had been employed as a seamstress had fallen in love with her and had brought her to Canada, to this lonely homestead near the swamp, where he had left her while he went to work on the railroad. She was not a common person, and could not adjust herself to the life of the farm women. After her husband was killed, she withdrew herself from the life of the community, with the exception of appearances at weddings and funerals. Her isolation gave rise to many malicious rumours; some even spoke of driving her from the community.

Lilli watched the face of the woman as she stood by the window and looked out over the swamp lands where the storm was abating. She seemed to be listening, and at the desolate look on her face, Lilli's heart contracted. She had heard the farm women relate that Tamara's husband had not been properly buried, since he had died in an explosion on the railway. Without proper burial, his spirit was doomed to wander disconsolate over the earth. Tamara continued to stare out of the window, as if she were looking for something.

"Sometimes the lights come," she murmured. "They are the souls of those unburied, yet dead. I have seen them walking through the swamps. . . ." The expression on her face became more intense as she mused, "I fear he is wandering along a dark road."

As Lilli listened to the woman's distracted speech, she realized that Tamara lived thus in constant communion with her dead, whose spirits she thought came to her at twilight from the swamps. Living alone with the memory of her dead family, she had become obsessed with their fate to such an extent that they replaced for her normal social intercourse with other members of the community. She herself was tonight sombre and brooding, "like one of the dead who walk the earth," thought Lilli.

That was why the widow had set the table as though expecting her family of dead to come to supper, and had placed a candle in the window to guide their souls. "He comes at night," she explained to Lilli, "and asks me to pray for him."

She showed the girl pictures of her husband, of the place where he had been killed, marked by a white wooden cross. There were also photos of her children in their small white coffins, and of Dunia, the youngest and dearest.

"Dunia, Dunia," she kept on repeating, and the melancholy sound was like a lament.

She spoke of dreams in which the shades of the departed had appeared to her and tormented her, beseeching her to give them ease. "There is no escape from them," she sobbed distractedly. "They follow me wherever I go."

The pressure of the woman's grief weighed heavily upon Lilli. She felt she did not yet possess the maturity to probe its depths nor to pacify it. Tamara, seeing the terror in the girl's eyes, feared she would lose the affection of this one person, who was her last link with humanity. In a kind of frenzy, she kept urging Lilli to stay, overwhelming her with endearments, offering her gifts.

"Stay, stay," she begged. "It eases my heart to speak with you. If you knew how they pursue me! There is nowhere to hide."

A sudden stillness ensued, broken by the sound of tortured sobbing, as the woman, exhausted, fell to her knees.

"When will he find forgiveness! When will he find forgiveness!" she exclaimed.

She dragged herself before the holy pictures and prayed desperately, her dark hair falling dishevelled about her white face. "Lord have mercy! Lord have mercy! Lord have mercy!" In a paroxysm of woe, she trembled, started, sang a few lines, then stopped and began to cry again. She got up from the floor and walked about the house, picked up the photos of her dead, and pressing them to her face, kissed them. Then she rushed to the mirror and looked at it, as if expecting to see her haunt, according to the old peasant superstition. On the table, the candles flickered, their flames shot up tall, shuddered.

Then the woman came over to Lilli, who cowered in a corner, and seizing the trembling girl by the arms, urged her again and again to stay.

"Don't leave me," she implored. "Do you know what it is to be alone?"

"I know," replied Lilli sadly, and spoke some words of comfort to the woman. Touched by her sympathy, Tamara began a recital of her life with her family, recalling how one of the girls had brought her a bouquet of flowers, how her husband had shown some token of affection, how Dunia had been preparing for her first communion when she was taken mortally ill. She even produced the flowered veil and headdress which she had prepared for the little girl.

"She never wore it," grieved the heartbroken mother as she placed the headdress on the table and stroked it again and again.

When the rain had ceased, Lilli, with a promise to come again, mounted on her pony and rode off across the fields, followed by the wild tragic music of that disordered personality. She looked in the direction of the swamp and saw the faint glow of the will-o'-the-wisp. It became brighter as it assumed the shape of a coal oil lamp and approached, following Lilli, or so it seemed to her, whichever way she fled. It came down lower, almost over her head, and in panic she urged her pony all the way home, although the swamp fire had long since disappeared.

5
PEASANT BOOTS
❦

ABOUT three weeks after this encounter with Tamara, late in October when Lilli was back home with her family, there came one day to the house a delegation of farmers to discuss with Anton and Zenobia the reports concerning the activities of the witch woman. Lilli's aunt and uncle were there, and she, recalling the five years of servitude she had spent in their home, shrank at the sight of them, although her aunt was effusive enough and commented at Lilli's improved appearance.

Outside, a throng pressed, wagons kept on arriving, the house swarmed with visitors as farmers in great sheepskins and their wives in embroidered boleros came into the Landash home.

They all sat around in a circle, about a dozen persons, men and women of varying ages. Such faces are not seen any more, except among primitive people, as though hewn from stone in rough, bold strokes by some imaginative but inexpert sculptor. Their hands, too, shaped like tubers by constant contact with the soil, revealed power in every gesture, so that you were conscious these hands had kneaded dough, woven cloth, broken the soil. They had great strength, even at rest.

As they looked at the feast which Zenobia spread, their eyes glistened, and they began to eat with great relish and noise, while Lilli hurried about with jugs of ale. As each dish was emptied, Zenobia replenished it from the pots on the kitchen table: rings of garlic sausage, loaves of braided bread, pickled mushrooms, stuffed cabbage.

Zenobia, wearing her yellow boots, coral necklaces and embroidered white blouse, her brown hair coiled in braids about her low brow, appeared to advantage that night. She was an admirable hostess, showing flashes of spirited humour, attendant upon the guests without being obtrusive, and a good listener.

"These pickled mushrooms are a treat!"

"Remind me to get the recipe, Zenobia!"

The talk, at first, was random – the harvest, the price of wheat, the rumours of matchmaking. It was common talk, rich as a mushroom dumpling, flavoursome as a dill pickle, sprinkled with the spice of proverb and parable.

Then, as the evening wore on, the visitors fell to relating folk tales and fables, and somehow the query arose whether supernatural beings had survived the migration to the new world.

"What do you say, Bartholomew?" queried Zenobia. "Do you believe spirits are able to live in this country, where ways are strange to them?"

All the visitors turned now to Bartholomew Charivnyk, for he was considered an authority on the demon world. Yellow and lean as a death's head, his face was like a cavern of horror. Indeed, all Bartholomew's conversation was tinged with melancholy: he spoke of corpses, shrouds dyed with blood, open graves. He performed constant rituals to ward off the evil eye, and still he was a man marked for misfortune.

He recalled now an instance where a vampire had taken up residence in a Manitoba village, and this vampire had caused great commotion in the lives of the villagers:

"The vampire made great noises, swooped into houses, rattled dishes and ceilings until at last in distraction the priest was called in to exorcise it. It was then discovered that the vampire was the guilty soul of a man who had died unshriven."

Bartholomew paused to swallow a pickled mushroom and then went on, "The body must be dug up and transferred to unhallowed ground," ordained the priest. So three of the villagers volunteered to dig up the coffin, the bravest men in the village. It was the dead of the night, black as the mouth of hell. Not a creature stirred. To light their way, the men carried torches and a stake blessed by the priest. Each step, as it fell upon the ground, caused their flesh to shudder."

"As the coffin was unearthed, a creaking was heard, and before the horrified eyes of the men, the lid commenced slowly to rise. . . . The men shuddered, their spades fell from their hands, they dropped to their knees and tried to pray, but the words froze. . . ."

Here Bartholomew's whisper stopped dramatically, while a chill of horror shook the teeth of the listeners. They looked fearfully at each other; pimples arose upon their flesh.

In a sepulchral voice, Bartholomew continued: "It was the vampire rustling within, trying to escape. . . . A sudden rush of wind from above put out one of the torches, as though blown out by the breath of the accursed spirit. The souls of the diggers froze with fear, and they began to pray, "Mother of God, preserve us!"

"Still the lid continued to rise, soon the vampire would be free of the coffin and would escape into the world to plague the villagers. But one man with a great presence of mind, raised his hammer, drove the blessed stake through the lid and pierced the heart of the vampire. A cry of anguish was heard, as the power of the vampire was destroyed. The coffin was transferred to unhallowed ground and the cursed vampire was never heard of again."

Faces paled and the story tellers were speechless at this tale, which was made all the more terrifying by the lugubrious voice of the narrator. The primitive voice has a peculiar quality which it loses in civilization. It has a greater range, from shrill to bass, and has a mastery of assonance. There is rhythm in the telling, a relic of the time when the ancestors had danced and sung in chorus – rhythm of labour in the fields, rhythm of seasons, rhythms of the wind and clouds.

Lately the appearance of the swampfire had roused much discussion in the district. A neighbour riding on a horse had seen the swamp lights and the horse had reared and nearly thrown the man. Upon his making the sign of the cross, the light had disappeared, proving that it was an evil spirit.

The most dreadful experience had been that of Lilli's own uncle, Artemas Gudzyk, who now undertook to relate his recent encounter with the swamp lights. He had run for miles, he said, pursued by the fiery ball, and when he arrived home, half dead from exhaustion, he was naked to the waist and shivering.

"The swamp lights pursued me for miles," he panted.

"Lord save us!" ejaculated his wife. "What did you do?"

"I struggled to get away. I could feel the spirit hands reaching at me, and felt blood from their scratches trickling down my shirt. I put my hands to my chest and they came away covered with blood. . . ." The sweat broke out on his face.

"It's a mercy you escaped!" gasped the listeners. "What happened to your shirt?"

"I tore it off and buried it in the ground, as it was cursed by the swamp lights," said Artemas Gudzyk.

Lilli, as she saw the faces of the visitors change before her eyes, did not know whether it was the excitement, the food or the light, or a combination of all these, but it seemed as though in each face, secretive forces, formerly hidden, were now released, and these persons, whom Lilli had known in ordinary life as farmers, housewives and petty tradesmen, now became transformed. Artemas Gudzyk was certainly an insignificant man: there was scarcely anything in his everyday appearance that would remain in one's memory. Yet here he was now, malice gleaming in his small green eyes, his tiny hands twisted in fantastic poses to give point to his tale, his untidy little wisp of moustache perked up at both ends, giving his face a leer like that of the wicked ogre in the fairy tales.

It was about this time that Lilli detected a change in the atmosphere: a premonition made itself felt, and as she heard, surreptitiously, the name of Tamara introduced into the conversation, she shivered, as though an unwholesome draught had blown in from the swamps.

Old grudges, old resentments, old fears and envy – every unexplained mischance which had occurred in the district for years back, were dragged out on display, like musty clothes from a forgotten trunk. Mildewed, moth-eaten, these memories were now shaken out until the air was foul with their rancour.

Yet Lilli noticed – and felt gratified because of it – that her mother did not participate in the chorus of disapproval, and that her father, also, was reluctant to join in the indictment. Zenobia all this while bustled about with platters of food, hardly uttering a word, for she was more closely acquainted with Tamara than were the other women, and disturbed as she was by the charges – for she was a superstitious woman and could not entirely discount them, neither could she bring herself to accept them without question. Then, too, she feared to attract censure to herself, for it was not so long ago that she had invited Tamara to participate in Fialka's wedding rites, and also she had been present on the night Lilli herself lay dying. Torn between loyalty to Tamara, and her own belief in the supernatural, Zenobia had already resolved that she would not join in any action against the widow. This was for her a courageous decision, since in all the years to come it would be held against her, although she was confirmed in her determination by the knowledge that Anton's sentiments were not too dissimilar to her own.

She listened with a perturbed countenance, therefore, while the house rocked with the tumult.

As each speaker chimed in, one phrase giving rise to a balanced counterpart, the voices swelled in a crescendo of fury, until at last all joined in the scoffing chorus:

"She sends balls of fire bouncing across the prairies – "

"She looked upon a sheep of mine, and caused it to pine away – "

"Many have seen her at her ungodly work in the evenings, plaguing cows and milking them so they give no milk – "

"After she visited me in early summer, my tomato plants shrivelled up, three dozen promising plants which I had just set out – "

"She diverted a locust plague from her own fields, and they passed over mine instead, and ate all the grain, everything – not a stalk was left. They spread like a blue blanket of ruin upon my crops. Yet her own fields escaped, and she, the witch, stood by and laughed at me."

"Akh, cholera upon her!"

Their hatred mounted in a kind of chant as they lashed out at Tamara, each seeking for some accusation by which to discredit the woman, as if hoping to gain esteem thereby. Faces grew redder and shone with sweat, jackets were thrown off, comments heard about the increasing heat:

"Like dancing on top of a hot stove in a steambath."

Lilli, meanwhile, who had retreated into a corner beside the clay stove, became more and more sombre as the clamour grew, thinking of Tamara, recalling the passion and sorrow within the woman's heart, and as she thought, that maturity whose lack she regretted only recently made itself felt within her, she knew compassion, tears flowed as she realized that Tamara was one such as herself, as she might have been, born in other circumstances.

"All these stories are lies," she thought. "They have only one thing against Tamara – that she lives alone and has no one to defend her."

Meanwhile the people in the room – the great circle

shifting with the colours of their silken shawls and embroidered sheepskins, became more animated, the hum of their voices grew like a swarm of angry bees as they tossed Tamara about on the prongs of their dislike.

The most telling charge was made by the widow Agapia, whose husband had committed suicide a year previously under mysterious circumstances, and this was considered a great disgrace, as his body was not permitted burial in the churchyard, but was laid away in unhallowed ground.

Agapia was homely as a potato, with a great nose upon which resided a family of warts. Crooked teeth in a lopsided mouth gleamed yellowishly in contrast to her shining red complexion. Her ugliness was further accentuated by the beauty of her costume. She had donned for the occasion her white linen shirt, with the most exquisite embroideries, and it was difficult to believe her coarse hands had executed that fine handiwork.

She spoke now, with intent to stigmatize Tamara irreparably: "She cast a spell upon my husband, and drove him to madness, so that in distraction he took his own life."

At this charge, a burst of indignation came from all.

"How much longer will we permit this woman to plague us?" inquired Lilli's uncle. "She is a disgrace to our community."

Restraint was now thrown off as all pricked their minds to wilder, more fantastic charges. Finally Anton, who was alarmed lest responsibility fall upon him, because the affair had come to a head in his own home, tried to intervene:

"Let us try to reason with this Tamara," he suggested. "And ask her to stop plaguing us. Perhaps she has a grudge against someone, something, not great, that may be set right."

"Who can reason with a witch?" scoffed Lilli's uncle. "She will swear her innocence and then revenge herself upon you. You will wake up one morning with the withering sickness – "

Anton, who realized he would lose caste with Jensen and

MacTavish if he participated in this affair, made one more attempt to reason with the crowd.

"Let us bring her to trial in a proper manner and have the case in court," he proposed. "All this can be done according to the law, and no blame will be attached to us."

But his reasoning had no effect upon the visitors, whose emotions, inflamed by the recital of their grievances, had now become uncontrollable.

"Who will testify against her, since all fear her retribution?"

"She is a cunning one, she speaks like one of the gentle folk."

"She twists about like a chip in a whirlpool."

And now the people, roused by the memory of wrongs, real or imagined, gave voice to their wrath, the condemnation coming from all: "We must drive her out. Yes, drive her out, drive her out!"

As one by one the wagons were filled and the people rode off, Anton stood among them because he still hoped to moderate their course of action. Lilli, watching with her mother at the window, noticed how the lanterns lit up their faces, so that they became distorted, with exaggerated noses, their eyes reflecting the flames with borrowed light, while their figures in their bulky sheepskins loomed larger than life as they shifted about in the closely-packed vehicles. The creaking of wagons in the night – which Lilli had once thought musical when she had heard grain wagons in the velvety softness of an early autumn evening – now grated on her senses. There was one wheel especially which wheezed and groaned, "like an evil spirit in torment," commented Zenobia. The shaking and jolting of the wagons, too, seemed to increase the excitement of the people, as though their reason had sunk to the bottom of their minds like silt, and to the top floated the effervescence of passion. Even when they had gone some distance, their loud voices could be heard, as their frenzied desire grew to arrive at the home of the witch woman.

Long after the departure of wagons, Lilli continued to stand by the window, tormenting herself with thoughts of what she might have done to prevent this. Even if she raced now, she reasoned, she could never arrive in time to warn the woman, and where would Tamara hide if she left her home? In their rage, the people would comb the countryside for her, and there would be little hope of escape. While she was thinking thus, the wagons disappeared finally from view, the voices were no longer heard, stillness fell upon the night so that the fiddling of frogs in the nearby slough could be heard. The night was soft, swathed in the misty veils of Indian summer; a copper-coloured harvest moon, as big as a washtub, hung in the sky; forms and shapes moved through a haze, as though tranquillity were the only possible mood on such a night.

Darkness, a mellow darkness came, and still Lilli watched, straining her eyes to see if she could catch a glimpse of wagons returning down the road. The smaller children had long ago been put to sleep, even before the arrival of the guests, and the older ones, who had been outdoors around a bonfire, had also come in and gone to bed. Sniffles, puffs and whistles arose from the sleeping forms where heads blond and dark reposed upon the pillows. Lilli, as she looked upon the downy faces of Petey and the twins, envied them their innocence, for tonight, she who was fourteen, the eldest now, had been suddenly thrust into the adult world of emotions, predestined for her people by centuries of ignorance and superstition. Up to this evening she had not questioned the old beliefs, but now a great rent appeared in them and she exclaimed to herself, "Lord, what darkness is in their minds!" Brought up on this isolated homestead, Lilli had had no basis for comparing her parents' world with the outside world, from which came only dim echoes, sometimes, in the speech of MacTavish or a visitor. Nevertheless she felt by intuition that another way of life was possible, that this thing which was happening in the darkness as she waited might have been prevented; that a day would come, not too long distant, when such tragedies would no longer be possible.

Yet when Lilli actually saw, in the direction of the swamp, a column of fire and smoke arise, rolls and welts billowing upward and illuminating the sky so that the countryside could be seen for miles about, she did not immediately relate it to the procession of wagons which had departed an hour back, and it was not until she felt her mother beside her, and heard a gasp, did she understand the truth. "No, no!" she cried out.

The two stood looking at each other and the icy fingers of apprehension crept over their hearts, but neither said a word. Lilli could see a muscle in her mother's face twitching, and her trembling fingers buttoned and unbuttoned the front of her jacket, as though unable to control herself. Lilli had in her hands a silk scarf, and this she folded and unfolded and folded and unfolded, while she continued to stare at her mother, both seeking refuge in these meaningless gestures, for the feelings which they dared not express in speech, until Zenobia had ripped the buttons off her jacket from top to bottom, and Lilli, looking down at the scarf, found she had torn it to shreds.

When Anton finally returned, it was close to midnight, and Lilli was in bed, but the sound of her father's heavy tread awakened her.

Landash's aspect was grim as he stood uncertain, breathing in rasps, as though each breath passed over a file in transit. His eyes, fixed on the floor, were furtive, surprisingly so, for Anton was a straightforward fellow, not given to subterfuge, and his habitual gaze was candid.

"What have you done, Anton?" cried out Zenobia as she waited for her husband to speak, but he could not, or would not, and all that came from him was that stentorious sound, like an admission of guilt. "What have you done?" she demanded again, advancing upon him. "Did you set fire to the woman's home?"

"Fire?" inquired Anton, as though in a trance.

"I saw the fire over the swamp. It reddened the sky for miles."

Anton looked at his wife, and put his hand to his mouth as if to pull out his voice which had got stuck there.

"That was done by herself."

"Have a care, Anton," warned Zenobia. "In this country, you cannot take the law into your own hands." Landash began to pace about in agitation and then came to a stop before Petey's bed, and as Lilli had done earlier in the evening, he stood looking at Petey's face as if wishing to transfer its innocence to himself.

"I can't believe she would fire her own home," said Zenobia, but she was beginning to be convinced by Anton's sincerity and vehemence.

"Yes, she did." Anton walked away from his son's sleeping form and threw himself down on a chair. He admitted his own exhaustion, although he often boasted of his strength and was accustomed to working late into the evening, long after his neighbours had sat down to rest.

"How, and why?" asked Zenobia. "I demand to know the whole story." She sat down opposite her husband, and Lilli could see how the skin had been drawn tight about her mouth, which trembled uncontrollably, thus distorting Zenobia's speech.

"It happened this way," began Anton, and he seemed relieved that he was able to unbosom himself. "As we approached, we could see the woman at the window in an attitude – as of prayer or meditation, for there was a candle beside her, and the blind was not drawn. . . . Before we reached there, she appeared to notice us, and opened her mouth as if to cry out. Then, while we watched, she took up

181

the coal oil lamp and removing the glass chimney, she set fire to the curtains, then, rushing about the room, set the flame to all she could . . . and, before our eyes, as we sat in our wagons unable to move, she rushed out of the door, still grasping the lamp, her black hair unloosed and streaming over her shoulders, and for a moment, we saw her face in the flame, a fine face, eyes glowing themselves like two lamps, but with a wild expression, as if she had lost her reason, then, hastening the opposite way, she ran in the direction of the swamp until the darkness swallowed her up. . . . Meanwhile, the flames shot up and we perceived that the house was all afire within, so that we were forced to withdraw to a distance, and nothing could be saved."

All the while Anton was making his recital, Lilli, listening in her bed, was tortured by the memory of that hapless woman, for she could not doubt that Tamara had met her death that night. What was this kinship between herself and that woman, a bond that held her to this mysterious figure, mysterious with her dark loves and hates and her futile protest against society? Tamara had been defeated, but by her defeat she had pointed out the way for Lilli's own rebellion. Tamara, Lilli recognized, was an exceptional woman, a woman who in other circumstances might have blossomed into a brilliant and productive personality, but, placed in this primitive community, could only dash her head against a wall of prejudice.

Meanwhile, Lilli could see, in the dim light, the regret of her mother that she had not made firmer defence of the woman.

"God forgive us!" exclaimed Zenobia, clapping her hands together. "It will be long before people forget this."

"It is not my fault – I tried to persuade them. I tell you, I tried to persuade them!" he reiterated and stamped his foot, as he tried to convince himself he had no complicity in the matter.

Anton then did something which Lilli did not at first

understand, for her father was not usually a fastidious man. Pouring out a basin of water from the pitcher, he thrust his hands into it and scrubbed them repeatedly as if endeavouring to scrub off the guilt, muttering to himself all the while, "I am not to blame, I am not to blame." He dried his hands, and combed his hair, scrutinizing his countenance meanwhile in the mirror as though endeavouring to erase the traces of guilt.

As he was about to take off his leather jacket, his hands went into the pocket, and a shamefaced expression came over his face. He stifled an exclamation and made as if to thrust something back.

"What is that, Anton? What have you there?" Zenobia held out her hand and demanded in a tone that could not be denied, "Show me what you have there."

"It is some bit of finery which the woman dropped as she hastened off, and I, in my excitement, picked it up and put it in my pocket." Anton held up the bit of net and flowers which had been destined for the head of Tamara's daughter.

At the sight of this religious object, Zenobia drew back in consternation. "A little girl's veil! A communion veil! I had heard how Dunia was preparing to receive communion before she died – "

Anton, as if fascinated, stood looking at it, as if he could not rid himself of it, as if it symbolized the innocence of the woman, and by its survival, gave the lie to all their trumped-up charges of witchcraft.

Then suddenly exclaiming, he threw it down upon the floor and stepped upon it, shouting in a hoarse voice, "Ech, curse her for a witch!"

That last thing that greeted Lilli's eyes before she fell asleep was the sight of Dunia's flower headdress being trampled beneath the heel of her father's great, tan peasant boot.

PART FIVE

The Grandparents

1
GRANNY'S LAST STORIES
ơ

MONTHS HAD passed and the story of Tamara had already passed into local legend, when Lilli dressed in fresh white blouse and red skirt set out on a summer morning to visit her grandparents who lived in the village. She met her grandmother on the road, and the old lady inquired, "Well, and how are you, little daughter?" Lilli replied, "Fine as could be, God give you health." The old lady was pleased. "The girl has a grown-up way of speaking," she thought.

They stood looking at each other, communicating silently as the very old and the very young are sometimes able to do, and then Granny Yefrosynia stretched out her hand to touch Lilli's cheek.

"How good to touch a young person" she exclaimed. "As downy as a chicken!" Her own face, smocked with wrinkles, was like a map of human experience.

The two walked together down the road, Granny waddling rather than walking: everything shook up and down like a jelly. Her three long skirts, striped and spotted in various designs, showed as she moved her nimble little feet. She wore a coarse white shirt under her black leather bolero, which was embroidered in red and green, and she had a yellow silk shawl over her hair.

Suddenly a great uproar and commotion were heard, and a motorcycle came charging down the road, heading straight for Lilli and Granny Yefrosynia. The old lady screamed and stood still, as though she had been frozen into a pudding.

Meanwhile the motorcycle plunged on, scattering chickens and a cow and hurling up clouds of dust and fumes. The young man on the motorcycle smiled and waved to Lilli, shouting to the excited villagers, who had rushed out to see what was the matter.

"This is the end!" exclaimed Granny Yefrosynia wrathfully. "This is the end of the world!" She shook her fist at the motorcycle.

"Maybe he will take you for a ride," suggested Lilli mischievously, her bare feet dancing grey imprints in the dusty road.

"I shall perish before I ride on that machine – it is the invention of the Devil!" Granny spat after the motorcycle.

When they neared Granny's home, she lifted the latch of the gate and turned to Lilli: "Some people from the city were here one day to take pictures of our home, and they took one of me, too, with my pipe in my mouth. I had to show them how to make a light from the tinder box, they didn't know how."

Granny paused at the doorway to stir the rose petals and camomile flowers which were drying out in the sun. As she stirred the leaves, they gave off a scent which intensified in the hot sweet air. Lifting a handful, she sniffed. "Some women stuff these into pillows and sleep on them," she said. "Maybe they dream of fields covered with roses."

"Sit down," she invited Lilli as she lifted her three skirts and plumped her well-padded posterior upon the doorstep.

Lilli bent down to examine her foot, on which she had discovered a scratch.

"Scratch your foot, little daughter?" Granny clucked her tongue sympathetically. "I know just the thing." She disappeared round the house and came back with a puff ball which she applied to Lilli's leg with a cloth. "Draws out the poison, Lilli."

They went within, and Lilli looked about. The interior of

Granny's home was crowded with objects of interest and originality. Plants stood in the window sills, mostly geraniums and sweet william. Christmas and Easter cards were hung in a wire frame, side by side with lithographed calendars. Numerous sacred pictures, depicting the martyrdom of saints covered the walls, some decorated with ears of wheat or crepe paper flowers. The beds, laid with feather beds, were spread with embroidered coverlets and crocheted pillows.

Before they had lunch, Granny called in Grandfather Nestor to administer a herbal concoction, as he was suffering from some ailment which kept him at home.

"But Frosia," wailed the old man. "This mixture tastes like, like – " he looked at Lilli and hesitated. "I will not name it in front of Lilli."

"Drink it down in one gulp and you will not taste it," commanded the old lady. Although she was generally quite kind to the old man, she never left him in doubt as to who commanded that fortress, and this amused Lilli, as quite the reverse was true in her own home.

Grandfather Nestor wore an enormous curly cap of sheepskin, with two huge flaps anchored over his ears and this cap he did not take off even when at table. Beneath the cap emerged a smallish face, wrinkled as a dried prune, but nevertheless with a look of craftiness in the two small eyes, set deep beneath overhanging eyebrows. These eyes at present had a mournful, dejected expression. Grandfather had swallowed the tonic, but the after-effects lingered bitterly within him.

For dinner, however, there was a treat. Granny had parboiled mushrooms in salted water then fried them with butter, onions and garlic. When the whole mixture was a simmering stew, she poured cream over it and made a thick sauce. Sometimes the Bukovynian women put fish in with the onions and mushrooms, and cooked them with oil, omitting the cream.

As they ate, Granny described a wedding which she had attended some months back. The old lady loved dancing, and could out-dance women forty years younger than herself. She made small, dainty turns, dancing with great vigour, her rotund body shaking like a ball as she stamped in time to the music.

After the meal, Grandfather Nestor paused by the window to watch the children across the road, bobbing up and down in their calico dresses and flying pigtails, and he exclaimed, "Like flowers springing up from the earth are these children."

"A pity we can't water them and let them grow," said Granny. Lilli chuckled: "A pity we can't, Granny!"

"And now," said Granny, settling herself in her rocker, "And now, let us tell stories."

Lilli brought a stool which she placed near her grandmother's chair and took out a piece of knitting while she prepared to enjoy herself. Her grandmother's stories seemed to her to be drawn from some dark deep well of legend, as though she had only to let down her bucket into an accumulated stock and bring it brimming to the surface.

Granny doted on stories in which the central figure was the frightened little human forced to extricate himself from embarrassing situations. Thus her first tale concerned the concession of a pious grandmother to the patronage of Old Nick.

"A granny came to church one day and lit candles before the picture of each saint. One candle remained. Where would she place it? Here was a painting of St. Nicholas gripped in battle with the Prince of Evil. 'Aha!' she said. 'Here's a place!' And lit a candle before the Devil! People gazed in wonder and pointed out her mistake. 'Look, Granny, that's the Evil One!' Then Granny turned around and spoke: 'Don't judge me harshly, I pray. Either in heaven or hell we'll spend eternity, so everywhere, since we can't tell, it's good to have a friend!'"

"Aha, he's a clever fellow, Satan," wagged Grandfather Nestor, who by now, with the fried mushrooms consoling his interior for the insult they had received from Granny's physic, was quite his sprightly self again. "And I'll tell you a story of how he first behaved on this earth."

The old man relished stories describing the activities of the Devil, who was represented in folklore as a shrewd, prankish fellow.

"This story I heard from a neighbour, a learned fellow, who said he read it in a book, but I also know it is an old story among us, as my own grandfather first related it to me."

Grandfather Nestor paused to refresh himself with a glass of ale, and then wiped his whiskers with a red bandana.

"Everything on this earth," he narrated, "all wisdom, all cleverness, all that sort of thing – comes from Satan. Everything you see about you – wagon, horse, music, violin, mill or house – Satan invented them all. And all that God did was to steal everything and give it to the people. What a smart one, that Satan!"

"You have to rise early in the morning to fool him," quipped Granny Yefrosynia.

"Well," continued Grandfather Nestor, "One day Satan got cold and invented a fire. Along came God and saw the fire warming Satan. The sly fellow knew from past experience what God was going to do, so he cried, 'No, I won't let you. You have stolen everything from me, but this you won't.' But God paid no attention to him and proceeded to build his own fire. So Satan became angry and spat in disgust on the fire. The spit caused smoke to rise from the fire into the air. The first fire, you know, was clean, it didn't have any smoke, but from that time on it smoked."

When he concluded his tale, Grandfather Nestor helped himself to a handful of sunflower seeds, which he shelled rapidly one after another, separating the kernel from the shell with teeth and tongue and gulping it without swallowing the husk. The Bukovynians called sunflower seed their "newspaper" because much news and gossip were exchanged over a dish of sunflower seeds.

An absorbing point of discussion to Lilli's grandparents

was the question of the existence of imps and spirits in Canada.

"I have heard," offered Granny Yefrosynia, "that many water nymphs perished at the bottom of the river when winter came."

"Perhaps," suggested Grandfather Nestor, "they are not able to live in this new country, where the ways were strange to them. Telephones, electricity, automobiles – all these things are distasteful to spirits."

"Tell about nymphs who live in the water, Granny," interposed Lilli. These nymphs because of their beauty, fondness for music and mischief-making were great favourites with the people, and Lilli loved to hear about them.

"It is said that they are the souls of drowned maidens and unchristened children," explained Granny, rummaging about a dish of pumpkin seeds which she cracked as she described the activities of nymphs. "They live in the sea, in streams, in wells, whole colonies of them, in their crystal palaces. Ah, they are beautiful, with blonde or green hair reaching to their knees, green or black eyes. They are clad in transparent shifts and wear green wreaths upon their heads. Sometimes they appear in maidens' dresses – in white linen skirt and blouse and red beads. They live in water all year round, but come out at midsummer and from then on, they play on the earth until autumn. During that time, they run over the meadows and forests and valleys, they play on the banks of streams, they cling to willow branches. Whoever hears their songs is drawn irresistibly after."

Granny paused while she filled her long-stemmed slim-bowled pipe with tobacco and lit it from her tinder box.

"Here's a match, Granny," offered Lilli, but Granny waved it off, and puffed contentedly for a while.

"And do they never love, as other maidens do, Granny?" queried Lilli.

"Whatever love a young man has for them is straightway followed by his destruction," replied Granny Yefrosynia.

"They love dancing, for example, and on one occasion enticed a shepherd lad of our village to play the flute all night while they danced. In the morning, the villagers observed a fairy ring in the grass where the nymphs had danced . . . but the shepherd lost his wits, poor lad."

During that long dreamy afternoon of story-telling, a magic atmosphere was created, full of the life of invisible creatures, a whole past was resurrected. Lilli was drawn from the real world to the world of fantasy, where the gods of nature were reincarnated again. It was like gazing into a mirror and seeing a parade of past generations, a backward-looking mirror, if such a thing could be, thought Lilli. All the while she listened, she had etched on her mind, as in a notebook, every detail of the proceedings, every word, every expression and gesture, every story. Some day, she would use the memory of these things – How? She did not rightly know, yet, but when these stories had become obsolete and forgotten, dim in the memory of ancients, they would still glow in her mind.

The telling of riddles was always an exciting feature of any story-telling. These were not ordinary riddles, but offered a challenge to the imagination and a mastery of tradition. The subject this time was the "Thunderer."

Granny Yefrosynia gave, without hesitation, her interpretation: "Behold the Thunderer! The Thunderer is a farmer who ploughs his field with a golden plough dragged by six oxen. The stars in the skies are like sheaves in the field. The Thunderer stands among the sheaves like the moon among the stars."

This poetic conception, coming from an illiterate farm woman, revealed the delicate touch of the artist. Lilli was enraptured. She would never again see the stars in the sky without thinking of Granny's exquisite simile. How many of her peasant ancestors had stood with heads uplifted to the skies and seen sheaves of wheat in the vast fields of the heavens!

Grandfather Nestor now followed with his interpretation,

which arose from his life as a shepherd in the Carpathian Mountains. He often said, concerning his childhood, "I was suckled by the ewes." Now he spoke: "The Thunderer is a shepherd who herds sheep in the lofty hills. He has three flutes of gold, copper and maple. When he blows into them, his voice resounds over the valleys, woods and meadows."

Thus the voice of nature spoke in musical tones through a flute. Lilli had heard those tones of gold, copper and maple in times of storm on the prairies. Each of the portraits represented some aspect of beliefs once held by the ancestors of the story-tellers, at a time when the young soul of man, still not able to think logically, called fantasy to assistance, and transferred earthly happenings to the sky.

As the afternoon wore on, Granny, seemingly tired by the exertion, laid her head against the back of the rocker. She looked very frail that day, thought Lilli, recalling that her mother had said only the previous evening, "Your grandmother will drop soon from the tree of life like a leaf in autumn," and had muttered something about a growth which was poisoning the old lady's system. Impossible to imagine, thought Lilli, that Granny Yefrosynia could ever die – Granny, bristling with bossiness, apt to mischief, teeming with legend as a bee with honey. She was timeless, she was meant to go on and on, like a continued story in a newspaper. . . .

But it was the last of Granny's story-telling, for Lilli never again saw her grandmother alive.

2
THE KEENERS

OVER THE VILLAGE and through the surrounding district the funeral bells, rung by a bereaved old man, tolled the melancholy news that Grandmother Yefrosynia had died.

Within the house, the women were preparing for the two-night vigil, as the dead was not buried till the third day. Lilli and Zenobia had lit many candles at the head and feet of the corpse; a dish of water had been placed on the window sill so that the dead woman would be able to quench her thirst. Zenobia, attired in a black robe, looked about to see if everything was in order. The corpse had been laid out near the window with her feet pointed to the door. All the mirrors were muffled, so that the soul would not wander lost around the house.

"Lilli, have you hung willow branches on the doors, so that people will know we are in mourning?" Zenobia called to Lilli as the girl stood draping an embroidered towel over the window. "It is all done," replied Lilli. Her face was pale, with dark smudges beneath her eyes. A warm affection had grown between herself and her grandmother, and its loss left a feeling of desolation in her heart. She came over to watch her mother making the corpse candle of beeswax. First Zenobia measured a length of wax the thickness of a finger, to correspond with the height of the corpse, and while the wax was still warm, she rolled it round and round like a snail, until it formed a platter nine inches in diameter. Then she took up a little wick from the centre to burn. "Someone must always sit by this candle and pull up the wick," she said as she placed the corpse candle beside the body. "It must never be left alone for a moment until the corpse is taken out of the house."

Stillness had fallen over the house, disturbed only by the shuffling pace of mourners, the deep sighs of women, the creaking of benches and the whispered prayers muttered by all. The shadows of the candles quivered across the dead woman's face, shunted back and forth across the bereaved.

Zenobia, standing by the coffin and contemplating her dead mother's countenance, was heard to murmur, "A stranger – far from home." At this, the heads of the mourners nodded, as they felt within themselves the consciousness that they, too, were strangers away from home.

The long tapers, with their points ablaze, shone upon the mourners against the wall, and brought into relief: faces with rough seams like ore veins in the earth; hands misshapen or gnarled as tree stumps left in a field, going through the motions of the crucifix, raised in supplication, or pressed upon the knees; eyes, rheumy with age, enfolded in skin laps; drops of sweat oozing out of foreheads. On all these the light played, accentuating each detail. Heads bobbed up and down, hoary heads of ancient ones, blond heads of young folk. Grandfather Nestor sat, a puzzled frown on his forehead, as though convinced that this was a play and not a real funeral; any moment, now, the actors would step out of their parts and Granny's laughter would ring out again. Lilli, too, looked about as though expecting any minute that Granny would appear in her orange blouse and green skirt, chuckling triumphantly, "A fine trick I've played on you!"

The conversation was carried on in hushed tones, and related to the beliefs of the Carpathian mountaineers regarding the souls of the dead: "It is said that the soul travels on horseback and the road is beset with obstacles and strewn with thorns," contributed one woman. She drew her black shawl closer about her face, one of those ancient physiognomies which was like an aged parchment written over with stories of a vanished age.

"Everyone knows," continued another, regarding the deceased, "that the soul roams about the world for forty days before it sets out on its journey to the other world."

"Sometimes it plays practical jokes on the family," observed an elderly man. "Rattles the window panes, misplaces the kitchen pots and pans, and such." He looked nervously about him as a gust of wind rattled the windowpane. "Listen." The mourners hushed momentarily at the sound. "It is the soul of the dead talking to us."

The thoughts of all turned sombrely to speculation concerning the life hereafter, the old folk brooding with the thoughts of the imminence of death, the young intimidated, as though by some awful presence, unseen but felt. The older folk related what they had heard of the life hereafter from their forefathers, as though striving to reassure themselves that the great unknown was not such a terrible prospect after all. In heaven, they said, people occupied houses exactly like those they had left behind, and they ate food like their daily diet.

For Lilli, the scene was like returning to a place where she had been before. The face in the coffin was familiar and yet not familiar; the departure of the warm breath had left only a dried husk, the colours faded and like a parchment. "She will not sing again," thought Lilli, looking at the lips, which were thin and silent now, and this appeared to her the greatest deprivation. Grandmother had sung so many songs, had told so many stories! Those were the hands which had baked the batches of bread, which had woven tapestries, had ministered to the sick and dying. Now, waxen, they lay folded across her chest, never to be animate again. Lilli strove to break that silence, arouse the dead woman, as if she could call her back to life with a word.

Deep sighs arose on all sides, increasing in intensity like a wind, in an atmosphere of growing emotion. Upon the dead face, with coppers covering the eyes, the light of the candles became more intense, every wrinkle, every blemish and discolouration was apparent. The smell of burning wax became stronger until it filled the house.

Suddenly the voice of Zenobia, the chief mourner, broke through the growing murmur as if in a shrill wail she commenced the invocation to the dead woman:

> When shall I spread a table before you, O my mother,
> You will not be here in the time of great snows,
> Nor in the heavy rains,
> Nor will you ever appear on earth again.
> Oh, when shall we expect you?
> Will you come by the road?
> Will you fly through the sky?
> Would I knew where to await you,
> O soul wandering like a bird upon a dark road!

Her lament assumed a more urgent tone as she solicited the dead woman, "Arise, mother, take a few steps so we will remember how you walked; speak a few words so we will remember the sound of your voice; wake up and teach us how to live. Who will come to us on Easter Sunday, on Christmas Eve, on the Sabbath to direct us?" Zenobia threw herself upon the floor beside the coffin, repeated the admonition, elaborated upon it, called to the dead to return.

As her mother's voice failed, Lilli, too, fell upon her knees and continued the exhortation to the dead: "Sing to us, grandmother, but one little song, sing of the joys of summer, sing of old times. Do not lie silent there. Open your lips and rejoice our hearts with only one song."

The mourners nodded in approval: "How well they lament!" Now they began, one by one, according to custom, to recall the life and deeds of the departed. One ancient crone, older than Grandmother Yefrosynia, recalled pasturing sheep with her on the Carpathian Mountains when both had been girls. Others described her youth and marriage in Bukovyna, her migration to Canada, her pioneer work on the homestead. Anton Landash, who had been fond of the old woman, recited her good deeds, how she had helped the poor, struggled with storms, fought with the land, laboured to clothe and feed her family. Lilli, for her part, told of the old woman's musical skill, her knowledge of lores, her way with a tale. All this, she knew – for it was a tradition – was to keep the soul of the old woman company, to prevent its loneliness by reviving memories of youthful days. Somewhere in this room that soul was still present, listening to the pleas of the mourners, taking comfort in their sorrow . . .

After some hours of this, the mourners suddenly reminded themselves that they must not add to the grief of the wandering soul by being too sad; there must be some merriment to cheer the departed. They began to tell jokes, to relate some of the lighter moments in the life of Grandmother Yefrosynia. Zenobia invited them to partake of the funeral repast: boiled wheat with honey and cherries, cabbage rolls, fish with oil, cooked beans, mushrooms, prunes, brandy. The mourners lined up in a row, and each, as he passed by the table, dipped a wooden spoon into the bowl of boiled wheat and tasted of it.

Beneath the shadow of the candles, which were smoking furiously, the corpse seemed to be left alone, save for a few old crones who still remained beside it. Lilli, watchful of the corpse candle, whose wick she lifted continually as it burned, prolonged her scrutiny of the dead woman, fascinated by the mystery of death. Was the soul indeed flying about like a bird of passage in the night? Was life, as the old woman had once said to her, like the brief flame of a candle, the song of a bird, a blossom in spring?

She watched as the corpse candle shrank into itself, coming at last to its own end. . . .

3
THE ANCIENT BARDS
❦

AFTER the death of Granny Yefrosynia, Lilli went to live in the village of Prairie Dawn, to keep house for Grandfather Nestor, who was the sexton of the church, charged with ringing the bells and making the unleavened bread for communion.

Ian MacTavish was leaving the schoolhouse one autumn day when he saw a figure flying up the road toward him. "O Mr. Mac! Please wait!"

It was Lilli Landash, panting and laughing. She stood for a moment, trying to regain her breath. Beside the road, the throb of a threshing machine sounded as it cut through a field of bearded wheat, filling the air with powdery particles of chaff.

"Well, I haven't seen you for a long time," said MacTavish, pleased as always to see her. He noted how she had grown, there was a sparkle of mischief in her eyes, a new confidence in her bearing, for life with her grandfather was much more pleasant and secure than her life at home had been. It was as though Nature, an artist, had decided by a few touches here and there to improve a rough sketch made in a moment of enthusiasm and then carelessly thrown aside. "How you've changed, Lilli I hardly recognized you."

"Maybe it's my hair," laughed Lilli. She put her hands to her hair, which she had done up in a braid, interwoven with red hanks of wool.

"Very becoming." He noted with approval the fresh white linen blouse, the trim red jumper of calico, with straps over the shoulders. Lilli wore her clothes with more dash than any of the other village girls.

"I have invitation for you." Lilli looked demurely at the teacher as she got out the big word, spoken very carefully. She was anxious for him to notice how much improved her speech was; living in the village had added many new words to her vocabulary.

"Invitation?" repeated MacTavish. "To visit your house?"

Lilli shook her head. "I don't live at home now. At Grandfather's. You know where he lives in the village?"

"I've passed there once or twice. Near the church, isn't it?"

"Yes, Grandfather takes care of the church. He wants you to come to supper and after he will show you, something beautiful, something which you never saw before."

Lilli paused, a smile trying to break through. She knew what an impression she had created on MacTavish, and it pleased her. He was always one to note any improvement, however trivial: all the families in the district had noted this quality in the teacher. If a family acquired a new calf, if they painted a barn, if a pupil made progress, MacTavish would be certain to comment.

The girl stooped to pick a plume of goldenrod from the grass by the road. "And I will sing for you," she promised, "a song you never heard before."

"I'll be glad to come," said MacTavish.

That evening, as he approached the home of Grandfather Nestor, the old man, dressed in a white smock and homespun trousers, was waiting for him on the *pryspa*, a bench built, old country fashion, around the sides of the house, where the old folk used to sit in the evenings and gossip.

As the men sat smoking their pipes, Lilli appeared from the house with a stringed instrument in her arms. "My grandfather will sing and play for you tonight, some old country songs," she said as she handed the instrument to the old man. "Maybe you never heard such songs. He learned them long time ago from his uncle, who sang all over the country, walked from one place to another and sang. Uncle was blind man, but sang wonderful. Some songs he sang were five hundred years old, maybe. Grandfather wants to sing for you these songs."

"Where did you get such an instrument?" marvelled the teacher.

The old man caressed the instrument with a loving hand and spoke to MacTavish in his native tongue, which the teacher understood fairly well by now. "Nobody has such an instrument in this country. Only our blind singers in the old country."

"Where did they sing?" asked MacTavish.

"In the market place. On streets. Sometime people asked them into the house." The old man plucked a few chords. "These singers are now disappearing," he commented sadly. "Perhaps their song is no longer heard in our country." He strummed with little bone plates attached to his fingers. Carved from a single piece of willow, the instrument had thirty-six strings, and resembled a cross between a harp and guitar, with a tone like a zither. "A primitive type of lute," thought MacTavish.

As the old man tried out a few preliminary notes, MacTavish started at the sound of his voice. Although all the Landash family had good voices, MacTavish could see now that it was from her grandfather that Lilli had inherited the style and cello quality of her voice. This discovery pleased the teacher, as he loved to trace the origin of characteristics, and had already divined how many of Lilli's qualities had been passed on to her by her parents and grandparents.

"What a singer you must have been in your youth!" he exclaimed.

"Yes," admitted the old man. "It is true that as a young man, people did speak well of my singing, but I am nothing compared to my uncle. He was a *kobzar*, a blind minstrel, and known all over the country, for he composed his own songs."

MacTavish watched the spatulate fingers of the old man as they strummed nervously across the strings, gathering momentum in an urgent tempo, to prepare the mind of the listener for the narrative which followed.

In an elevated voice, like recitative, using a free rhythm to induce a mood of passion, the old man began to sing the "Lament of Slaves in Turkish Captivity," and the song was a living thing, each stanza a picture set in relief by the muted accompaniment of the instrument, which permitted every word to be heard distinctly. Through the voice of the singer, MacTavish could hear the rattling of chains, the shock of waves on the Black Sea, the howling of the tempest, the desperate cries of the slaves. Thus, enclosed in the prison of his own blindness, the minstrel who had originally composed this song had summoned from his imagination a whole racial experience to preserve the poetic chronicle of a people's slavery.

Deeply stirred by the music, MacTavish looked now at Lilli and saw how the girl's face had become transformed: her eyes, always large, had become dark and sombre, tears trembled on the lids, even the shape of her face seemed to have changed to accentuate the high cheekbones and Slavic aspect. The music, like a hand, had swept across her face and erased from it all traces of Canadian life. It was obvious that her emotions were at a high pitch, aroused by something out of a past distant and alien to MacTavish, but to Lilli, and to her grandfather, recent and recognizable. "I've never seen her before, really," thought MacTavish. "It's only at a moment like this that you can look into the heart of a person like Lilli and recognize the past that created her."

When the old man had at last finished, no one spoke for a few moments. Then MacTavish inquired, "How long since your people were in serfdom?"

"How long?" The old man's voice was harsh as he

answered. "I remember my father telling me, as a boy, of the day when the serfs were freed."

"Three generations from serfdom," thought MacTavish. "It's not easy to eradicate the traces of the slave."

Another song of Grandfather's repertoire was the tragedy of a woman who was driven from her home by her sons. After she had cursed them, they were shunned by people and misfortune dogged their footsteps.

"The story has the grandeur of a Greek tragedy," thought MacTavish, "with its relentless pursuit of fate and grim ending." He felt as if he had heard the last of the ancient bards, the heir of Homer himself. These were songs from the childhood of the human race, yet they had depicted a complex struggle for the human soul; the basic human motives were dealt with in the grand style of the ancient minstrels.

At last the old man laid down his instrument. "Ah, if you had only heard my uncle sing those songs!" he sighed. "He could sing,, for hours, sometimes two hundred verses of one song he knew.

"How could he remember such long songs?" inquired MacTavish.

"If he forgot something, he replaced it with something new," said the old man.

"Then these songs must have lived long in the hearts of the people."

"Oh, yes!" exclaimed Lilli. "Nobody remember who made those songs Grandfather sang for you, Mr. Mac. Every time a new singer sings them, he adds something of himself."

"Like a leaf which falls in autumn and in the spring a new one grows," interposed Grandfather Nestor.

Grandfather Nestor, seeing the interest of the teacher, now went into the house to fetch something else which he thought would surprise MacTavish. He appeared shortly, carrying what appeared to be a bagpipe. "You see, Mr. Mac," chuckled the old man, "you are Scottish, and think that this is maybe an instrument of your country only. But we in our country have the same thing, and our shepherd boys play this in the hills."

"I have heard that people in Central Europe play the bagpipe," said MacTavish, "and that it was there the instrument was invented, but this is the first time I have ever seen any proof of it. I can imagine what my own granddad would say."

"I will tell you one thing about this instrument," related the old man, as he handed the bagpipe over to MacTavish for examination. "One time, years ago, we had a concert at our school, and I brought this to play there. We had one man, Scot like yourself, and he was very excited. He climbed on the stage and said, he must play on that pipe!"

Lilli looked triumphantly at the teacher, as though expecting him to play some tunes on his instrument, but he shook his head. "I can't play this bagpipe, Lilli. Probably your grandfather is a better piper than I am." He thought, "I imagine that the early Scottish settlers in the Red River Valley must have been like these people – rough, vigorous, clinging to old folk ways."

As Lilli took up the lute and played, MacTavish realized, "She sings like a woman, not a child any more." Her voice haunted and disturbed him; it had the moving quality that epitomized her race, "a contralto dark with a sense of human tragedy," thought the teacher. "For these people, song is part of their daily existence, their unwritten record and history. And it's only against her own racial background that you can understand the personality of the girl."

4
A SUMMER NIGHT
❦

IN THE summer evenings, as the sun was going down, the young people of the village strolled in couples up and down the road, conducting the first stages of their courtship. Later they retired to more private spots, beneath trees and in the shelter of bushes and haystacks.

Lilli, having finished her work, rushed out to take part in the procession. She had braided her hair in coils over her ears and put on a fresh embroidered blouse. She walked daintily, with head up and a little swing of the hips as she had observed other girls do. Her eyes shone with excitement and she licked her lips a little to make them red. Already several of the village boys had noticed her and passed around the word that she was a tidy lass. On the doorsteps sat old men puffing their pipes and grannies cracking sunflower seeds. Women in scarlet and yellow shawls hastened to church as they heard the bells ringing for vespers. Someone was singing a sentimental old country tune, then another caught up the melody, and another joined in, and another.

Lilli had not gone far when the sight of a familiar figure caused her heart to skip a beat. She turned rosy and paused to flee but it was too late. It was Vanni, with his hair slicked back and a clean white shirt, looking, as always, immaculate and full of ardour. Hastening to her, he seized her hand and pressed it. "You thought you would run away from me, eh, little one?" He joked. He put his arm about her and they walked slowly down the road, following other couples.

Vanni looked with admiration at the trim figure beside

him: "You're a young lady now, Lilli." He chuckled. "All the boys in the village ask me, "Who is that Lilli? Whose girl? Will she go to dance?"

"You're joking, I think." Lilli tossed her head to hide her pleasure.

"I think you know," said Vanni, looking slyly at her. "You look at them sideways and think, aha, you like me, you want to follow me." As they walked, they heard the sound of activity under trees and bushes – sighs, kisses, slaps and laughter. "Everything, everybody, is making love, Lilli."

They sat down side by side under a tree, cheek to cheek, hardly daring to breathe, and tried with awkward phrases, shy kisses and timorous gropings to express the first awakening of desire, tender and warm as the first spring rains. The hot sweet scent of hay, the ecstasy of the evening songsters, caused strange feelings to rise in their hearts. Afraid of these new emotions, which they did not rightly comprehend, they withdrew a bit, and sat, their hearts throbbing, but their hands still clasped. Then Vanni recollected something and his face grew sombre. "It is true, Lilli, that you are going to the city?" His voice trembled.

"For a long time, now, I thought I must go," confessed Lilli. "Each time I see a wagon go down the road to the city, with a boy or girl from our village leaving, I think, 'Some day my time will come.' But that will be a long time yet, Vanni, maybe one year, maybe two."

"You are making plans and in them there is no room for me?" the boy asked sadly. She averted her face. "I'll never forget you, Vanni. Never." She leaned over and pressed her face against his.

Boys and girls rode by in wagons, shouting and laughing. Nearby, the sound of the *tsymbaly*, played by some old man, arose, weird and high-pitched, in so compelling a rhythm that all who heard it were stirred by that primitive music. Vanni began to sing: "What a glorious night!" His tenor voice was

soft and resonant; it caused Lilli's heart to quiver. All his soul
was revealed in his open countenance, the trembling of his lips
as he sang, the tender look of his eyes as they wandered over
her face.

"You have two dancing devils in your eyes, Lilli," he said
when he had finished. "What do you want of life, that you are
going so far to look for it?" He nuzzled her cheek.

"What do I want?" A sense of longing filled Lilli. Longing
for what? What was she seeking of life? She sighed and stirred
restlessly. "I don't know exactly," she confessed. "Only that
there's so much I must learn, and I can't learn it here."

"What do you think of when you sing, Lilli?" the boy
asked.

"So many things – " she meditated. "I think of wheat fields
with the sun on them, of sheep crunching in meadows, of
leaves turning in the wind – I look at the faces of people, and
in each heart is a remembering, of something that makes them
happy or sad – " She stopped suddenly.

"That's why your song is so rich, Lilli," said the boy. "Not
like a singer who thinks, how can I make my voice loud so
everyone will say, what a big voice he has! Your voice is big
because your feelings are big – that is different." He paused
while he caressed Lilli's hair and then went on, "Once to the
village came a big singer from the city. She was so proud, so
big! Everything was big, blue eyes like glass, big smiles full of
big white teeth, red dress too tight to show how big her bosom,
big voice like tin horn. Some people, not knowing, said, "Like
an angel, she sings!" But all the time she sang, I thought of a
donkey who makes a big noise but doesn't know why. People
went away empty, there was nothing to warm them."

Lilli laughed as she reached over and tugged Vanni's two
upright curls. "You think that, and you wonder, why is it Lilli
wants to learn?"

Vanni sighed. "You are right, Lilli, you must not stay here.
When you have something to give, it's wrong to hide it." A
lump arose in his throat and for a moment he could not

continue. A big tear squeezed out of Lilli's eyes and rolled down to her mouth. She licked it in with her tongue and swallowed it. Then the song of a whip-poor-will, breathless, mysterious, in the pale moonlight, resounded in a thicket, as if expressing the poignancy of young lovers soon to be parted.

Vanni began to speak, eyes fixed on Lilli's face as though he wanted to memorize it. "I have so much to remember about you, Lilli, pictures I'll never lose, because they're in my mind." He stroked her hand. "How you put a red cap on Petey's head, and sat looking at him with love in your eyes, and kissed his cheeks. . . . How you cracked my egg with your big one. . . . How you jumped over the burning straw cross at Christmas, and Petey flew through the air like a fat little pigeon. . . . How young, how fresh I felt that day, frost on my cheek! You had a white wool cap and your eyes shone like two green lamps. You pulled off my mitt and ran away with it. . . . I remember the colour of the fire against the snow and the smoke and boys and girls laughing. . . ." He paused while he recalled all the sensations, all the sights of that glorious winter day, then, as he finished, his voice broke: "Don't forget, you belong to me."

"I don't know if I belong to anyone," sighed Lilli. She felt the light golden hairs on Vanni's wrist. "Who knows what life will bring us?"

"Whatever it brings, we'll be together," said the boy positively. "Some day, maybe in a few years, or many, I will be walking in a strange place and I will see a girl, not too big, singing, and a crowd of people will be listening, and I will know it's my girl. . . ."

Sitting cheek to cheek, arms intertwined, they listened while the primitive harp still sounded, as the old man played on. "You are sad, Lilli?" She shook her head. "Then why are you crying?" he demanded as she brushed a tear away. "I always feel sad when I hear music." He brushed her lips with a light kiss. "I understand," he whispered. "I won't keep you now, Lilli. And some day, when you sing, the whole world will listen."

5
THE RAILWAY BUILDERS
❦

IT WAS a late afternoon in June and Lilli, walking across the prairies, was surrounded by a mass of bloom. The wild prairie roses, streaked with red, held up fiery torches on all sides. Sunflowers, poppies, tiger lilies and violets – like a group of Bukovynian peasant women, their dress varied in shade from orange to rose to purple, and yet all blended. Scents, too, were more discernible – the fragrance of hay and wild mint arose from the meadows and sloughs so that the very air had a tang of honey. Lilli stood still for a moment, overcome by the beauty of it. With a lifetime of living on the prairie, it seemed to her that she would never exhaust its infinite variations; why did her mother find it monotonous?

At that moment, the soothing hum of the prairie – the wind, the insects, the call of birds – was suddenly disrupted by a great bustling, an ear-splitting din, and echoes on the flat plains, with hissing of steam, buzzing saws, clanging hammers, booming timbers and the calls of men. "It's the railroad gang!" thought Lilli with great excitement, recalling that only the previous evening her grandfather had mentioned that a gang of workmen were building a new spur of railway in that district. "I'm going to see them!" She began to run in the direction of the noise, curious to see the building of this path to the outside world. Railway building was one of the most dramatic chapters in the history of the Canadian West, and the speech of the Bukovynian homesteaders made constant reference to their experience on the extra gang.

As she approached, the din grew louder and a great gang of men became visible – about two hundred in all, all working, calling, laughing, their voices harmonizing with the metallic ring of their tools. Perspiration oozed off their faces in great streams, the sound of their breaths came in deep rasps as they heaved about the great timbers. The gandy-dancers – trackmen who handled the shovels, were executing a kind of jig as they tapped the ties with foot on shovel and their legs moved up and down in rhythm. The spikers, wielding their eight-pound spike-mauls in a circle about their heads, stood with both feet outside the rail to spike the track. Like a down-beat came the call of the foreman, chanting directions to the toiling men, and in rhythmic response, the hammers replied. As they worked, Lilli saw the slim steel ribbon growing across the prairie before her very eyes.

When she was a few feet away, she could see that the gang was preparing to cease work. One of the foremen, a Swede, was the first to notice the girl. "Well, well, here is a girl come to visit us." Lilli approached, curious about the appearance of these men, who were to her like beings from another world. Their faces were wild, and many of them were bearded. "Come here, don't be afraid," urged the foreman. "What's your name?" She stood off a little as she replied, "Lilli." His freckled face presented no threat under its thatch of sandy hair. "Would you like to have supper with us, Lilli?" He grinned to hear her eager reply, "Oh, yes!" She stole a glance at this great gang of men who had assembled in the wilderness from the four corners of the earth.

"Get on the hand-car with us, and we'll be the first there."

With a gesture of his hand, the foreman summoned a group of about eight men, who along with the Swede and Lilli crowded on the hand-car, which was set in motion by pumping it up and down, so that it slid along the steel rails. It was a ride of some two miles back to the dining-car. At that moment, the stop-work whistles blew and the men of the gang, dropping their tools with a great clatter, made a wild rush to the hand cars, and in groups of eight or ten crowded on the cars and set off down the rails. Back and forth went the handles in frenzy as the workers in the first car exerted themselves to draw from the other cars, which swished along the tracks after them, while the sound of wheels and the pumping of handles mingled with the calls and laughter of the men. The big sweaty bodies crouched on the cars as they swept through the countryside in a clamorous procession. Along the route, people in the fields stared and pointed at the sight; children laughed and shouted. "Speed it up! Speed it up!" the men urged, so that they had scarcely time to wipe their perspiring brows. "Let 'er go!" called the men in the leading car. "Let 'er go!" From one car to the next, down the entire line of twenty cars, the men called, "Let 'er go!" Looking back at the racing cars behind her, Lilli shouted. "We're far ahead!" She laughed with delight as the wind blew through her hair and billowed her blouse at the back like a balloon. Every so often she caught the scent of prairie roses or traced the wings of birds etched in copper on the sloughs over which they flew.

Within a short while the leading car was at the diner, and the men jumped off, taking Lilli with them. Supper was a tumultuous affair, due not so much to conversation – for the men scarcely paused to say a word in their eagerness to gobble the huge messes of bacon, beans and pie on their plates – as to the rattle of the tin cups and plates, the clink of knives and forks, and the smack of thick coffee mugs as they were banged down on the table.

After supper, Lilli watched as the men separated into various groups to transact their domestic duties. Some washed out their shirts and socks and hung them up on an improvised clothesline between two scrubby trees. Others sat around rolling cigarettes while they listened to Vasyl recite his popular tale, "How I Fell in Love for the First Time." He chose each word carefully and economically, as though he were buying it, but each word was like a jewel. He was a born storyteller; the men never tired of listening to him. Roman, the linguist, was the letter-writer for the whole group and specialized in writing and reading letters in any language; he was now writing letters home for two Italians, using a phonetic system which he had invented. "Bene, bene," said the Italians with excitement as they bent over the letters. Ivan, a trumpet player who had taught himself to play by means of a correspondence course, was now playing long, lonely notes which seemed to express the nostalgia of the men on the prairies. Sandy, a Scot, was teaching a Ukrainian how to read the English Bible. Two Swedes, freckled and red-headed, were engaged in a wrestling match. A crowd looked on, including the cook in his white apron. A few Hungarians with looks of swarthy melancholy were playing poker for matches, the slap of their dirty cards sounding at intervals against the wooden crate on which they were playing. Lilli took a deep breath and looked about her. "Like a gypsy camp," she thought, as she watched the throng of two hundred men moving in the twilight about the camp fire. Above the general hubbub, the mournful notes of a whip-poor-will sounded from time to time. The workers, clad in their khaki-coloured or blue denim work shirts, presented a study in racial differences – German, Irish, Ukrainian, Scottish, Italian, Scandinavian – their powerful physiques were outlined in statuesque poses against the open prairie.

Suddenly a call for attention was heard. "Make way for the dancers!" A space was cleared, and three young Bukovynians, their bronzed bodies naked to the waist, began to dance, forming beautiful sculptured movements with arms and torso while they shook their long waving manes. One caught up a scarlet shirt and manoeuvred this like a cape, with expert and precise movements. Beating time with their feet, the undulations of their bodies increased to a frenzy. They had the delicate chiselled features of the Carpathian mountaineers, yet there was a certain fierceness of expression revealed in the quivering of the nostrils. As she watched them, Lilli's senses throbbed, her pulses pounded in rhythm. The dance was now accelerated in barbaric intensity, the dancers jumping first on one foot and then on the other until the ground reverberated beneath them. As they danced, the men watching pounded out an accompaniment with feet and hands, and one played a drum instrument, consisting of a leather skin stretched over a frame, with bells attached. Then the dancers ceased, a shudder passed over them and they motioned to the water boy who threw buckets of water over their glistening bodies. The other workers, who lay exhausted after their work, were stupefied by this display of ferocious vitality. "Bravo, bravo!" they clapped. "The devil take them! Here we are too tired to move after work and see how these people can dance!"

Lilli stared as though hypnotized during this performance. Unconsciously, she had been imitating the movements of the men, swaying her body as they swayed theirs, moving her long hands with grace as they moved. When she realized that the men had been watching her, she stopped and laughed. "O to dance is a wonderful thing!" she exclaimed. "All over you come to life." Her spontaneous outburst caused chuckles from many of the men. Each, as he looked at the young girl, fresh in her blue blouse and red skirt, thought of his own family – his wife, a daughter, a sweetheart, for despite the harsh life of the extra gang, these men, beneath their rough exterior, were amenable to the appeal of sentiment.

When the evening grew cool, the men built a bonfire and lounged about it, their tongues unloosened, while they told stories of the Klondike gold rush, of the building of the transcontinental across the Rockies, of dreadful accidents which had taken a toll among the immigrants, of lonely graves beside the railway. These were the men who had travelled across Canada ahead of the steel, who had worked in the bush and logging camps; who knew the western country from daily living with it, as a worker does, from mountains blasted to make tunnels, from swamps filled in to make roadbeds. They spoke of death by violence, of strange chances, of fortunes made overnight, of the motley, tragic procession to the Klondike gold fields. They mentioned such names as Persia, Turkey, Romania, Alaska, Yukon, Oregon, for these men were great travellers. They spoke the language of the common man, full of descriptive phrases from their occupations. They spoke of the mushrooming of prairie towns: "In one week Main Street appeared, with barber shop, bank and restaurant." They recited anecdotes of their adventures; they told of how Scottish lads worked on a cooperative system and "taught the rest of us how a grade ought to be built." They spoke of the track-layer which they named "the gibbet" because of its resemblance to gallows. They spoke of the difficulties of building the railway – of fighting swamp, forest, rock, quicksand, blizzards in the rough country. This was how they had come to know Canada, which to them was a pitiless wilderness. Some pointed to missing fingers or toes, relics of old accidents. They spoke of men lost in snowstorms, or entombed in swamps or slush on the lakes. One told a grim story of conveying a corpse on a sleigh through a forest, until he nearly went out of his mind. They told how they had talked, sung and prayed in loneliness and isolation. They spoke of dynamite and flying rock responsible for the death of many a "rock-hog."

There was one man, an Englishman, obviously a cultured man, despite his muddy, torn patched khaki trousers and brown flannel shirt, who described his reason for leaving England and coming to work on this railway gang: "I should have starved as a clerk in London."

The singing now became general. There were songs of nostalgia, of the homeland, of loneliness for wife and children. One would commence to sing some snatch of song, dimly recalled from the old country, and then, his private ache eased, lapse into silence, while another took up the tune. Sometimes two or three joined together, harmonizing while the rest kept

215

time by tapping their feet. As they sang, the men turned often to look at Lilli, and their rough faces would soften, recalled to a mood of tenderness by her presence. Seeing her here among them, with her neat figure, her eyes shining with excitement, her brown braids gleaming in the light of the fire, they became conscious that somehow they were pleasing her and giving her something that she valued as few girls of her age would have valued.

When they had sung for a while, one of the workers, a Scot, asked, "Will you sing for us now, Lilli?" The men cried out in chorus, "Yes, yes, let the girl sing for us!" Sensing the drama of the thing, more and more men drifted to the campfire until a great circle of over a hundred men had formed around Lilli. "What song do you like?" Lilli asked, pleased at being the centre of attention. "How about Annie Laurie?" suggested the Scot. The men murmured approval. "Give us Annie Laurie! That's a beautiful song, now! Do you know that one?" Their eyes were fixed with expectancy on the slight figure of the young girl. Lilli got up and stood by the fire where the flames illumined her face, and with a blanket draped about her, she commenced to sing, while the men hushed. They were expecting the small, sweet voice of a schoolgirl, and were astonished when the rich, low voice poured from her mouth. As she sang, the men joined in softly, the girl's voice soared against the background of chording male voices, then descended in a graceful swoop to a deep, thrilling note at the end of the song. The men were profoundly stirred. "Bravo, bravo!" they called, clapping and stamping. They liked the simple old songs, which had a strong emotional appeal to these workers exiled from home. "Big voice for small girl," commented the Swede. "We Swedes had a singer like you once, Lilli - also not too big. She was called the Swedish Nightingale and she had wonderful voice! But you - " He paused before he bestowed the accolade - "You are the nightingale of the prairies." The Scot found this comparison a little too much for his sense of humour. "It's only in Canada you'd find a little Bukovynian girl singing a Scottish song like a Swedish nightingale," he chuckled. His sally aroused roars of mirth from the men; their laughter resounded in waves over the prairies, the men laughing not so much at the witticism, as in enjoyment of the situation; the girl's performance had pleased them mightily.

As the men sang on, Lilli ran out from the circle to stand a little apart, on the steel track, looking into the distance and remembering that night – how many years ago – four or five? When she had ridden on the jigger with her Irish friend. It seemed impossible that she had been that sickly child. She felt that nothing could conquer her now. O how strong! O how full of life! O everywhere beauty, beauty! she thought as with head uplifted to the the prairie sky she vowed, "Some day I'll travel down this steel track to faraway countries, some day I'll travel all over the world, gathering songs."

6
THE LAND FIRST

ON AN evening not long after, Anton arrived at Grandfather Nestor's cottage to make a proposal regarding Lilli's future. She had forgotten how overwhelming was his authority until his great untidy presence stood in their tiny immaculate kitchen, and as Anton strode to the table and threw himself upon a chair, his big muck-covered boots left tracks upon the floor which Lilli had recently scrubbed. As she looked at him, an uneasy feeling, growing like an unhealthy fungus within her, told her that his attitude of smugness portended something ominous for her.

"Well," he said, smacking his lips after he had stowed away the excellent supper of dumplings which Lilli had prepared. "I have a match for you, Lilli, and such a match!"

Lilli's heart began to thud unevenly, and she clutched the edge of the table.

Anton continued, crossing one leg over the other, and scratching his left ear, "I have been speaking to Simon Zachary, and we have made a deal. Lilli is to marry him, and in exchange he will give me some acres he owns at the south end of our fields. Think what a bargain! He is not even asking for a dowry." Anton slapped his hand on his thigh with gratification, then looked across at Lilli, although previously he had been addressing Grandfather Nestor, almost as though Lilli were not involved in the matter at all. "You remember him, Lilli? He was at Fialka's wedding. A big, fine-looking fellow."

Remember him? Yes, Lilli remembered those lascivious hands pinching young girls' rumps and breasts, she remembered the wet red lips parted over the jagged yellow teeth, and the dirty frayed moustache stained with grease and tobacco juice. Remembering, she shuddered.

"I don't like him." She spoke through stiff lips, unable to collect her forces for a defence.

Anton threw his head back and roared as if Lilli had just made a joke. "You will learn to like. What is it to me, if you like, not like. My mind is made up to have that piece of land."

"But father," protested Lilli, aroused now as she realized the seriousness of the situation. "That's my life you're trading for your fields. As long as I live, I'll be paying for those acres. That's too high a price. Let me work out," she pleaded with passion, "I'll send you money. You can buy land, as much as you'll get from Zachary. Only let me be free, don't trade me. I'm a person. So many years, and I'm only sixteen!"

When she had finished, she looked about the room and thought how every object had assumed a sinister shape, how their secure little home had suddenly become converted into a prison cell.

Her father listened unmoved throughout, as though discounting her opposition. After all, it was traditional for girls to protest against marriage, it established their modesty, but in the end, they all gave in and resigned themselves well enough. But Lilli, watching his face, was reminded of a previous occasion when Anton had worn that same expression, compounded of sadism and satisfaction, and this had been when he was taming his new horse Diamond. "He looks at me with the same eyes," thought Lilli, "as though he'd like to tame me to his will, but he won't."

Anton meanwhile rubbed his hands as he calculated what a good bargain he had made.

"You're of an age to be a wife," he said with a coarse grin. Putting his hand into the pickle jar, he fished out a dill pickle, bit into it, and then made a wry face. "Something too much of salt here," he said, but he finished it off and then wiped his hands on his shirt front.

Grandfather Nestor, who had been listening with a perturbed expression, now intervened on behalf of his granddaughter. "This Zachary has a bad reputation, Anton. They say that he beat his last wife when she was carrying a child, and as a result, the girl died in childbirth. A young one, too, not yet twenty. It is only six months since she was laid in her grave. This is not a good thing, Anton, to give Lilli to him. You may regret you ever laid eyes on that land."

As her grandfather was speaking, Lilli recalled the pale, frightened face of the girl who had danced so reluctantly with Zachary at Fialka's wedding, and the story of her tragic death which was still whispered about among the women. So short a time the girl had had before her, and her fate had already been marked out, in the midst of that merriment!

Anton could no longer conceal his impatience. "Does Lilli expect an easy life, to live as a lady?" he asked. "She must learn that life is work, hard work. Here in this country there is no room for ladies. The land takes before it gives. Simon Zachary is a good farmer, one of the best. Lilli will be lucky to be his wife. She can help him in many ways – cook, sew, clean – oh, I commended her to him! He was so anxious to have her, he could scarcely wait! He is fond of jellied pigs' feet, and when I told him how you prepared it, with garlic and spices, the spit ran from his mouth." Anton laughed at the memory.

"But father," said Lilli, trying to control her panic so she could reason with him, "a person is more important than a piece of land. Isn't that so?"

"No!" Her father pounded his fist on the table. "Land comes first, always. That is why I was born, that is why you were born – to serve the land. For Peter, for my new son, this land will bring a better life."

"Am I, too, not your child?" inquired Lilli desperately, and she felt the weight of his dislike in the glance he gave her.

"You – Gypsy!" Anton spat on the floor then wiped his mouth with the back of his hand. "Who knows where you came from! That in my family should be such a gypsy!" He laughed, then extended his forefinger. "You will do as I say, or else – " He doubled his hand into a fist, and shook it at her. "I will take you to him, if I have to drag you by the hair, in the sight of all."

The words lingered in the air, chilling the atmosphere. Lilli shivered, and held up her hand to her cheek, as if to protect herself. She drew a long breath, so sharp it was audible, like the sigh of a person about to surrender his soul.

Anton, feeling some compunction for his daughter, tried to cajole her; "Ech, Lilli, cease blowing up your face with pouts. Zachary is a good enough fellow. He has a home all made of bricks, with a stove half as big as this room. Pots, dishes, you have never seen the like! And a new copper kettle he just got from town. You can be the grandest housewife in the district, a nest just made for you."

"If he is so grand," said Lilli bitterly. "Why is it no girl will marry him, but all tremble and hide when they see his matchmakers coming?" She made another spirited attempt to persuade her father: "Fialka had her choice," she pointed out.

"Fialka!" A sound of disbelief issued from Anton's throat. "You are not one such as Fialka! Look at you – small, wretched, eyes as big as potatoes. What boy would take you? Fialka is a beautiful girl, who could have her choice of all the young men in the district, and she chose wisely. For you, there is no choice."

"Vanni Karmaliuk – " began Lilli, and could have bitten out her tongue for her indiscretion. Her father turned pale with anger beneath his deep tan. "Karmaliuk!" he breathed. "Karmaliuk!" he repeated incredulously. "Never will I permit a daughter of mine to marry a Karmaliuk. Besides, do you think he will marry you?" Anton snorted. "I have heard how he met you secretly at night. He also meets other girls. . . ."

"No!" cried out Lilli, unable to conceal her feelings. "Vanni would never do that. He is a good, true boy!"

Her father smiled. "Aha, you speak for him, do you?" His face became sly as he realized how he had caught her. "Let me tell you, Lilli. Vanni wants only one thing from you, and when he has that, he will run away, as his father has already matched him with a fine, plump blonde." Anton made a gesture to indicate a buxom figure. "People are beginning to say that in our district, every farmer has an unmarried daughter with a baby. I will not have this said of my family, not even of you. You are not to see this Vanni any more. No, that is enough," as Lilli opened her mouth to speak, but she was not to be deterred.

"In Canada girls can marry whom they please." In spite of herself, the words burst from Lilli's mouth, impelled by a bursting heart.

"In Canada, I am still head of my family," replied Anton. "And I won't hear any more talk from you. Get your things ready, for he is coming in two weeks to fetch you. . . . Your mother, who is pleased about this, I can tell you, has been sewing late into the night for you, for she never expected to get you off her hands so soon."

"Two weeks!" exclaimed Lilli in dismay. In two weeks, her life would be sold, all doors closed, all music stilled. She would be given, like a piece of machinery, to slave for this man, to share his most intimate life, perhaps to bear children to him. "Two weeks!" she repeated, and the sound of her voice caused even Anton to blench. "So soon!" she cried. "So soon!" she wailed in a higher, even more distracted tone.

The old man protested: "Why this haste, Anton? Give the girl a chance to get used to the idea, she may become reconciled to it. But this unseemly haste is bound to cause talk among the neighbours."

Anton stirred uneasily. He did not wish to admit how

sordid a bargain he had driven, but pressed now for an explanation he had to admit: "Zachary is in a hurry as he must get some one to help him with the harvest, to cook for the harvesters."

"I will not – " began Lilli, but she was cut short by her father, whose stubbornness increased at this unexpected opposition.

"No more words from you!" He slammed his great hand on the table, so that the dishes fell off to the floor.

The silence which followed was like a hand gripping Lilli's neck. Her eyes became dark and huge, her nails dug deeply into her palms so that they bled, her throat choked off all speech. She felt that her life had been snatched from her. All that bad sprung to life in the past years – affection, understanding, laughter, music – suddenly withered as though a blight had fallen. One last time she must try, and her voice was hoarse with anguish as she choked out, "Father, this marriage cannot be."

"Cannot!" Anton snorted, getting up preparatory to leaving. "Can, and will, as you will see in two weeks. Parents still have power, as you will find out if you try to cross me." Anton strode across the room to the door and the beat of his heavy heels, as they struck the floor, were like hammers crushing out her hope.

Lilli remained still only until the footsteps had died away, telling her that her father was out of hearing, then she turned to the old man, stretching her hand in a gesture of supplication. "Grandfather!" she appealed. "Grandfather." Again she spoke and came closer, but the old man turned away, even though her touch on his shoulder was like a reproach. He shook his head, as though wishing to be rid of this bad business.

"He is your father, you must obey him."

That evening, which Lilli spent quietly in the company of her grandfather, Lilli said farewell, in her thoughts, to the community which had nourished her. Although outwardly acquiescent, her course of action had already been determined. Her father's laws were made in the old country, she reasoned, but she, Lilli, had been born in the new. Her need for Anton's approval vanished, and how much she had grown with this knowledge. She was strong now, strong enough to revolt against his authority. Rebellion that had been growing within Lilli sprang up and took shape. Tiny seeds sown by MacTavish, by Vanni, by others had taken root, spread deep, more so than she had realized. She simmered as she thought of it. Her fresh young body given to the uses of that man! Her strength in the services of his greed! All the years of her life taken from her, the rightful owner, and bestowed on this gross stranger! As she looked at her grandfather through deep, secretive eyes, she said inwardly, although she spoke no word, "This marriage will never be."

The old man, as he sat near the lamplight carving a wooden box for Lilli, was thoughtful that night, obsessed with reflections of old age and death, and with regret at the injustices of man.

"What is life?" he mused. "Like the brief flame of a candle or the song of a bird, or a blossom in spring. Old age isn't happiness. To wait – until the Old Man from Up Yonder comes to you with a letter from the next world, or kicks you from behind into eternity. Ah, Lilli, youth is sacred, and when you are old, everything falls into decay. You go about, not as if you were preparing to live, but as if you were waiting for a summons, and had little time to put your house in order."

The words of the old man, repeated over and over, began to fall into a kind of funereal cadence, and the phrases united in rhythm. What is life, the voice within Lilli repeated. Like the brief flame of a candle, like the song of a bird, like a blossom in spring. Sadness overwhelmed Lilli, but within her the song became more persistent, and the lines repeated themselves:

What is life,
Like the brief flame of a candle,
Like the song of a bird,
Like a blossom in spring.

The stern jarring note of personal discord, alternating with the rhapsodic nature of her grandfather's meditation, wove a melody in Lilli's mind, a theme of conflict, now harsh, now melancholy, now bursting forth in protest.

Finally, as she still sat up and the old man slept while the clock struck farther and farther into the night, something like calm began to assert itself in her spirit, although the current of her discontent still ran dark and deep within her.

Two evenings later, Lilli waited secretly by the schoolhouse and waylaid MacTavish as he was locking the door after the last of the scholars had departed.

"Mr. Mac, I must see you." The urgency of her voice, as it came from behind him, startled the teacher and he turned around to look at her.

Her face, framed by the flowered blue silk shawl which had once been Granny Yefrosynia's, was of a sick pallor, and her eyes were smudged beneath with dark circles, as though she had not slept. MacTavish knew at once that Lilli was in grave trouble.

"Come back into the schoolhouse. We can talk there privately." They went within and Lilli sat down in the bench near the window, where once – for how brief a time! she had thought to be a scholar. With what wonder she had examined the globe, the blackboard decorated with chalk, the books, and taken delight in the magic of their shapes and uses, and now that magic was replaced by dull regret, and she was a young woman faced with the urgent problems of womanhood.

Lilli looked at the teacher, at that thin foxy face which was certainly not handsome, if handsomeness were merely a matter of physical regularity, and tears hung trembling in the corner of her eyes, tears of gratitude that in her life she had been fortunate enough to encounter such a man.

"Well, what is it, Lilli?" said MacTavish, assuming his brusque, dictatorial manner as he saw that emotion had made her dumb. "Speak up, you have no cause to fear." He got out his pipe and rammed it into his mouth with his odd, authoritative gesture.

Lilli gulped twice, to swallow the bulge in her throat, and then spoke. "Father want me to marry Simon Zachary."

MacTavish took some time to examine his fingernails before he spoke. "I see."

"You know him?" Lilli's tenseness relaxed under the influence of MacTavish's casual behaviour.

"Yes," said MacTavish, who had already sized the whole situation up and was now busy working out a solution.

"Zachary will give father piece of land for me." Lilli explained the bargain her father had made.

The teacher listened, heart wrung by the pathos of Lilli's dilemma as reflected in her intensely Slavic face. How quickly she had reverted to the melancholy of the peasant! He wondered how long it would take for these people to work out from their souls the remnants of serfdom, to dispense with those ways of life incompatible with existence in the new country? All the weight of a semi-feudal heritage hung in the balance against Lilli's future happiness.

MacTavish knew that Anton Landash, for all his brutality, had many admirable qualities, and these were qualities necessary to the pioneer in his struggle for a better way of life. Land was the only good that Landash knew, and for him, all progress had to be related to it. But sensibilities, as MacTavish knew them, had early been trampled out of these people, who had been ground into the earth, and indeed they might have been a hindrance in the brutalistic life the settlers had to endure in those years of new breaking.

If he acted rashly now, MacTavish knew, he might arouse against himself, not only Landash, but also the entire

Bukovynian community, and then all his chances for assisting progress would be destroyed. He would have to proceed with caution, but in this he was helped by Lilli, for she now asked him, as though intuition had told her what stage his reasoning had reached.

"What is law of Canada, Mr. Mac – must girl marry man her father choose?"

MacTavish started, as though his mind had been read. He replied, "The law is that a girl over sixteen may lead her life as she wishes, apart from her parents' home, if she supports herself."

Joy ran over Lilli's face, rubbing out all her dismay. "Then I don't have to stay – I don't have to marry Zachary – "

"No." MacTavish made his tone definite. He added, "It would help, of course, if you were away from here, and working – "

"Yes, that I must do. Go away. Now, before too late," said Lilli. "Leave grandfather, leave home, leave Vanni – " Lilli's voice broke at the thought of her young lover, and she buried her face in her hands.

Why was it at this moment MacTavish suddenly thought of two opposite images – the image of Anton's great, tan peasant boots as MacTavish had seen them tramping across the furrows of his newly-broken earth, and the contrasting image of the dancing yellow boots of Fialka, as he had seen them at that wedding – how long ago – three years? The ruthless strides of the pioneer, beating out their harsh rhythms, crushing anything delicate that might come into their path, and the exuberant rhythm of dancing boots, tracing a pattern of joyous colour: these two pictures symbolized for MacTavish the beauty and brutality in the heritage of these people. Was it not asking too much of these unlearned immigrants, he thought, that they should pause in the midst of their pioneering labours to decide how much of that beauty they should retain, how much surrender of their brutality?

He turned now to the task at hand of instructing Lilli in

the business of leaving the village and obtaining employment in the city. When they had discussed the practical aspects, and made a plan, he said to her,

"After you leave the village, and the affair has died down, I'll speak to your father myself. He may be in a mood to listen to reason by then."

Lilli arose from her seat and stretched her arms above her head with relief. "After I leave!" she breathed. "Oh, yes, after!" It was really possible, then, she had regained the right to her own life, she could still work out her own destiny. How good were the long years ahead of her, stretching beyond a hundred!

"Oh, Mr. Mac," she exclaimed, trying to express her gratitude. "If I could do something for you – if I could give you something, but I have nothing."

As MacTavish rose to accompany her to the door, he said, "You've given me a great deal, already, Lilli. Meeting you has been one of the great experiences of my life."

Before returning to his bachelor shack beside the schoolhouse, MacTavish stood for a long time and watched Lilli walking down the road, her dark silhouette standing out against the brilliance of the Manitoba sky. As he turned away, the incongruous thought came to him that Lilli in the end would prove to be stronger than her father, and the words flamed in his mind,

"There's something about her can't be beaten."

7
NEW HORIZONS
❦

BEFORE she left the village, Lilli felt she must say farewell to Vanni, and they met secretly one evening on the bank of the river. Vanni was not long in discovering that Lilli was not her usual self.

"Well, *malenka* (little one)," he said, "what have you for me today?" He hugged her to him and put his hand beneath her chin. "What is this face so full of clouds? Not like my Lilli. Why nothing happy makes? No songs? No jokes? No smiles?"

"I have something sad to tell you, Vanni, tonight."

Vanni looked at her closely for a long time. "Yes, I see something is the matter." He took her arm gently and motioned to sit down on the ground. "Come, tell me."

In a heartbroken voice, Lilli began to tell him the story of the match her father had arranged for her, and as she was speaking, Vanni interrupted with frequent exclamations of rage.

"Well, what do you say, Vanni?" she asked when she had finished.

Vanni's face was serious, as he knew Landash's reputation for stubbornness. "If your father make up his mind, he will carry this through."

"Yes," agreed Lilli and she looked and looked at him, for the last time in her life, perhaps. He had been devised exactly to Lilli's taste – tiptilted nose, broad at the end, sunlit eyes full of prankish freckles, rosy skin as if peeled off an apple, and dearest of all, his two forelocks, obstreperously curly, despite applications of vaseline.

"I wonder who make you like that, Vanni?" Lilli asked, after drinking up his face with her eyes.

"Like what?" asked Vanni, regarding Lilli as if she were a cheese dumpling, ready to be devoured.

"Exactly the boy I like. This, this, this." She touched his nose, eyes, cheeks, and then added, "Even these," and she pulled his two locks. Then suddenly she burst into tears and buried her face in his shirt.

Vanni tried to comfort her: "Think, Lilli, in the city you will learn so much, all you dreamed will come true, you will meet new people, forget me, maybe."

At this, Lilli seized his hand and cried out in protest: "No, no, Vanni, I'll stay here. Never mind about city, better to live on prairie with you, listen only to what my heart tells me." Even as she spoke, Lilli knew that she could not stay, that this was their last meeting. Her eyes overflowed and she sighed.

Vanni took her face in his hands and said: "Face all wet? From where come all those tears? Come, I'll sing one more song – " He cradled her head on his arm so she should not see his face, which was as wet as her own, and began to sing, with uneven voice, "Farewell, thou sad word, farewell. . . ."

Lilli, face buried in Vanni's sleeve, thought: "Why so heavy, heart? Why tears will not stop? Why I can't say good-bye? Why can't look, even, at him, so hurts me inside?"

When he left her at the gate, his eyes were no longer wet, he smiled and his voice was full of courage: "Good-bye, Lilli, don't be sad you are leaving me. Because everywhere I look, you'll be there. Not one thing on the prairie there is, which you didn't look at once with your eyes. All my life, I'll have you with me; where I go each morning, there I'll find you, everything will live with a different life, when I think that once I was there with you."

Not long after, Lilli made preparations to leave for the city.

She had gone back home the previous day to see Petey for the last time and to give him a rubber ball which she had bought in the village. There was anguish in her heart as she looked at the big log house and took farewell of each tree in the yard, that one, near the window, to which she had listened so many times on sleepless nights. . . . But Petey was inconsolable. Lilli stopped and put her arms around him, covering his fat face with kisses, and tears streamed down her face.

"Petey, little Petey," she murmured over and over, heartbroken at the thought that she might not see her little brother again. His stout little body felt so good pressed against her! Then she put him from her and resolutely marched down the archway of trees for the last time, without looking back. The small stout legs endeavoured to keep up with her and finally lagged behind. Then the boy sat down on the ground, and crying dolefully after her, lamented, "Lielana! Lielana! When are you coming back!"

She got up early next morning before her grandfather was awake, put on her navy blue jacket, and went down into the village to meet the market gardener who was to take her to the city. At last he came, jolly and red-faced, with sandy hair and a comical grin. His sheepskin coat must have been brought over from the old country, so bedraggled was it, but he wore it with an insouciant air. He placed the suitcase under the seat. "Well, you are going to the city today."

"At last." Lilli looked down the road which had taken so many other young people from this community which had nourished them, and had set them down in the alien city, to encounter – what fate?

She smiled tremulously, not daring to speak any more as she got into the back of the wagon and sat down among the milk cans and stone crocks containing sour cream and cottage cheese. It was a cool and fragrant morning and the early autumn landscape was beautiful. The clouds kept on drifting swiftly in the brilliant autumnal sky and impelling Lilli to follow them. The wind increased in strength and the leaves rustled. She looked back and saw the village vanishing, with all its familiar landmarks. She might never again see it, never again see Vanni and he would grow up and she would grow up and not know each other. If they were to meet on the village road ten or fifteen years hence, she thought, they might pass each other and not recognize that this was Vanni, that this was Lilli, that this stranger's face and mind concealed those memories shared, that affection aroused once, and perhaps not even remember the day of Midsummer on which they had pledged their youthful troth. The swamp would lie steaming in the summer sun and she would not be there to listen to the churring of insects, the call of gulls. The whispering pines would sing in the wind and she would not be there to listen to their song. She took farewell of every object as she passed by, trying to memorize its outlines so that it would remain in her memory. She looked long at the church with its silver domes and recalled the Paschal Night and the procession of singers about the bonfires. She thought of Petey, Petey who would grow up day by day, learning something new each moment, developing some endearing quality, laughing in the sunshine, and she would not share those joyous moments.

At first she had looked back at the road as familiar things disappeared, but now she directed her attention to the road ahead and to the new sights which appeared on every side. They passed other wagons on the road to market. A woman with a scarlet shawl turned to look at Lilli and smiled: "Are you going to the city?" And Lilli exclaimed: "Yes!" with delight and amazement, as though the whole world must know.

"Where are you going, Lilli? To what address?" inquired the driver.

"I don't know." She scarcely heeded him, so engrossed was she with the adventure before her.

"You are going to the city and you don't know an

address?" The driver was worried. "The city is a very big place. Are you going to visit?"

"I am going to find work." Lilli looked at the poplars at the side of the road as they shivered in the wind, and thought, "Like ladies dancing and shaking their hair."

The driver, however, was not to be put off. "What kind of work?" he asked.

"Housework. Sewing in a factory." Oh, there would be plenty of work, Lilli did not doubt. She could not imagine a situation where work did not exist for able hands, and hers – she looked at them, recalling how she had been ashamed of their knotted appearance, but now, those hands gave her a feeling of confidence – with such hands, she could not starve!

"You are a brave girl to go so far by yourself," the driver said. He meditated a while. "Tell you what, I'll take you to a friend of ours, a widow. She'll keep you a day or two, until you find a place." He looked back at the girl to reassure her. "Enjoy the ride, Lilli. It will be a few hours yet."

One person watched Lilli for a long time as the wagon in which she was riding disappeared down the road. It was the teacher, Ian MacTavish, who was out on his horse early that morning. As he followed with his eyes that courageous little figure sitting upright among the milk cans, he was conscious of a feeling of deprivation. Something had vanished from the landscape which had given it warmth and colour and vitality. MacTavish wondered what future lay ahead of the young girl. Would she lose those original qualities which formed her chief attraction, or would transference to an alien environment constitute a challenge to her? With her leaving, a chapter of his experience had come to a close. It was she who had first made him aware of her people. Without her, how many months it would have taken him to understand them! Surely, in the city, fate would place in her path those persons who could help her talent to fruition. A life such as hers must count, there was too much in her to go for nothing. As MacTavish turned back to the village, he lifted his hand in salute to courage, thinking that this was not good-bye, some day their paths would cross again. The conviction grew within him that Lilli was one of the strong ones, that she was destined to survive, that something of that fire and originality must surely pass into the heritage of the race.

PART SIX

In Search of a
Lost Legend

1
BUILDERS OF THE CITY
❦

THE RAW young city of the Red River Valley lay on the Manitoba prairie like a temporary intruder, a guest on that immensity only recently snatched from the wilderness. Faces on the streets of the city could provide a study in racial contrasts, for the population was one of the most cosmopolitan on the continent – Ukrainians, Poles, Jews, Icelanders from the great Northern lakes, Scottish Canadians, Métis, Mennonites, Hungarians, even gypsies. These people, through living together, through vital experiences shared – marriages, births, deaths, the land, harvests – dreamed common dreams, forged common bonds, built the foundations of the city. It was full of longing young people, aching with the ache of youth for life, trying to find themselves here in the city of the plains, not quite of the old world and yet not entirely accepted by the new. Lilli was one of these people as she walked down the broad central avenue – the broadest in the world, its citizens boasted – on a day in early winter. It was Thursday afternoon, known as Pot Wallopers' Day, because all the domestics of the city enjoyed a free afternoon, and the streets were thronged with domestics, most of them girls from the country like Lilli.

In the city, thought Lilli, you couldn't see the sky except in bits and patches, shining here and there through the buildings. There was never a clear great view of its immensity, as on the prairie. People spoke of things, bank, job, car, factory, their language was clipped and mechanical. Things obtruded, houses and buildings and machines. Nobody ever stopped to look at cloud formations, only at shop windows, cars, other people. As they hurried down the street, frowning and tight-lipped, they gazed with hostility at each other, or looked with anxiety at their own reflections in the plate glass windows, always this anxiety, as though misfortune were walking behind them, ready to tap their shoulder.

A light snow powdered the pavement with a sparkling lustre, like star dust, thought Lilli; sleigh bells jingled from the sleighs which dashed by, people hurried past in excited swarms, Ukrainian farmers burly in their sheepskin coats, policemen in buffalo robes, their six feet of height increased by eight inches of furry hat; Mennonites in black wool costume, Slavic women in flowered shawls, city girls with rosy faces against their dark furs. Lilli loved the smell of perfume which drifted from the furs of these women, she loved the feel of the oversize snowflakes as they stuck at random in her hair and eyelashes, like jewels.

There were certainly many sights to be seen along this avenue, not only the wealth of shops with their enormous plate glass windows, and the variety of goods displayed therein, but the avenue itself – stretching west for miles into prairie country. If one followed that trail, Lilli had heard, one would eventually reach the city of Edmonton. The city was so immense, so breathtaking, so indomitable in its youth and in the diversity of its population, that it flung a challenge to all the young people who came seeking there. Its citizens, with their vigorous gestures, polyglot conversation, uninhibited laughter and peasant physique, certainly gave the impression of a city of pioneers.

Lilli, caught up in the impetus of the crowd, rushed along with them, although she would have preferred a more leisurely pace to examine, for example, a display of silk lingerie in pastel shades like a rainbow. Did women really wear such things beneath their outer garments? In the country all the farm women had undergarments made of flour sacks, or if they were well-to-do, they ordered substantial knitted wear through the mail order department of the big city department stores. Lilli thought she would love to know the feel of such garments next to her – cool, sleek, not scratchy, giving a sensuous thrill to the skin. She noticed everything – how the city women walked, for example, with light, almost dancing steps on their high heels, not heavily, with feet spread apart, like the farm women; how they talked, laughed, dressed. There was one display in a jeweler's window which attracted her eye and she stopped before it – an array of brilliant jewelry, necklaces, earrings, and most dazzling of all, a circlet for the head. Lilli moved her head so that her reflection appeared just beneath the circlet, and thus seemed to be crowned by it. She smiled dreamily, stood on tiptoe to be taller and looked at herself through half-closed eyes. Thus seen, the circlet seemed just to touch her hair, like the snowflakes which also glistened there. The tears in her eyes created a mirage through which she saw her own face, only lovelier and more mature, as she might be, a few years hence. She was so eager, so naive in her delight, that people laughed indulgently, sympathizing with the extravagant dreams of the young girl. There were some, too, who envied that youthful desire; it was so long since they had felt it in their own hearts! Her revelry was shattered by the laughter of two callow youths who came up behind her to watch her as she moved her head back and forth before the window. She appeared a grotesque little figure to them, worthy of ridicule, with her coat – a gift from her mistress in lieu of her first month's wages – dragging to her ankles, and an enormous turban sagging around her ears. "Hey, Mary," they cackled, bursting with their own wit, "Hey, Mary, it's not Hallowe'en. Go back to the farm." Lilli turned to face them and replied with dignity, "My name is Lilli, not Mary." At this, the young men guffawed more uproariously than ever. They felt sophisticated and city-wise in the presence of this raw country girl. "The little girl is wearing a coat too big," commented one woman to her companion as they passed by.

They could not touch the girl's exuberance. Everything was new, everywhere was discovery. Those whose minds were staled by the boredom of satiety might have longed to exchange places with her, to enjoy for a few moments, the fresh impact of life upon an unsophisticated heart. Lilli was happy.

She wandered about, as if in a big department store, looking at the dazzling array of merchandise which life had to offer.

2
A SCOTTISH BALLAD

❦

THE house in which Lilli was employed as a domestic was an old red brick one on the banks of the river. Formerly the residence of a pioneer English settler, it had, like others of its kind, been purchased by a prosperous business man who wished to establish himself as a solid citizen in the community. His wife, Rebecca Green, furnished the house with deep-piled carpets, upholstered furniture, massive mirrors, draperies, china, silver, in such quantities as to give an impression of magnificent bad taste. She economized on one item, however: her maids' wages and their living quarters – Lilli slept in the basement and Maggie, the cook, had a room in the attic. Mrs. Green, a portly, handsome woman with dark abundant hair and rich colour, was fond of rich food, rich clothes, embroideries, metallics, velvets and furs. She had an abundance of everything – colour, figure, furs, jewelry and voice, a coloratura soprano trained in an out-moded style of singing with exaggerated trills and tremolos. One afternoon, as Lilli was waxing the floors of the livingroom, Mrs. Green sat down at the piano to practise, feeling that she was accomplishing twice as much as usual, as she could thus direct Lilli's work at the same time. Her performance was punctuated at every line with a command to Lilli, giving an effect somewhat as follows: "I would that my love – a little more in the corner, Lilli – could silently flow in a single word – push that chair out of the way – I'd give it the merry breezes – don't rub so hard, girl, you'll wear out the floor."

The kitchen was a domain ruled over by Maggie, a Scottish cook who, because of her excellent cooking, could defy even Mrs. Green's edicts. In the matter of uniform, for example, Maggie insisted on wearing red shoes and red earrings with her black uniform, which fitted skin-tight over her full bust. A big, rawboned girl with frizzy red hair, red cheeks and large white teeth, Maggie regarded Lilli with exasperation, amusement and affection. When she discovered that the young girl had no nightwear, she supplied the lack from her own wardrobe. Lilli entered her room that evening and found on her bed an article of clothing whose purpose she could not guess.

"What that is, Meggie?" she finally inquired after she had stared at it for some time.

"That's a pajama, Lilli," Maggie raised her eyebrows. Had the little monkey never seen a pajama?

Lilli held up the garment. It was certainly an odd shape, the like of which she had never seen before.

"What for is it? Like overall, maybe? For work in kitchen?" It was too small for a man, she thought, and besides, it was pink with blue flowers.

"You put it on at night when you take off your clothes after you wash yourself all over," Maggie informed her.

Lilli was amazed. "People have special clothes for night time?" She held up the pajamas to herself and exclaimed: "Wonderful to live in the city! Think, only three days here and so much I have learn already!"

And several weeks later, returning from a party at two in the morning, Maggie had noticed a light in Lilli's basement window, and had gone down to investigate. There, in the little bare room, she had found Lilli on her knees praying at the window, her face upturned to the handful of stars she could see in the sky visible to her. Her body was swaying back and forth and she was fervently chanting in a language unintelligible to Maggie.

"Go to bed, you'll catch your death of cold," she had

admonished Lilli not unkindly, sensing that the girl derived consolation from this simple rite which kept her from feeling too abruptly cut off from her past. "I'm sure the Lord won't mind if you take a rest," she said with good humour.

The next day Maggie discussed the incident with her friend the milkman. "My granny is a person like Lilli," she began as she made preparations for baking. "In her time all folks believed in spirits, charms and such, but how can the girl, when we've a telephone and radio in the house!" She pounded the dough on the kitchen table with exasperation, as though she were dealing with Lilli, and resumed, "You think you've taught the little monkey civilized ways, then you turn around and catch her at it."

"At what?" questioned the milkman as he helped himself to the cookies, then stole up behind Maggie and squeezed her arm.

She slapped his hand a stinging blow and continued, "Singing those queer songs, with a look on her face, I never saw the like except on my Gram. It haunts me, that's what Gram says, her songs haunt her. And the looks of those big eyes of hers – they're strange eyes. I don't know whether they're pretty or not. Too big, I think." She opened the oven door to inspect the baking and added, in justice, "She catches on quick, though, been here only a few months and knows all the routine." She slammed the oven door. "But I was sorry for the poor little thing when she couldn't have Christmas Day off; she'd been counting on it so much."

Lilli had looked forward to Christmas, hoping that she might find a Greek Orthodox church where she might attend the Christmas service. On Christmas Day, however, instead of having the day off, Lilli was set to clearing the snow off the walks, as Christmas Eve had been stormy. As she shovelled the huge snowdrifts, piled several feet high in places, Lilli recollected the sacred Christmas dinner when the family returned home from the glorious Christmas service. Petey would be there, round cheeks puffing out as he ate his egg with big gulps, getting the yolk in golden whiskers about his firm little mouth; the baby would be making dimples in his high chair, Masha and Tasha would be sniffling with identical sniffles as they dipped their spoons into the big ceremonial dish of *kutia*.

Lilli heard the church bells ringing from a distance, and paused to listen. People began to hurry past to the Christmas service, brushing the snowflakes off their new hats which seemed incongruously gay in the wintry weather. The whole pageantry of the Christmas festival passed before Lilli's eyes, and she saw, as in a mirage, the village church, its silver domes sparkling in the winter sunshine, the crowds of people in their sheepskins and shawls streaming out of doors. In the throng, she saw the figure of her mother and father and Petey; she saw Vanni with his rosy face and golden freckles; she saw people climbing into their wagons. The mirage was so real that she could discern the features of neighbours, hear voices, the chiming of bells and shouts of "Christ is Born!" Then, having cleared the walk Lilli went within, eyes swollen with tears, to make preparations for Mrs. Green's Christmas cocktail party.

One day Lilli had come into the kitchen all glowing after a walk in a nearby park and described to the cook the flight of wild geese. "Nobody was looking at them except me, Meggie," she exclaimed in a breathless voice. "Wings shining in the morning sun, hundreds of them, in two big V's across the whole sky, calling to each other and waving big wings. . . . People coming and going. . . . This so beautiful thing in the skies, and nobody saw."

The Scottish girl listened with an indulgent smile. "People in the city don't get excited about such things as you do, Lilli," she said as she whipped up a batch of biscuits. "They've forgotten about the land, most of them, though if you go back a bit, you'll find, sure enough, that most of them were farmers once, or were the children and grandchildren of farmers. . . ."

She added, with a kindly pat of Lilli's shoulder: "It's good to hear you talk, though, Lilli. Strange, but I've always the feeling of listening to my Gram when you're around. Don't let anyone take what you have from you, it's something beautiful, right enough."

On their day off, Maggie suggested to Lilli as they were making preparations to leave the house: "I'll take you to see my Gram, Lilli. You should get along with her, with all your talk of spirits, charms, and those queer songs of yours."

"How old your Gram?" asked Lilli as Maggie adjusted a purple velvet beret upon her red curls.

"About one hundred years old," said Maggie, but she was exaggerating, her grandmother was only seventy.

The old lady, whom they found sitting in her midget parlour surrounded by plants, was a half pint of pepper and snuff, wrapped in a grey maud, and tolerating no nonsense from the younger generation.

"Well, you're small enough," she conceded with one look at Lilli, as though from such a small parcel of goods no great harm could come. "Neat," she commented, sucking a peppermint. "Except that your clothes are too big," she went on, scrutinizing Lilli further. "Like a small pea rolling around in a big pod."

After she had offered the girls a seat on the horse-hair sofa, and exchanged a few remarks with them, she inquired,

"Do you know, Lilli, I've noticed that you've a bit of Scottish accent. How is that?"

Lilli paused in the act of devouring a piece of shortbread to reply, "Because my school teacher, Mr. Mac, was Scottish and I tried to talk like that. I thought, that is the right way."

The two found it a bond that they both pronounced Maggie, Meggie; good with a good long "oo" and "very" with a Scottish burr of three r's.

"I hear you're something of a singer, Lilli," the old lady remarked. "Know any Scottish songs?" She settled back in her rocker and regarded Lilli from the top of her spectacles.

"Annie Laurie?" suggested Lilli, reaching for another piece of shortbread.

"Like to hear some more?" Gram inquired. She thought Lilli was eating too much, and removed the plate from her.

"Please!" exclaimed Lilli. "Meggie told me you know many, many Scottish songs." She pulled the plate back to her.

"It'll chill your blood to hear her," warned Maggie. "It'll make your hair stand on end."

"Nonsense," scoffed the old lady. "I'll have to admit the old songs were strong stuff. Ay, they could tell stories in those days! The songs of today – no blood in them, no blood at all!"

"There's certainly blood enough in your ballads, Gram," said Maggie, tossing her red curls. "Gore all over the place."

Gram ignored her granddaughter's impudence. "I'll sing you something I think you'll like, Lilli. It's called Twa Sisters of Binnorie. A grand song, Lilli, and an old one. The Scots in Canada seldom sing it now, perhaps because young people have become tame."

The ballad concerned the murder of a girl by her sister and the transformation of the victim into a musical instrument. Gram's voice, which ranged from a strident soprano to a hoarse whisper, instilled a sense of horror into the hearts of the listeners.

"It gives me the creeps," shuddered Maggie, but Lilli revelled in it. All during the performance, she could not take her eyes off the old lady, as though by looking at her she could absorb the essence of her personality. She knew she must make herself like the old lady, to sing that song as she did. "Never think to hear in the city such a thing!" she exclaimed when the old lady had finished. "Only our people in the country sing like that." A frown appeared on her forehead. "You know, Gram, we have something the same story in our language, we call it, Cranberry Flute. My Granny told this story to me when I was small girl, once I was sick. Question, how from Bukovyna to Scotland flies that story? This I am interesting to find out."

But she did not find out from Gram, for the time of her afternoon nap having arrived, the old lady dismissed the girls abruptly with the command, "Bring the little gel again, Meggie."

As the two were walking home, Maggie remarked, "I've never seen Gram soften so quick to anyone, Lilli. Most times, she stings them like pepper. But you – you've certainly got something – " She paused to wink at a young man who was gaping at her fiery hair.

"You know why?" Lilli glowed all over with the memory of the visit. "Because your Gram and me, we are same kind peoples, so we like each others, is that funny?"

"But you get so excited about a song," objected Maggie, "the way I'd get about a hat or a new dress."

"Because I'm getting rich inside," replied Lilli. "Never I forget this song your Gram sing. Like magic, all old time come back."

Maggie was not satisfied. "You see, Lilli," she pointed out with some logic, "it's not normal for a girl to be one hundred years old when she's only lived sixteen years upon this earth."

"So what to do?" inquired Lilli. "How to get young again?"

"Come in here – we'll enjoy ourselves." Maggie pulled Lilli into an ice-cream bar.

"Oh, I like to enjoy!" exclaimed Lilli, clambering upon a stool in eager anticipation of enjoyment to come.

"Come, what'll you have?" asked Maggie, admiring herself in the colossal mirror. "I'll stand treat."

Lilli looked about her at the people, debating what she should say. Not only had she never been in an ice-cream bar, she had never tasted ice cream. So she parried: "What you have, Maggie, so I."

"Chocolate, then, two doubles."

A look of amazement appeared on Lilli's face as she tasted it. "MMM! So good to eat!" she exclaimed as one spoonful after another vanished.

"Delicious!" Maggie said. She smacked her lips.

When Lilli saw her empty dish, she could not believe it. "Where went that so good stuff?" she cried out, scraping at the bottom.

"Come, have another," urged Maggie. "It's worth it, just to watch you. What flavour would you like?" She winked at the clerk.

"What kinds are?" Lilli peered over the counter into the cans.

"Chocolate, vanilla, strawberry, maple."

Unable to make a choice, Lilli turned her head from side to side, mouth watering. "All," she gasped. "I want all." Her eyes bulged.

"Four dishes of ice cream, all flavours, for the young lady," ordered Maggie. She shoved a spoon into her mouth to keep from laughing.

With the four dishes in front of her, Lilli ranged happily from one to another, consuming that delectable confection a spoonful at a time, smacking her lips with joy and murmuring to herself,

"Delicious, delicious, delicious, delicious!"

3
VARIATIONS ON A
FOLK THEME
❦

A FREQUENT visitor in the household was Sam, who played the piano. As soon as he came into the house, he would walk straight to the piano and commence playing. He came at any time without announcing himself. The first time Lilli heard him, she was dusting the living room. This took a great deal of time, as the room was filled with numerous objects – curios, bowls, figurines, lamps, pictures. She had time, therefore, to listen to the music which, with its intricate harmonies did not resemble the simple folk melodies she knew; yet they were not entirely unfamiliar. Sam would play for hours, oblivious to the presence of other people in the room, not speaking, and then as suddenly as he had come, he would get up and rush from the room.

"Who is that man?" Lilli asked of Mrs. Green as she arranged a great mass of deep red roses in a cut glass vase.

"That is Sam." Mrs. Green's hands fluttered about the flowers as she rearranged them to her satisfaction. She stepped back to get the effect. "Not so bunchy, Lilli. You see, how much better now! You have to be an artist to arrange flowers."

"What does Sam do?" persisted Lilli, getting out a silk cloth to polish the furniture.

"He plays the piano," replied Mrs. Green. Her shrug relegated Sam to the company of wastrels and incompetents.

"We once thought he had talent, and now – " She shrugged again. "He looks like a rumpled bed."

In appearance, Sam was a pudgy, plain man, with mussed hair, soiled shirt and hunched shoulders, but his hands riveted the attention, being firm, large, of extraordinary mobility, the one vital feature of a disintegrating personality. Through them, music flowed from his body in a continuous stream.

Lilli looked forward to Sam's visits. When he arrived a week later, she was busy waxing the floor. Pretending to ignore his presence, she went over the whole surface three times in order to defer the time when she would have to go to the kitchen and so be out of range of the music. When she got behind the piano, she remained concealed there. Suddenly she recognized a passage which he was playing. It was part of a song which her mother used to sing. Lilli was puzzled by the appearance and disappearance of this melody in the piece which Sam was playing. It seemed to have been altered, and sometimes it was completely submerged in the rest of the music, then the tune emerged again, and before it could disappear, Lilli caught at it and sang out in a loud voice which could be heard over the thumping of the piano.

Sam stopped playing, and becoming conscious of Lilli, peered at her through the back of the piano and poked his finger at her. "You, girl, what are you doing there? Stand up. Come out."

Lilli cowered, head hidden in her arm. She felt humiliated to be caught in such a position.

"Don't be afraid." Sam's fat, pale face smiled sadly, as he reached his hand down to her. "Look at me, I am only a fat man who likes to play the piano."

Lilli emerged, bumping her head against the piano, and stood before him, cheeks flaming, eyes downcast. Sam appraised her for a moment, then took his cigar out of his mouth and waved it at her: "What were you singing under the piano?"

A tiny smile flickered around the corners of Lilli's mouth. "A song."

Sam grunted. "I know, a song, but what kind?"

Lilli thought she should feel ashamed, but instead, a feeling of mischief exhilarated her. Somehow, she knew she was pleasing to this man, so she stammered, "Old song. We sang in the country."

"Sing it to me," Sam swung around on the piano bench and placed his hands on the keys.

"Mrs. Green will not like it," Lilli whispered, as she did not know whether Mrs. Green had gone out.

"Never mind Mrs. Green. She is not here. Come, sing."

He looked at her through his thick glasses, pursing up his fat lips to make a note. Lilli, not daring to lift her eyes, sang the little song through. A silence followed, during which Sam puffed at his big cigar and regarded her with amused and cynical eyes.

"Sing it again," commanded Sam.

Lilli sang the song in another version, slightly different. She sang the whole verse, and then a chorus.

"That is not the way you sang it before."

"No," admitted Lilli. "Some people sing it this way, some the other way."

"Aha, it is a variation."

"A – what?"

"A variation." Sam waved his large hand. "A different way of singing the same song." He looked curiously at her. Why was a girl like this doing housework? Who had put that unbecoming uniform on her, as if to hide the grace of that fine, slim body? He frowned. "You should be in school, learning to read, write."

"I'd like to go to school, but you see, I must work." Sam nodded, his head sagging to his chest. His dull, hopeless eyes made him look more than ever like a sad clown. A relentless melancholy gnawed at him; even when laughing, no gleam

251

showed in his eyes. He leaned his head on his hand and thought for a moment. "Tell me, what do you want to learn – you do want to learn, don't you?" He swung around on his stool to get a better view of her. "You look like a bright girl."

Lilli's face glowed with colour as she replied, "I know what I want to learn – music."

"Music, eh?" Sam pondered. "Let us see how you understand music." He smiled a moment, thinking of what Lilli had said, his face touched with tenderness, so that it lost momentarily its appearance of despair. Then he began playing a pastoral air, watching Lilli as his hands moved over the keys.

"Tell me, what is this?" Lilli saw the Maytime, saw the scholars dancing and jumping with wreaths in their hair.

"Children playing in the springtime."

"And this?" Her excitement grew as the music created pictures of life in the country.

"Sheep skipping around. Wind through oats."

"And this?"

"A shepherd playing his pipe."

"You come from the country?" Lilli nodded. The pianist realized that for this girl, everything had its counterpart in the natural world, in the harmony of nature's sounds.

The fat man became melancholy and absorbed in his own thoughts. Lilli's singing had reminded him of a time when he himself was so certain, so fresh and full of faith, a faith which had become a dried up thing in comparison to the young faith which now confronted him. He seemed to have forgotten Lilli's presence, then turning around, he looked intently at her from sleepy lids and said, "All music comes from the people, people like you. Don't forget that." With that, he got up and went off abruptly. Lilli ran to the window to watch him go. His shoulders were hunched, he walked awkwardly and swung with an odd jerk those large, mobile hands.

She ran back to the piano, caressed it, touched its keys, whispering to herself, "All music comes from the people. Oh it does, it does! That piece he was playing, there are different parts, different sounds, like the sounds I heard in the country, and they all fit together in a pattern."

That evening, Lilli asked again, "Why does Sam play the piano? I mean, why is he so sad about it?"

Mrs. Green replied, this time with a touch of malice, "He fell in love with Becky, my daughter. She's a beautiful girl, and she laughed at him. Who would have such a fat man, without money? Now he comes here and plays and dreams about her. But she never thinks of him. Poor Sam!" She stood before the hall mirror, adjusting the oversize corsage on her lace evening gown, exuding a sense of triumph over the wretched musician. She was one of those people who delight in the misery of others.

Lilli, however, did not think of Sam as a person to be pitied. She listened to his conversations with Mrs. Green's friends, always on music; he rarely spoke of anything else. The language was like a foreign language, but occasionally phrases enlightened Lilli. They were discussing the piece which Sam had been playing: "I have found the basic folk melody; the servant girl was singing it as she cleaned the floors under the piano. Listen, it is a thing of great beauty!" He played it, but it was much richer, with its accompaniment and variations. "It is a wonderful discovery – to trace it back to its original source in folk song. It must have wandered over many countries, or possibly the composer heard some immigrant sing it."

The whole affair aroused the greatest interest among Sam's friends. Indeed, it was only because Sam had a wide acquaintance in music circles that Mrs. Green permitted his visits at all, since she was ambitious to be known as a patroness of music.

One afternoon in early winter Lilli was standing by the window, watching a light snow fall, her body quivering with light dancing movements in response to the dreamy waltz music which Sam was playing. The fire in the hearth of the living room caused ripples of light to gleam on the piano, creating a romantic atmosphere through which Lilli floated, imaginatively, in a sensuous dance. A soft voice interrupted her musing: "What do you think of when you look like that?"

"Like what?" she asked guiltily.

"You look as if somebody had turned a light on inside of you," said Sam.

Lilli's eyes beamed with laughter. "Oh, I'm always with lights."

Sam beckoned to her, and she approached the piano with diffidence. "You like this?" He waved his hand to indicate the room and its contents.

"I don't know."

"What's wrong with it?" Sam persisted. "Come, tell me." Lilli remained silent. "Costs lots of money, doesn't it?" Lilli swallowed, and then nodded her head. "But you don't like it?"

"It's too much."

Sam laughed; for the first time, he sounded as though he enjoyed laughing. "Too many carpets, eh? Too much silver, too much china. Too much of everything, except one thing – too little taste." He began to thump angrily on the piano, raising his hands up high and then bringing them down to crash on the keys. "They think an artist must behave so – they have the souls of barbarians!" He struck a discord.

"People who need these things," he went on with scorn, "think that rich furniture will make their lives rich – but it won't make up for the cheap furnishings of their minds and hearts. You and I know that, don't we, girl?"

Lilli, to hide her embarrassment, had been tidying the ash trays which Sam had filled with cigar ash.

"Leave that," ordered Sam. "Those things don't matter. Lilli, that's your name, isn't it? I have news for you. Come here, don't try to disappear into the wall. You can't, you know. Stand up straight near the piano and let me look at you, head up." He appraised the body of the girl, so perfect for its size that it reminded him of a Greek figurine. "I'd like to see you some day in different clothes," he mused. "Do you always wear dresses eight sizes too big for you?"

"This dress belonged to another maid," Lilli explained.

"Ah yes," sneered Sam, "Mrs. Green is very thrifty. And then, if you wore a pretty dress, people might confuse the maid and the mistress." He reached out and touched the skin of her face. "Don't shrink from me, I won't hurt you. Women in the city don't have skins like that – an olive skin with a tinge of red under the surface. Somebody should paint you, Lilli. In two or three years' time you're going to have an amazing face – not yet, most of you is still under the surface."

For some reason, the musician appeared to be in an unusually communicative mood. He went on talking, more to himself than to Lilli, as she didn't understand thoroughly all his remarks. "If only you could retain that naivete – like taking the bloom off, when you lose it. But they glory in their artificiality."

These abstractions were beyond Lilli, but the moment of intimacy was so breathtaking that she stood listening to him with lips parted, eyes widened, and a flush on her cheek. Sam now took her hand and drew her to him.

"You are interested in learning to sing?"

"Yes," whispered Lilli.

"If I tell you where to go to learn, will you take my advice?"

"Yes," replied Lilli, somewhat bewildered.

Sam struck a few haphazard chords on the piano, then wheeled about. "A friend of mine, Matthew Reiner, the leader of a choir in town, is looking for voices. He will hear anyone who cares to go to him."

"Anyone? Even me?" Lilli put her hand to her throat.

"Especially is he interested in people like you." Sam poked his finger at her to emphasize his point. Lilli's eyes fell.

255

She did not believe that Sam could guess the extent of her ignorance.

"But I know nothing."

"You know enough to sing one song, yes? That is all he needs. He will teach you everything else."

"But I have no money."

"It makes no difference." Sam dismissed her objection with a wave of the hand. "He is looking for people who can sing – and you have a voice. You will get your training free, and sing in his choir. Now, do you want to go?"

Lilli hesitated. Emotion made her mute, emotion, and uncertainty of her ability.

"Listen to me, girl." Sam gripped her shoulder hard. "If you are afraid, you will never learn anything. You must have confidence, a little vanity, even. Come, you know you're good, don't you?" He tilted her chin with his finger, and detected the change in her face. "Come, Lilli, be sensible. What can I get out of you? Are you afraid?"

She shook her head with determination. "Tell me where to go."

He scribbled the address on a slip of paper, telling her how to reach the place. "What is your day off – Thursday? Good, you can go this week, in the evening."

She folded the slip of paper and placed it in the pocket of her uniform. "I want to thank you – " she began shyly, but Sam stopped her.

"Don't thank me," he said. "Today I got what I thought I'd never get again – a look of tenderness. That's enough for me – a great deal, in fact." He stood up and briefly touched her cheek again. "So, good-bye, my wildflower. Don't lose your bloom too quickly."

4
THE IMMIGRANT'S
NOSTALGIA
❦

MATTHEW REINER had come over as an Austrian immigrant to Canada in the early 1920s and had organized a choir from among the needle trades workers in the city. There were singers of many national origins in it, but Reiner knew several tongues and had a good knowledge of folk lore, because his old home town had contained people of many races.

Before learning a new song, Reiner told his singers what he knew about the background of the song, something of the history of the people who sang it, and the traditional interpretation.

"Do you have to teach them all these things?" inquired one skeptic. "Will they sing any better?"

"Yes, they will," answered Matthew positively. "It will enrich their understanding. They will be singing a song and not merely a tune."

The choir leader had faith in the capacity of the common man to respond to beauty and art, even to create art, for where did music originate, if not from the people? He would argue, "It's my theory that you can find talent everywhere – lying in wait to be discovered. Sometimes it is never discovered. A man who could be an artist works all his life in a pants factory. I will find my singers in the factories, working at machines. What they do not know about music, I will teach them."

It was a day in February when Matthew Reiner set his

bachelor apartments in order while awaiting a friend of his who had arrived in the city the previous night. This was Willie Schmidt, a wealthy clothing manufacturer, formerly a music student at the same Austrian conservatory where Reiner had studied.

When a knock sounded, Reiner opened the door to a short, roly-poly man whose dimples and tuft of light hair made him look like an adult Puck, full of suppressed pranks. He was overjoyed to see Reiner. "Matthew!" he threw open his pudgy arms. "Come in, come in," invited Reiner. "Here, take off your coat." Willie bounced rather than walked in and took a look about the place. "Tch, tch!" he commiserated as his eyes took in the shabby rooms in which only one object – the piano – appeared a relic of more palmy days.

"You have become prosperous, I see," commented Matthew pointedly.

"You mean this, ha, ha," laughed Willie, indicating his brilliant teal blue suit. "I like colour, you know. Not like you. You look like an undertaker in that black suit."

"Suits my subdued personality," said Reiner.

The two men sat down and regarded each other with affection, as it had taken only a moment to regain their former intimacy. "Same dark brown eyes, warm and full of poetic fire," thought Willie as he scrutinized his friend to see how the years had dealt with him. "But what a thin face! Something is lacking in Matthew's life."

Willie, who possessed the intense Jewish interest in the family, the home, the wardrobe, had with one glance summed up his friend's austere and lonely life. "I'll have to stir him up somehow," he thought, recalling Reiner as a gay and prankish lad. "He's become too serious – he needs a family to soften him. Every year he'll grow more and more narrow without realizing it, for all his choir."

He asked, therefore, "Don't you feel you're wasted here, Matthew?" He waved his hand to indicate the room. "You were the brilliant one of us all."

"No, I've found my place," replied Reiner with composure. He was not disturbed by Willie's pitying appraisal of his worldly possessions. Poverty had become a way of life with him, a state he accepted in exchange for other, more compelling values.

"But your talent – "

"Composing, you mean? I have a knack for arrangement, not original composition."

Willie banged his pipe impatiently on the arm of his chair. "Tell me, what satisfaction is there for a man of your talent to waste time on such an enterprise – this folk choir?"

"The satisfaction," replied Matthew with great feeling, "of making lives so much richer, of satisfying creative instincts which otherwise would remain dormant."

"But you can't have any singers of real talent," objected Willie. "Who are your choir members – mostly factory workers, aren't they? What can you accomplish on such a level?"

"You'd be surprised," replied Matthew with spirit, "at what level we do work. It seems to me sometimes that I'm learning more from my choir than they are from me." Then, recalling his friend's sentimentality, Reiner sat down at the piano and began to play.

"I heard that song somewhere before," remarked Willie as he came over to the piano. "It arouses a mood of nostalgia."

Matthew nodded as he continued playing. "It is called Watching the Wild Wheat, a Welsh folk song. You should hear my choir sing it."

"Hm, a beautiful melody." Willie went over to the window and looked out, his fingers beating in time against his palm. "What does it remind me of? Something I did when I was a boy. I know – " He turned excitedly to Reiner. "Remember when we went out into the country and heard a crowd of peasants singing as they made hay in the meadow?" Willie became animated as the details returned to him. "I have that feeling now, as though I were a boy of fifteen. The smell of hay, the girls in their red skirts, the sun flashing on their scythes, the sound of their singing like a choir – they harmonized naturally. Remember, Matthew?" He sat down and closed his eyes, as though to capture the memory in a mental image. "That's one of the brightest memories of my life. That girl who laughed and called at me – I can recall what she looked like – exactly! Like a little madonna, she had a beauty spot on her cheek, her black hair was braided in a pigtail, and her eyelashes so long they made smudges on her cheeks. Yes, and what's more," continued Willie with relish, "I can even remember the sound of crunching as she bit into her apple." He sighed. "My only regret is that I didn't jump into that field and kiss that girl."

"Apple and all," commented Matthew drily as he stopped playing and turned to his friend. "But you know, Willie, your reaction to that piece illustrates my own argument regarding the purpose of my choir work."

"And what is that argument?"

Matthew got up and walked about excitedly as he expounded his favourite ideas to his friend. "Here, to this city, to this country," he began, "have come immigrants from Italy, Germany, Bohemia, Scotland, Austria – what do they talk of when they get together? The old country. Do you remember, Fritz, or Ivan or Moishe or Pietro, do you remember, they say, what we ate, how we sang? This city is full of exiles and all, in their hearts, are sentimental. Believe me, I know. The day comes, for all of them, when they long for the old country, at least in spirit. What I mean is this, people don't want to lose their roots. Underneath the skin of every person who comes here is an exile, a stranger who longs to go back, at least in memory, to his native land. Do you know how many groups are represented in my choir? Over a dozen. I have the benefit of the musical traditions of a dozen countries."

"But surely," objected Willie, although he was intrigued by his friend's passion, "don't you have trouble with so many nationalities? You can't tell me they all get along."

Reiner laughed as he recalled the early days of his choir. "At first, I had trouble enough," he admitted. "I thought the League of Nations had minor woes compared to mine. Immigrants were swarming into the country when I first started out as a young man, after the war, in the early 1920s, and they didn't always appreciate each other's good qualities. Later, as they learned to understand various racial traditions, it became an asset."

Reiner flung himself down in his dilapidated armchair and crossed his long legs. "We need racial understanding, Willie," he said with urgency. "Each person, as I said is at heart an immigrant. What is our common ground – music. You have no idea how my choir has altered lives, expanded horizons."

"Still," objected Willie, "you live like a pauper, when you might be comfortably off – " He held up his pudgy hand, on which an enormous expensive ring glittered like a symbol of success.

"You're a materialist, Willie," chuckled Reiner, who found his friend's complacency more amusing than provoking.

"And you're a sweet fellow with impractical notions about humanity," countered Willie with affection. He got up and went to the dresser to pick up a portrait of a young girl. "Naomi?"

Matthew's voice was scarcely audible as he turned his face away to conceal his emotion. "Yes."

"Naomi was a lovely girl, Matthew," said Willie with great sympathy, "but are you going to let the memory of a dead person dry up your juices until you are a creaky old bachelor? You might make some girl very happy, if you'd only stop looking for Naomi's twin. How about your choir girls?"

Reiner smiled, a rather pathetic smile, his friend thought. "Those girls think I'm an institution and not a human being. So perhaps I've got into the habit of acting like one."

Willie clicked his tongue. "You spend your evenings

developing the creative instincts of factory workers and then come home – if you can call it a home – " Willie took another look about the drab room, "to sit and look at Naomi's portrait. What a waste, Matthew, what a waste! And you're only thirty-one!"

"It needn't be a waste if – " began Reiner and then stopped abruptly.

"If what?" enquired Willie, thinking, "What is Matthew hiding?"

"If, as I hope, some day I'll discover an instrument for my ideas, a real artist," burst out Reiner.

"And if that artist should be a girl," observed Willie with a sombreness unusual for him, "you might go overboard, Matthew."

Reiner shrugged. "My life is my choir, my gift teaching. To mould and shape one hundred singers is a brilliant enough destiny for me."

"You know, this intrigues me, Matthew," admitted Willie as he arose to go. "Will you promise me one thing?"

"What is that, Willie?"

Willie turned, and his face was more puckish than ever: "I'm sending you a light suit, Matthew. Wear it and remember, you're still young."

After he left, Reiner stood at the window, watching the figure of his friend as it receded, and pondering upon his words. Something that had been dormant for a long time began to stir, and he realized that his choir, indeed, was no longer enough. "You can deny the emotions so long, and then they have their revenge," he thought. He laughed at the memory of the peasant girl, but associated with this memory were other memories of himself as a gayer, younger person and he was what – now? Recalling Willie's warning, he was more intrigued than disturbed. It might be interesting, he thought, to go overboard . . . after so many years . . . perhaps it was time!

5
THE FOLK CHOIR
🍎

WHEN Lilli reached the hall Thursday evening, she stood at
the door for a few minutes, trying to reassure herself by
recalling Sam's words. She put her hand on the doorknob,
withdrew it, then pressed her ear to the door. The sound of
voices rose like a muffled hum. With heart bouncing like a
rubber ball, Lilli pushed the door open and went in. The hall
had a stage at the farthest end; the ground floor, usually filled
with seats, had been cleared for the rehearsal. A few people
were busy on the stage.

Lilli stood, clutching her long coat, an odd little figure,
scarcely daring to lift her eyes, when a dark-haired young girl
came up to her and said, "You've come to try out for the choir,
haven't you? Come with me." She led Lilli to a group of
chairs where the candidates were seated and left Lilli with the
words, "Wait here. Reiner won't be long."

The people in the hall, mostly factory workers, were
gathered in groups, constantly shifting in an atmosphere of
camaraderie, for all seemed to feel as if they belonged. Lilli
buttoned and unbuttoned her coat, pulling it up from the floor,
her hands clammy despite the heat of the room, her vision
distorted by a haze of cigarette smoke. The merry-go-round of
faces, lights and music whirled about her – doors opening and
closing, cries of greeting, bodies moving about. One couple
was doing a polka, another group was discussing a song, still
another was laughing hilariously at a funny tale related by a
young man with a comic face. Scraps of various languages –

Jewish, Polish, German and others – reached Lilli's ears. As Reiner had said, if a Jewish girl should sing Bonnie Dundee and a Scotsman learn Eli, Eli, they came thus to a closer understanding of the common dreams of humanity. These scraps of conversation drifted like coloured balloons over Lilli's head, and she snatched at them, examining each speaker's face in turn.

"Oof!" As each newcomer arrived, he shook off the snow, pulled off cap and mitts, stamped his feet and then walked over to the crowd, where he was immediately absorbed into one of the groups. At the piano, Reiner was talking with one of the candidates. He was asking questions, playing a few bars of music, joking with animation. Lilli, as she watched, ached to talk to someone, but nobody appeared to notice her. She swallowed painfully. What if she had come for nothing?

Next to her sat a big, burly young man of about twenty-five, who smoked cigarette after cigarette while listening. Lilli liked him at first sight. He had a muscular physique, an ugly face and an ingratiating grin which gave an impression of a warm personality. Lilli wondered how he would sing, and she thought his singing would have the vitality of his appearance. In this she was not mistaken. He was not nervous when he went up for his audition and spoke a few words to Reiner, who called him Tim. Pointing to a low note on the piano, Tim released a prodigious bass voice which rumbled across the hall like a billiard ball, and Lilli laughed aloud. "See how easy?" he bent over her as he returned. "Now you go up."

Lilli slipped out of her seat and shakily walked over to the piano, which seemed very far away, followed, as she thought, by the looks of every person in the room. Matthew Reiner watched her as she came up, apparently not noticing the long, dragging coat, but looking instead into her eyes. His face, which she had not seen clearly before, combined the strength and softness of the artist, the strong planes of his cheekbones and chin contrasting with the soft curves of his mouth. His eyes were deep-set, of an intense brown almost chestnut; his movements decisive, as those of a man of intense purpose. His speaking voice was sympathetic; like a good reader of poetry, he brought emotion to his simplest phrases. He smiled with a rare tenderness at the girl, and she sucked her breath in sharply, so susceptible was she to tenderness.

"Well," said Reiner, "did you like the singing?"

Lilli nodded, her eyes devouring him. "I liked the big funny man. He had a voice like – " She hesitated.

"Like?"

"Like very old frog which was practising long time and can sing good," she finished triumphantly.

Reiner banged a bass note on the piano. "I don't know whether Tim will appreciate that, but I am sure you intend it as a compliment."

To break down her nervousness, Reiner played a bit for her, while she looked at him with such a depth of longing, almost worship, that he was deeply touched. "Where did this grow?" he thought. Aloud, he said, "Do you sing, young lady?"

"Yes," the word came out almost in a whisper. "I came to – oh, will you please let me try, too?"

"Everyone is a candidate for our choir."

Lilli tugged at her hat which had fallen over one ear. "It's a little too big," she said apologetically.

"Take it off, you'll feel better," Reiner suggested, and she obeyed. "Stand beside me," he said. "Come closer. Am I so frightening?" She shook her head. "Most beautiful piano." She caressed the dark wood. The slight flush on her cheek, the naive look in her eye made her appear like some wildflower half opened. "Her shyness is a lovely thing," thought Reiner.

"What is your name?"

"Lilli Landash."

"Lilli? I am Matthew Reiner. Now we are friends." He extended his hand, thinking, "There is something about her –

that light in her eyes. She looks as if she could sing. There is an intensity in her body, as though she were under compulsion to express some great longing." He said aloud, "Come, stand close to the piano. Don't be afraid."

Lilli approached him, her body tense, fearful that she would not be able to sing a note. The chorus of talking, laughing voices in the background formed a kind of screen, however, and she felt protected, thinking that the others would not notice so much if she failed. Reiner now played a series of four notes, difficult to remember because they were dissonances, and nodded to her, "Sing." Thus encouraged, Lilli took the four notes effortlessly, without flaw. Reiner, recognizing the quality of her voice, was surprised to hear such a rich, deep voice from a rather small girl. He looked at her curiously and then played four more notes, to test her low voice.

"I'm glad you're a contralto," he said, as he made a notation in his notebook. "I need contraltos. Every girl wants to sing soprano."

"Is that all? So easy?" exclaimed Lilli with relief. She had no idea that she had passed a difficult ear test. She relaxed, let out a deep sigh, then looked eagerly at the group of people near the stage. Soon she would know them all by name, soon she would belong. When she came into the room, they would call her by name, maybe some young man would seize her and dance a polka with her. All her expectancy was written on her face with such transparency that Reiner could almost read her thoughts.

"What an interesting type," he thought. "I have not had anyone like this in the choir. It will be good to have her with us." Aloud, he said, "Well, Lilli, how would you like to stay and practise with my choir? I always ask my successful candidates to stay for a rehearsal."

"You will let me sing with your choir?"

"Yes, we'll put you in the contralto section. That's the

weak part of my choir, so you'll give us the strength we need there."

"Oh, how wonderful to sing with your choir!" cried Lilli, clasping her hands. "I promise, I'll work hard!"

"I was right," thought Matthew Reiner as he saw her rapture. "This will be someone to watch."

The talking, singing and dancing ceased, the crowd of singers now filed into line and walked up the stairs to the stage, where they arranged themselves in rows. Lilli followed at the end, looking with fascination at the old scenery, piles of lumber and apparatus back stage. Reiner put her in the front row, the better to judge of her ability.

"What an interesting face she has," he thought. "So young and so naive, yet so full of human experience."

Before commencing rehearsal, Reiner delivered a brief lecture attacking such faults as exaggeration, shrillness, vulgarity, falseness of gesture and voice. "We cannot sing the bare words of a song and hope to reach an audience. First we must feel what the words say before we can hope to pass that feeling to those who hear us. When we know we are singing the truth, the audience will believe us, and we shall move them. While relaxing, we must keep full control of our emotions. When singing a song, do not think only of the sounds coming out of your throat; do not admire the beauty of your own voice, but think of the meaning of your song."

Despite these words, the rehearsal went badly that day. Reiner had introduced a new song entitled "The Cranes," a beautiful, melancholy air about which he had been enthusiastic, but the choir members did not respond to it. Most of them were factory workers, and were too far removed from the natural background of the peasant to understand its spirit or tempo. Where the song was melancholy, in a minor key, they were slow, ragged, and off-pitch. The "croo, croo, croo" representing the call of the cranes they found ridiculous; some of the girls tittered. Finally the song seemed to degenerate into sheer dissonance. There were murmurs of disapproval: "Give us something happier to sing, Reiner."

Reiner was disappointed, until in the second attempt he distinguished one voice which appeared to be singing the song as it should be sung. It was the newest recruit to the choir, singing with such intensity that everything came to life in her face. Reiner tapped his baton on the back of his chair as a signal for the choir.

"This is not how a song of the cranes should be sung," he addressed the choir. "There is only one person here who understands the meaning of this song – this young girl." He indicated Lilli. All the choir members turned to look at her. "Let us hear you sing this song, Lilli – and all the rest of you listen and learn from a singer who sings from the soul, as the birds sing. Come, step out."

Lilli, astonished at being singled out, stepped to the front of the stage, and for a moment could not make a sound. Then she took a deep breath and began to sing, face uplifted as though following with her eyes the flight of cranes: "Look, where the cranes are flying!" With the first line, Lilli established the symbolism of the song: the wandering of cranes over the earth and their annual return to their home. There was a deep hush as the beauty of the song was revealed. One felt the presence of the cranes, the beating of their wings was heard, the strange melancholy of their call penetrated every heart.

Wing to wing they fly together,
Singing as they fly,
Croo, croo, croo,

The "croo, croo, croo," echoed exactly the call of birds in flight, swelling from a mere whisper of sound as the birds approached, then dying away as they vanished far in the distance. There was a feeling of foreboding, that some would fall in flight and never reach their goal; there was the mournful sound of the wind as the cranes soared with it. When Lilli had finished, there was a moment of silence, then a kind of collective sigh. "But it sounds so different when she sings it!" exclaimed one young man. "Perhaps because we didn't see the song before at all, and what you don't understand, you can't sing," observed an older member. The choir members crowded about Lilli, congratulating her, asking her questions about herself. Where did she learn to sing like that? How glad they were she had joined the choir! They did not appear to notice her queer clothes; they looked at her and saw what she really was, within. "Sam was right," thought Lilli. She felt as though she had left her old life behind her, and would never return to it.

"She has the soul of a singer," exulted Matthew Reiner. "The voice, yes, that is something extraordinary, almost a cello tone, like the great contraltos, but without that soul, that fire, she would be just another singer."

After the rehearsal, he singled out Lilli and Tim, and requested them to remain behind. When all had left, he invited Lilli into his study, which he used for individual instruction. Taking her hand; he led her up a musty stairway into a cosy room at the head of the stairs. She stood at the doorway, looking shyly about the room, almost with a feeling of recognition, as though she had been there before. The room contained a small piano, books, records, a gramophone, fresh flowers, a mirror, two easy chairs, and piles of music. "So much music in this room," she said, turning to Reiner. He led her to one of the easy chairs; and sat down in the other, close to her. For a while, both said nothing, happy to have discovered each other.

"Well, Lilli, do you think you'll be happy with us?" Reiner said at last. She nodded, eyes full of tears, choked and turned her head away, still ashamed of a display of emotion. He bent over and took one of her hands.

"Now, tell me something about yourself."

"What is there to tell?" asked Lilli. "I'm from the farm, I never went to school and I can't read music. There, you know now." She looked at him, as if frightened of the effect her revelation would have on him.

"That is nothing," Reiner assured her. "The mechanics of singing – how to read notes, how to breathe properly, how to stand on the stage – all that I can teach you. But the essential thing you have already. Tell me, where did you learn to sing like that?"

Her eyes widened as though in surprise at the question. "On the farm we always sang. I remember singing at church, on Christmas Eve, at Easter, funerals and weddings. For every holiday, we had a song."

He thought of her interpretation of the song of the cranes: "You have a strong feeling for nature, Lilli. You love to be outdoors, yes?"

Again she showed surprise at the question. She could not yet understand the antipathy of city folks to nature; it seemed as though they were anxious to get away from the natural scene.

"Oh yes," she replied, "to watch the clouds running across the skies in the fall, to listen to the leaves on the trees, every tree with a different note. The poplar rattles like spoons in a dish. The pine tree whistles, like when you suck your breath through your teeth."

Reiner watched her face intently, thinking,

"Her eyes always light up when she speaks of what she knows intimately; she is not shy then." He came now to another question which he knew concerned her closely: "What do you do for a living?" He had guessed, however, by looking at her hands, which were scarred and rough. She extended them now to him.

"Housework – see my hands?"

She extended her hands, looking at his face in expectation of the reaction. Reiner studied them without any trace of shock, then said, in a matter-of-fact voice, "This is not a permanent condition."

"What means that, permanent?"

"It won't last. Once you stop doing housework, your skin will clear up. As for these – " he touched a callous. "A little pumice and hand lotion should clear that up."

But," said Lilli in surprise. "Everyone laugh because they are so long."

"Length of hands is often considered a sign of beauty and strength."

"Beauty? Strength?" Lilli looked down at those hands which had always been a source of shame to her. "How, beauty?"

"You will grow up to your hands, Lilli," the choir leader assured her. "At present, they look older than you do. My advice is, forget them for the present. Later, I will teach you exercises to give your hands grace and pliability. A singer must know how to use his hands, since they're an instrument of expression. You don't know what to do with your hands, do you?"

"No," confessed Lilli, hanging her head. "All the time, I want to hide them, because I am ashamed."

"If you are ashamed, inside of yourself," pointed out Reiner, "it will come out in your voice. That can't be hidden."

He touched her hands again, feeling a pang as he contrasted their blemished surface with the smooth skin of her face.

"We'll have to find something else for you to give you more freedom, so you'll have your evenings free. Let me see – " he mused. "Most of my singers work in factories. Do you sew? Know how to use a machine?"

"Yes, I learned in the village from a Swedish woman."

"Good." Reiner made a note on a pad. "We'll get work for you in a factory. You'll have more time, more money, you'll be able to meet more people. In the evenings, you can go to night school, come here for choir practice." He stopped talking when he saw her expression of concern. "Is there anything the matter?" She twisted her coat in her hands, unwilling to speak. "Come, don't be afraid. I'm your friend. What troubles you?"

She spoke at last: "I must tell you something – It's this, I can't read, only a little bit, I hardly ever went to school."

"Is that all?" Reiner patted her hand reassuringly. "I was just going to suggest that you go to night school."

"But I'm too old," said Lilli. "Sixteen."

"There are people two, three times sixteen who go to night school," said Reiner. "These classes are for grown people who never had a chance."

Lilli drew a deep breath. It seemed miraculous that all her problems should be so easily solved. She was reluctant to leave the beautiful room; it did not seem possible that she would be here again and again in the future. Reiner, as though guessing her thought, said, "You will be here many times, I hope, Lilli, and have many chances to look at the books and pictures."

As she rose to go, Lilli tripped over her long coat. She jerked it up with an embarrassed gesture. Reiner touched her shoulder: "Don't worry about clothes, Lilli. The girls in the choir will tell you what to wear. Do you know, you have a pretty face?" He placed his hands gently under her chin and lifted her face to his. "Especially when you smile; it gives life to your appearance. You must smile more often, now. I think you will make many friends here."

Later, when Lilli had left, Reiner discussed her with Tim. The two men relaxed in their big easy chairs, smoking comfortably and feeling warmly attracted to each other; for them, too, it was the beginning of a friendship.

"I could hardly believe my ears," said the big basso. "She sings like an artist. What other singers take years to learn, she knows by instinct."

"It is as I have always believed," asserted Reiner. "You can find a voice anywhere. She looks like a farm girl, yet what a miracle she has in her throat! Without training – she can't read a note of music. She is wild; speak to her, and she is almost in tears. Isn't it fate that brought her here to me? I have often thought of such an experiment – what could be done to develop a human being of great ability, but of almost absolute ignorance. Well, here she is. What she may become depends on us."

When the two men finally left, Reiner looked back at the room and commented, "We will see Lilli many times in this room. You know, it has made a difference, already." And Tim, as they left the hall, said. "It's easy to see that this girl and music are really one."

6
A BIRTHDAY PAPER
❧

DAYS, months followed of lessons, work, companionship with Tim, wonderful Tim. Each meeting with him was a voyage of discovery, a step forward in life. What was commonplace, became, shared with him, an occasion.

In the spring, a great event occurred in Lilli's life. It came about as a result of a chance remark which Tim made to her when they were going to choir practice.

"I'd like to have a birthday party for you, Lilli," he said. "Dancing, music – " He was so sure she would be pleased that he could not understand why the gaiety in her face vanished. "She looks almost frightened," he thought.

"A birthday party!" Lilli said slowly with an odd catch in her voice. "Lovely idea, Tim, but you see, I have no birthday."

"No birthday!" repeated Tim. "But everybody has!" He thought she was joking, but her face was serious. "When were you born?"

"Don't know, Tim," said Lilli hanging her head. "So many of us, my mother forgot."

"Do you know what time of the year it was?"

"Like now, Tim – spring. On a Wednesday in Lent, mother said once."

Lilli heard no more of the matter for a couple of weeks, then one late afternoon in spring she found Tim waiting for her at the factory entrance, an enormous parcel under his arm.

"You are shining all over, shoes, tie, face," she remarked as she held out her hand to him. "What is it, a holiday?"

Tim grinned. "Yes, special declared by the Government for Lilli." He had an air of mystery, smiled often, chuckled to himself, pinched Lilli's arm.

They walked down the street, laughing for no good reason, admiring the flowered hats on the heads of all the girls.

"Tell me your secret, Tim." ordered Lilli, squeezing his hand so that it hurt. "You have a secret, I know, it's popping out all over."

"Ouch!" He pulled his hand away as if in pain. "Well," he said, "I can't keep it from you. So if you must know – " He stopped and looked at her as if he were addressing some curious child: "Today is your birthday." Then, pleased with his surprise he executed a shuffle.

"This day, this very day?" asked Lilli, tugging at his arm. "I can't believe it!" Her eyes, enormous under her red beret thrust question marks at him. Big tears hung suddenly under her eyes.

Gently he drew her into a little cafe where they often had dinner together, and as they sat down in a corner booth, he put his hand into his pocket and said, "I have your birthday paper." It was an impressive document printed on crackling white paper, with a big red seal on it, and a picture of a buffalo. Lilli took it from him with an expression of awe. "Where did you get it?" Her fingers trembled as she held it.

"From the Manitoba Government," replied Tim. "You see Lilli, everybody is born, that is how we get into the world." He winked.

"But never before did I know that I got in with a paper," she countered, unfolding the document. "Oksana Landash! Who is Oksana? Never heard of her! This is a mistake, Tim!"

Tim smiled. "No mistake, Lilli. Oksana Landash is you. That is your real name, so now you know." He chuckled at her puzzlement.

"Nobody ever called me that!" protested Lilli. "What

happens to Lilli? I am used to Lilli! Oksana is a nice name, but doesn't sound like me."

"You have both names now, Lilli," Tim assured her. "Fancy like a real lady. You are Oksana like in the poem Shevchenko wrote – Oksana, dearest of all strangers to me, who taught me how to smile, and live and love. . . ." Tim's voice became husky with emotion. He pulled a cigarette out of his pocket and rammed it into his mouth.

Lilli's face cleared. "Oh, Tim, it's too good to be true!" Then she burst into sobs and burying her face in the paper she kissed it again and again, saying, "A birthday, a real birthday!"

When they had finished their meal, and the table had been cleared, Tim brought forth his big parcel and untied it, revealing a heap of lesser parcels, all wrapped in pink tissue.

"Birthday presents for Lilli." Tim lit his cigarette and sat back with a smug expression.

"So many! Who gave?" Lilli's curiosity got the better of her and she reached for the nearest.

"From me, Lilli. Seventeen presents, one for every year. Saved up because nobody ever gave you any before."

She began unwrapping the gifts one by one. An emory pincushion in the shape of a strawberry, a tape measure which disappeared into a tin case, a powder box, pearl earrings, a book of foreign stamps, a pocket dictionary – all from Woolworth's. Finally she came to a jewel box. "What is this?"

"Diamond ring," snickered Tim. "Extra big stone."

The stone, indeed, was of a staggering size.

"How much you paid?" Lilli demanded as she put the ring on her finger.

"Very dear," jested Tim. "Twenty cents, but I thought, for Lilli, I must have the very best." He reached out and put a record on the gramophone nearby, gypsy music which Lilli liked especially.

She sat back overwhelmed, examining each gift in turn. "Oh, Tim, never before anybody thought to make me a birthday! To give so many presents! So wonderful! In all my life, I won't forget. When I have grandchildren, I will tell them!" Tears splashed over the diamond ring.

Tim became serious now, looked long at her. "If ever you marry, Lilli, where would you like to live?" His brown eyes touched her all over with affection.

"In a tree, or tent, wherever my husband lives, so I."

"Your husband will be a lucky fellow." He sighed, then reached over and pulled a curl from her beret. "And curls, too, now you have, where never grew any before – "

Lilli pushed back the curl as she replied: "To marry, I don't think now, Tim. Too much to learn, too much to do. I'm growing too fast, can't settle down." She sighed as she thought of the long way she still had to travel.

"Friends, then, we'll be – " said Tim. "In your heart, save a special corner for Tim."

"A whole room, I have for you," said Lilli. "Corner is too small for such a big fellow."

Tim reached again into his pocket. "I have one more thing for you, Lilli – a letter from my brother who is a sailor."

"A sailor – in a ship he travels?"

"All over the world, Lilli. He has sailed the seven seas and crossed the equator." He showed her a thin envelope with a Chinese stamp. "Once you told me you wanted a letter from China, well, here it is. See, your name on the envelope, Lilli Landash, and the postmark is China."

"I can have this letter, Tim?" She seized the envelope and examined the stamp. "Oh, my friend, you gave me so much today!" Her eagerness was like that of a little girl with a new doll.

"Lesson for today, Lilli," said Tim. "Wait long enough, and all your dreams come true – birthday, curls, letter from China, everything."

7

THE DEEPENING STREAM

SHE had been a bit fearful at first, Reiner recalled months later as he waited in his studio for Lilli to come for her lesson, a bit fearful, and afraid to let herself go. It had taken much patient teaching before she acquired confidence, he thought as he looked at his watch. It was fifteen minutes past the hour and Lilli was, contrary to her usual habit, late. He paced up and down the room, wondering at his own impatience. Perhaps he had not realized before how much he had looked forward to those lessons, in spite of much drudgery involved in teaching her to read music, to breath properly, to relax. He thrust the chintz drapes aside and looked out at the spring afternoon. Fluffy white clouds waddled across the sky, like ducks shaking their fat rumps. A wisp of breeze stirred the sticky buds on the poplars. There she was now – he could hear the tapping of her high-heeled patent slippers, quite different, Reiner thought, from the clumsy boots she had once worn. Her beret came into view, cocked on one side of her brown curls, and her green dress with its round white collar. All the prettiest dresses, the factory girls assured him, came in Lilli's size; it was surprising how often "samples" turned up in the factory, which only Lilli could wear. There was a rush of feet on the staircase and Lilli stood breathless at the door, holding out a bunch of flowers.

"At school, in the country, we used to bring flowers to the teacher."

"For me, Lilli? They're beautiful."

"I went out to the prairie to pick them for you. Look, violets, crocuses, buttercups."

"They're like you, Lilli," said Reiner. "that delicate wild beauty. Here, we'll put them in a vase on the piano so we can look at them."

Lilli came up to the piano and stood, a little tense because of her excitement.

"Relax. Take it easy," he admonished her. "You are trying too hard."

"How? Show me."

"Come here." He placed her before the mirror so that she could study every one of her movements, and showed her how to relax by making her stretch and smile, yawn and shake her head. "When you're happy, you feel good, yes? You must feel like a cat. Watch a cat – how he jumps, how he stretches, how he walks. Everything is easy for him. You should look and feel like him." She went through her exercises with the grace of a ballerina, betraying a naive vanity in the image which the mirror reflected – she had not yet got used to this new self. "How do you like when I make like a cat?" she asked, turning to Reiner for approval. "Maybe I should purr, too?" Reiner tried to conceal his amusement. "If you like," he agreed. "If it gets you into the right mood – purring is a sign of content, isn't it?" She quivered in rhythm, like a cat's back when his purring sings through him. "That is what people want to see, Lilli – your happiness. Of course," he went on hastily as he saw that she had taken quite a relish to these new gymnastics, and did not seem willing to stop, "you don't have to make those motions all the time; simply keep the feeling of them inside of you. Look into the mirror when you go home and sing," he continued. "Watch yourself as you sing, especially your eyes. Your eyes are the mirror of your soul. The eyes can't lie. Whatever your eyes look like, that's what you feel like. If your eyes stare, your voice is stiff; if your eyes gleam, your voice will be full of life."

"Oh, I'm always full of life when I sing!" exclaimed Lilli. She placed her hand on her hip and stole a look of sly coquetry at him – a new trick she had recently acquired. She was continually surprising him with some word or gesture which was not entirely in keeping with his conception of her. Anxious to appear like the city girls, she imitated their behaviour, especially in some detail of manner or speech which appealed to her. She tried these out on Reiner, with astounding results – like a little girl trying on her mother's clothes before she's big enough to fill them, thought Reiner.

On one occasion, being out with Tim for a walk, Lilli observed that he seemed to admire the sophistication of a woman dressed, as it appeared to Lilli, in a most elegant costume such as none of the factory girls wore. For weeks Lilli made plans to impress Reiner, and worked nights devising a similar costume. Then one day she appeared for her lesson attired in a black suit trimmed with monkey fur, a white satin turban, purple suede gloves and a long cigarette holder.

Reiner regarded her for several moments without speaking. He was truly amazed at the transformation and touched at the pleased expression on Lilli's face as she looked to him for approval. What to say which would indicate her error without hurting her? The naive gesture of handling the cigarette holder, the mature turban on top of that guileless countenance, the purple gloves on Lilli's work-roughened hands, and above all, the monkey fur sitting on those childish shoulders – all these appeared pathetic to Reiner, and tears of pity and amusement filled his eyes as he turned away.

"You are attending a fancy ball tonight in that costume, Lilli?" he asked.

Lilli put down the cigarette holder and took off the turban. "I – I borrowed it to see how I would look," she lied.

"We can wait a few years for this suit," suggested Reiner. "Next time, wear the green angora dress."

The subject was then dropped, but Reiner never saw the

black suit again, nor anything like it on Lilli.

Now he watched her as she opened her music case. "What will we practise today?" she asked.

Matthew took up a piece of music, a look of speculation on his face. He had long planned to introduce Lilli to Schubert. Was she up to it? "I have a song here which I think you will like, Lilli, Schubert's 'Shepherd on the Rock.'" He thought a moment of how he could create a proper background before commencing practice. "Did you ever take care of sheep when you lived on the farm?"

"Many times," replied Lilli eagerly. "I took them into the valley, when the clouds were floating, and the leaves were turning and I heard a sound – like a pipe."

"How would that be?" asked Reiner, pleased at Lilli's swift response.

"A little sad, a little sweet. Like this." Lilli sang a few notes in a flute-like progression, tenderly, sadly, a song or youth and love. She sang with her whole body, poised in a beautiful line which Reiner never tired of watching.

"Where did you hear that?" inquired Matthew with curiosity.

"From Vanni Karmaliuk."

"Who was Vanni – your sweetheart, perhaps?" He got up from the piano and came to her.

Lilli flushed and nodded her head. "You don't have to be shy," he said, kissing her as he would a delightful child.

"Vanni's father played those pipes when he went as a shepherd to Romania."

"Let me hear."

Lilli made the motion of blowing over the top of Pan's pipes. "Like this." She imitated the sound – a few bird calls, a shepherd song. With the spring sun streaming through the studio window, she had induced, in those few notes, a poignant mood of nature. Reiner was struck by the primitive nature of music. "It is something archaic," he thought,

"Something out of the childhood of the human race." To Lilli, he said, "You must learn how to use the memory of the things you have lived and loved to make your song rich." He sat down at the piano. "As you have used the memory of these pipes to interpret the feeling of a shepherd lad. Remember, you must not sing one note unless you feel compelled to do so. When you sing of nature, remember spring, remember how you loved to watch the clouds running across the skies."

While singing the Schubert song, dozens of pictures arose before Lilli's mind and became incorporated into her song of clouds floating in autumn, of leaves turning on the silver maple, of wild geese arising from the swamps, of her own loneliness. She drew on her background to create images which she translated into the musical idiom. "She's like Schubert." Reiner thought, "in this naive quality, and like him, a child of nature. The joy simply pours from her."

Matthew Reiner was continually striving to get Lilli to tell him something about her early days, but her reticence sometimes baffled him. She was communicative up to a certain point, but beyond that she retired and became almost hostile. On the subject of her parents she was noncommittal, and Matthew could get nothing pertinent from her regarding her family life. "Tell me about your childhood," he urged.

"I had no childhood," Lilli replied, her face assuming a closed-up look he had begun to recognize almost as soon as it began to form.

"What do you remember of your early years?" he persisted.

"Work," was the monosyllabic reply.

"What kind of work?"

"Milking cows. Ploughing the land. Cleaning out the stables. Making hay."

"But that's work for a grown man."

"Where we live, it's work for anyone who can do it." Lilli showed by her attitude that she was unwilling to continue the conversation and he discontinued his questioning. Strange, he thought, that he could not sound the depths of this naive little country girl! She withheld so much from him, yet in her singing she could express herself with so much freedom! He tried another approach on another occasion:

"What does the prairie mean to you?"

"Do you mean the land?"

"Well, yes."

"The land – I hate the land."

The soil and the tilling of the soil, Matthew realized, were not romanticized by Lilli as they were by those who had no intimate acquaintance with pioneering life. The only escape from a brutish existence, Reiner gathered, was through holiday festivities, and these Lilli delighted to describe – the immigrant carollers, the Paschal night, Fialka dancing in her yellow boots, a whole series of peasant paintings such as would have delighted an artist.

Little by little Reiner came to realize what her existence must have been, and he wondered that her sensitivity could have survived, but coupled with this sensitivity was a toughness of fibre which made her endure prolonged rehearsals and lessons without a sign of fatigue. One evening, after a particularly difficult lesson, when he had driven her, as he thought, to the point of exhaustion, he asked her, "Aren't you tired?"

"No – I'm strong," replied Lilli. She seemed surprised at the question, and turned a fresh, happy face to him.

"The work has been difficult tonight," he remarked as he held up her coat for her.

"Work?" Lilli stared at him as she buttoned up her coat. "This isn't work!" With expert hands, she arranged a beret on her head. She had a flair for style, and especially did she love the unusual in hats, creating something individual with the most unpromising materials.

"What do you want, Lilli?" Reiner tried to detain her, unwilling to let her go.

"Want?" She looked at him as though not understanding.

"Of life, I mean." Reiner felt pleased that he had snatched a few more moments of her time. For a while she did not answer. "It's too big a question to answer in a few words," she said at last. "All those years, before I met you, I was living like in a little closed-up room, and now I see big halls, full of things I never knew of. I walk around, and can't take it all in." She laughed a tremulous little laugh. "Still a country girl, you see."

She was that no longer, thought Reiner; in spite of the rags and tags of hastily assumed mannerisms, he could see a change, an integral change, like a preview of what might be. He inquired, as though teasing her: "How about love? Have you ever been in love, Lilli?"

"Maybe. Boy and girl love, with Vanni."

"Tell me about it."

Lilli lifted her face to Matthew and he could see her eyes were shining. "It was June. That is what Vanni is always to me – June. Oh, to walk through the valley holding his hand, to play the pipes, to run around the hay wagon and shout – I'll always remember that." For her, Vanni would always remain a boy; he would always walk on the prairie, playing his flute. Did she ever want to see him again, or merely to retain the memory of what he had been?

"Do you still love that boy?"

"In a way, yes, what he meant to me. He was my friend, and I was very lonely. Those few hours with him – there were not many such in my childhood."

"You know, I'm jealous of this Vanni," said Matthew, thinking how much brighter the studio was since Lilli had entered. "And now, there are other young men, I suppose –"

Lilli shrugged as she picked up her music case. "Tim and a few others. We are not in love, it is only that we are young and like to play." She winked with one eye. "You know, it is only for fun."

"You're changing rapidly, Lilli." He recalled the girl who

284

had once been too shy to look at him. "Each time you come here, you have something new added to you."

"I'm finding myself, Matthew." Lilli became serious. "I once thought this person might be, and now I have so much to learn, so much to live, so much lost time to make up for – you see, I haven't decided what I am, or what I want, yet."

"You certainly are growing in many ways," said Reiner.

"You see, Matthew," Lilli explained and her green eyes expanded as she looked at him. "I was like a plant which had been set in a dark, narrow place and grew crooked, and then this plant is suddenly removed into sunshine and space, and told to respond to its new environment. . . . Well, at first I was bewildered. I couldn't adjust myself. I tried many strange things, grabbed at ideas you'd laugh at."

"That costume, for example?" Matthew's lips quivered as he recalled how she had appeared in it.

Lilli looked abashed. "That was one thing," she admitted.

"Whatever happened to it?"

"I gave it to the Salvation Army."

"I see," said Reiner thoughtfully. "They must have been surprised."

"Yes. . . ." said Lilli a little dubiously, and then hurried on as though anxious to forget the incident. "I made other mistakes, as bad. Bright, glittering things attracted me for a while. . . . I loved long words, and sometimes used them without understanding them too well."

"For example?"

"Well," said Lilli with a glint of mischief, "I once told my night school teacher I was interesting to be an education lady because I so enjoyment to read what from books makes people culturally."

Matthew burst out laughing. "And what did she say to that?"

"She said," replied Lilli quite seriously, "that she agreed I was interesting, and that enjoyment of reading would no doubt make me some day a lady of education and culture."

"Her prophecy has come true."

"After so many mistakes!"

"Making mistakes is part of life, Lilli, and sometimes, when we look back, a necessary, even enjoyable part, for how else can we find our true selves, if not by experiment?"

Lilli nodded and went on: "To leave off those old ways, those old beliefs was not easy; they were too much a part of me. Sometimes the changes were so swift and unexpected that I hardly knew myself how I was being transformed. Dreams I dared not dream at home, I now permit myself; new ways of thinking and behaving have become so natural that I did not realize they were replacing old, cherished things."

As he watched her, Reiner thought, "She's like a flower springing to life after it's been trampled on," and he realized, "How much more satisfying to observe this growth than to waste my life on dead regrets."

"But what was so difficult, Matthew," continued Lilli, "and I can't grasp it yet, was to realize this way of life need not be. People can be free in spirit." She paused and there was a profound silence. "Do you know what that means, Matthew, to a person who did not own himself?"

The question threw Reiner off his guard; he could not conceal his emotion, and try as he would, was unable to speak. "If she had deliberately designed it, she could not have hurt me more," he thought. "Never before has she so deeply revealed herself."

But Lilli, as she spoke, felt that at last she was growing up to Matthew, that the distance between them was lessening. How to compare the feeling she had for him with her affection for Vanni? She could not rightly estimate it as yet, it was still in the process of becoming.

8
SCHOTTISCHE

❦

THE STREETS of the city were crowded on Thursday afternoons with the daughters of immigrant farmers who had come into the city to go into domestic service. You could distinguish them by their happy, unrepressed voices, their cheeks which had not lost their country freshness, and their clothes which betrayed the naive gaiety of the country girl lost in the wealth of city shops. Some did not speak English very well, often with a touch of Scandinavian, Polish or Ukrainian, but they picked up city ways and within a few months felt at ease. Growing up on homesteads in primitive conditions, these girls, most of them elder daughters, had become inured to hard work – milking cows, pitching hay, stooking, cooking for harvesters and taking care of younger children. They were considered good workers by the city women, as they were healthy and strong, and had no sense of money values; consequently, they worked long hours and were miserably underpaid, an arrangement which was satisfactory to their mistresses. With this background, the girls matured young; they had a grasp of the realities of life through their early struggle and had ambitions for a more comfortable future. Many of them sent money home to put the younger children through school, or to buy machinery for the farm. On Thursday evenings they thronged to the public dance halls, where they met their young men, some of them farm boys who had come to try their luck in the city; others were workers in the factories or petty tradesmen. Many of the girls were beautiful, and all possessed great vitality, being exuberant dancers who could dance long hours, even after putting in ten or twelve hours at domestic service.

Passions were free, and the blood was hot and wild and young in the veins of the strong, lusty boys and girls who stamped, whirled and shouted their way through schottisches, polkas, mazurkas and square dances. A pair of trim and skillful ankles were more highly esteemed than a pretty face. There were hundreds of tunes and improvised steps, which were the delight of the skilled and the discomfit of the inexpert. The girls in their bright taffeta and crepe dresses, patent pumps and earrings, had arranged their hair into stiff artificial waves and spit curls; the men were dazzling in shirts of many colours; and together, they formed a gay picture as they whirled about. Not yet inhibited by city ways, they were determined to show they had come to dance and had put their heart into it.

Tim and Lilli had formed the practice of attending these weekly dances. The big basso was an enthusiastic dancer, and, despite his size, one of the best dancers on the floor. Lilli was so anxious to begin dancing that she raced up the stairs ahead so as not to miss a dance.

"You look like a kid with a Christmas tree," Tim said to her as he watched her delight at the glistening wax floor, the coloured streamers, mirrors and potted plants.

"I love country dancing!" exclaimed Lilli, pulling off her coat with a gesture of impatience. "It's so free – not stiff, like people in the city. Here I can let myself go and be as wild as I like."

"You like being wild?" smiled Tim. "Come, let us see how wild you can be," and they flew off in a schottische.

The band leader was a clever young man who had a knack for picking up tunes and arranging them. He had discovered through the requests of the patrons that many wanted to dance their own familiar country dances, so he had searched the music shops for them, got records and sheet music and made his own arrangements. Years later, when those girls and boys looked back, it appeared a wild, happy time, as they recalled how vigorous were those dances, how enthusiastic those courtships.

When the first dance was over, Lilli put her hands on her hips and whirled a couple of times to show off her accordion-pleated skirt, made of six yards of red chiffon, her low-necked sheer white blouse and red shoes.

"Nobody else could wear a dress like that," commented Tim with admiration. "So many of the girls here put everything on their dresses, tinsel, ribbons, flowers, frills. You'd think they were going to a fancy dress ball."

"That's because they couldn't have very much on the farm," said Lilli. "Some of us wore boys' clothes all year round and had no shoes, so we couldn't develop our taste. Still I think those clothes suit our girls. Suit their personality, I mean. When you see them on the street, they look so fresh and full of colour. The city girls look pale beside them. I suppose they're like a big bunch of wild flowers, all colours mixed up."

As the fiddler scraped three times across his strings to indicate the beginning of a new dance, shrill cries were heard from all over the hall as young men and women surged forward to take their positions for the dance. The couples whirled madly round the room, increased their speed, spun in a rainbow-coloured mass until the walls vibrated with the strength of their stamping. Lilli danced with a wild impetuosity which was a challenge to every young man who looked at her. She was giddy and gay; despite her fierce exertion, she never felt fatigue. As she danced, she slid her eyes in long, provocative glances, not only at her own partner, but at other young men. They smiled back, resolved to dance with her at the first opportunity. In a twinkle she had forgotten everything, she had given herself up to the mad rhythm of the dance, she invented audacious new steps, she had something new every time. Tim never tired of dancing with her.

"Where did you learn to dance like that?" he asked on the way home from the dance. She told him something of her life on the farm, the weddings, games, dances. "People worked so hard on the farm, Tim, they had to find some release. So they danced, sang. But in those days I didn't think the boys would like me. I was a plain little girl."

"You're not plain now," said Tim, as they crunched the snow beneath their boots, stopping occasionally to look at a whitefaced, lopsided moon. "As if it had toothache," commented Lilli. "Although it's bright. . . . Reminds me of a saying of our people."

"What is that?"

"Let the moon shine for me, and I shall gather the stars in my fists," quoted Lilli.

"Tonight, you have both fists full of stars, I think," said Tim. They paused for a momentary scuffle in the snow. "Like two kids on the first day of winter," said Tim, as Lilli pushed him into a snowbank. They both loved physical contact – dancing, tussling, hugging.

"It makes me feel young and strong," glowed Lilli.

"When you come into the room, there is life," said Tim, as they resumed their walk. "*Joie de vivre*, the French say. You take each moment and paint it full of colour and music, Lilli. That is why people are rushing to you. They want to know, what is this excitement? They want to share, to warm their hands at your fire. You said once you were a different girl when you lived in the country. Do you know why, Lilli? You were in a cocoon. Who thinks that beauty is in the cocoon? It hangs, grey and without life, from the twig until it is ready to burst. So Lilli. You have found your wings and you are surprised that you can fly, too."

Lilli pressed the young man's hand warmly as she replied, "Tim, you opened that cocoon for me, you taught me to fly."

9
FACTORY RHYTHMS
ೡ

THE FACTORY in which Lilli worked was a modern one, well-lighted, with big panes of glass and modern machines, clean and spacious. It had a lunch-room where the workers gathered at noon to drink coffee and eat sandwiches. This room was a place of social gathering, centred about a piano of ancient and unwieldy design which some person had once donated to the factory workers. A couple of chintz sofas and several comfortable if dilapidated armchairs created an atmosphere of camaraderie. The owner of the factory, considered one of the most progressive men in the business, encouraged this social life, since he felt it raised the morale of his workers, and consequently their productivity. Every noon the workers, after disposing of their lunch, gathered around the piano for a sing-song. Some of the older workers recalled songs they had sung in the old country regarding exploitation within the European factories – the terrible speed-up, the whip of the foreman, the child labour, all these aroused gloomy and terrible memories of sweatshop and ghetto. The words of these songs were harsh, there was no softness in them, the music dragged heavily on the spirit, as relentless as a foreman's whip. "If you desire to know grief," they would sing, "Come into the mills with us. You will work all day long, and you will come home sorrowful and hungry like a shadow. When old age weakens your strength, they cast you away, like a rag." These songs interpreted for Lilli the fatalism on those faces which she saw around her – the beaten, haunted looks of men and women whose youthful lives had been blighted by servitude to machines. She listened, absorbed, as these older people related stories of their life in European sweat shops, the whip, the bundle system, the crowded firetraps of basement and attic workshops. The resignation which was stamped on every lineament contrasted with the younger people, those born in Canada, who were gayer, more spirited and fond of lively modern tunes.

The time came, inevitably, when someone would call out, "Come, Lilli, sing for us," and Lilli would clamber on the table, which was their stage, to sing, sometimes popular melodies for the young folk, sometimes a folk song of Europe, and sometimes, with sly coquetry, a song of amorous mischief which amused both old and young. The workers had taken Lilli to their hearts; as a kind of accolade, they had bestowed on her the title of their songbird.

A Japanese girl, Mitsui Toyama, one of the most skilled workers in the factory, was once called upon to sing a Japanese song. "Come, Mitsui, a Japanese song," the workers urged. Mitsui, who looked like a china doll, with hair black as though painted in two wings on either side of her porcelain pink face, was pulled onto the table-stage and in a bell-like tone sang, with an Oriental rhythm, the following song:

Nen-nen kororiyo okoriyo
Nen-ne no o-mori wa doko e itta
Ano yama ko-e-te sato e itta
Sato no miyage ni nani moro-u-ta
Den-den da-i-ko ni sho no fu-e
O-ki-a-gari koboshi ni i-nu hariko.

"How pretty!" exclaimed the workers, clapping. "What does it mean?" "It's a Japanese lullaby," explained Mitsui. "My mother used to sing it to me when I was small." "But what do all these words mean?" insisted Lilli, pushing her way through the crowd to Mitsui, who by now had gotten off the table. "It's a promise to give the baby toys if he goes to sleep," replied Mitsui. "I'd like to know the words in English." Lilli was excited, as always when she heard something new that pleased her. Mitsui translated hesitantly:

> Lullaby, baby, lullaby, baby,
> Baby's nursie, where has she gone?
> Over those mountains, she's gone to her village,
> And from her village, what will she bring?
> A tum-tum drum, and a bamboo flute,
> A tumbling doll and a paper dog.

"I like that!" cried Lilli. "What is that tumbling doll?"

"A little doll, with a weight in the bottom, that you can push over, but it won't stay down."

"I think I remember such a doll once," said Lilli, trying to recall it. "Yes, I know now, my father once brought such a doll for my younger sister one Christmas, long ago."

"I had a tumbling doll, painted red and black, when I was little," recalled one of the workers. "What fun, to push it down, and it always came up! Like magic!"

"If you like, Lilli, I'll teach you this song," offered Mitsui. They sat down on one of the chintz sofas. "But I'd like to learn it in Japanese, to sing as you sing it, everything, the way you hold your hands, the way you close your eyes, the way your voice sounds when you sing – "

"Listen," said Mitsui. She sang the song over and line by line, word by word, Lilli imitated her in intonation, gesture, expression.

"You even look Japanese when you sing," laughed Mitsui. "I think it's your eyes." As she spoke, she was aware of a change in Lilli's face. "Mitsui," Lilli gripped the girl's shoulder. "Listen, I have an idea. I am going to make myself look like you." Mitsui's voice tinkled with laughter. "How, Lilli?" she asked. "Your face is quite different." "Wait, you'll see." She took from her purse a makeup kit. "I got this for Christmas

from Tim. Look, lipstick, eye shadow, mascara, everything."
She began to work on her face, all the while keeping her eyes
on Mitsui. She combed her hair back, slicked it down with
pomade, exaggerated the slant of her eyes, heightened the
curve of her cheek. Then she removed Mitsui's pink chiffon
scarf and folded it about her waist like a Japanese obi.

"Well, what do you think?" She turned her head from one
side to another, assumed the expression she had noted on
Mitsui's face. The Japanese girl giggled. "People will think
you're my twin." "Now, how is this?" Lilli made a few
gestures with her hands. "Like this," Mitsui corrected.

The workers crowded about the girls, laughing and giving
Lilli advice. "You'd make a good actress, Lilli," one suggested,
offering her a bottle of pop. "It's hard to tell which is Mitsui
and which is Lilli now," quipped another. They insisted that
the girls both get up again on the table and sing the song as a
duet, the pianist meanwhile pounding out what he considered
an appropriate Japanese tune.

"If you can change your face so easy," remarked one
worker at the end, "We'll never know who you are."

At the stroke of five each day, Lilli pulled on her coat and
beret and ran down the stairs quickly, so that she could take
her place near the front of the building, standing on a platform
slightly above street level, so that she might look down as the
vast throng of factory workers flowed by her, for in ten minutes
the street was empty again, and nothing remained of the
moving swarm of humanity. It was a wonderful sight. At first,
a few came straggling, singly or in couples, and then, the
factories on all sides burst open their doors, the sound of
footsteps on the pavement increased to a roar, the whistles
blew, the street was thronged by a dense mass of men and
women, pushing, hurrying, gesticulating, jabbering, the babel
of tongues audible for blocks. In this city, which had formed
the crossroads of the nation during the period of immigration,
immigrants from all over the world had paused, and many had

gone to work in the factories, so that on the basic Scottish complexion of the original valley settlers had been superimposed overtones of the Jewish, Slavic, and Nordic races. They were all represented now in the crowd which Lilli watched, a crowd which was sad rather than joyful, for a feeling of melancholy prevailed, although many were laughing and joking. Lilli looked eagerly at each person as he went by, trying to judge his race by expression, gestures, features and intonation of voice. On the faces of some, notably older women without families, was written loneliness as they went off singly to their furnished rooms, yet even these for a few moments were united in the vast crowd, and then the main stream divided into numerous currents as the workers streamed off in various directions.

Next day, while working in the factory, a musical phrase drifted into her mind and commenced to torment her. It was not like anything which she had ever heard before, based on some kind of driving rhythm, rather than on melody. She could not explain it; it puzzled her and kept recurring. Unconsciously she began to hum it, and beat her feet in time to it. The tune had a powerful hold on her imagination, growing and developing within her during the next few weeks, especially during the five o'clock rush. The rhythms of the factory, too, began to obsess her – the throb of machines, the flying shuttles, the whirr of wheels. She began to imitate these sounds, weaving melodies, shrugging her shoulders, pounding her feet, whistling, stitching, humming. She found she had created a rhythmic pattern which absorbed and revealed the life of the factory worker. She recalled the sounds of workers on the extra gang. She recalled the sound of the jigger when she rode down the long trail of steel. She imitated the sounds and rhythms of the city as she had once imitated the sounds of nature. In that industrial section, the sounds of industry were many and varied; the noises of street workers, the screaming of factory sirens, the hum of dynamos, the throbbing of machines.

On her next visit to Reiner, Lilli tried to demonstrate some of the rhythms of factory life. Reiner was intrigued. "What is this, Lilli?" he asked.

"It is how I hear the factory," explained Lilli. "Workers and machines, that is what makes this music. How they are, what they think, how they sound and feel and look when they are leaving the factory. How the workers and machines become one."

Reiner experimented with her tunes on the piano. "You have caught the spirit exactly," he commended. "It is true, composers have written themes based on factory life, some new and modern work, but this is the first time one of my own choir members has felt the music of the factory."

Was this how the true folk artist translated work rhythms, whether on the land or in the factory? "She has made the transition," thought Matthew, "and without losing her natural touch." The peasants who were forced off the land into European factories, the peasant immigrants who had gone into American industry, leaving their peasant background behind them – all had been faced with disorientation – the inner rhythm had been lost, naturally enough, reflected Matthew. He had seen the effects, not always happy, in the lives of his own choir members. "You can't predict what Lilli's reaction will be," he thought, "except that it will be a true reaction, in conformity with the soundest instincts of her nature. With her, there never has been any permanent maladjustment."

About a year later, Matthew and Tim had a discussion about Lilli, as the two men strolled through a park near the hall. They often met here, for Matthew had formed a warm friendship with the big, friendly young man. "Tim is like a St. Bernard," Reiner used to think, "big, affectionate and loyal." They walked now in a leisurely fashion past shrubs of flowering honeysuckle as Matthew expounded his opinion of Lilli: "Such singing," he pointed out, "would be crushed in a conservatory of music. The average singing teacher regards art from an academic viewpoint, analyzing technique until he makes an empty skeleton of it. He does not bring forth the living soul of music; instead, his training is such as to make the singer self-conscious. The spontaneous desire to sing is ruined; the singer loses his self-confidence and his bird instinct. He becomes aware of pitch, and obsessed by fear of the highest note in the scale. He doesn't think any longer in terms of human song, but of tone." Reiner paused to break off a branch of blossom and tucked it into his lapel.

"How does that apply to Lilli?" asked the big basso, puffing at his cigarette.

"Well," resumed Reiner as they stood watching a bowling game on the lawn. "Take Lilli and put her through the mill of a conservatory. You would crush the originality of that talent. She would become like a thousand other singers. A teacher can't run his pupils through a mill. You must be a sensitive psychologist to lead people. It's necessary for the teacher to live within the pupil; and teaching is not primarily concerned with vocalization."

They sat down on a bench and watched a red-headed boy on a bicycle, singing "O Sole Mio." His voice was cracked, his face ugly, but his happiness was so infectious that the two men burst out laughing.

"He's a bit like Lilli, isn't he?" asked Tim.

"In his enthusiasm, yes," agreed Reiner, his eyes following the form of the boy. "You know, Tim," he returned to his favourite topic, "I've always felt that Lilli was a child of fate. Wasn't it fate that sent her to me? She had the urge to come, to express what was within her. Was this the action of a simple country girl with a pretty voice? No, it was the desperate compulsion of an artist." He fixed his dark eyes on the good-natured face of the young man. "I have never seen such a striving for perfection, such passion for detail in any pupil. Not one looked so completely for truth and beauty as this country girl." There was something about Tim's expression which worried him, but he continued with increased enthusiasm: "These are the marks of an artist, and they are not always recognized as such. Most people confuse a superficial technical facility with true talent. They are generally disappointed when such a performer fails to develop, as indeed he cannot, for he lacks inner resources which he may draw upon as he grows spiritually and artistically. The capacity for growth – this is the basic quality of the artist. What is essential, therefore? Merely that Lilli develop her original capacities to the point where she can command attention on any concert stage – for she has something unique to offer. Present to her any folk song, and in a short while she has mastered style, idiom, feeling to perfection. The tiniest detail in interpretation will not escape her, and she is never satisfied. Each interpretation is not static, but grows, and this is a phenomenon of folk art – it has been acted on by individuals over whole centuries."

During this long harangue, which Matthew Reiner delivered with considerable ardour, Tim listened without interruption, an expression of intense interest in his face. He did not speak for a few moments, and when he did, his eyes were averted from Reiner: "Aren't you giving Lilli big ideas?"

The question disconcerted Reiner. He had not anticipated an unfavourable reaction from his friend. "What do you mean?" His tone betrayed surprise.

"I think Lilli should be free." There was a look of dogged determination on Tim's face.

"Isn't she free?" Reiner pulled the flower from his buttonhole and began to tear it to pieces.

"You're going to dazzle a naive little country girl before she has a chance to grow up." Tim shifted uneasily on the park bench. He watched a group of young girls pass by, voices raised in a popular song, smiles directed at him, then continued, "Yes, I know how you feel about Lilli. It's exciting to find a voice and develop it, but remember, the voice belongs to a young woman, and there are emotions attached to it; it's not a mechanical box for reproducing sounds."

"I've never discounted Lilli's emotions." Reiner was hurt, angry at the injustice of Tim's accusation.

"Yes," said Tim, "you're free with her, too free, you kiss her, pet her, hold her hand – she's such a charming thing."

"Don't you do any of those things?" Reiner smiled at the recollection of numerous embraces which he had witnessed between Tim and Lilli.

"Of course! Every chance I get. Sometimes I make chances." He chuckled then went on more soberly, "But it's not the same thing."

"Why not?"

"Because for us it's only play when we laugh, kiss, hug. With you, it's different. She thinks you are a being apart. Lilli is especially susceptible to an emotional appeal, because her life has been so harsh. She's with you often, looks up to you, you've great influence on her – "

"You mean," said Matthew incredulously, "that you think I'm using that influence to her disadvantage? That's a serious charge, Tim." For a moment, there was a feeling of tension between the two men, as though the prelude to a quarrel. Then Tim broke it by placing his hand on his friend's sleeve. "Let me put it this way, Matthew," he said. "Lilli looks at everything with new eyes. Everything is fresh to her. Her appreciation has not become stale. She's beginning to discover her potentialities, and it's exciting to her. She doesn't know what to grab at next. When she's in a bright, glittering atmosphere, surrounded by people, she has a look of pure happiness such as I've seen only in a child, a child with a copper to spend looking into a wonderful candy window. Let her stay that way for a while, Matthew." He met Reiner's glance with a plea in his soft eyes. "Don't give her ideas about a career that may not be realized."

Reiner could not speak for a while, so moved was he by

Tim's appeal. "I have faith in her talent – I think she'll succeed." He could not easily surrender his plans for his protégé.

"You have no assurance of that, have you?" Tim persisted. "Think of her background. Would competition break her spirit? She hasn't as much confidence as you think."

The effect of this argument on Reiner was chilling. He was more deeply distressed than he cared to admit. His voice trembled as he replied: "Since Lilli came to us, I've thought constantly of making an artist of her."

"There are small artists and big," said Tim. "Let Lilli find out for herself which she is. If you don't push her too far now, she'll be satisfied no matter which it turns out to be. I'm asking you, Matthew," Tim put all the urgency of which he was capable into his voice, "don't use your influence to form her life. Let her develop of her own self." He stopped to look with compassion on his friend, then continued, "We're still friends, Matthew – don't let these remarks make any difference."

"You're right, Tim," Reiner held out his hand to his friend, and they clasped with warmth. "Of course you're right, a thousand times right." He paused to take his cigarette case from his pocket, so as to hide his emotion from his friend. "How could I have been so blind to it!" Then he began to talk, as though trying to explain himself to his friend.

"When one has helped to create something, one can fall in love with that creation. You've made me doubt, whether I'm in love with the real Lilli, as she knows herself, or something in my own mind. She has some aim, I know, but what does she want?"

"I'm sure she respects you, Matthew." Tim, realizing how harshly his criticism had affected his friend, now tried to make amends.

"No doubt about that," commented Reiner drily. "But you see, respect sometimes creates a gulf between individuals, so that a real intimacy is not possible."

"I know she feels a real affection for you, Matthew." Tim tried again as he began to realize the depth of Matthew's feeling for Lilli.

"The kind of affection one feels for a museum," replied Reiner with bitterness in his voice. "Do you think I don't envy you your friendship with her? Your naturalness, the way you act and talk with her, dance with her, throw snowballs. . . . For me, it would not be dignified. I'm encrusted with dignity. Yes, I'm with her often, all the time realizing that I'm fifteen years older than she is . . . that her gratitude is no substitute for natural affection." As Tim listened he knew that their rivalry, if you could call it such, had not set them against each other, but had only served to bring them closer together. Matthew felt this, too, for he was encouraged to make an even more revealing confidence:

"One day she came in, Tim, laughing because she had tied a sunflower on her head with a yellow taffeta ribbon in place of a hat. She was so young – a child, it seemed, about twelve years old. What could I say, except to think, with an aching heart, that some day she would be taken from me by some young fellow closer to her own age – this Vanni she speaks of, or you, Tim – because your understanding is the understanding of very young people; your high spirits, something that I lost years ago. When you come into the hall together, your faces glowing with youth, my own facial muscles ache, and I can feel every line, every wrinkle, every year that separates us."

"You are not such an old fellow, Matthew," said Tim, placing his hand on his friend's shoulder. "Does it trouble you that Lilli might find someone else?"

"So much so that I can't stand the thought of it," admitted Reiner.

Yet in spite of his own interest in Lilli, Tim was moved by some instinct to make the prophetic remark: "You know, Matthew, I feel that in the end, Lilli will turn to you, because it's with you she can grow."

But as he looked at his friend's face, Tim thought: "He needs a personal life much more than I thought. I've made the mistake of thinking of him only as a teacher. It's true, he's a wonderful teacher and is able to bring out the best in each pupil, but he has denied himself too long; that's why he's taking this affair so much to heart."

10
A SONG OF ENCHANTMENT
✌

AFTER AN absence of two weeks from her lessons, due to a throat infection, Lilli showed up at the studio to find Reiner at the door, looking concerned.

"You look pale," he scolded as he helped her off with her coat, noting the woollen muffler wrapped around her throat.

"I'm not often ill," said Lilli. Except for a slight diminution of her usual vitality, she did not appear much affected by her illness. Reiner unwrapped the muffler with an angry gesture.

"I suppose your voice will be hoarse."

"All better, I think." She sat down in an armchair, a sweater draped around her shoulders.

"How did it happen?" Reiner went to the window to stop up a draft.

"Too much dancing with Tim," smiled Lilli. "Afterwards we walked the streets all night singing. Oh, Matthew, it was glorious! Worth a cold." She looked at him like a child asking forgiveness for a fault.

"I must tell him to take better care of you," growled Reiner, as though unwilling to be appeased. He was jealous, too, that he had not shared this experience with her.

"Please don't say anything to him," begged Lilli. "He'd be terribly upset. Truly, it wasn't his fault. I urged him on, and kept him going when he said I should be in bed."

"You must take care of yourself. I can't afford to lose you. You're my best pupil." As he spoke, the prospect of actually losing her caused him a sharp pang.

"I promise it won't happen again."

Somewhat mollified, Reiner sat down on the piano bench. "Do you enjoy dancing?" He strummed a polka.

"So much!" exclaimed Lilli. "I look forward to it all week. I can't dance enough." She added, with an impish smile, "Especially polkas."

"You're very young, and it's natural you should want companions of your own age." He was conscious of the disparity in their ages. "Are your music lessons becoming a chore?"

"Never that, you know," she assured him. Then, with an impulse of shyness: "I've brought you something, Matthew." She took a sheet of music from her case. "What is this?" He looked at it. "I've searched a long time for it, Matthew," she replied. "This was the song I heard Sam playing – you remember, I told you about it."

"A song of your people?"

"Yes. It is a song of enchantment, of a woman who poisoned her lover through jealousy."

Reiner played the four opening notes, each accentuated in the song with a long vowel, as though uttering some grim warning. "From the first four notes," he remarked, "I can tell she means no good."

Lilli leaned over his shoulder and laughed: "I suppose you could translate it, in popular language, "Watch out, she has her eye on you!" He turned in time to detect a mischievous gleam in her eyes. "It is an old tale of the people," she went on. "And has been made into a folk operetta, very popular with us."

"Let's hear you sing it." The tune was vaguely familiar, and Reiner could not shake off the feeling that he had heard it before, somewhere. With the dark premonition of the first notes. Lilli established herself as the jealous peasant woman plotting revenge on her fickle lover; she revealed, with brooding savagery, the feeling of outrage of the sensual woman who has been scorned. The rich vibrations of her voice, combined with the exotic vowel sounds, gave an effect of haunting antiquity. Every line of her face and body betrayed defiance, jealousy, passion.

"You sing with deep conviction," said Reiner when she had finished. "I didn't think you were capable of it. Could you translate for me?"

"There is a translation," replied Lilli. "You'll excuse me if it's a little clumsy – I don't remember the exact words." She recited:

> Beware, young man, the evening's revelry,
> That black-browed maid, an evil enchantress, she,
> With brooding looks she feeds her jealousy,
> In secret plots a dreadful fate for thee.
> Within a forest dark, she digs beneath a tree.
> Well does she know each herb's malignancy,
> Distils from them the poisoned cup of tea
> With looks of love she gives the drink to thee.
> Beware, young man, the charm has potency,
> A dark, dark house of planks, a grave for thee!

Reiner listened, marvelling at the peasant economy and capacity for creating pictures. "You frighten me, Lilli," he said. "I didn't know you had all that primitive passion in you."

"I sometimes think you don't know me, Matthew."

He had known, he thought, that she was capable of emotional depth, but he had overlooked passion. "It's a demoniac creation!" he exclaimed walking excitedly up and down.

Lilli nodded: "My mother told me, once, that this song was made by a peasant woman who had been disappointed in love. Her first name, I know, was Maria, and the song is very old, maybe two hundred years or more. They say it all happened."

What a genius that peasant woman had, thought Reiner, to

compose this legend of the people which had a life of centuries! "She must have been very much like you, Lilli."

"Like me?" Lilli was pleased.

"Why not?" said Reiner. "If you had lived in her time, been subjected to the same influences, lived in the same surroundings – " He added, as an afterthought: "Do peasant women treat their lovers so when they're jilted?"

"Yes, they do," Lilli said. "They poison them." He could see that she was speaking in jest, but at the same time, she was brooding over those circumstances of the past which had brought such women into being. "I'd almost believe you'd be capable of it." With a quick reversal of mood, Lilli smiled: "I made a charm once, on Vanni."

"How did you do that?" He tried to match the levity of her tone.

"Put a sugar lump under the water of the creek at midnight and then gave it to him on Midsummer Day."

He chuckled: "Did it work?"

"Of course!" She wondered at his disbelief. "He couldn't keep his eyes off me."

"I don't think you need a sugar lump," said Reiner. "You have, let us say, other charms." This was a propitious moment to examine them at close range. Her face, Reiner thought, was a little fuller, her figure more mature, her use of makeup more subtle – all these changes in themselves were not great, but how different the total effect! The country girl had disappeared. Her inner growth, too, disturbed him. "The Christmas tree phase is over," he thought.

"You don't really believe in witches, do you?"

"In a way, I do," Lilli surprised him by answering. "They're women who live apart from society because of something tragic in their lives. I knew such a woman once – she was not happy." She sighed.

"You baffle me – " Matthew exclaimed in exasperation, unable to follow her wanderings from the modern world into her private cavern of superstition.

"There are some things you can't explain," Lilli maintained stubbornly. "I've seen things – " She checked herself. "No, I won't tell you, you'll only laugh."

How difficult, thought Reiner, to tear her from her ancient faith, even if it were desirable, and was it? Would he destroy the unique thing she had, and was she a better artist because she guarded herself against the destruction of that faith?

Lilli felt she possessed complete understanding of the woman whose story she had related: "This woman shouldn't be judged as if she had committed a terrible crime. In those times, many cruel and ugly things happened, people had to fight continually for their lives." The song, Matthew understood, had to be considered against a background of wars, conflagrations, national disasters, when violence was engendered in the nature of the people. To understand an individual like Lilli, he thought, one would have to know the historical background for centuries back.

"Why do you look at me?" She brought him out of his reverie.

"You've grown into quite a young lady," he said, trying to sound casual.

"You're surprised?" She pulled on her gloves with a slow, graceful motion, not with the clumsy vigour of a child trying on its first mitts, as she had done with her first pair of gloves, he recalled. With this single gesture, she symbolized, somehow, her new-found sophistication.

"I shouldn't be, I suppose," he replied. "Maturity is a normal process. Perhaps I had the habit of thinking that you were my discovery, my property, so to speak. I was taken aback that you could develop independently, without asking my permission." He held the door open for her. "I'm glad you brought it to my attention, however," he said as she went out. "So I can take measures to protect myself against those charms."

When she had left, Reiner went back to the piano and played the song over and over, unable to understand his feeling of discomfiture. A woman's jealousy was the last emotion of which he would have thought Lilli capable. He had formed the habit of thinking of Lilli as a naive girl, yet inwardly she had been developing a woman's passions. Confronted with her new maturity, it was he who was disconcerted, not she; she wore her new poise naturally. He recalled her laugh, and how he had been thrilled by it without thinking about it – the head thrown back, the mouth slightly parted, the eyes alight, and the slight toss of her head at the end, like a point of emphasis – yes, she was certainly using her charms. He continued to play the tune, musing, "It's haunting – no wonder it captured Sam's imagination. He knows a good thing." How much more had Sam seen in Lilli? "More than I did," realized Reiner. "Even Tim understands her better." He speeded up the tempo of the song, composed variations, improvised. "It lends itself to composition," he thought. "That damnable tune – it has a morbid fascination. I'll be hearing it in my sleep." He got up from the piano and went to the window to look out at the lilac shadows of twilight. Did he regret that he had seen the last of Lilli's naivete? "I'm not sorry," he thought. "Her naivete was a charming thing, but might become cloying." As he lit a cigarette he thought of the look of mock challenge on Lilli's face when she had said, "Watch out, she has her eye on you!" He chuckled: "I could swear she meant it." He looked forward to the exciting changes which the future might bring to their relationship.

11
MIGRATIONS OF MELODY
❦

LILLI'S life for the next three years had been devoted to her music lessons, solo work with the choir and her ambition to set up her own dressmaking shop. As her taste developed, she began to design costumes for the girls in the factory, then for women who attended the choir concerts, and with an increasing clientele, she spent her lunch hours looking for a suitable location for a shop. When she finally found what she wanted, she left the rooming-house where she had lived during her factory years and established herself in a small dressmaking shop in the theatre district. She made it attractive by stencilling designs on the walls, painting the furniture in bright colours, and placing four candles in carved sticks on the mantelpiece.

One late winter afternoon, Matthew Reiner dropped in to visit Lilli in her shop, carrying a box of roses from a nearby florist. As he stood inside Lilli's sitting room, his coat and hat covered with snow, he could not understand the burst of laughter with which she greeted him. "Why are you laughing?" he asked as he handed over the box. "You look like Father Christmas," she explained, pulling off his beaver cap and shaking the snow off.

"It's cosy in here," said Reiner, advancing into the room. "You have a fire in your fireplace today. I thought that was just decoration."

"Draw up a seat and relax," Lilli urged. "I'll be free soon. This is the only dress I have to work on tonight."

Reiner sat down before the fireplace and took out his pipe. There was only one item in his surroundings which displeased him, and that was Lilli's dress, an affair made of black woollen material, high-necked and severe.

"That's not a very becoming costume," he frowned.

"I know." Lilli looked up from her work. "You see, my customers wouldn't like it if I competed with them in dress. In this, I look five years older and they have more confidence in me." She turned up the hem of the gown on which she was working and whipped it with fine, small stitches. Her deftness did not surprise Reiner, as he had already noted her manual dexterity, but he had not expected that she should work with such imagination and daring, draping folds of brocade like a sculptor.

"You've decorated this place in a most original manner, Lilli," he commented, looking about the room. "Is this your design?" He fingered the black drapes, which had a complicated design in lilac, green and buff.

"Not exactly mine," replied Lilli. "I had a bit of Bukovynian tapestry and I copied the pattern."

"You like working with your hands, don't you?"

"Yes," replied Lilli. "I'm like my granny in that way. It's satisfying to make something of my own design, it helps to get away from the machine. People don't seem to have time for such things any more."

She appeared serene and composed as she worked – a simple, natural woman, Reiner told himself, whose function was to create a comfortable atmosphere for her man. As always, he was impressed by her natural dignity of speech and gesture.

"Do you have many visitors?" he asked, stretching his legs out before the fireplace.

"Mostly customers." Lilli held the dress up and appraised it.

"Are you doing well?"

"Quite well, Matthew. Enough to keep me busy." She

waved her hand in the direction of the rack of half-finished dresses. "Mostly evening gowns for concerts. They seem to like my work."

Matthew was surprised to feel a pang of jealousy that he knew so little of Lilli's life outside the choir. When were these people who demanded her attention and energy? Probably society women who pestered her with their demands, probably spoiled creatures who imposed on her.

"They're difficult to satisfy, I suppose."

"A few – most are pleased."

Lilli's work had attracted many customers, because she had inventiveness in devising new styles and suggesting new colour combinations. Her workmanship was superb; purity of line was her first concert. She loved working with rich materials, and lavished all her skill and imagination on brocades and velvets. Reiner could understand that Lilli would not tolerate shoddy workmanship.

"It's a pity the work takes up so much of your time."

"Sometimes I begrudge it," admitted Lilli, regarding Reiner with a look of naive candour which made his heart contract. "Sometimes, inside of myself, I rage, but then, you know, I've learned much from them."

"What could you possibly learn from such women?" Reiner got up to examine the carved wooden candlesticks on the mantelpiece. He could not explain his sense of irritation.

"Speech, poise, manners," replied Lilli. "They made me feel at first like a clumsy little gawk."

"Clumsiness is the last thing I'd accuse you of, Lilli," replied Reiner. "You have a natural grace." He stood admiring the precision of her fingers. "How do they teach you?"

"I watch them," confessed Lilli with a grin. "When they go away, I practise before a mirror – the way they walk, stand, laugh, talk, enter a room. Oh, I have fun when I'm alone! Then I try it out on my customers."

She went on to tell Reiner how she had attended the recital of a so-called folk singer who had been highly praised in the local press. The woman had a high, light voice, not unpleasing, but with many artificial gestures and trills. Her arrangements violated the true spirit of folk song. Lilli could not conceal her disgust. "Is this the way people want to hear folk song?" she asked indignantly. "Not as these songs are sung by their creators, not as we sing them, but with all force gone, like watered wine."

"The wine, undiluted, might go to their heads," suggested Reiner.

"I prefer the rich, strong draught," protested Lilli.

When she had finished her work, she went out to change, and came back wearing a soft woollen dress of an odd shade of blue. She had a genius for colour, thought Reiner. Any other women, in that blue, would look sallow.

"What are you going to do now?" he asked.

"Work at a costume." Lilli showed Reiner the Bohemian costume on which she was working. The cloth for the skirt had been woven on a hand loom which she had purchased at a second-hand store. As she embroidered the muslin blouse, she told him how she took pains to get even the slightest detail exact. "People often ask me, why do you take so much trouble? Who will see? Who will know the difference? And I always answer, I myself will see. I myself will know the difference."

Reiner picked up a piece to examine it. "It must have taken months of work to make this."

"That's the way peasants work, Matthew," said Lilli. "To last a lifetime. To express something of their own reaction to the beauty of nature. See this?" She held out the embroidery to him. "This design was made by some peasant women in Bohemia, maybe one hundred years ago. I wonder what she would ever think if she saw it now."

"Probably be overjoyed to think her work had travelled over half the world," said Reiner.

"It's strange that you should say that, Matthew."

"Why?"

"Because it fits in with something I thought of today." Lilli laid down her work and looked eagerly at Reiner. "Did you know that a folk song or story can appear in the lore of different people? Well, when I first came to the city I heard an old Scottish lady sing the same story my own granny had told me when I was a child. Could it be this same story travelled from Scotland to Ukraine?"

"That's the case with many songs, Lilli," said Reiner, returning to his seat before the fireplace. "The migration of melodies has been studied by many musicians. It has never been satisfactorily explained, but I suppose that travellers from one country to another could carry songs with them."

"You mean, songs are wanderers? Oh, I like that!" Lilli's eyes gleamed, as always when she hit a truth through her own intuition. "So you might find the same song in many different countries!"

"Yes, there are many known instances," continued Matthew.

"For example, an old song which tells of a child speaking in dreams with a dead mother. We have many versions of this story – German, Greek, Romanian, Bulgarian, Finnish – I don't know how many. Much of the poetry produced by the people was scattered by itinerant minstrels. They changed details to suit the country; an orange tree in Spain appears as a cypress in Greece, or a briar in England."

"And I suppose in Canada it would change into a pine or maple."

"Probably."

"And the flute of my story changes into a harp in the Scottish song," suggested Lilli with growing excitement.

"Or lute, or bells, as in the Chinese version." Reiner smiled at Lilli's enthusiasm. "Give her a hint and she'll gallop away," he thought. She was quivering with an intense physical reaction of her face and body, and when her eyes met his, they were alight with discovery. "Such a poignant reaction to a mere point of knowledge!" mused Reiner. "In an ordinary

313

young women, that physical response could mean only one thing. How can any onlooker remain calm in the face of such passion?" He sighed uneasily. "I wonder if the little wretch knows how she torments me?"

"Did you know the story yourself, Matthew?" Lilli selected a skein of rose-coloured silk from the basket at her side.

"It's one of the best-loved legends of the human race, Lilli," replied Reiner, "and one of the most widespread."

"Why do you think people loved it more than others?"

"Perhaps because it embodied some essential truth."

"It does haunt me," said Lilli slowly, "but what is that essential truth?"

"Offhand, I'd guess the story might be a way of explaining the musical voice of an instrument: a young girl's body is transformed into an instrument, and her voice is then a part of it. Or it may be a simple story of revenge – that is always satisfactory to the human sense of justice."

"It proves that a there's a similarity of feeling, melody and rhythm in all songs, doesn't it?"

"All of humanity has the same emotions," replied Reiner. "It's the local sky, vegetation and climate which create the variations." He leaned back in his armchair, looking through half-closed eyes at the flames.

"You are fortunate that you have this background, Lilli," he said, sensing that now might be an appropriate time to probe more deeply into Lilli's past. "Tell me something of your people."

"When they talked," said Lilli, "it was in pictures. When they sang, it was truly the voice of nature. When I first began to work in the factory, I found the noise of the machines confusing. It seemed ugly and monotonous. I was unhappy, because I felt I had to hear the harmony of natural sounds. Later, as you know, I began to feel rhythm in the factory."

Psychologically, Lilli had had to re-orientate herself, just as all peasants who had left the country to go to work in the factories. Unlike them, however, she had not lost in the transition.

"You know that song you were teaching me the other day, Matthew," Lilli went on, in what was for her an unusual burst of confidence, "Schubert's *Der Tod und Das Mädchen* – it could have been written for me."

"How is that, Lilli?" Matthew became alert as he sensed that here was one of the many untold chapters in Lilli's life, hidden from him by her primitive silence and dark reticences.

"When I was a little girl, about eleven," recalled Lilli, "I was very sick, everyone thought I would die. There were even two women in the house to mourn for me. I saw Death close then, and know what these lines mean, 'Death will not halt because he hears a voice crying – Tarry, I am still so young'!"

Looking at those brilliant eyes, that passionate face, Matthew found it hard to believe that this young women, so full of life, had once approached the threshold of death. He had sensed this knowledge of death in her, and not knowing its origin, felt it as a disturbing element in her personality. She was becoming more and more herself, reflected Reiner, casting off that borrowed personality which had been inflicted upon her. Each time he saw her, something new was revealed. Like watching an exotic plant come into blossom, he thought. This was an aspect of Lilli's character which most intrigued Reiner; how could he piece together all these disparate pieces and make a composite portrait of Lilli satisfactory to himself? "The minute I think I have her analyzed, she changes, and reveals another pattern, like a kaleidoscope when you move it. I suppose because her idea of herself doesn't accord with my idea of what she is. I wonder whether I'll ever really know her."

She still seemed a bit of the wild country girl to him, as she sat with her Bohemian embroidery, humming softly to herself.

"What is that you're singing, Lilli? A sad tune, isn't it? Is that the way you're feeling tonight?"

"Not really, Matthew," relied Lilli, looking up at him and smiling. "I used to hear a family of Bohemians sing this song in the village, in the evening, and always I had a feeling of – what is that word which means homesickness?"

"Nostalgia?"

"Yes," replied Lilli. "That was the song of their homesickness – nostalgia, I mean. All those voices – there were about a dozen of them in that family, one with a big bass voice, like from a barrel, my grandfather used to say, singing that sad song! Everyone in the village sat quiet to listen, as if each person were asking in his heart, 'Where is my home?'"

"Were you so much attached to your home?"

"I wasn't attached at all, really." Lilli recalled the huge, untidy log house, where there was never a corner she could call her own. "A home in which I never felt at home," she sighed. "I was the odd one, the gypsy, in the family. My mother thought I had magic powers because I was born at twilight." She paused to rummage in her work basket. "Sometimes I wonder whether what she believed about me helped to make me what I am." Her face took on a brooding expression, like an alien mask suddenly applied.

"That's an odd thing to say, Lilli," frowned Matthew. "I'm not sure I know what you mean." He looked around the room, as if to relate its decorative details with the alien element in Lilli's character.

"I mean," said Lilli, "that what people think about you sometimes changes you." Matthew felt himself baffled again by her constant retreat into primitivism, her disconcerting fatalism.

"Don't look so cross." Lilli came over to him and passed her hand gently over his face.

"Am I cross?" Matthew trembled at the sensual thrill her touch had aroused in him.

"You're frowning, as if to say, what a strange girl, she behaves like a savage."

316

"Not at all," said Matthew. He got out his cigarette case and extracted a cigarette. "I was simply thinking that you have a life behind you that I know very little of, really."

"Maybe it's hard for you to imagine such a way of life, Matthew," said Lilli, drawing up a stool and sitting close to him. "My people had a long way to go. When they came to Canada, they had so much to make up in so little time. The road other people took centuries to travel, they had to cover in a few decades. It was the same with me, too, Matthew." Her voice trembled. " I know I'm not what you want me to be, but give me a chance to learn. In a few years, I can't unmake my whole life." She rested her head lightly on his sleeve.

"I wouldn't want you to, Lilli," he said, stroking her hair. "Then you'd be somebody else, and I'd miss the real Lilli."

"Nobody to worry over, nobody to scold," her muffled voice went on.

"A dismal prospect." Reiner, realizing what Lilli meant to him, pushed her head gently aside and stood up near the mantel, his face turned so that she could not see it. Some day he would have to face that fact that he would lose her, to Tim or one of her young men. He knew, by the ache in his heart, that he was not willing to give her up. "If the day ever comes when you leave me," he said. "it will be grey, covered with clouds, cold and dismal. I'll close the door of my study and play funeral marches. I'll look out of the window and think that I won't wait any more for Lilli to come to her lessons, or listen to her high heels tapping on the pavement. Soon I'll turn into a crabby old man and when young girls come to see me, I'll snarl at them."

Lilli laughed, her credulous child's laughter. "Do I mean so much to you, Matthew?" The emotion in her voice touched him. "Lilli!" He turned to her and held out his hand. For a few moments, they stood with clasped hands, Matthew wishing dreadfully to prolong the moment without developing it to its natural conclusion. How could he confront her with a mature passion before she had found herself? By her own admission, she was not yet ready. He squeezed her hand, as though in jest, and then withdrew his own. He kept looking at her while he fought within himself to make some decision.

"Continue to grow, Lilli," he said, placing his hands on either side of her face. "You've come a long way."

"And I still have a long way to travel, haven't I?" The candour of her eyes compelled an honest reply from him.

"The most interesting, the most rewarding part of the journey is still before you."

"How far do you think I'll go?"

"We won't set any limits," replied Matthew, striving to keep his voice light, as he recalled Tim's warning about giving Lilli big ideas, and permitting her to lead a natural life. "You'll always find people to listen to you. Does it matter, who is the audience? For you, the important thing is not success in the conventional form, is it, but to keep on learning, keep on reaching out, keep on developing yourself as an artist. With that in mind, you don't have to worry about competition, failure, success. You will, in time, find your level, and whatever it is, I think you'll be content." Having thus, as he thought, solved the dilemma, Reiner congratulated himself on his narrow escape.

"I'll be content if you're there." Lilli's sudden frankness upset him. Wondering whether he had made a right decision, he hesitated momentarily, strongly tempted to settle the matter right there.

"Will you, Lilli?" He assumed again the comradely tone. "You have no reason to fear I won't." He patted her hand. "I can't look ahead and see the future where you and I won't be together." He could not take his eyes away from her, so appealing was she in her soft woolen dress, so dear to him.

"Well," said Lilli, "have you examined me enough? This is all me, it won't rub off. Look. Can you suggest any improvements?" She turned her face from side to side.

"I don't know if I want you to change, Lilli," replied Reiner. "I suppose you must, but it seems a pity. All that glow dimmed. That's what they call progress – when individuals become as much alike as machine-made goods."

"And what am I?"

"You're as unique as your grandmother's tapestry. An original design."

"If you like it, Matthew, I won't change." Lilli bustled about, getting out her tea things, which, like the rest of her possessions, were unusual in appearance. She had two peacock-green cups trimmed with gold design which she had purchased in the local Chinatown. These she placed on a little table before the fire-place, along with honey, toast, and strawberry preserve. Teatime was always a great ceremony for her. She poured tea from a samovar, also purchases, she told him, in a second-hand store.

"You must haunt the place," said Reiner, sipping the delicately lemon-flavoured tea.

"Every noon," replied Lilli, spreading honey on a piece of toast. "I got this honey from a Mennonite farmer in the marketplace. He's an old friend, I often talk to him there. Do you know, Matthew, I'd like sometimes to visit those people in their community. And others, too – those Icelandic fishermen who come in every week with their fish. How could I get to know all those people?"

"It's a coincidence you should mention that." Reiner helped himself to the strawberry preserve. "I've been thinking for a long time, Lilli, in fact that's the main reason I came to visit you tonight. How would you like to go on tour?"

"Oh, where, Matthew?" Lilli set down her cup so hastily that the china rattled.

"Of rural communities, and later, perhaps, if it can be arranged, to points all over the country. They have been writing to me to send them one of my singers. Would you like to go?"

Lilli's eyes sparked. "More than anything!" she exclaimed. "How could you ask?" She got up from her chair and began dancing about the room.

"They aren't elegant audiences," Reiner explained with caution, not wishing to raise her hopes too high. "You'll sing to common people who are hungry for music and would appreciate your coming to them. There are some fine musicians among them, and you'd have a chance to get their opinion of your talent. At the same time, you might pick up some songs to increase your repertoire."

Lilli, as though scarcely hearing him, was at the chest, pulling out costume after costume. "I'll take all these along with me," she planned, her cheeks scarlet with animation. "And my songs – which do you like best, Matthew?"

"I think you should make the choice yourself." Reiner laughed as he saw how his idea had aroused her. "Could you take time off from your work?"

"Oh, yes, I can shut up the shop whenever I please. I'll choose a time when business is slow." She spread the costumes on chairs about the room and stepped back to admire them. "Think of the opportunity to speak to all these people – Icelanders, Germans, Ukrainians, French, and to try out my songs on them!"

How many men would find her beautiful, thought Reiner as he watched her preparations. Excitement had stimulated her; she always responded to an occasion. Well, he conceded, he had never wished Lilli to become one of those austere women whose lives, meagre of personal love, were dedicated to the cause of art. Lilli could never survive without an earthly passion. For years he had monopolized her attention, and now that time had come to an end, the time of learning, the time of discovery.

"You won't need me much longer." He spoke abruptly.

"What do you mean, Matthew?" She turned around and looked at him in surprise.

"I can't do much more for you," he replied. She continued to stare at him as if she did not understand. "How many years since you came to me – seven, is it seven or more?" He thought of the lessons, rehearsals, concerts, and how they had strengthened the feeling which he had for her.

"Everything I know I owe to you, Matthew," she reproached him. "And I can't imagine a time when I won't need you."

12
PRAIRIE CONCERT
❦

OF THE whole tour, the richest, most rewarding experience came when she least expected it. What was there about that evening that held such enchantment for her? No matter how often she recalled it in after years, the memory never lost its glow.

She had no premonition of what was coming when she got of the wagon, after a long, tiresome ride, at the huddle of shacks in the middle of the prairie. The community hall was little better than a wooden shack, with all the paint peeled off, its stairs askew as if blown in by the wine. Lilli felt chilled: had she travelled so many miles to come to this drab place?

The driver was apologetic: "Perhaps this isn't the kind of audience you're used to. They're poor people here."

Lilli straightened her shoulders as at a rebuke. "The poorer they are, the more they need what I can give them." She marched into the hall.

The crowd of people within seemed still covered with the dust of depression and drought, but the faces, as they turned to her were full of strength and curiosity, the voices rising in a murmur of polyglot overtones.

"Already I feel warm," said Lilli as she looked at them. In this audience, she thought, were the people who had composed her songs, who had fought the wilderness, built the railway – the primary creators.

What was it that inspired her to give as her first song, "Lament of a Hebrew Mother for Her Lost Child?" Was it the sight of a Jewish woman's face, speaking the loneliness of a stranger among strange folk? Singing in Yiddish, with each inflection and gesture copied from life, Lilli created so vivid a picture of grief that even in that foreign tongue, the audience did not require interpretation.

Before each number, she selected one person in the audience and sang to him whichever song she thought would touch him most closely. An old lady with a face all in hard planes as if chiselled from the rock of the native Scotland moved Lilli to sing and eighteenth century Scottish lullaby:

O can ye sew cushions
Or can ye sew sheets?
Or can ye sing Ba-loo-loo
When the bairnie greets?
And hee and ba-birdie
And hee and ba-lamb
And hee and ba-birdie
My bonnie wee lamb.

Hee-o, wee-o, what would I do wi' you?
Black's the life that I lead wi' you.
O'er mony of you, little for to gi'e you.
Hee-o, wee-o, what would I do wi' you?

When afterwards the people came crowding back stage, Lilli felt surrounded by the stuff of her songs – as though the characters in them had come to life and flocked about her.

Her old Scottish lady was the first. "It's forty years since I heard that song," she told Lilli, gripping her hand. "In the old country, it was – I sang it to my youngest." There was no sentiment in her face, but her voice communicated her feeling to Lilli. The two women stood looking at each other for a moment, then the old lady released her hand, and said, "You're a bonnie lassie," and was gone.

She was followed by Mrs. Rosenberg, the wife of a local storekeeper, the only Jewish woman in the audience. The emotional response of the Jew pouring out in a rich, warm stream like wine, she embraced Lilli again and again as she exclaimed: "Thank you, thank you! How long since I heard the songs of my own people. You understand, here we are alone, we do not get the chance – where did you learn that song! As though you were singing for me, my little girl who dies – I thought I must come, I must tell you what it means! May you have luck! May you sing for many, many years! You don't know what you have done for me!"

"Or you for me," retaliated Lilli. How could she ever have thought this place drab?

She was surprised to be approached by a young girl, perhaps thirteen, whose skin had the blond transparency of the Scandinavian.

"Oh, tell me," the girl begged with colour flushing through her white skin. "Where did you learn to sing like that? I, too, want to sing, but it is so hard to learn, here – How did you find your first teacher?"

Lilli knew the answer: "The wind was my first teacher. I heard songs all around me on the prairies, carried by the wind."

The girl clasped her hands and her face lit up. "Oh, that is the way I hear the prairies, too!" she cried, and Lilli answered, "For those who can hear, there is always a teacher."

How much later was it – an hour, two hours – when Lilli finally left the hall and took her place on the wagon seat beside the driver. As she rode along that anonymous road with the anonymous driver – she didn't know his name and she didn't want to – Lilli abandoned herself to sensation. Where was she? Did it matter? Somewhere on the prairies, wit the prairie sky above her, hearing the creak of the wagon wheels, the voice of the driver beside her, reliving the memory of theat concert and the people. . . . Each sense was alive, like an ear pricked up, to catch the most fugitive vibration of her surroundings. She threw her head back to look at the stars. "Like home – " She paused. A surge of nostalgia gripped her.

"You were brought up on the prairies?" The voice beside her startled her. Almost, she had forgotten she was not alone, so deeply immersed was she in reverie.

"Can't you tell?"

The driver scratched his head. He seemed to her like the prairie itself, with his bleached hair like stubble, his face golden as if it had absorbed the essence of prairie sky and sun. "You must have been like Lilly Svenson, our little Swedish singer," he remarked. "She was here tonight."

"I spoke to her." Lilli murmured, feeling the wind on her cheek like a velvet paw.

"She was determined to talk to you," continued the driver. "A strange child, always walking around the prairie and singing to herself."

"We understand each other," said Lilli. She was pleased to think that there would always be on the prairie some girl like herself to listen to the music in nature. "I used to be like that," she went on. "Suddenly the wind catches you up and in your mind you are rushing across the prairies, wanting, that terrible wanting that you feel when you're very young, before you've had the chance to try out your wing. You look back in later years and you think, was it really like that? It's so hard to feel as you did then – except at some moment like this one." She savoured the emotion again, like some delightful food once tasted and now by chance offered to her again.

The driver pursued the train of thought. "That's exactly what you did tonight," he pointed out. "You gave each person something he thought he had lost."

"I only gave them back what I got from them in the first place," said Lilli.

"But how full of colours, how strong you made it!" He sighed at the remembrance. "They will not forget you soon." His face, in the light of the lantern, was oddly distorted and he looked like some mythical personage, Lilli thought, not quite real, something out of a fairy tale.

"You must come again."

13
RETURN HOME
ੴ

WHY was she going back, on this train through southern Manitoba? Lilli sat in a crowd of farmers' wives returning home from the city, and speculated. All during her recent tour the words of that Czech song had kept running through her mind, "Where is my home?" She felt incomplete, especially when she met all those people to whom their own past was so dear, and she wanted – what? To claim her own inheritance? To return to her origins? What was drawing her back?

She looked out the window. How changing were the prairies, so many colours, sounds and movements, thought Lilli. She had heard people call the prairies monotonous, but she loved their bigness, as if one could not have mean thoughts there. The landscape was breathing with hidden life for her.

When she got off at the station, everything was changed. There was a gasoline station, a drug store with plate glass front and a groceteria. Her lovely little village, mourned Lilli, which artists used to paint, vanished beneath a veneer of chromium! She stood, uncertain, looking for something familiar whose sight would set her memory aflame.

Then, feeling like a stranger, she set off to walk to her father's farm, noting on the way that the land had lost much of its shagginess. It was trimmed, orderly; new buildings had replaced the old whitewashed cottages. Occasionally she saw a tractor driven by some bronzed farmer.

At last she came within sight of her old home and for a

while she hesitated, afraid to go near, remembering so many things of her childhood. There was the old outdoor bake oven, now crumbling in decay, there was the archway of trees which led to the house, and Petey, where was he? She wanted to summon him by crying out, as if across the years he would come running to her gain, hands full of flowers, crowned with radiance, not one day older.

As she approached, a man came from behind the house and stood silhouetted against the fields, on which there were no wild acres now. All had been broken to the plough, and broken, too, the man. Diminished by all he had given, he looked at the soil into which his young strength had been ploughed.

This could not be her father, thought Lilli, staring at him, chilled that the years which had added so much to herself had made of him an older, paler edition, like a worn copy of some favourite childhood book.

The man turned to look at her. "Lilli, is it?" Almost timidly he peered from beneath grizzled eyebrows, out of eyes like dim coals, his hand extended – as though uncertain. "Well, Lilli, you are a lady, now, a fine lady." Always able to recognize quality, he knew what level his daughter had reached by her bearing, the elegance of her grey suit, the leather, even, of her shoes. "We are plain people here but we have heard of your singing, and are glad."

"Father!" Lilli choked. She ran to him and they clasped hands. Anton saw from her eyes how he had changed. "Yes, age has sprinkled many snowflakes on my head. A hard struggle with the land, Lilli. I thought to beat it, but look, it has beaten me." He smiled, with a touch of the old bravado. "We learn, sometimes too late."

Was he apologizing to her? Lilli felt ashamed. "No, not too late," she insisted. "We still have time to know each other."

Never a man of sentiment, Anton shrugged. "It is good

that you have come back to see us," he said. "You will stay awhile? Your brothers ands sisters will be glad to see you."

They came running out now, how many – all those heads, those long legs – she could not count them. "Are all these my brothers and sisters?" She was excited as the girls and boys thronged about her, giggling, pushing, striving to attract her attention. When small, thought Lilli, they had not occupied so much space. Now grown large, they filled the yard with themselves. She recognized the twins, in blue gingham dresses. One face she looked for in vain. "Petey?" She scanned the boys hoping for some response.

"Look up," said Anton, pointing upward. "Petey is no longer a small boy – "

"Of course!" exclaimed Lilli. "He must be how old – seventeen? But which one?" She looked around her while the crown laughed. "Guess, guess!"

The door opened and Petey came striding out, much enlarged, much matured, but still undeniably Peter. Lilli ran to him. "Peter!"

"A giant!" chuckled Anton. "Six feet tall is our Peter." Lilli looked up and down and around and then flung her arms around her young brother. "He goes to agricultural college," said Anton with pride, "a scientist. He knows from where come possl, how to make bigger the melons, what kind of wheat keeps off rust. . . ." Anton related while Peter grinned only and said nothing, because nothing had to be said now. Looks were enough for now. Afterwards would come the talking, he indicated to Lilli with a lift of his eyebrow. So let the old man go on. . . .

Anton continued, "Yes, Lilli, many things today young people know and we old ones, like blind, tried to live without science." He sighed. Imprisoned within the limits of his ignorance, he knew he would not seek that science. "I am now myself, old possl," he winked at Lilli, but the pathos of the jest hurt her, and she turned her head from him.

One person was still missing. "And mother?" she asked. "Where is mother?" One of the girls assured her: "She'll be out soon. When she saw you from the window, she ran upstairs to dress."

Even as she spoke, her mother came from the house. There was timidity in the woman's eyes, timidity and the desire to please. She wore a city style dress of purple crepe which sat awkwardly upon her peasant shoulders. Her brown hair, not streaked with grey, was arranged in a premanent wave not so becoming as her old style of braids had been. She wore silk stockings and shoes with high heels which were uncomfortable upon her broad feet, used to the comfort of barefoot walking. This, then, was Lilli's mother – as Lilli remembered her, a harsh women, full of superstition, fanatic in her devotion to ritual, yet behind that drab face, that awkward figure was a lifetime of intense living. The two women appraised each other, Lilli from her new status, her mother almost humble.

At last Zenobia spoke. "I am an old woman, you think Lilli?" She touched her hair. It was the old vanity of woman who does not desire to grow old, and it was the betrayal of this human weakness that finally broke down the barriers of Lilli's reserve. She knew now what to say. "You have a good skin, mother," she told the old woman. "Clear, like a girl's."

Zenobia bridled with pleasure. "Come in, Lilli, come home. We have much to show you. So many new things!"

Lilli followed her mother, accompanied by the procession of her brothers and sisters, and stood within the house again, looking about as though memories were embedded in the very planks.

With pride her brothers and sisters pointed out the latest improvements. They showed her the phone, the radio and refrigerator. Everything was hygienic. One could not imagine any spirits, evil or benign living here. What had she been expecting? She could not explain the sense of disappointment. Progress had been made in material things. She listened abstractedly to talk of improvements and realized that the old world had indeed receded far away.

"The poplar – what of the poplar that used to whisper beneath this window?" she asked, a lump in the throat. She had planned to sleep beneath that window and listen to the clatter of the flat, sibilant leaves.

"We cut it down to let in the light," her brother said.

Let in the light! Yes, the light of modernization had come even here and something had been lost, something poetic had gone when the machine came.

"We have an upstairs now," said Zenobia as she led Lilli up the stairs. In one of the girls' bedrooms she helped Lilli to remove her coat and hat, all the while pointing out the fixings of chintz and ribbon. "Well, Lilli, how is home?" Zenobia asked as she watched Lilli comb out her hair. "You like all this?" There was a hint of wistfulness in her voice as she indicated all the modern improvements.

Lilli hesitated. "Everything is changed." How could she tell her mother without hurting her that the change was not all to her liking? "The new range must have cost a lot of money."

"But you like it?" persisted Zenobia. "You like better than old?"

"I don't know. . . ." Lilli would not commit herself. "I wanted to see something of the old life, to find what I left behind me. It's strange to find it's so different."

To Lilli's surprise, Zenobia's face lit up with relief. "Oh, I am so glad you said this, Lilli!" she exclaimed. "Don't tell the girls," she lowered her voice, "but for me, these new things do not satisfy like the old. . . . With the hands is nothing made now," she explained. "Everything from factory, shoes, clothes furniture. How can person put in his work what he feels inside of him, when always he must live with machine? Old beauty is now disappearing. What is there for the – " she stopped.

"For the soul?" Lilli did not hesitate to supply the word.

"The girls would laugh at such a word," said her mother, a

little shy, "but what soul is in a machine?" She sat gingerly on the edge of the bed, fearful to disturb the chintz ruffle, and the words poured out: "If I could tell you, how shameful what the girls did with those carpets, embroideries, dress up and laugh! Costumes wear out and new ones not made. Girl will not spend time to embroider when she can order from mail order catalogue, so cheap, so fine!" Zenobia wiped a tear and sighed. "Not new style, mother," girls say. "We must be like others, have lazy daisy cushion. . . ." "Lazy daisy!" Zenobia said scornfully. "No more kilims on wall, all, all, taken off and instead put on wallpaper, curtains from mail order, range where was old stove, so good to bake bread!" He voice broke and she buried her face in her hands.

"It's all right, mother," Lilli assured her. "You have one daughter still who loves the old."

Zenobia held out her hand in an imploring gesture. "You are not still angry, that we did nothing for you?"

The last trace of bitterness disappeared as Lilli replied: "I learned everything I needed to learn, and you see, I haven't lost. Perhaps it was better that way, I'd be like the others, all for the new."

Zenobia's face shone. "I made promise to you, Lilli, and now I am keeping it." She went over to the carved chest standing in the corner of the bedroom and fumbled within for a few moments before coming forth with something glistening, something orange and sleek.

"The yellow boots!" exclaimed Lilli. "Oh how often I thought of those boots, mother, and wondered whether you still had them!"

"Maybe they will bring you good husband, like me," said her mother slyly as she handed them over to Lilli.

Lilli sat down on the bed with the boots, thrilled by the sheen, the touch of the leather, the craftsmanship. What memories were attached to those boots, of her mother's courtship, of Fialka's wedding, of all the beauty that had been!

"You will save these things for our people?" Zenobia pleaded as she left the room and Lilli nodded, hugging the boots to her.

When Lilli came downstairs some time later, she saw that the living room was full of people. "Here she is! here she is!" they cried out. Music sounded and three players advanced to her, one of them the old fiddler who had helped her spy on Fialka. People swarmed about her, people with vaguely familiar faces. People who had once been boys and girls with her and now were men and women. Lilli hesitated to ask about Vanni, although she examined eagerly the features of all the men to see if she could find any resemblance to her childhood sweetheart. How could she say, "And Vanni, what of him? Where is Vanni?"

Zenobia took her aside and spoke to her: "Many people heard you were here and came to see you, Lilli. Everybody wants you should sing. You will sing, eh, Lilli?" She seemed anxious. "People came many miles to hear you, Lilli. It would be good if you could say something to everyone." Lilli smiled at Zenobia's respect for appearances. "That's what I came for, mother, to see and speak to all my old friends, and to sing for them."

Coming to her now was Fialka, still beautiful, with her three children, and Marko. Fialka was dressed in black satin, which had the effect, as usual, of making all the other women appear dowdy.

"Fialka!" exclaimed Lilli. "What a beautiful gown!"

Fialka smiled, pleased at her sister's tribute. "My littlest one is called Lilli, after you."

Lilli was touched. She was stirred by the friendliness of her family as she never thought she would be. Face to face with them, she found her resentment had disappeared; she could remember now only the many beautiful things of her childhood; the ugliness had vanished.

Although she hesitated to ask about Vanni, one thing she had to know: "What of Zachary, Fialka?" she inquired. "Whom did he get?"

Fialka squeezed her hand sympathetically. "That affair was too bad, Lilli. Afterwards, we were all sorry. But you'll be glad to hear that Zachary married a widow who controls him with an iron fist."

One person in the assembly intrigued Lilli, and this was a youth with an astounding forehead and dark brown eyes behind thick glasses.

"Whoever is that boy, Fialka?" she asked her sister. "He acts as though he owned the place."

"In a way, he does," laughed Fialka. "Don't you recognize those dimples?"

"Of course!" exclaimed Lilli. "It's the baby. How did he grow up so soon?"

"Johnny is in his first year high school – not a baby, Lilli."

"But he's only eleven!" exclaimed Lilli. Where had she been at eleven! She turned her face away to hide her emotion. What a wild, untaught little creature she had been! All her new-found sophistication dropped momentarily from her, and she became again that desperate little girl surrounded by hostile forces seeking to push her out of the world.

Zenobia now summoned them to the table and all the women looked at Lilli, half embarrassed, half expectant. The table was spread out the length of the room, and was laden with mushroom dumplings, cabbage rolls, smoked sausage, beet soup, pancakes with cottage cheese and sour cream. There was some constraint among the guests at first, as though they feared their manners would not be polished enough, but Lilli, seizing an enormous dill pickle, crunched it noisily, and laughter and natural conversation then broke out.

Zenobia was relieved at Lilli's hearty appetite. "The girls wanted to make English pudding, rosbif and out of tin cans everything but I said, no, Lilli wants old style."

"You were right, mother," sail Lilli. "I never get the chance now to eat Bukovynian food."

During the meal, which lasted for two hours. Lilli spoke of the places which she had visited on her tour, the people she had seen, how she had sung to an extra gang, how the songs she had learned here on the farm, in this very house, had been taken to the hearts of people in immigrant communities all over the country. She described how she had hidden behind a piano to hear a fat man play and had gone for an audition to the Folk Choir.

When all had finished and had pushed back from the table, Lilli sensed an undercurrent of excitement, a light trembling in the hand of her mother as she adjusted the brooch on her dress, a clearing of the throat from her father, a scraping of feet from her brothers and sisters. It was like the atmosphere in church before the choir commenced singing. Lilli smiled at them all and then quietly without announcement she began to sing, as though on sheer impulse, as though from the heart in the manner of the people, and the song was the song of the highlands – "Rich is this land, for it's nurtured with song dew!"

Songs poured out one after another, all she could remember, songs that had not been sung for how many years? Incredible, thought her listeners, that she remembered! Before she had finished, they all joined in with her and the young people, too, found a new beauty. It was strange, Lilli though, that she who had fled that environment had built her life upon all the old traditions which had constituted its essence, while those who had remained behind had yielded to modernism.

In the evening, the boys, who were proud of their car, wanted to take Lilli for a ride, but she insisted that she wanted to ride in the old wagon. The young people piled in and sat on the hay, all excited at having Lilli as their companion. Lilli, sitting half-buried in the hay, began to hum and soon all the young people had joined in. The singing continued as the twilight deepened and the wagon moved through the dark and secret countryside.

Lilli asked about Tamara's place. It had been taken over by a thrifty Icelandic farmer and now in place of Tamara's cottage stood a modern clapboard bungalow, before which a little blond girl was playing. From within, a radio blared. A Ford car stood in the yard. There was nothing left of Tamara's beauty, except a legend in the memory of old-timers, nothing of the dark and fearful passion which had once burned in the heart of a woman. Yet something of terror still remained in Lilli's heart, and when a shout went up: "Look, there's the swamp fire!" she shuddered.

From the direction of the swamp arose the jack o'lantern, the glow deepening and brightening, swung to and fro, now approaching, now receding. Peter spoke up scornfully: "Gases from decayed vegetable matter. Those stories of the old folks about evil spirits swinging lanterns make me think of the Stone Age."

This, thought Lilli pensively, was the little brother whose childhood she had nourished with fantasy!

Early next morning, Lilli arose and went out walking over the countryside, fresh with the spring dawn. She picked a handful of crocuses into which she thrust her face, as though by contact with their cool, moist petals she could make herself a young girl again. Now, apart from her changed and changing family, she wanted to establish contact with her childhood. Here were her roots; here, always, would be something of herself.

From a distance, she saw a figure on a tractor, her young brother Peter. He waved and called to her, and came chugging in her direction. When he got off, he came up and stood by her for a few moments without saying anything. How beautiful the prairie spring! The wind running with light feet through the grass, the blue glass dome of prairie sky, the horizons where one could stretch one's soul after the confines of the city streets!

Lilli laughed. "I keep on looking for another Petey, small and with curls like a buttercup. How you've grown! When I look at you, at all my brothers and sisters, I feel as if somebody had given me a legacy. All that mine, I think!"

Peter grinned. "I suppose we are overwhelming, there are so many of us, and now that we're grown, it must seem as though we've been multiplied by three."

He looked at her with shy eagerness. "I'd like to show you my grain seed," he said. "I'm thinking of entering it in the provincial grain show. That is, if you want to see it, if it would interest you – "

"Of course," said Lilli. She poured the reddish kernels through her hands. "Marquis?" she guessed.

"A descendant of Marquis," replied Peter. "There are many improved kinds now. Do you know, Lilli – " he smiled as he felt the old bond between them had been re-established. "My first lessons were from you – it was you who taught me to observe all the hidden life around me. For you, that feeling for nature led to music; for me, to agricultural science."

"But it's still poetry," said Lilli.

"Yes." They were silent for a while.

"How do the young people strike you?" Peter asked.

"They seem more alert and worldly. They speak good English." Lilli did not deceive Peter, however. He knew what was in her mind.

"Our people no longer live as peasants," he pointed out. "We're mechanized. Every farmer has a tractor; every house has a radio."

"Hasn't it been too swift a change?"

"Yes, we've lost something. Maybe we've become modern too quickly. In ten years we had to cover ground that other people took fifty years to travel. So perhaps we're losing our individuality. For instance," he turned to her and smiled, "you never see a wedding like Fialka's now. All the girls wear white satin, the latest style out of the mail order, and they get a jazz orchestra. We've forgotten even how the old songs should be sung, and conditions are not possible to create new songs as our parents did. Many of those songs you sang last night haven't been heard at all by some of the younger people. They were ashamed of their past, but now you've come, they've been talking and thinking, maybe there's some good in the old things after all."

As Peter was speaking, a great wedge of geese appeared in the sky and flew majestically overhead. Suddenly their imperious flight was interrupted by a great honking and clamouring, the symmetry of the wedge was broken, and the geese in confusion scattered off in all directions.

"What's happening?" cried out Lilli. "I've never seen anything like that before." She scanned the skies for some explanation.

"Look there," Peter pointed to the horizon, where Lilli could make out the form of an airplane, which shortly came into view over them. "They heard the noise of the motor before we did and that was what alarmed them."

Thrilled by what she had seen. Lilli looked, first after the retreating geese and upward at the airplane.

"See what I mean?" said Peter. "The invasion of modernism."

"Yes, it's symbolic," agreed Lilli. As she followed the flight of the plane Lilli wondered, was she singing of a vanished world? Something that even now had passed into history? Why did she think it would undergo no change, while she herself had become transformed?

"He's flying over Karmaliuk's farm," said Peter. He looked at Lilli as thou he had deliberately invited a query.

"Vanni?" Lilli's voice trembled and the blood rushed to her cheeks. "Why wasn't he here last night? Why didn't anybody say anything about him?" At last she had the courage to ask, but the old feeling suddenly sprang to life and overwhelmed her, as though the boy Vanni had suddenly materialized by her side.

"Vanni cared too much for you, Lilli," Peter replied. "He waited until a couple of years ago and when he heard about your success he decided to marry another girl. He's one of the best farmers in the district and plays the clarinet in the village band. We couldn't do without him."

Lilli felt she must know more, must take back something at least to console her. "Has he changed, Peter? Is he still the same Vanni?" She tried to conjure up the Vanni of the present.

"Much the same, Lilli, except that he's older, of course, settled down now. But you've changed, too, Lilli," Peter pointed out. "More than any of us. People who knew you as a little girl could hardly believe it was you. Remember, Vanni is still a farm lad. He was the first to say, Lilli must go on."

Lilli turned in the direction of Karmaliuk's farm again and strained for some glimpse of her friend. If she could see him, only for a moment, if she could make that memory alive again, but there was nothing, nothing! This, then, was how it must be, a memory only. Vanni would always be a boy to her, and she a girl to him. She sighed and the sigh carried something away, like a lost dream. Still, it was good to think that Vanni would always be here on the prairies, that if she herself had to leave her past behind her, he would still be its worthy guardian, and his children, too, would grow up here.

A meadowlark screamed with joy, his yellow velvet vest and black stock flashing from the fence post.

"It's so beautiful I feel like crying." A sob burst from Lilli's throat. With tears on her cheeks, she heard music around her, the music that haunted her childhood, only now it had a majesty, a fulfilment that it had never before possessed.

"What can I do for our people?" she asked Peter, turning

to face her brother, who was the future of her people on the land.

"Take back with you what is best in our past and preserve it for us," replied her brother. "The land, that is our job, mine and Vanni's, but yours is to cherish the old and give it new meaning. Through these songs, other people in our country can look into the hearts of our people, whom they once despised, and see what beauty is there. You'll speak for all of us."

When the time came for Lilli to leave, the family assembled. "Let us all sit down together for the last time and in our thoughts be close to each other as we may never be again." Anton motioned to the circle of chairs in the living-room and all the guests filed in slowly as though they were loath to take leave of Lilli. According to custom they sat down in the company of the departing guest, keeping silence, some with their heads bent, others with their eyes on Lilli.

As Lilli sang for them the song of farewell, she knew what her people had given her. Everything she had, everything she was came from them, the ability to endure, the love for detail, everything that made her an artist was inherited from them. She had all that before she ever left home, and didn't know perhaps how much she owed them. If she had had any resentment because of her father's brutality or her mother's harshness, if she had nourished a grudge, all had vanished. She felt light and free, her mind and spirit soared. She knew then that the ripe time had come, the time of fulfilment.

14
IN SEARCH OF A
LOST LEGEND
❦

IT WAS A day in early autumn when Lilli returned to Reiner's study, which was filled at this time with great bouquets of asters.

"You look like the spirit of fall yourself, Lilli," Reiner greeted her as she stood in the doorway, dressed in a wool crepe suit the russet colour of an autumn leaf, a cluster of bronze baby mums tucked under her chin. He watched her as she set down a bulky music case and drew off her suede gloves.

"Sometimes I think the air is sprayed with gold at this time of the year," she said, leaning out the window.

"The Canadian fall is always beautiful to me," said Reiner, coming up to stand beside her. "I never stop wondering at it – that absolute colour, that quality of space and excitement." He clasped her in his arms and drew her to him. "Lilli!" He looked down at her, marvelling at her capacity for radiance. "Everything comes to life when she entered the room," he thought. Aloud, he said, "I imagined you'd never return. You don't know how I tortured myself thinking of that Vanni! All those months and no letters!"

"You know I'm not much of a letter-writer, Matthew," said Lilli, eyes downcast. "I never really learned to write, not to express intimate thoughts, that is. Writing is still a chore with me."

"You've another outlet," consoled Reiner. "Perhaps more

compelling because you've poured all your self-expression into that medium." But he had touched her in a sore spot.

She broke away and went to stand before the mirror adjusting her flowers. Reiner watched the gestures of the long mobile hands in which was a knowledge of the life of the peasant, the tiller of the soil. The face itself, with its strong planes and sculptured profile, was like the reincarnation of a type no longer common. No actress, thought Reiner, could imitate the sense of affliction which appeared an integral part of her. Only a reminder of her difference, and it had arisen to the surface.

"Lilli – " Reiner strode across the room. "Have I hurt you?"

"How, Matthew?" Lilli's face was composed, no trace of self-pity.

He was disconcerted. "You've changed in some way – something in your way of responding. . . . What happened on your tour?"

Lilli sighed as if she could not decide how to make a choice of all the ideas which she had to communicate. "First of all," she began, "about the audiences. I loved them Matthew. I wouldn't exchange them for the audiences in those big city halls. They're warm, they participate with me, and afterwards, I feel as though I had added to myself."

"It must have been a great emotional experience."

"It was, oh it was, Matthew!"

"And what are you keeping from me?" Reiner insisted.

"Of course, I might have known I couldn't keep a secret from you," she said. "Let's sit here in front of the window and talk."

They sat for awhile regarding each other. The silence was pregnant with meaning as Reiner laid his hand on hers. "Tell me about it."

"You've often asked me, Matthew, about my past life," she began, "my background and so on, and I never wanted to tell you very much about it. It was too difficult, I suppose – how could I find words to describe that life to you? Besides, I wanted to leave it all behind and become a new person." She paused briefly and then went on: "What was it that took me back there? Nostalgia, I think. All during my tour the words of the Czech song kept running through my head, 'Where is my home?' I felt incomplete especially when I met all those people to whom their own past was so dear, and I wanted to claim my own background, and so I went back."

"Back home?"

"Yes," Speaking with impetuosity, under the spell of the experience, Lilli described her return home, the changes she had found, her reconciliation with herself and her parents. When she had finished, Lilli looked at Reiner, eyes full of revelation, as though she were at last giving herself to him.

"You'll never grow cold if you keep close to the fires of your rich experience," said Reiner, feeling that now he understood Lilli, that here indeed was her source.

"I think you sent me out purposely to find myself, didn't you, Matthew?" Lilli had suddenly realized that her confession had not taken Reiner entirely by surprise.

"It was partly your own idea, wasn't it, Lilli?" he countered. "What did you hope to accomplish outside of our trip back home?" He knew that she was still holding back something, that the main story had not yet been told.

"You see," she pointed out, "I wanted to test my songs – if they were wrong, these people would tell me."

"And what did you find out?"

"A few times, they did correct me. I remember reading somewhere, "You must stretch your work twelve times on canvas. . . ."

"Meaning what?"

"Meaning you must paint in layers to get that lifelike effect. One coat is flat, empty! The same song became richer, deeper, because I gave it to so many people."

Reiner was stirred and excited as he waited to hear what she had to say. "You can't foretell how she'll react to any experience," he thought. "It will always be something novel. She's never stereotyped in her emotions. And now, I can tell by the excitement in her – she always gives herself away – she's really becoming what I always thought she would become."

Lilli went on in a low voice to describe that memorable evening in the shack on the prairies: "On those faces, I saw a remembering . . . They had looked on the earth, the skies and fields. . . . Night came and day, the seasons, death. . . . They saw these things and they were filled with wonder. Their peasant ancestors couldn't read, so to express their feelings, they made them into songs. That's where their songs came from, that's why I could sing the, because I had heard them at the source. . . ."

Reiner paced up and down during this recital, uttering an exclamation of agreement from time to time. "The common touch, yes, we've lost that. We've gotten too far away from origins." He lit a cigarette and puffed. "But what of your big city audiences, Lilli? What success did you have there?" He looked anxiously at her.

Lilli seemed disconcerted at the question. She hesitated before speaking. "The critics said nice things about me. . . ." she began slowly. "I read and wondered, was that really myself? It sounded so different in their language! The people, too, were kind. . . ." Again she paused as though at a memory not altogether pleasant, and then went on. "To show me off to their friends, they invited me to a party in a most luxurious studio. I have never seen such a room, Matthew – each person, each thing wrapped in silk, full of importance. And I, as if in a silk-lined cage, sat like an interesting insect, observed by them. . . ." She laughed, somewhat bitterly. "I tried to tell them something of my background – the carollers on Christmas Eve, the watch on Easter Night. They exclaimed, 'My dear, how quaint! These peasants do have some picturesque customs. Like a picture by Van Gogh. 'The Potato Eaters,' I think.'" There was an edge to Lilli's voice as she commented, "They were polite with their masks, but underneath, was nothing." She shrugged in a gesture of disdain. "While they twittered, I could only think of that shack on the prairies, I saw all those faces, so lonely, so starved, each face as if carved from the earth, the people not afraid to expend their strength, not hoarding themselves preciously like these. . . . I remembered the swamp fire, the ride on the jigger, that wild country and my shaggy people in their sheepskin coats. . . . All those memories – why did they come crowding to me at that moment, so incongruous in those surroundings?" Lilli's voice broke, but she did not stop, she kept on speaking as though under the influence of an emotion too powerful to suppress: "Did you ever notice how, at some critical point in your life, the events of the past flash before you and come into a new focus – you can see a design that was never there before? That afternoon it was so for me. O Matthew, how I longed for one moment to get back to the prairie – "

Lilli stopped and looked at Reiner, her face alight. It was as if the look, feel, colour and fragrance of the prairie had come into the studio, as if Lilli had summoned all her people there, and given them flesh and a voice. While she was speaking, Matthew could not take his eyes off her, not a flicker of expression escaped him. What a privilege, he thought, to look into the most secret recesses of a life, to live with Lilli this moment of self-discovery! How deeply she had touched those areas of nostalgia in the immigrant, for were not all of us, in the long run, immigrants? The day comes for all when they long for the old country, at least in spirit.

For Lilli, on the other hand, all her experiences were intensified, because she was relating them in Matthew's presence. At last she realized how deeply he had entered into her being, how he had unobtrusively guided her talent, brought out all the latent wealth within. If it had not been for him, she thought, she would have been like an undeveloped negative, all the potentialities locked up. Only now, looking at him, did she know what it had cost him to restrain himself, to maintain always that teacher-pupil relationship, and this discovery was so overpowering that she felt she must have time to appraise it before they could, finally, come together.

Finally Reiner asked the question which had been tormenting him: "And Vanni? What of Vanni? Did you see him when you returned?"

She was not concerned as he had thought she would be. Her eyes were calm, her voice steady as she replied: "Vanni is married to someone else."

Reiner could not hide his gratification. "How do you feel about that? Any regrets?"

Lilli shook her head. "Maybe that was best – not to see him," she replied. "Vanni was my childhood. Perhaps, if we had met, we would no longer feel the same affection. Those years which meant so much to me – which developed part of me that he never knew – were lived by him in different circumstances, and he, too, took his own path. That would have separated us, even if we had seen each other. As my brother Peter said, 'Vanni belongs to the land.'"

"And you?" Reiner asked in a scarcely audible voice.

"I know now where I belong," Lilli replied without hesitation. "I've found out what I really want, is not fame at all, but simply to sing and be heard by these people – my people, wherever they are – "

Although it was not the answer he had been hoping for, Reiner concealed his disappointment and said, "I can hardly wait to hear you sing again. How about a concert in the city?" he asked. "Many people have been asking about you. They've been hearing reports, and are curious to hear you."

"Any time, any place," agreed Lilli. "This time, Matthew, you will hear me, as you always thought I might be."

On the morning of Lilli's concert, Reiner went over to her

apartment to encourage her, as he thought. "Though she'll probably end up by encouraging me," he said to himself. "Lilli being what she is." She was humming when she came to the door. "You look radiant," he said, clasping her hands. He took off his hat and coat and sat on a couch near the window. Lilli, too happy to sit, waltzed about the room. "Thanks for the flowers." She buried her face in them.

"Are you anxious?" He lit a cigarette.

"No, I'm looking forward to it. I know it will go well." She broke off a stem and thrust a rose in her hair.

"You've a glorious colour – is that real?" He kissed her lightly on the cheek. "There's a tang of frost on your skin – like the taste of a MacIntosh Red apple in the winter time."

"I went for a walk this morning." She rubbed her face affectionately against his, and then broke away again.

"So early?"

"Right after breakfast," replied Lilli, looking out the window, which had a view over the park. "The snow was so crisp, people were walking, girls and boys sledding, sparrows scratching on the ground. . . . I walked and walked and thought, 'This is a city of history and a city of immigrants. In some ways, it's a city of villages. The people here come from the same countries as the people I knew at home on the farm, so they'll like the same music. Go back far enough and you'll find that same peasant background.'"

"And don't we all yearn, at some time, for our heritage?" interposed Reiner, thinking that he had never seen her look so lovely.

Lilli continued, "I met a Japanese lady with her baby, and I sang her a bit of my Japanese lullaby – you know the one, Matthew – she could hardly believe it. There were tears in her eyes."

"You have a gift with people."

"Because I never think of them as strangers."

"To you, they'll never be." Reiner watched her as she

arranged the flowers in a vase. "What else have you been doing?"

Lilli stood before the mirror and admired the effect of the flower in her hair. "I've been recapitulating, Matthew, everything that's happened since we first met."

Reiner got up and crossed the room to her. "I'm trying to imagine what you were like before then," he said. What memory was most poignant? Perhaps the swift, impetuous tap of her footsteps up the stairway, almost like a dance, he thought, the sound always brought a rush of anticipation to his heart. "How did you feel about me then, Lilli?"

"At first, shy," she replied, smiling at him. The smile transformed her like the touch of a match. Reiner loved to watch her face. It had the plastic qualities of the actress, he thought, so swift was the change of mood, and the shadows which played over it, from intense to subdued. Sometimes she was almost plain; it was this lighting of expression which constituted her chief beauty.

"I never thought you could really like me," she went on, still evading him. "A rough ignorant country girl. I thought you felt sorry for me. What had I to offer you? I studied hard to please you, to speak well, to dress properly. . . ."

"For me?"

"All, all for you." He thrilled to the warm colour of her voice. "You touch me deeply," he said, "so deeply, it hurts." He relieved his feelings by a deep intake of breath.

"I wonder if I can explain it to you, Matthew." She sat down, a look of contemplation on her face. "I hadn't found myself. So full of curiosity I was, so eager to learn! I always thought of satisfying you, of trying to reach the standards which you set up for me. I was bewildered, dazzled." The words came now in a rush of feeling. "I wanted to explore, to find myself. It wouldn't be the same if someone else did my discovering for me. I was in the process of becoming. Now I wanted this, now I wanted that. The most commonplace

347

things that everyone else took for granted were new to me –
ice-cream, pajamas, silk stockings. I loved dancing. I loved to
tease the boys and make them fall in love with me. It was so
exciting when I discovered my power over them!" She paused,
breathless after the effort of self-revelation.

"And Tim?" Reiner paced up and down, trembling and
tense at what he was hearing.

"Tim was my balance," Lilli replied. "He was always the
good companion, never asking too much. I'll always be
grateful to him."

"You've been thinking all these things this morning?"
Reiner sensed what her remarks were leading to, now.

She nodded. "Then, when I came back home, I took these
out of my trunk and looked at them." She went to the closet
and took out a pair of high tan boots, which she held up so
Reiner could see them. "What are those?" She brought them
close so that he could examine them. "My mother gave me
these when I went home to visit. Feel how soft, almost like a
piece of cloth." She ran her hand over the surface of the
leather. "And the colour – that beautiful orangey tan which we
call yellow, with this scarlet leather overlay in scalloped design
– all hand-made, Matthew." She took his hand and rubbed it
against the boots. "My mother wore these to a dance – that's
how she met and married my father. My sister Fialka danced
in these at her wedding."

Lilli sat down on the bed, took off her pumps and pulled
on the yellow boots. Then she went over to the mirror, and
with her hands on her hips, began to execute a lively dance,
her yellow boots flying and whirling and tapping about the
room. "What a mood you're in!" exclaimed Reiner, admiring
the lithe young figure. "Floating. A good thing the windows
are closed. You'd float out through them." Lilli finished her
dance and threw herself on a chair, laughing and breathless.

"I suppose," she said, "Every immigrant family has
something like these boots – a talisman which they brought

from the old country – a pair of boots, a shawl, a carved wooden chest, a samovar, something they get out at family gatherings to symbolize their heritage."

"Meaning what?" Reiner felt the conversation was now leading to some crucial point.

"Well – " Lilli paused and her eyes met Reiner's. She smiled. "Maybe I need a talisman, too. You always said I was superstitious, didn't you? These boots brought my mother luck and maybe they'll do the same for me."

There was a moment of intense silence, then Reiner spoke, "I think I know what you're trying to tell me. Lilli. Come here." She moved slowly to him. "I think I've waited long enough for you to grow up," he said, watching her as she walked across the room to him. "Did you have to put on those boots to tell me?" She paused, uncertainly, half way to him. "How could I know?" she said. When she stood before him, he drew her down beside him on the couch. "You made a conquest the first time," he declared, putting his arm around her. "My life changed, too. I used to wait for you, and got impatient when you came late for a lesson. How I tormented myself while I waited for Lilli to find herself and come to me of her own free will." He held her face gently in his hands. Her eyes even yet seemed fearful, as though unwilling to believe his words.

"How could you like me?" she asked. "Such a ridiculous little person I was! With a long coat dragging on the ground and a turban falling over my ears. How did you keep from laughing at me?" For a moment, she was childlike, almost like the wild young girl he had first known.

"Perhaps," replied Reiner, "because I looked first in your eyes and there I saw the real Lilli. Coat, hat didn't matter. We take those on and off and they're not a part of ourselves." The last trace of her uncertainty vanished. "You look plastered with stars," he said as he saw the glow of her great, dark eyes fixed on him. "I am, I am!" exclaimed Lilli, her cheeks wet.

"Except for two big tears in your eyes." He drew her into his arms and felt her ardent response as the strength of her passion grew to meet him, returning kiss for kiss, embrace for embrace. "I've always wondered what it would be like to hold that body – so full of joy, so full of life, every line vibrant with meaning and grace, to share that joy of living with you – " He felt the warm impress of her lips on his. "You don't withhold yourself, do you? You surrender to it as to your song. I loved to watch your body when you sang. There was an intensity in the curve of your throat, the gestures of your hands, the lift of your breast." He kissed her with increasing intensity, while she replied with a strength he hardly believed possible. He drew back her face and looked at her. "So, the time of seeking is ended," he said. "What is that song you used to sing? Where is my home? Well, here it is, with me." He kissed her forehead. "How do you feel?"

Lilli roused herself as from a trance. Speech was difficult for her after such an expenditure of passion. "Happy," she whispered. "Too happy. An emotion too big as if I can't contain it." Reiner laughed exultantly as he pressed her close to him again. "You'll get used to living with it."

"I never want to live without it." She seemed unwilling to take her eyes from his.

"Now I know the difference in your face," said Reiner. "It's full of expressed emotions."

"They make me feel so strong," she spoke with conviction now.

"Because they're working for you, not against you."

She stirred in his arms. "Why didn't you tell me that before now?" she asked with a touch of petulance.

"Because I knew you were looking for something. To substitute gratitude for love was not what I wanted. I thought discovery should come from yourself." He looked down on her face, and saw that she was frowning. "The time wasted – "

"No, not wasted," he corrected. "The process of self-discovery is often a slow one, and can't be speeded up. Besides, there's so much time ahead of us, isn't there?"

Her eyes brightened: "I'll have to thank mother for those boots," she said. "You know, I think she was afraid I'd miss that . . . maybe that was what she wanted to tell me . . . in spite of her hard life on the prairie, she had romance."

"So, the circle has been completed," said Matthew. "Now you know the meaning of each link."

* * *

The crowd which attended Lilli's concert comprised a cross-section of the city's cosmopolitan make-up; an old-fashioned Lutheran choirmaster shepherding a dozen choir members, a noted Hebrew cantor, a Negro quartet, a band of Bohemian musicians, a troupe of Chinese actors, a Syrian cafe owner – men and women of almost every European and Asiatic origin, some of whom had not left the district in which they lived since they had come over as immigrants many years previously.

Matthew Reiner and Dr. Ian MacTavish, eminent anthropologist, were smoking in the lobby before the concert. They had met by accident and had discovered, in a random exchange of remarks, each other's identity. MacTavish, his read hair receding somewhat from his peaked forehead, did not appear much older than he had ten years before; he was one of those people who age well. A few years back, he had published a book based on the diaries which he had kept while a teacher in the community of Prairie Dawn; that experience, indeed, had formed the basis of his lifetime work.

"Do you understand all these languages?" Reiner asked him as they listened to the hum of voices.

"Between the two of us, we should cover most of them," replied MacTavish. "Look there." He indicated two elderly couples, a Jewish man and woman, both dressed somberly in black, the woman with a black shawl over her head, followed by a Scottish couple of about the same age.

"My people and yours," MacTavish grinned. "Wonderful faces, aren't they? Those strong bones and peasant features – they remind me of a group of Bukovynians at a wedding I once attended. Did you notice how many older people are here?"

"It's exactly right," said Reiner. "Lilli will feel at home singing to these people. She always did like old people, in fact she told me once they had richness and depth, a kind of flavour – salt, I suppose you'd call it. Their minds are curious repositories of folk lore. Once they die, the secrets of their art will die with them."

"That costume must have come out of an immigrant's trunk," MacTavish indicated a vigorous old woman in full Bohemian costume – huge puffed sleeves lace cap, woollen apron. "Looks genuine, doesn't it? All that lace, embroidery and weaving – "

"The photographer seems to think so." Reiner nodded in the direction of the excited photographer, who was busy taking pictures, murmuring, "Such a crowd! Where did all these people come from?"

"Listen – " They were silent for a few moments as the polyglot babel of voices soared about them. "Even if you shut your eyes, you'd have a good idea of the make-up of the crowd."

"The regular concert goers don't know what to make of it," commented Reiner as the two men walked through the bewildering throng. "Their usual dress parade can't compete."

They paused in a quiet corner to reminisce. Both felt their mutual interest in Lilli constituted a bond; in addition, each was curious concerning the role the other had played in Lilli's life.

"Tell me a little of her childhood," urged Reiner, anxious to get as much as he could of that unknown Lilli from MacTavish. "You knew her when she lived on the prairies. That's a part of her life that's only a second-hand story to me. You know, I feel jealous of you."

"There was always something about her that captured the imagination and set it on fire," recalled MacTavish. He was trying to connect the Lilli he knew with this warm, enthusiastic crowd of human beings who swarmed past him. "Some quality of excitement that arose from the bond which tied her to her natural surroundings. I wondered, then, whether that excitement would survive transplanting to alien surroundings, and what effect it might have on what we call the civilized mind."

"It will be interesting, then, for you to see the difference," said Reiner. He felt drawn to the lean Scottish-Canadian. "The first who really saw her," he thought.

MacTavish lit a cigarette and puffed. "I'm anxious to see what she has become, naturally," he replied. "But that other Lilli was more mine. There was an intimacy between us that we could never re-establish now. When I see her, and hear her, I'll have to share with so many others! Before, she was mine – my discovery."

As the singer was revealed to the audience, there was a murmur all over the hall. Lilli stood for a moment on the stage, immersed in the warm receptivity of the audience, which flowed to her in waves. Everything that she had been, everything she possessed, came to focus on this one moment. Her eyes, skilfully made up to enhance their size and lustre, were almond-shaped, of a curious hazel hue; her mouth, painted a deep carnation, was wide and curved; the high cheekbones, casting a shadow on the hollow of the cheek, stood out in relief, making each plane of her face as clear-cut as though from the chisel of a sculptor. Her hands, the hands of the soil-tiller and creator, conveyed with a single gesture the idiom of an entire race.

As the big, passionate voice burst upon the audience, they felt as though they stood in the presence of the first folk poet who sang of human things; and the song emerged with great strength and nobility, emotion expressed by the barest twitch of a facial muscle, the fugitive vibration of the voice, the half-suppressed sob, the classic pose of the singer.

Now, like childish laughter on a spring day, the singer's voice carolled forth joyous, impetuous, shrill. Sing the song of a prairie spring, of children greeting the Maytime. The crocus blooms on the prairie, the voice of the meadowlark is heard, children seize hands and twine in a circle. A troupe of Armenian gypsies runs into the market square and begins to dance, their mad rhythms increase to a frenzy, and a girl's voice rings out clear and mocking. Fast ride the dead by night as from the churchyard issues the Dead Battalion! Now it is the death song of the crucifixion, profound sobs are heard as the body is lowered into the tomb, and then, in an exaltation of sorrow, the crescendo which leads to the climax of resurrection.

"Remember?" That was a common word as the immigrants turned to each other, faces full of wonder at hearing a dance, a prayer, a lullaby, some precious incident of childhood revived. "Rosita – thus we were in childhood – remember?" The exile felt once more the memories woven into the fabric of his childhood. These memories tugged at his heart, they appeared as far-off glimpses of a country once beloved and long since deserted. Pictures arose before his mind of village dances, of the mock wars of shepherds, of the wild notes of flute and bagpipe, the gossip of women in the village square, his native earth and sky.

Aroused by this re-creation of their own vanished past, the people in the audience knew that this artist had sprung from them, and that her art was the art of the people. They acclaimed in many languages, as they stood up and cheered, shouted, stamped, "She is ours! She is ours!"

In recognition of their applause, Lilli returned to sing as her final number "The Song of the Cranes," and through the melancholy air, beat as the sound of wings, the nostalgia of the human soul for its ancestral home, for all the arts by which the spirit had expressed its ancient faith. With this song, she paid tribute to those countless unknown songmakers who had created the songs to immortalize the common incidents of their daily life, she added the hues of her own living to them, she acknowledged her debt to her own people for what they had given her.